P9-CDA-726

DOWN TO A
SUNLESS SEA

DAVID POYER

DOWN TO A
SUNLESS SEA

A Tiller Galloway Thriller

St. Martin's Press ❧ *New York*

Grateful acknowledgment is made to reprint from the following:
"I Don't Know a Thing About Love." Wade Driver, Rhythm Records. By permission.
"End of the Line," by the Traveling Wilburys. © 1988 Ganga Publishing B.V. By permission.

Library of Congress Cataloging-in-Publication Data

Poyer, David.
    Down to a sunless sea / by David Poyer.—1st ed.
      p.   cm.
    ISBN 0–312–14589–6
    I. Title.
PS3566.0978D68   1996
813'.54—dc20   96-3120
                                                                           CIP

First Edition: November 1996

10 9 8 7 6 5 4 3 2 1

To all my Florida friends
Especially those men and women who face mortal danger
In the most dangerous sport that exists
Not for pay, not for duty,
But simply because the caves . . . are there.
This is courage unalloyed.
This novel is respectfully dedicated to Carl Sutton, Roberta
Swicegood, Sheck Exley, Captain Robert McGuire,
and all the others who have died over the years
to push back the frontiers of darkness.
May they swim forever in unending light.

Save your life.
No matter how experienced an open-water diver you are,
NEVER ENTER A CAVE without formal cave training, a guideline, at least
three independent sources of light, and an air plan.

ACKNOWLEDGMENTS

For this book, I owe thanks to James Allen, Richard Andrews, Janet Borneman, Jennifer Brown, Edward and Ann Buniak, John and Pam Buscemi, Jeff Carson, Gene Chunn, Sue Crum, Mark Danziger, Page Edwards, Victor Fabiani, Amity Gaige, Frank and Amy Green, Kay Hart, Monica Hart, Steven de las Heras, Paula Hopper, David Jones, Hugh King, Mike McOwen, Will Miller, Kim Overcash, Rod Perry, Lenore Hart Poyer, Frank Richardson, Todd Rippberger, Ron Rippey, Lauren Sarat, Patrick Smith, Marian Stradling, Terrence Tysall, Hal Watts, Eleanor West, George Witte, David Wood, The Shore Squares, and others, who, preferring anonymity, still gave generously of their time and knowledge. As always, all errors and deficiencies are my own.

DOWN TO A SUNLESS SEA

Half a mile into the icy dark, the diver scraped to a stop. He tried an experimental kick and wriggle, then dug his fingers into gritty rock and hauled. He didn't move.

Held there, ribs and shoulders squeezed tight by the cave's walls, he realized he was caught.

Instead of struggling, he relaxed. He turned his light back on, and by its sudden brilliance pondered the pale pitted stone, dotted with the fossils of ancient scallops and sea biscuits, that glowed inches from his eyes. He tasted the sulfurous seep around his mouthpiece, and purged a spoonful of murky water from his mask. Then he brought his wrist up, focusing his eyes and attention on instruments and gauges.

The luminescent numbers told him he could breathe for fifty-two more minutes at this depth. The twin steel tanks on his back were cross-connected, with dual regulators in case one free-flowed or jammed. He had another regulator and stage tank clipped to a D ring on his harness. He'd already breathed it down, but that still left it two-thirds full. A fourth, smaller tank held pure oxygen, for decompression on the way up, after the traverse.

Calmed by the knowledge he had plenty to breathe, he concentrated again on the constriction. But no matter how much air he dumped from his buoyancy compensator, or how tightly he ground his groin into the smooth stone, he couldn't free his tanks from the ceiling niche into which they'd snapped like a rifle bolt.

1

He was caught, wedged tight as a mouse in a blacksnake's jaws. Trapped under the solid rock, alone, deep in the black labyrinth.

He began hyperventilating, sucking in gusts of dry, metallic-tasting air. His heart raced. The beast in his belly was waking. It wanted to tear off the mask and hood, yank the mouthpiece out, and claw its way up to the light.

But his mind knew there was no light above him, and no air. Just 30 to 60 million years' worth of Oligocene limestone and, above that, the muddy, leaf-strewn bed of a river. If he panicked, he was dead. It was that simple.

But *you* don't panic, he told himself. He'd mapped systems in the Yucatán ten times longer than this one. In fifteen years of cave work, he'd blown regulators, lost guidelines, burned out lights, snapped off valves, lost primary gas, had gauges implode and computers fail, even driven his Tekna into a rock wall at full speed once. And survived, every time.

Staring into the dark, he pulled out a memory he kept for times like this. A fall afternoon, many years before. The smell of burning leaves. His granddad's voice, telling him how much he looked like his dad, when his dad was little. The old house. He went inside and there was the mudroom, then the living room. The moose head. The big record player, and on it his father's tarnishing tennis trophies . . .

Gradually, his heart dropped back into a normal rhythm. His hands stopped twitching. He groped at his chest, found the squeeze tube, and took three quick gulps of Gatorade and honey. He thrust his mouthpiece back in, the rubber tasting mud-gritty and foul after the sweet liquid, cleared the regulator, and reconsidered his position.

He'd obviously gotten through here before; there was his guideline leading off into the dark. He must have eaten better than he thought over the winter. Amazing what an extra couple of pounds around the middle could do. Well, there was always slack somewhere, as Houdini used to say.

He took his primary regulator out again and shifted to the secondary, on the seven-foot hose. Then, wriggling backward as it came forward, he began working his tank harness up over his shoulders. His joints felt as if they were dislocating, but at last he was rewarded by a hollow clank. The manifold unlocked from the ceiling with a shower of mud and stone fragments. He grabbed for the guideline before it vanished in the murk.

He shoved the harness and gear through ahead of him, the tanks scraping and clanging like muffled bells. Then grabbed an outcrop and pulled himself after them, belly pressing loving-tight into the rock. He wriggled twenty feet, the jagged fossils ripping at his hands and suit, before the constriction opened out. Beyond it, his light probed blackness, tracing an oval passage walled with dark stone.

He breathed easier, and the beast closed its eyes. He checked his valves and slipped the tanks back on, then rested for a minute. He adjusted his buoyancy, centering himself in the six-foot-wide passage, and listened—to the silence, to the incredible peace.

No matter how quiet it was at the surface, if you listened, you always heard something—the rumble of traffic, the distant thunder of an airliner, the hum and buzz of refrigerators and air conditioners and telephones. But here no sound existed but the click and hiss as he inhaled, then the muffled roar of bubbles. And as he hovered motionless, the black silence swelled, grew enormous around his feeble heartbeat, the weak, transient spark of his light. As if this hollow in the earth lived and thought and breathed in its own way, throbbing with the slow pulse of water.

Then he moved on, finning forward again, reaching out occasionally with the tips of his fingers to guide himself around a turn.

He bored on steadily for the next few hundred yards, as the passage branched into fingerlike extensions angling off into darkness. He didn't remember this section, but there was his line, taut, reassuring. There were his own white plastic line arrows clipped to it. The water gradually turned murky brown, laden with solids. His light showed him a rough, bubbly reddish brown goethite, through which he tunneled like a worm in a Swiss cheese. He checked his depth: passing a hundred feet.

A wide, low-ceilinged room, floor littered with rock; then another fork. He followed the line into the right-hand passage. He swam slowly, deliberately, head down and feet up, stubby fins pumping in a cautious shuffle-kick so as not to stir up the silt. Still going down.

Fifty yards on, he stopped again, overcome by a sudden sense of danger. He drifted to a halt in the middle of a tunnel just wide enough for his outstretched hands to brush opposite walls. He floated midway between left wall and right, floor and ceiling. His wrist-mounted light played over a pile of breakdown. The tumbled rubble loomed up, partially blocking the way. The spot of yellow light flicked back and found the guideline. The braided nylon led on ahead, over the rocky pile. The spot flicked upward, probing into a vertical slot or crack in the ceiling.

He pressed his light against his chest, cutting off the beam. Blackness flooded in all around him, the absolute and eternal black of the caves.

He was lost.

But he *couldn't* be lost.

When he uncovered his main light again, it was noticeably dimmer. He shook it angrily and it went out altogether. He clipped it to his harness, groping for a backup as the darkness closed around him like a suffocating fist.

Light burst out again, reassuring, but not as bright as the bigger unit. His eyes narrowed behind the mask. There was his guideline, still leading on. But he hadn't recognized anything for the last fifteen minutes. Was he losing his memory? Getting narked? But he wasn't that deep. He felt focused, intent with the controlled paranoia of the trained diver. Had he screwed up somehow, gotten turned around? He couldn't think how.

When he checked his computer again, he saw the decision was already made. He'd used more air than he thought back there in the bottleneck. He couldn't go back. He had to go forward, trusting that air and light lay ahead.

Bubbles roared in his ears. The beast shuddered, stirred, and again he breathed deep and slow. He was sure now he'd never seen this part of the cave before. Maybe this *wasn't* his line. It looked like his, but maybe other divers had been in here. Somehow, he'd fouled up in the murky water, taken the wrong turn—there were lots of side branches—and gotten off his line and onto theirs. Wherever it went, now he was committed to it—more and more with each second that passed as he hung here, trying to make the right decision.

All in all, not a good situation. But he'd been in tight spots before. Even if this wasn't his line, it must lead to an exit—wherever the other divers had come in. Some obscure sinkhole back in the hammocks. The river, maybe, or a chimney up, a shaft or lift tube or syphon.

He glanced at his gauges again, hoping he found it soon. The passage had led gradually downward, and the deeper he went, the more air he used. He had fourteen minutes left in his main tanks. When they went dry, he'd shift to the stage bottle; after that, the oxygen. Breathing it would be swiftly fatal this deep, but he was running out of alternatives. . . . Don't fixate on that. Just keep going. Stay calm. Above all, he had to stay calm.

But he couldn't help thinking of the bodies.

He'd pulled out his share over the years. Open-water divers who came to Florida and decided caves couldn't be that tough. So beautiful, so innocent-looking, bubbling with millions of gallons of spring water clear and clean as liquid light. They'd just take a look . . . and the dark welcomed them, tempted them on. Then it struck, silent and sudden. They turned back, to find the way out blotted black by kicked-up silt. They lost their bearings, or their lights, or sometimes just their nerve. You found them wedged into the overhead, masks off, some with air still in their tanks. They'd panicked, sometimes just a few feet from escape.

But it wouldn't happen to him. He wasn't going to die. In the next hundred yards, or the hundred after that, he'd find a way back.

Breathing as slowly as he could, holding his spare light out at arm's length, he followed its fading golden beam down and down and down, into the reverberating black heart of the earth.

ONE

Galloway had felt savage all morning. Not just hung over, but close to desperate. He owed too much and there was no money coming in. With the general slowdown, the doldrums that had hovered over the Outer Banks for the last year, he felt as if somebody were burying him alive, a teaspoon at a time.

The weather didn't help: ninety-five in the shade, and so humid a mist squatted above the muddy chop of Roanoke Sound. The hot air stank of salt marsh and fish guts, diesel exhaust and welding. But mostly, it smelled of the low-priced bottom paint he was slowly and with abundant cursing rolling onto the battered hull planks of the forty-two-footer that loomed over him.

A drop of paint left the raised roller and fell straight into his eye. He muttered, "Shit," and tried to blink it out. It didn't blink out; it burned. Suddenly, he couldn't take it anymore. The narrow space he lay in upside down beneath *Miss Anna*'s teak hull was suddenly untenable, threatening, as if her massive suspended weight had shifted imperceptibly in the moment before it came crashing down.

He pushed himself out from between the splintering keel blocks and threw the roller into the drum of Sea Guard. On the far side, his partner was humming Hatteras High fight songs as he hammered caulking into a gaping seam. Across the boatyard, a fifty-ton Travelift whined as it extracted a trawler from the water like a rotten tooth from brown gums. Galloway dabbed at his eye with a handful of grimy T-shirt. Then his gaze lifted, tracing the soar of a herring gull, its cry coming down, then fading, faint above the man-made clamors of Mill Landing Marina, Roanoke Island, North Carolina.

"Hey, you ready for a beer?" he yelled.

"Still workin', Till."

He considered, balancing the need to get the job done against the suspicion it was futile. Finally, he hauled himself upright and rooted a Bud from the cooler. Leaning against a ladder, he stared up.

The 1954-vintage Chris-Craft had spent four months on the bottom of the Pamlico after being blown apart by an alcohol bomb. They'd raised her with oil drums and compressed air, then towed the hulk here.

Then they'd run out of money. While they'd gone to Louisiana for more, diving on the oil rigs offshore, the boat had waited patiently on blocks. She baked in the sun, soaked in the rain, and her planks warped and rust and rot crept into her heart. His own heart sank as he surveyed her now. The pilothouse was charred, windows blasted to blank stares. Crumbling caulking. Shattered glass. And inside her, wiring corroded to green powder, cracked timbers, frozen valves, split hoses.

"You okay, man?"

When he turned, Shadrach Aydlett was wiping his face with a fluorescent orange bandanna. His thick, scarred, muscular arms glittered with sweat, veins knitted like rope fancywork over smooth mahogany. He caught the beer Galloway tossed and tilted it back. When he surfaced, he said, "What's eatin' you today? You been awful quiet over there."

"Just thinking."

"Hey, I tell you 'bout Abe? He got some bee in his shorts about that land we use to own down on the beach, that they took for taxes. Got himself a lawyer and everything."

"Your dad always said he was the smartest one of you three."

"Uh-huh, right. Hey, don't look so down. Get this hull tight, we can drop her in the water. Tow her down to Buxton and finish up at the dock."

"I know. But then we got the engine work to do, the electrical, all the interior—"

"What you gettin' at?"

"I don't know if it's worth working on her anymore, Shad."

Aydlett said softly, "How much we got left?"

7

Galloway swallowed the last of the beer. He looked at the hammered lead sheet of the Sound, darkening under a bank of cloud. Studied the distant arch of the Oregon Inlet bridge, a curve of bleached bone beyond the sand hills and spoil islands that barred their way to the sea. Examined the black-and-white horizontally striped shaft of the Bodie Island lighthouse.

"Everything we brought back from Bayou City?" his partner said quietly.

He nodded. "And we still owe Dacor, and Seaquest, and the hospital."

Shad said tentatively, "We could ask your brother for a loan."

Tiller didn't answer.

"Anyway. Hey, at least Nuñez is off our backs. In jail outside Medellín, the paper said."

He nodded. Yeah, that was good, that they didn't have to worry about geeks with guns. But right now, he felt boxed in, nailed down, and stamped for shipping. He'd figured once they had a boat under them, they could make a living. Shad had suggested setting up a ferry service over to Portsmouth Island. They could take summer sightseers over from Hatteras, charge them twenty-five a head for an afternoon in a ghost town.

"How you boys doing this morning?"

The flat Massachusetts voice belonged to "Davy" Jones, the marina manager. Galloway shaded his eyes, held up the empty can questioningly.

The thin man with the red-and-gray beard shook his head. "This is business. Till, I got to have something on your lay bill."

"Next week, Davy."

"You said that last month. And you're into the marina store for five hundred bucks."

Shad said, "You can trust us, Mr. Jones. May be slow, but we always pay."

Jones took his hands out of his pockets. "Look, we been through all this before. I gave you the winter rate, gave it to you all last summer, too. I got to have a payment."

Tiller cleared his throat. "Well, fact is, we ain't got it right now, Davy."

"Then I'll have to take her. Take her and sell her at auction."

"Sell her?" Shad laughed. "Who's gonna buy her, shape she's in? Let us get her in the water, to where we can turn a dollar—"

"Then I'll break her up and sell the fittings. Won't be the first

8

time I've had to do it. This isn't a charity operation. If you can't pay, get out."

Galloway stood in the sun, sweat making rivers through the paint chips and grit on his chest. He felt something huge and angry growing in his gut.

He said, "You don't take a Hatteras man's boat."

Shad said softly, "Tiller."

Without answering, he went over to the ladder that led up to the main deck. He looked at Jones, but the manager didn't blink.

He went on up, hand over hand.

The blistered paint of the afterdeck crackled under his Dock-Sides. They kept their tools and supplies up here.

"Tiller," said Aydlett from below, louder.

Clear fluid splashed and then disappeared, sucked in by thirsty old wood. He threw the empty five-gallon can of thinner into the wheelhouse. He rounded the foredeck, kicking cans of enamel and hardener and varnish down into the open hatch. Coming back along the port side, he looked down into the engine compartment. At his feet was a can of acetone. They used it to clean fiberglass resin off their hands. He uncapped it and took a lighter out of his pocket.

"Tiller! What're you doin' up there?"

"Stand back, Shad. You, too, Jones."

He flicked the lighter. Held the pale wavering flame for a moment, looking the old boat over from stern to bow. Then he tossed it down into the hatchway.

Aydlett pushed his head over the gunwale, only to be met by a six-foot dragon tongue of fire licking up out of the engine room hatch. He muttered, "Aw shit," and dropped back out of sight.

When Galloway was halfway down the ladder, he heard the *whump* as the flammables in the forward cabin ignited. The boat groaned, as if sensing her impending end. He stepped off, to see Jones sprinting for the marina office.

A puff of smoke, and the crease and waver of heated air showed above *Miss Anna*'s pilothouse, hovered over her flying bridge, then drifted off to seaward. Looking up, he recalled making love to Bernice there one summer night. Better to remember the old boat as she'd been then, not as the gutted, hopeless wreck he'd been slaving over long past any real hope.

Jones came running back, with three other guys on his heels. Two had fire extinguishers. Jones and the fourth were dragging a heavy canvas fire hose.

Like a sleepwalker waking, Galloway suddenly realized that *Miss Anna* wasn't the only boat that might burn. On one side of her was Al Foreman's *Crystal Dawn,* laid up for a shaft replacement. On the other was a brand-new fifty-five-foot Davis, and beyond that trawlers and sportfishermen and a huge Beneteau with a yacht broker's sale sign. Already, sparks were shooting up from the old Chris-Craft. They hovered like fiery angels above the immobile boats, the baking decks, bone-dry or fresh-painted.

"You son of a bitch!" Jones yelled. "You burn down my marina, you're never gonna see the outside of a jail again! That's arson, mister!"

Galloway hesitated, looking up at the climbing smoke, the falling sparks. Then he ran for Shad's truck.

The pickup snarled to life. He backed it violently, then straightened. The row of boats loomed through the windshield. Then he gunned it.

The truck mowed down the first set of boat stands along *Miss Anna*'s side. He kept the pedal down and the second set went flying with a rattling thud. Sparks bounced off the windshield, danced on the hood.

Then he was past and braking as the big Davis towered like a gleaming, curved white wall. He twisted in the seat to see *Miss Anna* sag, hesitate, then give way, heeling to a last, invisible sea.

She toppled over onto the paint-stained ground, rebounded, scattering a fiery spray, and slid a few feet down the concrete ramp toward the water, as if struggling in her last agony toward the cooling sea. But her weakened strakes buckled and split. Fire spilled through the hull, then curled back to attack from outside, too. But now the gaping hatches and the torn-up deck boards lay open to the firefighters. They moved in, the lavender plumes of the extinguishers probing into the flames.

Jones was coughing as Galloway, on foot again, caught up to him. He wrestled the hose out of the manager's hands and pulled back the bail. The stream blasted out so hard, he almost lost it. He got a better grip and played the roaring cone of water back and forth along the Davis's side, till it ran a gleaming waterfall. Then he swept it around.

Bending over, he crab-walked into the roaring heart of the flames.

They worked together side by side for the next few minutes, Tiller, Shad, Jones and his men, others who came running from Coastal

Engine and the boatbuilders' and the seafood packers'. By the time the Wanchese Fire Department's white engine pulled in, the other boats stood dripping—safe, while *Miss Anna* had subsided into a steaming, hissing pile of charred teak, glowing metal, and two oblong black masses that had been Chrysler 318's. Fortunately, her fuel tanks had been empty. He crouched beside it, hands on his knees, coughing out the smoke. The still-radiating heat warmed his face, but his heart felt cold.

Aydlett came up, eyes dark with soot and anger. "You okay?"

"Uh-huh."

"That was about the goddamn stupidest move I ever seen in my life. What the hell was that supposed to do for us?"

"He was gonna take her."

"He took her, least then we wouldn't have owed him nothing. Now we got to pay all our other bills and that, too. Plus, you purely pissed the man off." Aydlett looked off across the tarmac, jaw set. "You're explaining this one yourself, my man. I don't want no part of it."

The green-and-white sedan eased through the gate and coasted to Jones's lifted arm. A pause, then it turned, tires squealing, and rolled toward where they stood. The window hummed down. A white-haired man with weather-beaten skin crooked a finger. Galloway straightened and sauntered over.

"Sheriff Austin," he said.

"You really do that, Till? Torch your own boat?"

"*Our* boat," said Aydlett. "And he done it, all right. The stupid shit."

"I'm talkin' to Tiller here, Shad. Till?"

"I did it, Bert."

"Uh-huh. Any special reason?"

He shrugged. The sheriff studied him a moment longer, then asked Aydlett, "He sober?"

"Sober as he gets."

"Uh-huh. Well, Jones wants you boys out of here. Now."

"Can I get my truck?" said Aydlett.

"Get him in it and take him out of here," said Austin. His slitted eyes followed them as they walked away.

"And don't come back," Jones yelled as they drove by him.

"Goddamn," Aydlett said. "You know, pretty soon we ain't going to be allowed in a bar or a marina anyplace in the Banks."

"Lay off, Shad."

"Yeah, lay off. . . . That wasn't purely your boat, man. That was half mine, what you burned."

"It was worthless. It was an albatross. We're better off without it . . . stop kidding ourselves."

"It was half my goddamn albatross. Least you could have asked me 'fore you torched it."

"It just got to me all of a sudden."

" 'It just got to me all of a sudden.' What a sorry-ass—" Aydlett slammed a palm suddenly on the wheel. "I don't know, man. Latricia says she don't see why I hang with you. And then you pull senseless shit like this. Sometimes, I swear, I don't think you got both oars in the water. When you gonna learn to think about somebody other than yourself? When you gonna grow up, take some damn responsibility?" He scowled through the windshield. "And look at my hood. Maybe it's time we developed us some other friends."

Galloway didn't answer. He looked out as they rolled through the chain-link fence. A small group had gathered there, locals from Moon Tillet's and Etheridge's and tourists diverted from the Fisherman's Wharf by the column of smoke and the wail of sirens. His eyes scanned the faces, then locked on one of them.

"Stop the truck," he said. "Shad! Stop the goddamn truck."

The boy was thin and lanky, with a scraggly Jefferson Davis beard and hostile pale blue eyes. He had studs in both ears and a black T-shirt silk-screened with copulating skeletons. He wore dirty, torn jeans and new black combat-style boots and had a nylon rucksack on his back. He came slowly over to the pickup.

"Tad?" said Galloway after a couple of seconds.

"Yeah . . . Dad."

"Who's this?" said Aydlett, staring down.

"You remember Tad."

"Oh . . . oh, yeah. Theodore! You grown up, last time I looked."

"Where's your mom?" He looked around for Ellie.

"She's not here. I come alone." The boy put his hand on the door. "I got in some trouble. Told her I didn't want to live there anymore. And then I took off down here."

Tiller didn't know what to say. He'd hardly recognized his son. It had been that long. At last, he jerked a thumb over his shoulder. "Well, get in. We gotta travel."

Clambering in, Tad said, "I saw you torch the boat."

"Oh, you saw that?" said Aydlett.

"Yeah. Why'd you do that?"

"It seemed like the right thing at the time."

"Man, it was killer."

Tiller asked him, "What kind of trouble?"

"What?" The boy flinched, blinked.

"You said you got in trouble. What kind?"

Tad fished a clipping out of his jacket. It was creased, as if it had been carried around and folded and unfolded, as if he'd been showing it off.

Youth Held in Property Destruction

A 15-year-old Prentis Park resident was held as a juvenile yesterday after going on a rampage Sunday, damaging his mother's vehicle and escaping after being placed under restraint, according to a report filed by police.

At 10:00 A.M. Sunday, Officer Neil Curran was dispatched to Des Moines Avenue in response to a disturbance. Upon his arrival, Curran drove around to the back of a mobile home at that address, where he observed a young man striking a new pickup truck with a piece of angle iron approximately three feet in length. When the officer approached the juvenile and instructed him to drop the bar, he stated that his mother's truck meant more to her than he did, so he wanted to see how much it meant to her now.

The officer was standing approximately eight feet from the juvenile when he advised him two more times to drop the bar. Holding the bar like a baseball bat, the youth took one step toward the officer, at which time the officer removed his chemical-agents canister from its holster.

The juvenile then dropped the bar and was placed under restraint. Officer Curran placed him in back of the patrol car and then entered the home to take the complaint.

After speaking with the mother, the officer came back out of the residence, to find that despite being handcuffed, the juvenile had managed to slide open the window on the cage between him and the front seat, crawl through it, and steal a .44 Magnum handgun that the

13

officer kept in the patrol car. At 10:51 A.M., the officer requested assistance from the juvenile correctional authorities and the K-9 tracking unit.

The juvenile was reapprehended at 1:20 P.M. one mile from the scene by another patrol team. At the time of his apprehension, the handgun was no longer in his possession.

The juvenile broke out the front and rear windshields of his mother's vehicle, destroyed the front grille, broke the headlights, the radio antenna, and dented the hood. Total damages were estimated at over $6,000. He is now in custody and awaiting an appearance in juvenile court.

Tiller coughed into his fist, then glanced up, to see Tad waiting for his reaction. "This is you?"

"Uh-huh."

"What was all this for?"

"It seemed like a good idea at the time."

Beside him, Aydlett made a choking noise. Tiller ignored him. He asked Tad, "So why aren't you locked up in some juvenile facility?"

"I was. But they let me go. Mom's still mad at me for screwing up her stuff. So I decided to come down here and see you."

"Where is she?"

"Who?"

"Your mom."

"Back home. I told you."

"Then how'd you get down here?"

"I stole a car."

Aydlett started whistling, looking out at the passing woods and homes as they neared the causeway to the beach. Tiller gave him a glare, turned back to Tad. "You stole a car."

"Uh-huh."

"Where is it?"

"Back at the marina. Where we were."

"Turn around, Shad." Aydlett gave him a sideways glance and pulled over. They waited for the traffic and made a U-turn, slid in behind an Olds with New Jersey plates. The bumper read BE A HERO, SAVE A WHALE. SAVE A BABY, GO TO JAIL.

Tiller looked back at his son's sullen face, his folded arms. He remembered the boy having a birthmark, but it was bigger and darker than he remembered it. The red print stretched over the

14

right side of his face from nose to ear and up onto his forehead, like half of a Halloween mask. He tried to imagine how he'd have felt at fifteen, something like that on his face. Probably not very good.

"So, what are you going to do to me?" said the boy after half a mile of stop-and-go traffic.

"I'm thinking. Tell me again why you came down here."

"Where else would I come when Mom don't want me around? To be with my dear old daddy. Besides, I never got to tell you what I thought of you. All about how bad you treated us and how worthless you are."

Tiller pounded his head slowly with his fist. He didn't need this. Not today. "Talk to me like that again, I'm going to slap the shit out of you."

"Just like when I was a little kid, huh?"

Galloway turned suddenly, grabbed the boy's T-shirt, and pulled him close. He hissed, "Yeah. Just like that."

Tad dropped back against the upholstery and looked at Shad. Aydlett shook his head warningly.

"Okay, here we are. Where's the car? Which one?"

The boy pointed sullenly. Aydlett coasted past it, a sporty red Dodge coupe. Just what a fifteen-year-old would steal, Galloway thought. He cased the fence.

"There's the sheriff. Gonna turn me in?"

"Shut up."

"So what are we gonna do?"

"Drive it out of here. Where's the keys?"

They came flying over the seat. Tiller caught them, muttered to Shad, "Coquina Beach. The parking lot." He rolled out of the passenger side, trying to look casual, and strolled toward the Dodge.

"We'll leave it here," he said, slamming the door after wiping down the wheel and the interior with his shirt. It left red smears of bottom paint on the black upholstery. Aydlett stood a few yards off, ostentatiously scanning the wedge of gray-blue Atlantic beyond the dunes. The wreckage of a wooden schooner, time-eaten timbers and ribs and bolts scabbed with salt rust, lay like a dinosaur skeleton half-buried by sand. "The Park Service'll find it here tonight, call in the plates. . . . Do I have to tell you how stupid that was? Stealing a car?"

Tad didn't answer. He slumped, eyes half-closed, as if all this was too boring for words. Galloway reached in and jerked him upright so hard, his head snapped back. "I said, do I have to tell you—"

"I heard you. I'm stupid."

"You got a bag? Clothes?" The boy pointed wordlessly to the pack.

"Till, I got to get going. Latricia—"

"Yeah. Thanks, Shad. Just drop us at Sam and Omie's, okay?"

The boy ordered a soft-shell crab sandwich, fries, and a Coke. Tiller didn't feel hungry, but he ordered a beer. He sat and watched his son wolf his food. He was trying to get a grip on the situation. Everything the kid said was a sharpened stick probing for his vitals.

But at the same time, he felt guilty.

He'd left Ellie and the boy years ago, when he was so drunk or stoned whenever he wasn't actually diving, he didn't know or care about anything else. Pay was good in the Patch in those days, but it melted like snow in summer when you had to feed the monkey. He'd lived on the crew boat for a while, then moved in with Nicolette, graduating from buying to selling as the company didn't seem to need him as much anymore. Then they'd caught him with the duffel of grass out on the rig, and fired him. The easy money was gone, and not long after, so was Nicolette. He'd gone from selling to smuggling, first with Steinberg and then Christian and Nuñez. And somewhere in there, he'd sort of lost track of his family.

"You'd better stay with me tonight."

Tad grunted, mouth full. Tiller managed to keep his voice neutral. "They keep cots for when the blues are running. I'll get them to put one in the room."

"Where?"

"Across the street. There."

The boy peered. "You live in a motel? Mom said you had a Jewish girlfriend."

"That's been over for a long time." He put a bill on the table, seeing only a couple more behind it in his wallet. "Come on. Let's go."

Gray's was the last of the little fishermen's motels that used to line the Nags Head shore like washed-up seaweed between Route 13 and the surf line. Most were fast-fading memories now, obliterated by block after block of time-shares and condos with rope-bordered signs and nautical names. The sand-worn planks of the

16

long porch creaked under his weight. Two fishermen were arguing over the open hood of a rusty F-150 next to Galloway's CJ6. That's next, he thought gloomily. Hang a FOR SALE sign on the Jeep.

He was bent over in front of number 15, searching his pockets for the key, when Tad said, "You got mail."

"What?"

"There's something stuck under the door."

It was a note. *Important you call your brother*, it read. *Message for you.*

His brother Otinus's office was in Kill Devil Hills. It was a mock-quaint replica of a Lifesaving Service lookout station, set back from the sea side of Route 158 behind a carefully landscaped arrangement of raked gravel, palmettos, and dwarf cacti. Beneath crossed oars and a life ring, the sign read FIND YOUR PLACE IN THE SUN WITH O. R. GALLOWAY REALTY. SELLING THE BANKS FOR OVER FORTY YEARS.

He stood at the door, trying to see if his brother was in the front office. But the glass was blank, reflective, impenetrable unless you were on the inside. He sucked a breath and pushed it open.

Icy air, potted palms, a big colorful LeRoy Neiman on the wall, and a blond receptionist with teeth any orthodontist would have been proud to take credit for. "Good morning, welcome to Galloway Realty. How may I help you, sir?"

"I'm Lyle."

"Nice to meet you, Mr. Lyle. How may I—"

"No. I'm Lyle Galloway, Otinus's brother. I got a message down at Gray's, something about a call for me."

Her smile stayed fixed, but her eyes widened. "Oh, Mr. *Galloway*. You must be the one who . . . I mean, yes, of course, I've heard you lived in the area. About the message—just a moment, let me check."

She got up and went into the back. He caught her murmur, then his brother's voice in reply. He hunched his shoulders, leaning over the polished waist-high barrier between him and the white corridor with the spotless fawn carpet. He looked at the pictures that lined the walls.

The officer in the white cap, white uniform: Adm. Lyle Galloway II, U.S. Coast Guard. A man of honor, a man of pride. He'd locked himself in his office the day the verdict came down condemning his son, the drug smuggler. And picked up a gun.

17

And just visible farther down, the engraving from the 1879 *Harper's Weekly* of Otinus Randall Galloway at the oars of a pulling boat, putting out from Kinnekeet Station into the worst northeaster in Banks memory. And in the offing, dwarfed by a fifty-foot surf, the dismasted wreck of the doomed *Floridian*.

Closer to the lobby, the wall was hung with framed photographs and certificates. Pictures of his brother at chamber of commerce functions, certificates of appreciation, shots of him shaking hands with Andy Griffith and Jesse Helms and Newt Gingrich.

The blonde came back without her smile. "You didn't need to see Mr. Galloway . . . your brother, did you?"

"Not unless he wants to see me."

"Well, here's the message. Tammy took it this morning. It took us a while to find where you were living. I'm sorry if it's bad news," she said in a rush, watching him read it.

"Uh-huh. Use your phone?"

"I'm sorry, our policy doesn't allow that. There's a pay phone over at—"

He slammed the door so hard on the way out, his reflection shivered in the mirrored glass.

He found a booth at the Exxon near Seagate North. The message said to call collect, so he did. "Tiller Galloway," he said to the electronic operator. The line went dead as it checked his acceptability, then came back on.

A woman's voice. "Hello?"

"Mrs. Kusczk?" He swallowed. "This is Tiller Galloway. You left me a message. About Bud?"

The voice on the far end of the line was extraordinarily precise, as if not far from losing control. "Yes, thank you. Thank you for calling back. I'm Monica Kusczk. You don't know me, but I understand you and Joel were good friends. I'm sorry to disturb you."

"That's all right. What happened?"

"They found him three weeks ago last Tuesday. It was a diving accident."

"An accident? Bud was the most careful guy I ever knew."

"I know. But in the springs . . . something must have gone wrong. He knew he was going to die. They found a few words on his slate, when they brought him up."

He felt unreal, felt as if he was being scissored in two by the cutting edges of his past. A face was taking shape, reflected in the

18

dirty glass of the booth. A young face, cowlick so pale brown, it was almost silver. The heavy Slavic cheekbones and jaw were masked by green camo paint. For some reason, it was looking back over its shoulder at him, as if Bud had taken point again. . . . He dragged sweat off his forehead and pressed the phone to his ear as a tractor-trailer rumbled past toward Belk's. "Like last words, you mean?"

The voice took an audible breath. "I'll read it. Here it is: 'Mon: Sorry I screwed up. Call Killer G for help. Always loved you above all. Bud.' "

"That was it?" he said when the line hummed empty.

"That's all. It wasn't a big slate. At first, I didn't know what he meant by 'Killer G.' It sounded so . . . But then I remembered him talking once about somebody nicknamed that, from when he was in the Navy. I found your name on the back of an old picture. But I didn't know how to find you. Then today I was looking through his desk and I found a postcard you sent him years ago from someplace called Hatteras. You were running a dive shop. So I called the North Carolina operator and they didn't have a listing for you, but they found a Galloway real estate office. Is that what you do now?"

"No. That's my brother. But they gave me your message. Look, uh, Monica, I'm really shocked to hear this."

"I know. I don't know how close the two of you were—"

He didn't say anything; she went on. "But he thought of you, there at the end. Do you have any idea why?"

"Well . . . no."

"Are you still running the shop down there? The dive shop?"

"Not anymore. No."

The voice took on resolve. "Well, I'm going to ask you a big favor, Mr. Galloway. You don't have to say yes. But apparently he thought you might."

"What's that?"

"He has—we had—Well, he left me a business here in north Florida—specializing in cave diving. Now that he's gone, I can't run it by myself. I dive, but . . . Anyway, would it be possible for you to come down for a couple of weeks and help me, help keep things running, help me sell it? I'll pay you, and pay for the plane ticket, and give you a place to stay."

He stood sweating in the booth, the clammy heat, too much like the Delta. He was having trouble visualizing Joel Kusczk dead. Bud had been ultracareful, ultrasmart, ultracool. Not that he

19

wouldn't take a risk, but he figured all the angles first. The squad had always figured him for the one who'd die in bed. But apparently, he'd slipped up somehow, deep in a Florida cave.

And now his widow needed help. Well, there didn't seem to be much left around the Banks for him. No boat, no job, even his partnership with Shad seemed to be fraying. But what about Tad?

"If you give me your address, I'll overnight you the ticket," said Mrs. Kusczk. And Galloway, clearing his throat, said, "How about if you send two?"

TWO

"Please remain seated till the aircraft comes to a complete halt at the loading gate. Those who are continuing south to Tampa and Miami, please remain in your seats. If you're ending your journey in Tallahassee, stand by to deplane, and thank you for flying US Air. The temperature in Tallahassee is ninety-two degrees Fahrenheit. . . ."

Tiller rubbed his eyes, looking past his son's slack face to the modern terminal that trundled steadily nearer. He'd dozed for most of the flight, though never going deep enough to forget where he was and where he was going. He couldn't count on having enough cash to get the Jeep out of the parking garage when he returned, so he'd left it in Virginia Beach—pawned it, essentially. The four hundred the auto broker had given him was all he had.

He sat there and thought again, with something close to dread, about cave diving.

Even the idea gave him the willies. It broke his lifetime rule: Never go anywhere you can't get out of. But he and Bud had fought together, in a war that had welded its veterans in a bitter bond all its own. Knowing he was going to die, Kusczk had laid the burden and debt of those fiery years on him. He owed it to Bud to help his wife out for a few days. He'd asked Shad if he wanted to go, but Aydlett had just looked at him and shook his head. Well, he was still mad about the boat.

He sighed and looked at his son again. Studied the closed eyes,

21

the pulled-back hair, the scowl lingering even in sleep. Remembering the three-year-old who'd thought his dad was God's boss. Now the kid blamed him personally for everything wrong with the planet. Shit, he'd paid for everything he'd done, paid double and triple.

Don't think about that, about prison and the succession of bad luck and bad company since. He rubbed his face. He'd told Tad he could either come to Florida with him or go back to his mom. The boy had just shrugged. Well, it might be good to get away, have a little father-son time together.

"Hey. We're here."

Tad opened his eyes. He looked out the window and sighed. "Where?"

"Florida."

"Looks just like home. Who's this bitch we're going to see?"

"Call her that again, you'll regret it," Tiller told him. "Is that how your mom brought you up? To talk about women like that?"

"That's what you used to call her—when you got drunk, when I was little."

He took three deep breaths. He didn't want to have to hit the kid here, on the plane, not with the gray-haired lady watching them from the seat opposite. "Who is she? She's the wife of a guy I was in Vietnam with."

"Oh yeah. The war you guys lost."

"That's the one. Like I told you, he drowned, and she wants us to come down and help her out. Her name's Kusczk."

"Coo-sick. Like *carsick*, huh? She wants you, not 'us.' "

"I could use some help. You like to work?"

Tad stared at him disbelievingly. The old lady smiled sweetly at Tiller—isn't he cute?—and he glared back at her.

They were going down the escalator to the baggage area when he spotted her waiting at the bottom: a red-eyed, tousle-haired woman in a high-necked black dress and heels, juggling a cardboard sign that said GALLOWAY. Anxious green eyes slid past him as they descended, then clicked back as he approached her.

"Monica?"

"Mr. Galloway?"

They shook hands. He noted a small chin, large eyes, skin that had seen too much sun. Reddish blond hair fell in waves below her shoulders. He glanced back, to find Tad hanging back, looking away from them. "Come over here," he said sharply. "Straighten up. This is my son, Tad. Tad, this is Mrs. Kusczk."

"Hi."

"Hi, Tad. How was your flight? Do you have luggage?"

"A couple pieces."

To be exact, one worn bag of well-used dive gear, and one scuffed Tourister with his clothes. He'd checked out of Gray's, just left the cheap utensils and the bread and bologna in the fridge for the next fisherman. They waited by the baggage station as it vomited suitcases and boxes and Tad's backpack. Then they humped their gear after Monica's quick stride out the automatic door and into a bright, hard wall of late-afternoon sunlight. "Sheez," Tad muttered behind them.

"Thanks for coming, both of you. I know you have things of your own to do. I really appreciate it."

"That's all right. This your car?"

"The green Buick. I'd better drive." She slid in, pulling her skirt down, and popped the trunk. Tiller stowed their stuff beside stacks of *Dive Training* and *Skin Diver*, a carefully wrapped transparent plastic package of jumper cables, starter fluid, tools and road-warning signs, and an unopened crate of Mobil 1.

"It's not specially hot today, but I'll turn on the air."

"Thanks." Not specially hot? He was already sodden. The sun glared down off the white terminal building, flashed from windows, grilles, and hoods as they pulled out onto a highway. Monica lit a cigarette and reminded them to fasten their seat belts.

He'd never been to Tallahassee before. It reminded him of Chapel Hill, or Durham, except for the palms. She drove slowly along roads that wound through low hills, whether because she always drove that way or to let them look, he didn't know. "This is Gaines Street," she said. "There's the Warehouse, where the Florida State students hang out. The rednecks play pool in front and the poets have readings in back. Like two completely distinct crowds—except for the redneck poets. These up ahead are all government buildings. There's the state supreme court. I used to work there, and in the legislature before that." He thought they all looked alike, except for the two monoliths with windows that looked like electrical sockets.

"You worked in the supreme court?"

"Legal secretary, years ago. . . . The capitol's on your left. The old capitol's the one with green striped awnings like a chicken franchise. The new capitol's the big tower, with the two domes on either side."

"Man, you know what that looks like?" said Tad.

"Shut up," said Tiller.

"Are you hungry? Want to stop at the Loop?"

"Thanks, they fed us on the plane."

"Tad, how about you?"

A negative mutter from the backseat. "Okay . . . I live north of town, off Thomasville Road. This used to be a beautiful canopied road, but they cut all the oaks down when they widened it."

"You've lived here how long?"

"Twelve years. We met here, Joel and I."

"I didn't even know he was married."

"Somehow, I thought you were closer. He never answered your postcard? The one I found?"

"He sent me one back. There's not much room on those things for the details."

They passed several expensive-looking subdivisions as traffic grew heavier. Tad stared out the window, looking bored.

Killearn Estates was in a wood at the crest of a hill. The houses were two-story, new, on plots so large, you couldn't see your neighbors through the trees. She finally turned off onto a winding brick drive.

"Is that your house?" Tiller said, leaning forward. He was thinking, Bud was doing better than I figured.

It looked old but wasn't, a reproduction of a Federal mansion. Beneath tall windows, azaleas frothed like pink foam. He recognized magnolias, crape myrtles, but there were a lot more. Cast-metal lawn furniture was set around a sunken garden. A pond rippled with orange-and-white koi. Beyond the detached garage, oak and dogwood stretched away, the shadowed ground beneath cool and dark and green as an underwater cavern.

"Nice impatiens," said Tad. "There in the shade."

Monica beamed at him. "That's right. You know flowers?"

"I like plants," the boy mumbled, giving Galloway a defiant glance.

She parked the Buick beside a showroom-new Land Rover, then took them inside, talking them through each room, then upstairs. The bedrooms were so clean and roomy and tastefully furnished, Tiller felt uneasy. "Go ahead and get comfortable," she said. "There are towels and things in the bathroom. If you see a cat,

24

his name is Lunker. That's short for Spelunker. He's a Himalayan. I'll be out in the garden when you're ready to talk."

The dark was a gradual infiltration through the treetops, a slow advance between the warped trunks of the screw pines. Showered and changed to khaki shorts and a Kitty Hawk Sports T-shirt, he looked around the garden. The verdigris-finished cast-metal benches and chairs were vacant. Beyond them, a path wound off toward where flames guttered yellow-orange back in the woods. He looked back at the house—Tad was downstairs, parked in front of a screen wide as his outstretched arms—then went down the steps and followed the path into the pines.

She lay on a chaise beside a pool. The blue-lit surface roiled slowly in the light of the torches. Night crept closer as he stood watching her, she not yet giving any sign she knew he was there. She was wearing a white terry-cloth bath wrap, not reading, not doing anything; just sitting there, staring off into the trees, where the fireflies flashed like distant buoys marking an unknown channel.

"Hi," he said at last.

She flinched, looked up, then smiled, but clearly it took an effort. "Oh, it's you. Find everything you needed?"

"Yeah, thanks."

"Where's Tad?"

"Inside. Watching TV."

"You're so lucky to have him. Bud and I once hoped . . . but it didn't happen."

She waved at a table beside her. He went over and examined the selection and finally poured himself a couple fingers of Jack Daniel's. "Cheers."

"Cheers. That's what Bud drank. Black Jack."

"Yeah?"

She put her hand over her eyes and he paced away, around the pool, letting her have a moment. When he returned, her head was tilted back. She said, not looking at him, "I'm sorry."

"That's all right. Don't apologize."

"The first thing you'll want to know is what happened."

"Sounds like a good place to start." He lowered himself to a chair beside her.

"Some campers noticed his clothes that night out at Emerald Sink. That's south of town, out toward Crawfordville. They called County Rescue when they didn't see anybody come back up by

25

the next morning. The rescue team saw fins sticking down from the ceiling, back in the cave. They brought him up in a body bag."

"Alone?"

"That's right."

"What was he doing there?"

"I don't know. He didn't tell anyone at the shop he was going out there. But he dove alone sometimes. Cave divers do that."

He said, "These are all freshwater caves, right? Freshwater springs?"

"That's right. The water table's high here in north Florida. You can get right into the aquifer through the springs." She glanced at him. "Or do you know all that?"

"All I know is there are springs here, and caves, and every once in a while you read in the papers somebody's died in them."

"Well, I don't know all the technical terms. But all this part of Florida is limestone. It's like a sponge. The rainwater filters down to it. Then it bubbles up again from the springs."

"How far down's the limestone go?"

"I don't know. Forever. And it's full of caves. Everywhere under us. When they collapse, it's called a sinkhole. They swallow cars, roads, whole houses." She shuddered, looking over the eddying surface of the pool. Light filled it from underwater fixtures, making it glow like a huge smoothly ground turquoise. "He took me into one once—into a spring. I didn't really want to, but I thought, Why not? So I took the courses, and we went out to Ponce de Leon for our first dive, to Vortex Spring.

"At first, it was beautiful. The water's so clear, it was just like flying, and all the fish following you. Then he took me down. Sinking down, everything was going blue. It was still clear, but everything got darker as we went down, and then the fish weren't there anymore. Just some little eels, the color of Grey Poupon.

"There was a cavern first, like a lobby. That wasn't too bad. It was shadowy at first, till your eyes adjusted. But down near the floor was a little hole, and past that, it was just black. That was the entrance to the cave.

"He went in first. I was supposed to follow him, but I was afraid. I didn't want to go in there. But he waited and held out his hand, and finally I did.

"Right away, it got really dark. We had lights, but they didn't really push away the black, you know? I could feel it all around, like it was crushing me. The roof came down lower and lower, and then it went up a little, but it was always there. It was just

26

so spooky, so *crazy*. You know there's no way up if anything goes wrong. And he kept going farther and farther, pointing things out to me, like the guide to . . . hell, or something. But there wasn't anything there to see. Just rock and silt, and hundreds of eels. They come up and nip you, to see if you're dead yet, I guess. Then the ceiling came down again, and we had to crawl through and not catch our tanks on the rock."

"How deep were you?"

"I don't know. Seventy or eighty feet. But it just kept going down. I was shaking. I kept thinking, What if I spit this regulator out? I'd die. And these slimy eels would eat me. I wanted to turn around, but I was afraid if I left him, I'd get lost. . . . Oh, I made it. I got to where you can't go any farther, where the roof pinches out. And then he patted my arm, like he was proud of me, and we turned around and came out.

"I've been diving since then, in Crystal River with the manatees, and down in the Keys. But I never went into the caves again. He asked, but I wouldn't go. It felt like there was something down there with us, back in the shadows. Waiting for you to make a mistake, so it could kill you. But the worst thing was . . . you almost *wanted* it to come out. Where you could see it."

He waited, feeling her necessity to talk like the pressure of cold springwater from deep underground. She took a deep, sighing breath and went on. "They called me . . . when they found him. The county called the shop, and they called me at home. Asked me to come and identify him. So I did. Went down to the hospital.

"The thing I can't forget is how cold it felt, leaning against that table. The coldness of that metal against his body. I wanted to cover him up, keep him warm. And when I touched him, how cold he was. Just like ice."

He didn't say anything. She looked off into the darkness, touched her nose lightly with one hand, pinching it. Then she got up, dropping the robe to the tile.

He looked at the curve of her back in the one-piece suit as she stood in front of the torches. Then she dove. A slim, wavering shadow floated beneath the glowing water, grew dim, then floated upward again.

She hoisted herself out, dripping, and came back to where he sat. She toweled her hair off, shook it out, then freshened her gin and tonic. Her lips were pressed together in a tight line. "Another?" she asked, holding up the bourbon bottle.

"Thanks. Yeah."

27

"Can you hand me that robe? And then let's talk about the business."

"All right."

"It's called Scuba Florida. Bud started it ten years ago. We've got two retail locations, one here and one in Orlando. Oh, and there's a grotto, a dive site he was trying to develop between here and Branford. The Orlando shop feeds us a lot of traffic, tourists, mostly. You had a retail store, you said?"

"Retail and charter."

"Have you done much cave diving?"

"My experience is mostly commercial. Oil-field work, wrecks, open water."

"I'm sure you can pick up what you need to know from the staff. They're pretty sharp. We have five people here in Tallahassee."

"Instructors? Or sales staff?"

"Our instructors *are* the sales staff. They do the training and the tours and the service work, too. They're all CDS-qualified. That's the Cave Diving Section, National Speleological Society. They certify cave divers and instructors." She paused. "Now, you must have some questions."

"Uh-huh." He sipped the whiskey, considering. "First, let's make sure you legally own the business. Did Bud have a will?"

"He was always careful about that. Anne Swerdlick—she's our attorney—there's no problem with that. It's mine, all right."

"Okay, I'll let you and her worry about the inheritance end. How about taxes?"

"There aren't any if it passes to the wife."

"Do you have any idea what the gross is, the profit picture?"

"You'll have to look at the books, and the tax returns, and talk to Colten. He's the manager. Bud said something about half a million gross once. And I think the profit's around twenty percent. But I'm not sure."

"That's a hell of a good gross. Twenty percent sounds too high for the bottom line, though. You draw a salary?"

"Yes. But I didn't really do much around the shop."

He nodded; it wasn't uncommon. "So there's retail sales, and training, and tours. Cave tours?"

"Dive services—cave and cavern."

"What's the difference?"

"Cavern, you can still see the surface light. Caves, you're in complete darkness."

28

"I get it."

Something rustled out in the woods. She said, "It's probably a raccoon. . . . The first few years, Bud didn't make any money. Then he did better, and then it really took off. The trouble is, it's so specialized. That might make it hard to find a buyer."

"Are you sure you want to sell?"

"I don't want to run a cave-diving business, Mr. Galloway. Or do you prefer Killer?"

"I haven't gone by that for a long time," he said quietly. "My first name's Lyle. My friends back on Hatteras call me Tiller."

"I loved Bud, not what he did. At first, I worried about it. Then as time went on and I realized he wasn't going to change, I guess I just accepted it. Caves fascinated him. He couldn't stop talking about them, going into them, surveying, exploring. He went to Mexico, Texas, Hungary, once even to Africa." She shook her head. "Anyway, I won't stay in Tallahassee."

"Where are you from?"

"A little town down in central Florida. I don't really know what I'll do. But the first thing to do is sell the business. I've already talked to some people about listing the house and the springs."

Watching her eyes closely, he said, "Did Bud have any insurance?"

She didn't blink. "We had a joint policy. A hundred thousand apiece."

"That's not a lot."

"No, not these days. He put his cash back into the business. The idea was run it till he was fifty-five, then sell it and do some sailing." She smiled faintly into her glass. "Anyway . . . maybe it won't be that hard to sell. We've got good demographics. Tallahassee's the state capital; there's a lot of well-off young people here. And the springs attract people from all over the world. We get Japanese, Germans, Italians, Dutch, Australians . . ."

"Okay," he said. "First thing in the morning, I'll go over, check out the store and meet your people. Get into the books. Where are they? The books?"

"Probably in Bud's office—at the store."

"I'll be looking for things we can do to make the figures more attractive. How are you fixed for living expenses right now?"

"The insurance check came in last week. There was money in our joint checking, too. Don't worry about that."

He sucked a tooth. "Okay . . . so we'll take you off salary starting tomorrow. Get everything cleaned up, make sure the books

29

are in shape. Then we'll put the word out to the business brokers and the dive mags, *PADI Journal, Sport Diver,* and so forth. Anybody you know might be interested in buying? Another shop, another operator, relatives, a rich customer?"

"I can't think of anyone. Colten might know."

"Last question: How much do you want for it?"

"I really can't say. How do you price something like that?"

"The shop, do you own the land it's on? Or is it rented?"

"It's rented. The only land we own is the house, and the grotto, down on the river."

"We'll let the real estate people handle that, then. Keep the business separate." He rubbed his face. "Okay . . . how much—the only real value is what somebody will pay, but we got to set an asking price. You can start with the furniture and fixtures and equipment, the compressors and rental gear and the other stock. But that's liquidation value; it doesn't really give you what a going business is worth. For that, you figure either in multiples of gross sales or multiples of the net profit. A business that's been around a while, a lot of repeat clientele, has what they call 'goodwill,' you'd be looking at maybe twice the annual gross, or seven or eight times annual profit. On the other hand, a lot of that would depend on Bud's reputation, his personal hustle and so forth. I'll have to look at the books, do the homework—but we might come out as high as half a million."

"Half a million! That seems like an awful lot."

"Well, that's where we'll start. If nobody comes out of the bushes, we can always drop back." He looked back at the house, invisible now in the all-enveloping night. "That, and the insurance, and the house—wherever you decide to go, you should be comfortable."

"I'd rather have him back."

He nodded silently. She hoisted herself out of the chair and stood, wavering. He'd counted four gin and tonics just since he'd come out. He wasn't all that steady himself when he got to his feet. He took her arm, afraid she might slip on the wet tile. Her hair burned in the yellow light.

She said, "The mosquitoes are coming out and I'm tired. I appreciate this, Tiller. I'm not sure how to say this, but . . . how do I pay you? Salary? Percentage?"

"Whatever you think's right. I'm mainly doing this for Bud."

She searched his face. "You were close."

"We were once."

"In the war?"

He nodded. They stood in silence, then she said, "I'd better get to bed. Good night."

"Good night," he said. Glass in hand, he watched her slim figure pace away, ghostlike in the white wrap, till she vanished among the trees. Then he reached for the bottle again.

THREE

The cicadas woke him. He lay motionless, listening to them and to the sigh of the wind in the trees. When he opened his eyes, the pale barred square of a window imprinted itself on his retinas. He couldn't remember who or where he was.

He knew he was too drunk to think clearly, but somehow he understood something he didn't when he was sober.

Time wasn't linear, like a Stoner magazine. It was like the cylinder of a revolver. And when you spun it, you couldn't tell what chamber would index when you snapped it shut and pulled the trigger.

Click.

Bang.

He was back in the Rung Sat Special Zone.

A patrol had located a Viet Cong base camp on the Rach Bau Bong. The next morning at first light, Lieutenant Commander Mc-Cormack sent them in on a helicopter assault. The camp was deep in a mangrove swamp. The Sea Wolves sprayed it with M60's and rockets as the SEALs hit the ground to the west. X-ray Platoon hugged the ground, watching the rockets blow the village apart. As soon as the fire lifted, they moved in.

Quartermaster Third Class Lyle Galloway, shit-scared in his first assault, carried a twelve-gauge Ithaca loaded with six rounds of double-ought buck. He couldn't imagine anyone surviving the storm of fire he'd just seen.

But someone had.

32

He could still see every line of the old man's face, and every detail of the weapon, an old French bolt-action rifle. The VC had fired from the hip and missed, the bullet blasting dirt off the reed wall inches from Galloway's ear. Galloway's buckshot had plastered the little man against it before he sagged into the mud, still staring at Galloway as death silvered his eyes.

Click . . . bang.

Central, in isolation after he'd stabbed the Horse. He'd never understood why the guy wanted to kill him. He hadn't scammed his cigarettes, didn't owe him money; it didn't seem to be a sex thing, either. But after the second time the guy tried for him, he hadn't had a choice, if he wanted to keep on living. Horse hadn't made a sound when the sharpened ball-point casing went into his neck, spraying blood like a water fountain. But the guards in the mess hall where it happened had made plenty.

He'd sat rubbing his wrists in a five-by-eight cell. It held a steel bunk with a paper mattress, no window, a stainless-steel toilet-sink combination. Its last occupant had vomited over it and the vomit was still there, dried but still contributing to that special prison smell. One wall was a steel-barred door. Four feet in front of the bars, well out of reach, was another door, this one solid iron. No window, no radio, no books, and damn near no air, since there was no ventilating system.

But there was sound. He couldn't see the others, but he could hear them, shouting back and forth, an incessant clamor that never ended, day or night.

He'd spent six months in that cell. It had almost driven him mad. He'd spent hours staring at his sheets. That was what inmates used to hang themselves. But when he came out at last, they told him Horse had killed another guy and been transferred. Being in isolation had probably saved his life.

Click. Bang.

The squad had been briefed about mines and booby traps before they deployed, but it was Bobby Charpeau being killed his first week incountry that got their attention. The VC had rigged the grenade so it worked backward, exploding when you pressed the spoon in instead of letting it go. In other words, it got you only if you saw it first and tried to defuse it.

They got real mine-conscious after that. The other side marked their toe poppers and spike traps so their own troops wouldn't walk into them. If you were alert, you could see them—in daylight. But in the dark, which was when the SEALs usually operated, you moved in a constant sweat, always dreading the hollow *pop* of a cap, the stomach-twisting crumble of earth at the edge of a punji pit, the tug of a trip wire. The SEALs spent as much time in the water as they did on land. But once they realized that, the VC booby-trapped the canals, too.

What you learned was that the squad was everything. A man might be black or Hispanic, nice guy or total asshole, but once you swam ashore and took the plugs out of your barrel, you had to trust him the way he had to trust you.

Click.

Click.

Click.

He lay grunting and flinching as the memories revolved, firing one after the other. Till it got to that night he'd killed the kids.

The Provincial Reconnaissance Units were Vietnamese, not U.S. A lot of them had been VC before they were captured, or turned themselves in as *chieu hois*. Others were criminals, their choice prison or PRU. There were two guys who'd been child molesters. The reconnaissance units were targeted against the VC infrastructure. They went into villages at night and snatched suspects out of their beds and either interrogated them or killed them. Occasionally, they killed their families, too. They dressed in black pajamas and carried Communist bloc weapons. It was classic terror. Near the end of their tour, he and Kuszczk had drawn an assignment as advisers. Galloway didn't like it, but he'd seen some of the things the other side did, raping and killing teachers and nurses, decapitating nuns. So black ops had seemed justified to him—till that night in the Ben Tre.

They swam into the village past midnight. The guy they were after was supposed to be a paymaster, but instead of cash and muster lists, they found a cache of arms buried in the dirt floor of his hootch. The PRUs had taken him down to the canal and were torturing him. Galloway and Kuszczk were squatting in the dark, weapons at the ready, when Galloway heard something from a little shed behind the hootch.

He found the two PRUs there with two dead women and two little girls. Phan had already been working on one. She was maybe four years old. Yen was holding the other one on his lap. His black trousers were pulled down. The squat little man was smiling down at her as she moved spasmodically against the knife.

Galloway's white phosphorous grenade had plastered the whole interior of the shed with a hell of sticky white fire.

That was the night Bud saved his life. After the screaming and the firing had died down and they'd been wading back, him on point, suddenly there was no bottom under him. His bare feet bicycled helplessly as he dropped away into black water. He was overloaded with the captured arms, and the slings got tangled in his fins. He couldn't get them on and he was too heavy to swim without them. The water had closed over his open mouth, and he'd thought he was dead, until Bud had come down after him and pulled him up again into the stinking, lovely black air of Vietnam.

Asleep, unconscious, he understood that was the only part of the night he consciously remembered now. They went out wired, strung out, and the combination of Dexamil and fear had erased the memory of the screaming, burning children into the soundless hiss of blank tape.

Except in his dreams.

"Hey, Dad. You gettin' up? She's been calling us the last half hour."

He lay motionless. As much as it hurt, he knew it would be worse when he moved.

He opened his eyes, to see Tad pointing a rifle at him.

He was out of bed and had the gun snatched away before his son could move. He stopped himself just in time from wiping the butt stock across Tad's astonished face. "Where'd you get this?"

"It was—it was in the closet of my room. Just hanging there."

"Hanging there?" He examined it, his hands shaking. He'd been dreaming Vietnam, and suddenly it had taken shape again. It was an SKS, the semiautomatic rifle the Chinese had supplied to the Viet Cong. The wood was banged up, but the metal gleamed with oil. He pulled back the bolt. The chamber was empty, but a live cartridge gleamed beneath it. He thumbed it back down, then eased the bolt forward and put the safety on. His head was hammering.

"Yeah, in the closet. Back behind the clothes."

"Put it back." He put his hands to his head and staggered into the bathroom.

When he came out, he smelled coffee and something baking. He pulled his shorts on and padded downstairs, holding the wall.

Halfway down, his drooping eyes lifted. He remembered where he'd seen that gun before.

Bud had brought it back from that last mission. A souvenir.

A huge bright kitchen. Monica was dressed and the table was set for three. Sunlight polished granite work surfaces and Mexican tile and copper pots and pans. "Can we draw those curtains?" he asked her. "Please."

"Sure. That better? I made biscuits and gravy. Coffee?"

He had two cups and then a third. He still felt disturbed. He didn't remember everything about his dreams, but they hadn't left him with good feelings. He didn't make much of a dent in the biscuits, but Tad ate for two. Meanwhile, Monica talked. He grunted occasionally to keep her going, so he wouldn't have to.

She said she'd grown up in Gotha, a tiny place west of Orlando, just a few houses, a post office, a store. Her maiden name was Scuyler. Her first marriage was to an Air Force sergeant. After the divorce, she worked in furniture sales, then telephone sales, then as the manager of an apartment complex while she went to a local community college. She'd been a legal secretary when she met Bud.

"So, you're going in to the shop this morning."

"Yeah."

"Are you going to wear those?"

He looked down at his shorts. "What's wrong with this? I'll wear a shirt—"

"Nothing, I guess. . . . Do you want to take the Buick? I don't need two cars. You can follow me in; then I've got some gardening to do."

When he went back upstairs Tad followed him. At the top, the boy said, "Hey."

"What?"

"What am I doing here?"

"You're here with me."

"Yeah, but what am I doing? Am I going to this dive shop with you?"

"Not this first day. Today, you stay here."

"With the—"

"Don't say it."

"Oh, man. I thought we were gonna do some diving."

"We will. After we get you qualified. Now listen." He clamped a hand onto Tad's shoulder, felt the sullen resistance to his grip. "You're on good behavior. Don't go snooping around in any more

36

closets. Go swimming, get some sun, help her out in the garden. Tell her what all her flowers are called."

The boy muttered something. Galloway put a crimp in his arm so hard, he cried out. He left him rubbing his shoulder at the top of the stairs.

Scuba Florida was on Gaines Street, in a shopping plaza with a dry cleaning store, an Italian restaurant called Val's Place, and an Eckerd's Drug. At 9:15 A.M., they had their choice of parking places. He pulled in beside the Land Rover and followed her in, tossing the keys before pocketing them.

The door jingled open on an empty sales floor. He stood at the counter, looking around as someone called from the back, "Be right out."

At first glance, it looked like a typical dive shop, maybe a little roomier than most. The front window with its papier-mâché palm trees, trays of sand dollars, draped fishnets studded with dried starfish, and placards for Cozumel, Belize, and Micronesia. Past that, though, past the colorful skin suits and mask displays, were tanks with the yellow cross of nitrogen-oxygen mixes, heavy steel Genesis-system bottles. The main counter had the usual displays of regulators and consoles, gauges and computers, but they were built more heavily than the sport models he and Shad had stocked. There were a lot of high-intensity lights and line reels.

A sample gear setup stood on a center table, and he drifted over to examine it.

Twin steel tanks were linked by a dual-valve manifold with machined brass knobs. The pressure gauges were brass, too, heavy and robust. An oxygen stage bottle rode on the right side of the rig, a green Nitrox tank on the left, clip-shackled to a flattened backplate and buoyancy compensator. The regulators were heavy-duty Neptunes. A battery pack the size of a loaf of rye bread was clamped to the back, in the position of a fanny pack. The light head was separate, a bulb and reflector at the end of a cord. Everything was streamlined and clipped or rubber-tubed into place.

"Colten? July?" Monica called.

Galloway drifted to the service desk and looked into the gear room. It was casually but neatly knocked together out of unfinished pine and knotty paneling. Tanks stood about near an inspection rack. He noticed a workbench, parts bins, drying racks with BCs and wet suits. His ear caught a voice: "He always ran a thirty-two Nitrox for deco. We were running fifty-fifty—you get a better washout rate. We're at a hundred and thirty feet and he reaches down for his Nitrox and pops it into his mouth. I slapped it out of his hand. Three or four breaths of that and he'd have had a seizure. He had the narcosis face; we're looking at ninety minutes of decompression—hey, I'm ready to bend an ego."

"Hey, in the back," Galloway yelled.

"Coming, I said."

The man who came out stood about six one, slim and blond, with muscular shoulders tapering down to thin legs. Veins stood out on thick forearms gleaming with golden fuzz. He wore his hair over his ears, with gold-rimmed round glasses, white shorts, a green polo shirt, Teva sandals. He gave Tiller a friendly smile. "Hi, I'm Colten Scovill. What can I do for you today?"

Monica came out from behind a rack of skin suits. "Oh, hi, Mon," Scovill said. "He with you?"

She introduced Tiller, saying he'd be managing the store and getting it ready to sell. Scovill went quiet. He said, "I'm the manager here."

Tiller said, "And you still are. Here's how it stands, okay? I'm an old friend of Bud's. Monica's decided the best thing for her to do is to sell the business. She wants me to check it over, make sure we look good to a buyer. You're still the manager; you're still in charge of the day-to-day operation, same as before. Far as I'm concerned, you do your job, you got a job."

"Nobody asked me about selling," said Scovill.

"Well, I'll get out of your hair," said Monica, moving to the door. "Call me at home if you need me. Bye, Colten."

Scovill didn't answer. He was leaning over the counter, focused on Tiller. Galloway took a grip on his brain, wishing he hadn't gotten so enthusiastic with Kusczk's liquor last night. He tried for a friendly tone. "Monica said some nice things about you. Colten, right? The decision to sell has nothing to do with you or any of the other staff. She just wants out, and I can't blame her. Can you?"

"Not for that," said Scovill, still staring him down.

"What for, then?"

"I'm part owner. She can't sell without my agreement."

He rubbed his face. "Oh."

"She didn't tell you that?"

"She's got a lot on her mind right now."

Scovill softened. "Yeah, she does. We were all pretty shocked when the county called. Bud was the best. Tell you what I thought when I heard it: If he got it, maybe I better ease back on the risk factor. Anyway. Mon wants to sell? I'll have to talk to her about how to handle my interest—"

"You can talk to me."

Scovill gave him a level stare. "All right. I took a low paycheck and participation. I've got twenty percent of the stock."

"That in writing anywhere?"

"Letter of agreement."

"Well, that could work out. Want to buy the other eighty?"

"How much?"

"I'm thinking of a sale price in the neighborhood of half a mil. You own a fifth already? Come up with four hundred grand and you've bought yourself a dive business."

The manager hesitated, then shook his head. "That's higher than I expected. If she wants to trust me for it, take a note—"

"Can you raise it? Got a girlfriend works for Barnett Bank?"

Scovill shook his head.

"Then we've got to put it on the market. But we'll factor your participation in. Now, how about telling me what you've got here."

The door opened to the back and a man and a woman came out. Scovill introduced them as Mark Daughtrey and July Toll. "There's one more staff member—that's Tony Montagnino. 'Sniffles,' we call him. We rotate; this is his day off."

"You're all certified cave instructors, Mon said."

"That's right. Mark's our new guy, but we've all got Abe Davis. You know Abe Davis?" Tiller shook his head. "That's a hundred cave dives."

"Tell me about the business."

"Well, there are four shops in the Tallahassee area. We're not the biggest, but we're the leader in what they call 'technical' diving, the cave diving and deep diving and mixed-gas work." Scovill took off his glasses and polished them with lens paper. "We've got the area exclusive for ScubaPro. Our secondary line's Beuchat. We carry DiveRite cave-diving accessories and Harvey's dry suits."

"What's your markup?"

"Keystone. A hundred percent."

"Sure it is."

"I'm serious. We don't do much discounting. And we're close to the manufacturers here. We can get product in one day, so we don't keep six regulators in stock. We have summer sales, but basically it's a hundred percent."

He said to the woman, "Tell me about the shop."

"We've got two thousand square feet here in town. Customer area, display, counter. Service center and rental department. In back, there's a classroom, storage."

"No pool?"

"You lose money on a pool," said Scovill. "Bud left the beginner certifications to the other shops. We do our training out in the springs."

"My son came down with me. Any chance of getting him a basic cert? Or should I take him to the competitors?"

"We can probably work something out. Want to look around?"

He went through the back, the classroom, the gear locker, the workbench. A little cluttered, but basically things looked ship-shape. He asked Scovill, "Where's the books?"

"On the computer."

"How do you run your desk?"

"We have five people—well, without Bud, it's four now. We work the floor eight hours a day, do the cleaning and inventory and so on. Then teach classes on a head basis."

"What's the pay rate?"

"Not too far above minimum wage. We're here because we like to dive."

"Insurance?"

"SSI group policy. Liability, building, contents, then there's the workman's comp and health insurance and stuff."

"Who handles that?"

"Bud; I helped him, and once a year we had an accountant come in and look at it, do our taxes and make sure we were ready for an audit. Dorothea's her name."

They got together back in the sales area. He was thinking he could already see some things he was going to change—you ran a business differently when you were trying to sell it—when the brown-haired girl, Toll, said, "How about you? You're a diver, right?"

"Uh-huh."

"But not a cave diver?"

He gave her the sanitized version. "I learned hard hat in the Coast Guard. Operated with the SEALs in Vietnam. Did commercial work for a while, then started my own business."

"What kind of certification?"

He shrugged. Scovill said, "You don't have any certification?"

"A logbook, that's all you need in the Gulf of Mexico. Ever heard of Sea Systems? Cal Dive? Global?"

"Have you got a logbook?"

"I lost it when my boat sank."

Daughtrey said, "Ever been in a cave?"

"It can't be that different from a wreck, or inspecting the inside of a platform leg."

"It can't, huh?"

"I've worked in tight places before. Taken people out of crashed helicopters at three hundred feet plus in zero vis. Welded pipelines at eight hundred feet. Taken wrecks apart from the inside with explosives. I don't think strapping on a tank and crawling into a hole's going to be that much of a challenge."

"This commercial diving," Scovill said. "You have what, a helmet? Hoses, surface supply? Topside crew? Telephone?" Galloway shrugged.

"We had some SEALs come down here a few years ago," Daughtrey said. "Two of them died in a cave. Then three more of their buddies came down and went into the same system, trying to figure out what happened."

"They died, too," said Toll. "Have you ever dived mixed gas? Nitrox?"

"If it goes through a hose or comes out of a tank, I've breathed it."

Scovill mused, "But you don't actually have any kind of qualification."

"Okay, I get the picture—it's dangerous as shit and you're all superheroes," he said in disgust. He'd seen this kind of arrogance before: in the SEALs, Special Forces guys, pilots, commercial divers, too. "When's your next dive?"

Scovill looked at his watch. "This afternoon. You can come along if you want, but you'll have to stay out of the—"

"Excuse me," he said. He took Scovill's arm and steered him through the door into the back and closed it.

"Let go my arm."

"Sorry. But you weren't getting what I was saying out there. Effective as of now, I'm the acting owner. You got a slice of the business? I suggest you protect it by cooperating. So why don't you just tell me everything I need to know about cave diving

41

in five sentences or less and off we'll go happily arm in arm."

"You sure you want to do this? I keep telling you, it's not like open-water work. Or commercial diving, or whatever else you've done before."

"It's my ass, okay?"

"Colten? You all right?" July's voice.

Scovill cracked the door. "Yeah, everything's fine, guys. Hey, how about putting a charge on that double in the table display."

He looked directly into Tiller's eyes. "Mr. Galloway's going cave diving with us."

FOUR

It was an hour-and-a-half ride to Peacock Springs, through largely rural countryside. Scovill drove. Galloway rode shotgun, while July Toll and the student divers curled up with the gear in back.

There were six students, four men and two women. The van was noisy and packed full and there wasn't much talking. Everyone seemed preoccupied. One dark-haired, knife-faced girl couldn't stop moving. Every time he looked back, she was jiggling a skinny leg or playing with her hair.

The roads were long, level, straight, and empty except for the occasional pickup or slowly trundling tractor. He stared out for a while at passing fields dotted with ant mounds, abandoned motels, horse farms, little backcountry churches. Then fished around in the glove compartment and came up with a cave-diving map.

Starting near Orlando, the springs stretched northwest in a broad band up into the Panhandle. There were divable ones pimpled across the northwest, but the biggest cluster was where they were headed, between Gainesville and the Gulf. There weren't any cities there, just towns he'd never heard of: Luraville, Branford, High Springs, Williston. He found Peacock, where they were going. The map said it was a state park on the Suwannee River, with a dozen sinks and springs.

He looked out again, to see Mayo going by, awninged brick storefronts along a main street, sidewalks empty in the glare of noon. A heavy man stared unwelcomingly at them through the

43

front window of an antique store. Scovill paused at a crossing, then turned left.

Past a weathered SITE OF THE FUTURE MAYO BAPTIST CHURCH sign, a modern blue steel suspension bridge x'd the sky. It looked out of place among the hammocks and pine woods. The Suwannee River. One of the students whistled a few bars of Stephen Foster. The dark-haired girl laughed, sandal flapping on her jiggling foot. Water the color of iced coffee swirled between vines, ferns, and wild orchids that grew right down to the banks. Past that, they made a right turn opposite the Luraville Country Store. They passed burned-over fields, acres of still-smoking char, as if a volcano had just erupted.

"We're here," July announced. "Cough it up. Park fee, dive fee, hand it up."

The students sat up, blank, inward-turned looks hardening. A round-faced guy chewed on a sandy mustache; sweat glistened on his forehead. They passed cash up front. Scovill folded it into an envelope and dropped it into an unattended box.

The Peacock Springs State Recreation Area was a sandy washboard road through deep piney woods. Scovill turned off at a wooden sign that read TO ORANGE GROVE SINK. A quarter of a mile on, he braked at a widening in the sand.

The doors slid open, the sound echoing from the trees, and they emerged into a dense, still, enervating heat. He was sweating, too, now. The forest was silent except for the distant shriek of a scrub jay.

"Here we are," said Scovill jovially. He slapped the back of the guy with the blond mustache. "How you feeling, Orr?"

"Fantastic." The man's adam's apple bobbed as he swallowed.

They pulled on wet suits and set up gear in front of another sign. This one informed them forty-five divers had died in these springs. Tiller handed out the students' equipment till the van was empty, then set up his own—tanks, regulator, BC, gauges. He swung it onto his back and humped it after the others past a rail fence and down a little root-choked path.

Past a tilted picnic bench, cypresses stood with outstretched arms. Palmetto fronds clicked in the faintest breath of wind. A bird called far off, harsh and startlingly loud. He rounded a clump of brush and there it was.

The spring pool was surprisingly small, a rough oval beneath a gnarled limestone cliff. He could have chucked a softball across underhanded. Fluorescent green slime lay bright and still under pin oaks and cypresses dripping long beards of spanish moss. The slime covered every inch of the surface, save for a small patch of slowly stirring dead black fluid.

"Yuk," a voice murmured beside him. Not the nervous girl, the other one—a stocky blonde with a broad face. Gloria, he remembered. Some kind of therapist, from Gainesville. "They want us to dive in that?" Another student, a thin fellow with a brown-and-gray ponytail, sat and began kicking his fins, driving the duckweed back. Slowly, the green curtain parted. Tiller squatted to peer through the surface.

Both the opacity and the darkness were illusions. Beneath the glare of sun, the water was clear and deep and green as old glass. Tiny black fish darted restlessly above a bottom of tumbled pale rock. He tested it with his hand. Cold compared to the summer heat, but not bitterly so. Near seventy, at a guess. He was wearing Farmer John bottoms and a long-sleeved jacket top. The thick black neoprene was already heating up even in the shade.

He swung his gear down on a patch of bare rock and went off to water the palmettos. When he got back, the divers were seated in a circle. As he came up, Scovill was saying, "Remember to illuminate the hand that's giving the signal. Down there, no one's going to see what you're saying otherwise. Basic hand-signal review: *Attention. Emergency. Okay. Look at that.*" He demonstrated each. "The other signals you need to know: *Turn around. Hold it. Slow down. Surface.*"

Galloway found a seat on a limestone outcrop. Scovill glanced at him and went on to review light signals. A circle meant *okay*; vertical movements, *attention*; rapid horizontal strokes, *emergency*. "Then, if you've got something more complex to communicate, you've got your slate. Everybody hold up his slate. Good."

They listened in silence as July outlined the emergency procedures: what to do in case they lost the line, had difficulties with their air supply, got stuck in a restriction, experienced silting, or lost their lights. She sounded distant, almost preoccupied. Or maybe he was reading something else into her dispassionate matter-of-factness.

"Any questions? Okay, the dive plan. Orange Grove Sink, which runs back under this cliff, goes back about a thousand feet to Challenge Sink. It interconnects there with the rest of the Peacock system. There are twenty-eight thousand feet of underwater passages. We will not take the complete tour today."

Toll waited out uneasy snickers, then went on. "Remember our two-thirds rule. We breathe our air supply down to two-thirds starting pressure, then turn the dive and head back. That not only gives you a safety margin in case there's a problem on the way out; it lets you take a buddy with you if he experiences a gear failure."

Scovill said, "Now, there's no reason to be nervous or not enjoy this. This isn't a test of either your *cojones* or your ability. Since this is y'all's first time in a close, real live overhead environment, we're going to take it nice and slow and not go in all that far. You read the cave description in your manuals, so you know what it's gonna be like."

"I didn't," said Tiller.

Scovill's mouth turned down. "Okay, quick review. The cave opening, and then the big room. Up near the ceiling of the big room, about seventy feet by your depth gauge, there's a corridor leads off in a northeasterly direction. We'll follow it to what we call the Throne Room. That'll put us about two hundred feet back, and that'll be our turnaround point. We should all still have plenty of air then, so if everybody's copacetic, we'll do some shared-air drills. Any questions?"

Gloria: "What if we need more weight, when we're on the bottom?"

July said, "You probably won't. Those steel tanks are a lot heavier than the aluminum ones you're used to. That's why we don't carry weight belts like you did in open-water work."

The third man, a freckle-faced redhead who hadn't said a word the whole trip up to now, grunted, "How are we organized?"

"You got your buddy, right, Kevin? Orr, you're his buddy? And Jack and Scott, so everybody's got a partner. Gloria and Kay are the lead team. Gloria's lead reel. I'll be 'up.' Mr. Galloway—" Their eyes turned to him.

"Tiller."

"July, how about we let Tiller take over the assistant instructor's position, let him follow the last team in. You can be our safety this first dive."

She hesitated, then nodded with the faintly sad expression he'd noted she often had. Scovill went over a couple more things, then said that was about it; they'd check their buoyancy and gear on the bottom before cave entry. The divers began buckling on their last items of gear.

Tiller zipped his suit and bent for the rest of his equipment.

Scovill had told him to take the display set he'd looked at that morning at the store. Twin tanks, dual manifold, dual regulators. He'd left the oxygen and the stage tanks in Tallahassee, since this wouldn't be a deep-penetration dive. For the same reason, he hadn't bothered with a computer. He hoisted it to his shoulders and finished the rigging, making sure everything was tucked back and clipped off, nothing dangled, and that he knew where everything was. A separate pouch held dive tables, a folding knife, two spare handheld dive lights, and a few plastic line markers.

He picked up his fins, then checked on how the students were doing. Kevin and Gloria were already in the water. His eye stopped on Kay. The dark-haired girl was jerking on her crotch strap and muttering to herself. Scovill frowned at him. Help her out, he mouthed.

He went over, told her to stand, made sure the straps were tight on her backpack, then bent to fix the crotch strap. She had heavy tanks, the same size as his, although she wasn't but half his size, and he could see her knees quivering. "You sure you're ready for this?" he asked her in a low voice.

"I'm all right."

"Better get in, then. Cool off, and let the water help you carry that."

She nodded quickly, managing a smile. As he watched her waddle away, he thought, Keep an eye on that one.

Back to his own gear, sweat running down into his eyes. The suit felt as if it were shrinking in the sun, shrink-wrapping him like a supermarket eggplant. He gathered up fins, mask, and line reel, then picked his way down the worn limestone shelf that led into the pool.

The others floated here and there in the water. The abrupt hisses as they tested their regulators echoed beneath the cypresses like the threats of dinosaurs. Steel clanged on steel as Jack backed into Orr.

"See you on the bottom," Scovill yelled. Tiller noticed he wore a yellow wet suit, unlike the others, which were black with colored accents. The instructor thrust his regulator into his mouth and sank from sight. Hardly a ripple marked where he'd floated. The duckweed stirred uneasily, closing in again. Then a gush of rising bubbles pushed it back again in a slowly widening circle.

Galloway stepped carefully down from rock to slick rock into the water and bent to slip his fins on. They felt tight over the booties and socks, but they'd loosen as he swam. He was checking his gauges when July surfaced. "Buddy check on the bottom," she said, and vanished again.

Suddenly alone, he rinsed out his mask and fitted it to his face. He looked around once more at the woods, the slowly stirring weed, the burning sun directly above. A crow cawed. Cicadas buzzed. He heard a distant crunching roar as a truck went by far off.

He tucked his regulator into his mouth, sucked a quick breath of dry air, and slid down into the blue.

Breathing slowly, he sank through a warm layer at the surface into a crystalline light that reached out in all directions. The water felt cold at first, iciclemelt filtering between his skin and the suit, the gloves, the booties. Then it warmed, held by the close-fitting rubber. He swallowed and worked his jaw, and his ears cleared with a fizzing snap.

Around him, moss that looked soft enough to pet waved slowly from tumbled white rock. The spring bowl sloped down into indigo depths where huge limbs and tree trunks lay woven into a crisscrossed jumble. He was astonished at the visibility. He could see every rock on the bottom, could see bubbles drifting up on the far side of the spring with perfect clarity.

Still sinking, clearing his ears again, he looked up to a wavering mirror. Sunfish and chub drifted in mobile clouds against the silvery green surface, the needle-nosed silhouette of a gar cruising slowly among them like some new high-tech weapon.

When he looked down again, the others were scattered across the bottom, hovering a few feet above head-sized rocks and white sand and fallen trees. Mercury jellyfish rocked upward from their bent heads, their exhaled breath racing to rejoin the outer air. They were checking one another's gear. Scovill swam among them, tapping a strap here, yanking on a fin. His faceplate flashed as he glanced up toward Tiller.

Galloway was looking past them, at the cave.

At sixty feet, its entrance was a malignant gape, an evil black grin. A waterlogged palm trunk was wedged across it, barring it like a last warning. It was just wide enough to drive a full-sized car in with enough room on either side to be comfortable. He looked back toward the surface, then toward the cave again. For the first time, uneasiness wormed down his spine. Past the mouth was nothing but black, rimmed by palely glowing rock and writhing weed. A fluttering curtain of fish glittered like rain in sunlight as they moved restlessly in the deepening blue.

He flicked his main light on, and the spot of hot light reassured him. He checked his pressure gauge next: 3,100 psi. Shit, he thought. Long as we've got light and air, what can go wrong?

Scovill, grabbing his arm, pointed toward the students. He nodded, getting the message. He pumped a little more air into his buoyancy compensator—no, the cavers called them "wings"—and swam toward them.

One diver rose, shrouded momentarily in the mingled plume of rising bubbles from the others, then fell again. It was Kay. She was floating upward, venting too much air, then dropping like a stone. Up and down, on the elevator. She stabbed clumsily at the dump valve, shaking her head. He waved, but she didn't seem to see him. He swam around in front of her and pushed his hand down, indicating, Slow down; take it easy. Dark eyes stared past him through her mask. Then they focused. He gave her the okay sign, and after a moment, she returned it.

Scovill pointed toward the entrance, beckoned, held up one finger. Hesitantly, the number-one team moved toward him: Gloria and Kay. Gloria had the line, a caged arrangement like an oversized fishing reel. She sank toward the fallen palm trunk, then fumbled there for what seemed like minutes while her fins kicked up a white hurricane of sand. When she rose again, the guideline was tied off, and a pale spider thread spun out. He wondered why Scovill let the girls lead. Then he thought, Shit, why not. It didn't strike him as that tough. What was so frigging dramatic about it?

The first team's lights probed the entrance, then darted inside. Finning slowly, reeling out the line, they went in. He saw their lights moving around, outlining weird knobs and hollows of rock with flickering shadow.

Jack and Scott went in next, with Scovill trailing a couple of feet above them. Then the last team, number three, Kevin and Orr.

His turn. He flicked his light back on, geared his breathing back to slow, and kicked slowly toward the entrance. Bubbles roared in his ears. The black mouth grew, yawning until it surrounded him, slowly drawing a cold barrier of shadowy rock between him and the last silver shimmer of the liquid sky.

*   *   *

49

His eyes searched the dark, chasing the spot of his light. He glided ahead slowly, following the flame flicker of fins ahead, craning around as his sight adapted to the grayish gloom.

He floated above an enormous room, falling away below him into a lightless depth. It looked big as the whole outer basin, though distances were deceptive in water this clear. The crystalline lens magnified each rock and outcropping as it thrust out toward him. But Billy Graham could have held a revival in this arched cavern, floored with canted flat boulders and the occasional waterlogged limb. The spring outflow was a steady wind in his face. He wondered, Did the current ever reverse? Maybe when the rains were heavy?

He peered at his depth gauge in the gloomy gray-blue light that still washed in from behind him. Eighty feet. He realized he was lagging, and followed his light downward.

The others were at the far end of the cavern already. Their lights moved slowly across tortured craggy walls of black-stained rock. He swam a little faster. As it grew darker, the water seemed to chill, as if a darker fluid were gradually replacing the liquid light that had first filled his suit. Craning his head upward, he saw air pooled in the irregular roof. It shimmered in the rays of his light, tiny silver replicas of the great bubble that was the world outside.

The manual he'd glanced through back at the shop called caves an "overhead environment." That was the overhead, right up there, and it was the reason so many people died in caves. In open water, you could bail out when things went to shit. You didn't even have to know which way was up. Just dump your weight belt, pop your buoyancy, and sail back up to the surface.

If things went sour down here, there was no quick way out.

He looked back, to see July silhouetted against the irregular crack of blue-silver light. The rays streamed in around her, outlining her body and gear like a painting of a descending angel. It was so achingly beautiful, he had to exert a conscious effort to turn back to the darkness.

Finning downward again, he checked his depth. The green needle nudged ninety, and still dropping. The room was deeper than he'd thought. The divers at the far end had to be a hundred feet down. And all around them, blackness, growing more impenetrable as each cycle of his fins drove him onward, as the walls and floor sucked in the last particles of light.

His light spot caught a white thread, followed its taut zigzag from rock to rock. Then he slowed, sinking as he reached the trailing team. A flash of yellow showed him Scovill. The instructor was pointing upward, making rapid hand motions.

Intent on him, Tiller flinched as his fin tip brushed the floor. He stifled his first impulse to kick himself upward and instead hit the inflator for a quick shot of air. He rose slowly, corrected, and came to a balanced halt four feet off the silty bottom. A flick of his light showed a rolling cloud of darkness where his fin had touched.

The two women, indistinguishable in suits and gear from the men except by their smaller size relative to their tanks, rose slowly along the face of the far wall. Their lights roved about, probed into recesses, then focused together on a saffron-colored guideline, already set, leading into an oval five-by-eight-foot blackness.

He finned slowly upward, eyeing the tunnel opening, suddenly conscious again of being a hundred feet back under the rock. If the air hissing through his regulator stopped, he'd either have to get help or make it back that hundred feet and up another sixty without another breath. His fingers searched his chest for the spare regulator, the "octopus." If he lost a first stage, he'd have to close the manifold valve fast or all his air would dump. What if he tore his wings on one of these rocks? He'd have to drop his weights. . . . No, no weights. He'd have to crab-crawl back along the bottom. He loosened the grip his teeth were indenting into the mouthpiece and forced himself on, following the student divers as one by one they filed into the tunnel.

Now the last remnant of light disappeared, and the only illumination was what they carried.

The passage was so narrow, he could touch both sides at once. It wound along, narrowing and opening, the ceiling dropping and rising. Bubbles skittered along it like live things trying to escape. He couldn't see the divers ahead, just the flicker of their lights and occasionally a writhe of fin.

He imagined the eight of them strung out along the length of the tunnel and was suddenly glad he wasn't in the middle, closed in above and below and to both sides by rock, and ahead and behind by other divers. Surrounded and walled in, and each individual isolated, separate, dependent on the steady flow of compressed air through valves and hoses and diaphragms for life itself. Shit, it was getting to him. His bubbles were roaring out too fast. He forced his breathing back to a slow, steady rhythm, put his light on his gauges, ran through the checklist in his head. Eighty plus feet deep, two hundred feet in, the guideline leading ahead into the darkness.

He was wondering how much farther it was to this Throne Room when the fins of the diver ahead suddenly flailed around his head, knocking his mask askew. He grabbed an outthrust of rock, clutching at his mask as he drifted toward the ceiling. When he had it adjusted and cleared, he pointed his light down.

Not the diver in front of him, but the one before *him* . . . Kevin, the big freckled guy. He was shaking his head, hand on his regulator, as if he wasn't getting air. Then he pulled it out of his mouth. It tumbled free, gushing bubbles for a moment before it cut off.

Then he saw the yellow circle of the backup regulator, and he relaxed as Kevin tucked it under his mask. His buddy, Orr, eased up on him, feeling for his own octopus. A plume of bubbles mushroomed against the ceiling as Kevin purged the backup regulator.

Then the redheaded diver was shaking his head again, craning it back, sinking toward the floor of the tunnel.

Orr didn't move to help. Maybe he didn't see. So Tiller swam forward, past and over him, jerking his own octopus free from the rubber keeper loop. He held it out as Kevin's mask came around. Bubbles roared up from his regulator, but Kevin was shaking his head again. As his widened eyes caught Galloway's, he made the slit-throat gesture: out of air.

Orr chose that moment to lunge in, and his head hit Galloway's left hand. It knocked the light head out of his grasp. It fell away, bounced off a rock, flared once, and went out.

Crap, he thought. But meanwhile, Kevin had reached out for his proffered regulator.

Now they were linked. He had to stay with the man he was sharing air with.

But to his astonishment, the big man shook his head again. In the flickering shadow, his eyes were white-rimmed. Great bursts of bubbles stormed upward, straight into Tiller's mask, making it impossible to see even if he'd had light.

He was marveling how rapidly things could turn to crap when Kevin lunged up and wrenched the primary from between Tiller's teeth.

He was on an out breath when it was jerked out, and his throat closed instantly against the flood of cold water. Galloway swallowed rapidly, floating upward as bursts of bubbles beat softly at his chest. Strange flickers lit the rock walls. The big redhead was yanking on Tiller's primary hose, pulling so hard that he had to roll with it, afraid the son of a bitch was going to pull it right out of the housing. Now everything was dark. He was losing his up-down orientation. He caught a flicker of the guideline, but that wasn't what he was worried about. He had to get some air in his empty lungs.

Kevin yanked on Galloway's hose again. Tiller reached back to his manifold, found where the whip came off the first stage, and ran his hand rapidly down it. His fist slammed into the other man's face. Then a hand gripped his, forcing it back. They rolled, locked together, crashing into the rock.

Tiller broke free at last, but he still didn't have any air. He swallowed. That usually helped, but it didn't seem to now. He couldn't find his octopus, though it had to be out there some-where. He jackknifed suddenly and shoved himself into where he figured Kevin was again. His outstretched hand brushed a regu-lator, drifting there in midtunnel.

He was groping frantically for it when he crashed into another soft body, and lost it. It was roaring bubbles- -he could hear it venting—but his splayed fingers scraped rock instead. Fire flick-ered around the edge of his vision. The dark contracted like a squeezing fist.

He hit another diver and grabbed, got what felt like a shoulder. Something smashed him in the face, almost cracking his mask. Something else closed around his shoulders and grew tight as he struggled. The black fist crimped down on his sight. He struggled weakly, staring into the dark.

Light burst around them, brilliant and white, flooding the tun-nel and showing him Kevin, Galloway's orange octopus in his mouth, his back against the ceiling of tormented rock. His light dangled free, illuminating a roiling brown cone of silt. Before Gal-loway could lunge, a yellow arm reached between him and the other diver. It carried a regulator, and it was only after Galloway had jammed it into his mouth and purged it that he recognized it as his own primary.

Scovill grabbed Kevin by the manifold and spun him around. He tore Galloway's octopus out of the student's mouth and jammed his own in. The redhead struggled, but Scovill just tight-ened the hammerlock. The instructor tapped his purge valve, giv-ing him bursts of air. Then, as the student's struggling lessened, Scovill slid around to face him. He stared into Kevin's mask, both hands on the other man's shoulders. He was holding eye contact. Without breaking it, he pointed quickly to Tiller, then pointed ahead along the tunnel and held up a clenched fist, indicating,

Hold them up. Then he pointed to himself and Kevin and jerked a thumb upward. We're surfacing.

Tiller nodded, sucking air with hungry rapidity. He tucked the broken light head under his harness and pulled out his spare. He swam rapidly down the line, till the tunnel opened again, widened, and the ceiling lifted.

The first two teams were hovering in the center of a large room, above a smooth dark floor littered with more fallen rock. Four faceplates swung toward him as he finned in, still sucking air so hard, his regulator squeaked and thudded. His heart was hammering so loudly that the walls of the cave seemed to vibrate. That had been close. . . . He gave them a quick thumbs-up, the signal to end the dive. They glanced at one another, then fell dutifully into line. He waved them on, checking each as he or she passed.

Gloria was the last to exit. She held the reel out, but he waved her on impatiently. She offered it again, then shrugged and moved off into the dark, the gears going *ratchety ratchety* as she cranked in the line. He glanced around one last time—the Throne Room, hell, he didn't see the attraction—and turned to follow her out.

His beam reached out two feet, then ended in a black wall of silt.

Oh shit, he thought. He lunged quickly toward the ratcheting sound and collided with her fins. The water was lightless, murky, making the lights useless.

He suddenly realized there were seven people between him and the surface now, in that pipe straw of a tube. And he was sucking gas like there was no tomorrow. He throttled back again, forced his frenzied consumption into a smooth in, out, in, out.

He followed her fins with one arm outstretched, back along the tunnel. When they exited into the main room, the silt cleared as if by magic. His beam leapt across it, picking out the silhouettes of the others making for the jagged crack of blue far above, outlined against the light as if they were ascending into a heaven gained despite their sins.

As he broke the surface, he squinted at his pressure gauge. He had four hundred pounds of air left.

When he pulled his mask off, treading water, Scovill and Kevin were sitting at the edge of the pool. The redhead looked shaken. Scovill was saying, "Yeah, but if you got a problem, you got to solve it right there, where you are. This isn't like an open-water dive."

"I done lots of wreck diving. Never had any trouble—"

"Well, this isn't a wreck. You feel better now?"

"I don't know."

Tiller got to the brink and pulled his fins off and threw them up onto the shore. He got his feet set and grabbed a rock and pulled himself out, then walked heavily, bent over, up to where he could unbuckle his harness and swung his tanks down to the ground. He still felt shaky.

Scovill came over and squatted down beside him. "Thanks, Colten," Tiller said, hating it, but knowing it was better this way, say it flat out. "Guess I dicked up."

"A guy starts to freak, hit him from behind. Give him air, but don't let him start grabbing on you."

"Okay."

"Or use a backup. I always carry one." Scovill swung his tank set down and pointed to a little separate bottle-and-regulator setup just the size, Tiller thought, of a fifth. "Hand 'em the Spare Air and back off. It won't last forever, but it gives them time to calm down. It's saved my butt once or twice. . . . But you kept your cool; you did okay for your first time in a cave." He unzipped his jacket and stood, raising his voice to the others. "Glory, you did real good up front. Kay, Jack, Scott—good dive; y'all looked fine down there. Orr, Kevin, let's go back to the van. I need to talk to you guys for a second."

They had to stay out for a while before the second dive, a surface interval till they dropped to a lower decompression group. Meanwhile, they had lunch. Tiller hadn't brought anything, but Gloria shared fried chicken and biscuits. "Take it. I need to lose a little," she told him. With the top of her wet suit off, he had a good view as she leaned forward, carefully dividing everything down the middle with a gleaming little dive knife. He kept looking toward the parking lot. He was curious to see how Scovill had handled Kevin. But when they came back, there was nothing to see, no fireworks. The redhead slogged along behind Orr and Scovill, not speaking any more than he had on the ride down.

"Want this last piece of chicken?"

"No thanks. So, what's with you and Kay?" he asked her. "Friends, or what?"

"You mean, are we lesbians?"

"Uh . . ."

"The answer's no. We just do a lot of stuff together. We took a

55

skydiving course, a yoga class. If there're two of you, it gives you more room to maneuver. You don't look so desperate."

He didn't really want a disquisition on the social life of the modern single woman, but he got it.

When their surface interval was up, they went in again, this time checking out a side passage and practicing emergency drills. July moved up as Orr's buddy. Kevin didn't go in with them on the second dive. He sat holding his knees by the pool. Tiller saw his head bent thoughtfully at the edge of the circle of light as they sank away, deeper and deeper, into the all-encompassing dark.

FIVE

I don't know about this. Maybe you better forget about me going," he said, scowling at his full-length reflection.

"Why? What's wrong?" asked Monica, behind him, in the walk-in closet. "I know it's—*here* it is." She emerged flushed, triumphant, holding up the cummerbund like a captured eel.

Tiller looked at his image again, then started to slip the jacket off. She closed in and pulled it back on with firm tugs, like an instructor adjusting a novice's gear.

"Are you sure it doesn't bind you?"

"No, it fits."

"You looked to be about Bud's size. Big in the shoulders."

He muttered, "Look, I don't think this is the kind of thing—"

"Well, I'm not going alone. You can just stay at the bar, if you don't want to mingle." She slid a drawer out, held up several sets of studs and cuff links. "Pick one."

"The gold and black."

"Those are the most elegant. See, you have taste."

He didn't answer, just stood straight as she leaned in so close he felt her body heat. As her fingers worked their way up his shirt, he breathed her perfume, the scent of her hair, stared at an edge of black lace. As she adjusted the bow tie, he had a sudden vision of . . . Knock it off, he told himself. He focused on a pin she wore, two dolphins that looked as if they were mating. It was heavy, a little crude, but a striking piece. "Nice pin," he said. "Is that silver?"

"Bud made it," she said, and that shadow fell across her face again. He bit his lips, wishing he hadn't said anything. "He used to make jewelry for me, back when we were engaged . . . made it himself . . . Then he stopped. Hi, Lunker. Coming in? Do you want to get dressed up, too?"

The cat stood in the doorway. It was a longhair, cream body, with smoke coloring like a Siamese. Its blue eyes stared at them expressionlessly.

"There you go," she said at last, stepping back. "Take a look."

As she sat on the bed to slip on her heels, he stared at a weird new Galloway. The sober black and white made his chest seem even wider than it was. He pressed his hair down in back and examined his battered blunt face doubtfully. "You really think it's all right?"

"You look very handsome. Now, let's get going."

He walked back to the pool to check out with Tad, but his son wasn't there. He went back into the house, yelling for him, but there was no answer. He wasn't in his room, wasn't in the entertainment room or the garage. They were standing by the car when he came out of the woods pushing a muddy mountain bike.

Tiller scowled. "I thought you were at the pool. Where've you been?"

Tad shrugged. He half-turned and called, "Come on out. They're harmless."

The kid who slouched out of the undergrowth was tall and lanky, with big hands and evasive eyes. He had on ragged jeans with burrs stuck to the torn cuffs, a windbreaker, despite the savage heat, and a black LA SWAT Team baseball cap. Tad said, "He followed me home. Can I keep him?"

"I've seen you around the neighborhood, haven't I?" said Monica. "Where do you live?"

The kid looked at the grass. Tad said, "His name's Ripper. 'Chain Saw' Ripper."

"Great," said Tiller. "Can he talk?"

"When he wants to."

"Where'd the bike come from?"

"It's his. He said I could use it."

"He's got two bikes?"

"He's got more than that. Any more questions, Officer?"

"Yeah, your diving homework. Get a good start on that and—"

"It's summertime. I don't do homework in summertime."

58

"We'll be out late," said Monica, slipping deftly in before he could start shouting. "You've got the key, right? Help yourself to what's in the fridge, Tad. You can heat up a pizza if you want to have something with your friend."

She hated driving in heels, so he took the wheel and she navigated. They headed south, out of town.

He couldn't stop remembering the cave, how he'd felt when Kevin had his regulator and he couldn't find his secondary, couldn't see, with nothing to breathe but black water. He shuddered. He turned his head to see her profile against the fleeing, shadowed trees.

"Tell me where we're going again."

"It's for the Friends of the Leon County Public Library. They have this Literary Lions event, the same kind of thing they do in New York and Miami. They invite famous authors, and people pay to have dinner with them."

"Why?"

"Well, to raise money. I said—"

"I mean, why do people pay to eat with them?"

"Some people enjoy that kind of thing."

"Why are we going?"

"I'm a board member of the Friends. So I more or less have to be there. Bud usually went with me. I'd skip it; I don't feel like going out. But this year, we got the Holders to open their family place on the Wakulla River. We've been trying to get their support for years."

"Rich?"

"You could say that. I've been to their house in town, but I've never been out to Apalachee Lodge."

"Oh, you know 'em?"

"Bud knew them. I'm not sure where from."

Dusk fell as they felt their way down long empty roads crowded by stands of slash pine and turkey oak and the unnatural uniformity of machine-planted longleafs. A fine mist began, turning the asphalt black and making the tires squirm. Monica clicked on the dome light to study directions. They found themselves in dead ends, rutted sandy paths where wild magnolias glowed back in the shadows of wild grapevines and palmetto scrub, clay roads that ended at sagging tin-roofed shacks or rusted trailers with lunging, howling hounds. At last, their lights traced a sign for the lodge. He followed another set of taillights down a canopied road.

59

It wound along an embankment through a marsh, then rose, twisting along a crest. As dark fell, he made out chimneys rising above the treetops ahead.

"Yaupon," he said.

"What?"

"Yaupon. It's a kind of . . . well, like holly bush. Grows on Hatteras. Looks like it grows here, too."

The roof was copper green, and as they got closer, he saw that the house was three stories high. A flawless lawn stretched out for acres in front of it.

"Jesus."

"This used to be a private hunting society. A man named Hiram Noble built it in '22. There were a lot of hunting camps here then—for wild pigs, and deer—and a little farther down the river, there are marshes and duck hunting. Only problem was, they didn't allow women. Mr. Noble's wife was from France, and she loved to shoot. She wanted to hunt with the men, but they blackballed her, kept her out.

"So Mr. Noble bought the Apalachee Club. Then he tore it down, and built this house on the same spot. Just for spite. He spent a third of a million dollars on it."

He grunted, looking up. For that kind of money, the old man had gotten screened-in verandas, custom dredging to a cedar-shake boathouse, and a formal garden that stretched down past the house to the river. On the far shore, the wilderness stood like a black rampart in the last skylight before dark. Monica was still talking. "Then the Nobles lost their money, and the Turlingtons had it for a while, and then it stood empty for years and years, falling down, rotting. Then the Holders bought it, not that long ago. They brought in an architect from New York. . . . Where are you going? Isn't that the parking, over there?"

"Thought you'd never been here before."

"I haven't. I see Blanche at the Friends meetings, but this is the only time I've had the chance. So I felt like I had to come."

He reflected sourly that the way Monica looked tonight, she should have come alone, picked up a millionaire widower. Her fire red hair tumbled to the shoulders of a modestly cut midnight blue dress. The dolphin brooch was the only piece of jewelry she wore. She was still quiet, but she didn't seem as depressed as she had the night before. As they made their way toward the main building, other cars were arriving, headlights beaming through the mist and sweeping over the gardens, the arbors. As he got closer, he could see immense windows, see people standing in groups and talking around laden tables.

He'd never liked parties much.

Half an hour later, he was standing on a second-floor balcony overlooking the woods, listening to a tall guy in wire-rimmed glasses and a tiger-striped tuxedo. He lived in Key West and wrote what he called "commercial novels." He was telling four admiring ladies with blue hair and pearls that the next book would be all about marlin fishing. Tiller listened with half an ear, swirling bourbon in a crystal glass.

Monica had introduced him to the host and hostess when they arrived. Billy Holder was pint-sized and pudgy, with flushed cheeks, receding hair, and a football player's handshake. His accent was Deep South but he didn't have much to say. Blanche Holder was taller than her husband, model-thin and emerald-eyed and craggy-cheekboned, with narrow lips and long honey blond hair. Galloway placed her closer to hardscrabble Kentucky than old-money Florida, and closer to thirty than Billy was to fifty. She held Monica's hand for a long time, telling her how sorry she was about Bud, how things like that always happened to the ones who deserved them least. Monica introduced Tiller as a friend of Bud's who was in town to help her with the business.

Mrs. Holder let him inspect most of her teeth. "Mr. Galloway. And where are you 'in town' from?"

"North Carolina."

"Raleigh? Durham? I have some dear friends in Durham."

"East of there, on the coast. Hatteras Island."

But she wasn't listening any longer, was turning her smile on the next person in line. Something about the Robert Kennedy Prize. Monica tugged at his hand. Tiller gave Holder a farewell nod—the guy had to be bored as hell—and moved off after her, toward the bar.

After getting himself an Early Times and Mon a white wine, he stood around, feeling stiff and self-conscious in the tux. It wasn't a young crowd. The women were either sun-wrinkled or face-lifted, and the men either loud and red-faced or silent and stooped. They didn't seem that interested in the writers, except for the tiger-striped Key Westian. He had simpering old ladies hanging on him like bluefish swarming to chum.

"Ever do any marlin fishing?" he asked Galloway. Tiller shook his head and moved off. He didn't feel like trading fish stories.

61

Instead, he circulated, looking the house over. It was even bigger than it looked from the drive. He couldn't believe the amount of handwork that must have gone into the carving on the ceiling, the archways between the rooms. An overweight poet with a braying laugh had her own coterie in the piano room. He peered out a window. Three levels of decks descended to the boathouse. The river flowed past black and lightless, bathed in the radiance from the windows but giving none of it back.

Eventually, he found himself shoaled up in a corner with a tall fellow with white hair and a gentle voice. Two or three others in his group were asking about somebody named Kate Duval, but he kept evading their questions. When the others left, Galloway asked the guy, "What was your name again?"

"I'm Page Edwards."

"Tiller Galloway. You one of the writers?"

"That's right." He nodded across the room. "There's John Jakes. One of his kids lives in Jacksonville. And you're—"

"Who, me? I'm nobody special."

"I'm Nobody! Who are you? Are you—Nobody—too? Then there's a pair of us? Don't tell! They'd advertise—you know!"

Tiller stared at him. What the hell? Finally, he decided it was a quote or something. "What do you write?" he asked him.

"Novels. Short stories."

"What kind? Mysteries? Science fiction?"

Edwards looked cornered. He said, "No . . . they're not mysteries. I guess you'd just call them literary fiction. The latest one's called *American Girl*. It's set in Saint Augustine, about a woman who inherits the Fountain of Youth."

Tiller had never heard of it. He muttered, feeling stupid, "Uh, I don't get much time to read anymore . . . sounds interesting . . . have to look for it."

"Nice house," Edwards said, looking up at the archway between the great room and an oversized salon looking out over the river. "But I guess if anybody can afford to live this way, Holder can."

"Who? Oh. What's he do? Besides have parties."

"What's he *do*? Billy Holder's one of the richest men in Florida. Ever heard of General Sugar?"

"Sure."

"The biggest producer in the United States. General owns most of the Everglades, whatever isn't state land. The Holders were the major stockholders, or so I'm told."

"Lot of money in sugar, I guess."

"Price supports and all. Hey, Pat!"

An older man with a seamed, leathery face was walking past with an attractive redhead with an Irish nose and shoulders like a linebacker. Edwards introduced them. "This is Patrick Smith . . . and Elisabeth Graves, the horror writer." Tiller muttered greetings. "Pat, I was telling Tiller here about General Sugar."

Smith seemed to be some sort of state historian. He sipped bourbon as he told them about the sugar fields back in the thirties. "Wadn't far from slavery," he said. "They'd promise cutters free food, housing, and when they got there, they were already in debt. Dogs and overseers to keep them in line, keep 'em from escaping. Now they use Jamaicans. They make trouble, turn down a piecework rate, General ships 'em home. No more labor trouble."

"I didn't know they grew cane up here."

"They don't. I'm talking about south Florida, south a Okeechobee."

"So what's he doing up here?"

"Billy pulled out of sugar a few years ago. Every crop uses up more of the muck, and they're gettin' close to bare limestone. Plus, he figured once Castro was gone, we'd be eating Cuban sugar again. Way I heard it, he sold out to some investors with less sense than money and came up here full-time."

"So he's retired now?"

"Not Billy. He looked around, finally bought some land down in Crane County. Started him a foliage business."

"Foliage?" He searched faces as they drifted by, looking for Mon. Another few minutes, maybe they could make a graceful exit.

"Garden plants. Poinsettias, forsythias, potted palms, scheffleras, ficus—the stuff they stock in nurseries, to decorate bank lobbies. Ship a few thousand tons of that north every year, you got a good income." Smith lifted his head. "Hey, there's Connie May."

The writers left, but Galloway didn't go with them. He sipped again, found his glass empty, and headed back to the bar.

A little later in a room done all in green velvet, he listened as Blanche Holder lectured a group on the merging of two somethings called the DER and DNR into one something called the

DEP. Everyone else seemed to know what they were, so he didn't ask. She said that now you needed to get permit approval from the governor, the cabinet, and three state agencies. That took an average of nine months. The new process would let corporations do one application to one agency, and cut the permit time to ninety days.

"One-stop shopping," an older women said. "Much more efficient. That should save everybody money."

Blanche said, "That's exactly why we have to fight the proposal. Environmental groups, like ours, feel it's a sellout to corporate interests. The governor promised us last session that if there was any streamlining, it wouldn't affect the permitting process."

A fellow in a graying ponytail said, "But there is one advantage to a superagency, Blanche. Dr. Trane thinks if we consolidate Game and Fish, water protection, et cetera, into one agency, we can coordinate the management of entire natural systems. Not have one agency handling the birds, one the land, another the fish, and so forth. Stop focusing on narrow issues and go for biotic diversity, saving entire ecological systems."

"That sounds good till you look at the way DER's actually operated. The corporations captured the state legislature years ago. They're out to gut the whole regulatory system."

A florid man in a gold cummerbund said, "At least then the jobs will stay here. Your ecofreaks take over, Blanche, every job in the state will go south. Puerto Rico, Mexico—"

"Tourism makes money, too, Wilkes. The Everglades attracts tourists from all over the world. Why shouldn't we? The Heritage Conservancy's not out to stop growth, or investment, or jobs. Just to make sure there's enough of the original Florida left that our grandchildren can see what it was like once."

"You mean, enough of it that's in your backyards. I love you, Blanche, don't get me wrong, but—like this Ormond Island thing. Now, that was smart. You buy half of it for a preserve. Low ball, the old Cracker who owns it throws his kids overboard, lets you have it for a song. Then hey, all of a sudden it turns out one of your board members actually owns the other half, going to put in a development and a marina—"

"Wilkes, that's nothing but a ghost development, so he gets a better write-off when he donates the rest of the island—"

Somebody cleared his throat beside him and Galloway turned his head, to see Holder again. The bored look was gone. He said,

"Tolbert, if you're going to say things like that, say them to me, not Blanche."

The fat man was suddenly a frightened puppy. "I didn't mean anything by it, Billy."

"If it makes any difference, I agree with you. This new preserve she's trying to put together, I'm against it. I've got two thousand acres there. If they clamp downstream water-quality standards on me, I'll have to shut the doors."

His wife smiled coldly. "You'll make it pay somehow, Billy. You always do."

"Now, Blanche—"

"How much of the wilderness do we have left? Very—damn—little. This last corner of Florida's it. From Crystal River to Wakulla. The rest of it's been drained, sold, and paved over. And what about the Indians? The Apalachees? That river, those springs are sacred to them."

"Indians? Those aren't Indians. They don't have any right to it—"

"Well, you sure as hell don't." Her angular face was flushed, and Tiller saw that the people around her were backing away, leaving Blanche Holder alone in the center of a little doughnut of space. Even her husband was outside it, staring at her expressionlessly.

"If they think they're so goddamned sacred, they should buy a few acres themselves," said the fat man, winking at Galloway.

He ran into Monica again back at the bar. A line engraved itself between her eyes as he shoved his glass at the bartender. "How many's that, Tiller?"

"How many what?"

"Drinks. And—are those doubles?"

"I forget. They're free, aren't they? Hey, some of these people are kind of interesting. You ever read anything by this Harry Crews character? The one with the tattoo that says 'How do you like your blue-eyed boy now, Mister Death?' "

"Are you diving tomorrow? Shouldn't you—" Then she stopped, biting her lips. "Sorry."

"That's all right."

"It's not. It's none of my business how much you drink or what you do. I owe you just for being here."

"Forget it." He waved it away, and an older woman jerked

back with a hiss; liquor spots dotted her silk gown. "Sorry, lady."

He was getting rid of some of the bourbon in a lovingly restored 1920s lavatory when he caught part of a conversation between two older men, one with rings on most of his fingers, except for two missing ones, the other wattled as an old turkey. They were both smoking cigars. "It's gettin' close, all right," the one with the rings said. "Between the tree-huggers and the gu-v'mint, there's not much room to turn around. Latest thing is, they say we got to *treat* the waste water before it goes back. Make it like that Perry-air, in the bottles, to drink." He coughed, hawked, spat a yellow oyster into the urinal beside where Tiller was zipping up. "First the feds were gonna do it. Split the costs, half the industry, half from the state, half from EPA. But we decided to do it ourselves."

"What for?" Galloway said, lurching into the conversation. "If the government's gonna give you free money."

He got a fishy, suspicious glance. " 'Cause if we do it ourselves, we get to keep that water. Reuse it. Want to do anything in this state—grow hogs, chickens, run a pulp mill—you gotta figure first where to get the water."

They left, and he followed them back out into the party. "Who's the fat nigger bitch in there playing the piano?" was the last thing he heard the wattled one say.

He circled a huge billiard room, watched a game in progress. Most of the players were terrible, but there was one woman worth watching. She was dark-haired, with a classic serenity to her face and an ass his fingers itched to cup when she bent over the table for a bank shot. When she straightened, a man put his arm around her, scowling at Tiller. He gave him a big grin and wended his way back to the great room.

The food was out now and a line stacked deep against the buffet tables. Uniformed serving women stood behind the dishes. A carver in a chef's hat played Michelangelo on a huge roast haunch. Tiller decided to let the crowd thin out some. He stopped by the bar again instead. By now, the bartender knew him. The liquor didn't intoxicate him, just made everything seem brighter and funnier. He felt clear and bubbling, like spring water. A little sloshed over the rim as he strolled away. Hell, the guy had filled it too full. He caught a glimpse of himself in a pier glass. Mon was right: He looked good in a penguin suit. Last time had been a rented one, the wedding, him and Ellie marching up the aisle. Too many years ago . . . He caught Monica's eye across a bobbing of heads and grinned at her. She shook her head, then looked away.

Was he embarrassing her in front of her friends? The thought sent him out onto the lower terrace, to stand alone contemplating the night. The rain had passed on, leaving the deck wet and dark as if it had just emerged from the river. The rising moon, orange as an orange, sent replicas of itself undulating across the black surface. It made the wall of forest or swamp across the river look even more savage and impenetrable. He studied it, sipping the drink as a bird screamed far away in the darkness, a loon or a heron. Splashes came from down along the shore: mullet or perch, helplessly attracted by the lights.

Suddenly, he felt angry. What the hell was he doing here, hobnobbing with the upper crust in his borrowed clothes? The more elevated the tone, the more uncomfortable he felt. The last fancy-ass blowout he'd been at had been in the Bahamas. At Bayou Serene, Nixon's place at Tanner Cay. Instead of sugar barons and writers, he'd been rubbing elbows with movie stars and newspaper publishers, prime ministers and drug lords and DEA agents in terracotta guayaberas. That whole Bahamas thing had ended in disaster. Nuñez had promised them a fat payday, but in the end he and Shad had been lucky to get out alive. And they'd been looking back over their shoulders ever since.

Just thinking about that made him angrier, and depressed, too. It was the same feeling of defeat and desperation that had made him torch *Miss Anna*. What a mess his life had been. No, still was.

He hadn't had a great childhood. Always in the shadow of his older brother. Always afraid of his dad's strap. His stepmother's cold arms had offered no refuge. About the only good thing he remembered was fishing with the Aydletts, running out two hours into the Stream.

Out in the blue water, you never knew what you'd catch, or run into. The most beautiful thing he'd ever seen there was a school of blue marlin. They'd thought first it was porpoises, and Captain Cliff hadn't even bothered to look when the boys yelled. It was in the small tuna season. The marlin were knocking them into the air, and then they'd jump. There might be ten or fifteen in the air at a time. The sun was shining, the water was running off their backs—he'd never seen anything as blue as that, and it shimmered and it changed—and when they went up, the sun would shine off them just like a deep blue rainbow. The guy in the tiger tux would never see that. The fish weren't there anymore. They were gone, like the empty beaches of his boyhood.

So there'd been some good times, too. And a lot of people started with a strike against them and still made something out of their lives. Why the hell couldn't he?

It seemed it had started off the rails the first time he picked up a drink. Though even then he'd been able to work, and dive, and he'd done okay for a while in the Coast Guard. But it had really gone to shit when he started using. Ever since he'd touched shit, his life had turned to shit. A tar baby he couldn't fight free of. Even now, when he didn't use anymore, he still wanted it. And it seemed wherever he went, whatever he did, it zeroed in on him, as if it could sniff out his need.

Shad said his approach was wrong, that he concentrated too hard on one thing. He snorted. But if you didn't? Tell me this Holder guy wasn't focused. All these fat cats, what the hell did they think about all day—how to help their fellow man?

Maybe this time he could come out a little ahead. He hadn't expected Monica to offer him a commission. But a few thousand would give him breathing room, let him figure out something to do. What did his brother get for selling other people's sand—six percent? Six percent of half a million would be thirty grand.

But then what?

Get another used boat? Start another diving business? He loved it, but someday he'd have to quit. He'd been bent too often; his back was shot. Maybe he should think about marine surveying. Crawl around under expensive yachts and write up glossy reports. It didn't thrill him, but everything else he'd tried since getting out had gone up in smoke. Chartering, oil-field work, his relationship with Bernie. He'd dicked up everything. . . . Okay, it was his life, but now he had to think of Tad. The kid was gunning it down the same road. He had to head him off, offer him something better. Present some kind of example. He rubbed his numbing face and laughed. Him, an example.

Christ, there had to be *something* he could do. He hovered above despair like a diver above an immense and lightless pit. He beat his fist slowly on the wooden rail, glaring up at the misty stars. There had to be *someplace* he belonged.

"So, you're Galloway."

The words were bland, but the tone was contemptuous. Galloway looked up at a man he didn't know. Near his age, but taller, in a gray suit and a watered silk tie dotted with what looked like little hostile eyes.

"Who the hell are you?"

"My name's Arkin. Timothy Arkin. I'm Mrs. Kusczk's attorney."

"I thought she had a woman lawyer."

"Ms. Swerdlick's one of my junior partners." Arkin looked around, then motioned with his glass. "Need to talk to you a minute. Let's go inside."

"You want to talk, do it here." He didn't like lawyers even at the best of times, and this wasn't one of the best. There was such a thing as hatred at first sight.

"All right. I understand you're taking over for Joel Kusczk. True, false?"

"I'm not 'taking over.' I'm getting Scuba Florida in shape to sell. At Monica's request. Got a problem with that?"

"Maybe. Maybe not. But why you?"

"I'm doing it because I'm—"

"I know, you're 'a friend of Bud's.' " The thin lips twitched, as if amused.

"Why ask, if you know?"

"How are you involved with Tartar Springs?"

"With what?"

Arkin leaned his elbows on the low railing. "The springs. The cave property," he said, louder. "The World's Largest Cow. Wrestle the Monkeys. The Devil's Bathroom."

"Look, asshole, I don't know what the hell you're talking about."

"I'm talking about the tourist-trap cave Kusczk bought."

"What about it? I don't know what she plans to do with it. Maybe you ought to go talk to her."

Monica appeared at the window, looking out into the night. He waved, but though he could see her anxious face plainly, she apparently couldn't see them. Not with the light shining out all around her, when he and the lawyer stood invisible in the dark.

"I thought she might have mentioned something to you about it," Arkin said. "Maybe a little pillow talk. Oh, I know what I wanted to ask you. Does she do that little trick with you? Where she sort of squats, and lifts herself up and down on your—"

He didn't think before he hit the guy. Maybe that was where he went wrong. Should have gone for the gut, not aimed for a jaw shot. Because he missed, and got him in the throat. Arkin

69

went over backward, tumbling over the railing. For a moment, it looked as if he was going to hit the roof of the conservatory, but instead a splash echoed from the river.

"Oh my God," said somebody from another terrace. A woman's voice. "Was that Tim? I don't believe he can swim."

Galloway grimaced. He was stripping his tux jacket off, getting ready to go in, when Arkin surfaced a few yards downstream. A few seconds of floundering; then he stood. The water was only waist-deep.

The attorney climbed up onto the bank, still holding his throat. He stared up for a moment, his mouth working. No sound emerged, but Tiller had to admit he'd never gotten a more unmistakable death threat. Arkin looked around, then moved slowly off, into the garden.

The door opened and Monica came out. Her voice when she reached him was like chilled acid. "Did you just *hit* Tim Arkin? Is that true?"

"Yeah. He was saying—"

"I don't care what he was saying. You don't start fights at charity parties! I don't care how much you've had to drink. No, don't bother telling me why. There is no acceptable excuse. I'll meet you at the car."

He stood wordless as she plunged back into the crowd. People stared after her as she passed. Mouths writhed.

He stood there, wondering if she could possibly be right. For a moment, facing her anger, he'd questioned himself. Should he have taken that? Just laughed it off? Then a cold voice he didn't hear very often told him: To hell with her. With all of them. With everybody who hasn't been where you've been, gone through what you've gone through.

In that moment, he hated them all. He gulped the rest of the drink, then went in.

SIX

The compressor was running, a muffled hum back by the air bank. The air conditioning breathed cold air across his desk. The icy wind fingered the edges of receipts and sales slips and tax documentation. It bathed his face, fluttered the maps and charts on the wall, then streamed out through his half-open door into the back rooms of the shop.

He sat at the desk, head in his hands, wishing he hadn't ripped and roared quite so much the night before. His eyes roved between the glowing screen of the computer and eight bulging accordion files. Occasionally, Scovill's voice drifted in; he was teaching a technical mixed-gas course in the classroom. "Argon narcosis is profound . . . different from nitrogen narcosis. When I was diving on the *Edmund Fitzgerald* . . ."

He tuned out with an effort of will, trying to concentrate on the February receipts.

He'd spent all morning hammering his brain against the accounts, and both his mind and his ass were going numb. The glamorous life of a pro diver, he thought. Playing bookkeeper for the upcoming quarterly Social Security, payroll, and income-tax submissions. It wasn't a task he'd enjoyed in his own shop, and here it was complicated by the discovery Bud had been keeping three sets of books. One was for the bank, one was for the IRS, and the third seemed to be what he actually ran on to pay the employees and keep himself straight.

You couldn't sell a business set up like that. He had to build

71

one single set of records that would hold up for everybody: the bank, the IRS, payroll, and anybody who might want to buy Scuba Florida. To do that, he had to have a clear picture of exactly what went where, where the cash came from, how each account stood on its own. He sat forward, gripped his pounding forehead, and forced himself back to work.

A dive business could be divided into five profit centers: retail, service, trips, air, and lessons. Retail was everything you sold in the shop or ordered for your customers. The goal was a 100 percent markup and a 50 percent profit, though he'd never been able to get there with the Hatteras shop. Maybe in Belize or Palau or Cozumel, some exotic place people went just to dive. Out of that, you paid labor and overhead, so actual profit came out around 5 to 10 percent. Scuba Florida was specialized; he figured it might come out near the high end of that band.

The service, air, trips, and lessons he checked independently. Ideally, each account should show a profit, though most owners were resigned at best to breaking even on air fills. Air wasn't free. You had labor costs, filters to buy, the compressor to keep running and eventually to replace. Training was another place you didn't expect a big profit. But without it, you didn't have customers.

He'd spent the morning working through the figures, not trying to slant them one way or another yet. Just getting an outline of what he had to deal with. Now they glowed like milling fireflies on the screen, and made about as much sense. He sat back in the chair, sucking a pencil and frowning. Once again, his eyes went to the photo.

He'd found it in the drawer when he was looking for a calculator. It was a snapshot of the squad, posed self-consciously war-like in front of a Conex. Bandannas and fatigue hats, flak jackets and Stoners and nine-millimeter Hush Puppies. Their Vietnamese guides flanked them, both smiling broadly, dwarfed by the Americans, who scowled grimly into the camera.

They looked so young . . . faces and names he'd never forget. Joe Rinaldi, A. W. Gaige, "Sal" Richardson, Matt Shear holding a Pabst. . . . There he was, "Killer" Galloway, the Coast Guard transplant, mugging with the rest. There was Kusczk, broad forehead smeared with horizontal bands of warpaint. No Charpeau, so the shot came from after he was dead. Yeah, Gaige had been his replacement. The photo was in color, but the hues were fading, running into a sallow mush of green and yellow, yellow grass, yellow sky. . . .

We never leave a man behind.

Scovill's voice eddied in again. "In its essence, cave and technical diving is an acceptance of risk. The recreational diver accepts minimal risk. He or she dives to enjoy. The technical diver accepts more risk. The explorer, like Jochen Hansenmayer or Mary Ellen Eckhoff, understands and accepts the risk of death as the cost of discovery."

Tiller got up and shut the door. Then he stood looking at the monitor, massaging circulation back into his butt as he thought.

The bottom lines on the spreadsheet didn't add up. As far as tours and classroom instruction, the place wasn't a big profit maker. Maybe 3, 4 percent. They were breaking even on air. Service and repairs was running a good dollar volume but not making much. There was income listed from some unspecified kind of overseas investments, but not much, less than a thousand a year. The Tartar Springs site was a dead loss. There was a stack of receipts for wood, concrete blocks, various building materials, but as far as he could see, not dollar one of return.

The big moneymaker was the gear-sales business, both in Tallahassee and at the Orlando store. The inventorying software was pretty user-hostile, so he hadn't yet worked down to exactly what was being sold. But he was getting something like a 110 percent markup and a 60 percent profit.

So the retail end was carrying everything else; and the bottom line was a very healthy 20 percent, just as Monica had said.

He went out into the back of the store, got some coffee, checked the compressor, started to go out front, then made a U-turn and forced his unwilling body back into the office. He picked up the phone, but nobody answered at Monica's. Shit, he hadn't seen Tad since before the party last night. Somebody was gonna get roasted when he came home. . . . He hung up, started to get up, made himself sit down again. He forced his reluctant brain back to the accounts.

It wasn't a bad place to start. He'd already figured out how to increase revenues in the other areas. Air, for example, was going for a flat fee per fill. It was smarter to sell it by the cubic foot. Customers accepted that; they could see the rationale for charging the guy who filled twin 121's more than the one who came in with an old steel 72. He could perk up service, run more ads, attract more people to the tours. But all in all, Bud had a good business going here.

The only thing was, he didn't see that the traffic through the front door matched the inventory walking out.

He sat thinking about that for a while, looking at the maps Bud had taped up around the cubicle. One was of the Tampa area, another of Crane County. A Florida Department of Natural Resources map showed the location of every spring in the state. There were pencil marks on the county map. Looking closer, he saw they bracketed a blue circle marked Tartar Springs. So that was where it was.

Had to keep his mind on business. He tried again to break into the inventory software, but it fought him off once more. "You bastard," he muttered to the computer. "I promise you, when it's time to replace you, you're going over the side in a thousand fathoms of water." The screen stared back contemptuously.

At last, frustrated, he went out to the classroom, and stuck his head in to see how it was going.

"Another difference is that self-reliance, nondependency is your goal down there. The farther out there you are, the fewer people you want out there with you. Beyond six or seven hundred feet in, buddy assists don't happen. You may have two guys, but they're both going solo."

Four guys were sitting on a wooden bench, elbows on the Formica table, eyes soldered to Scovill. The manager's back was to the door. Tiller reluctantly admired the slim, straight back, the muscles beneath his light T-shirt, the blond hair on the back of his forearms. There was no way Scovill could have seen him, but somehow he sensed him there. Maybe from the students, glancing past him. Because he said, "Take commercial diving.

"It's got its challenges, but the difference is, in commercial work, you have a lot of support, a lot of equipment. You have surface tenders, a chamber, a bell. You breathe through an umbilical. But in a cave, anything you breathe, you've got to carry in. Only you can breathe for you; only you can swim for you; only you can *think* for you. You can't jerk on a line when you dick up and have somebody come down after you. You keep your cool and figure a way out. Or you die."

He turned his head, registering surprise. "Here's somebody who's done both. Want to comment on that, Tiller?"

He hesitated, thinking about one midnight rush job on a Grace jackup twenty miles south of where the Mississippi River hit the Gulf.

Some barge jockeys had managed to lose an anchor in 210 feet

74

of water and black mud. The first diver down after it had gotten himself wound up in a massive snarl when the bottom current wrapped his lines around the tugger wires. Tiller had gone after him in total darkness, knowing that if his hose got into the snarl, too, neither of them would ever come up again.

Somehow, he'd found the other diver, limp and swaying on the end of his crimped hose. He'd grabbed him with one hand, and with the other started climbing his own umbilical. Both divers weighted down with lead, fighting a current so strong it whipped them around like kites, caroming him off the drill string so hard, his skull rapped the inside of the helmet. There was a time in there he didn't remember; his brain must have switched off. But the next thing he recalled was sitting on the edge of the moon pool, and the tenders were taking his partner's helmet off. Jaxon's face had been blue-green, like a newborn baby's, and for a while they weren't sure he was going to start breathing again.

"They're different," he said to the curious faces. "Sometimes you're as much on your own as you'd be in a cave. Most of the time, Colten's right, though. You got tenders and an assured air supply."

Scovill nodded. "Thanks, Till. Oh, and I meant to ask you—got anything planned for tonight?"

"Don't know. I'm kind of behind on sleep. Why?"

"Well, now that Bud's . . . not here anymore, we're one guy short on an exploratory dive out at Wabasso. Lamont Exmore's in charge. A deep-penetration push, some real challenging caving. Interested?"

He'd planned to crash early, make up for last night's alcohol soak. But faced with Scovill's half smile, he felt both annoyed and glad to be challenged, to have something to look forward to beyond playing accountant. "Okay, sure," he said. "Count me in."

The front door chimed and he glanced toward it, seeing July's slightly hip-heavy figure swing in. " 'Scuse me," he said, and went to ask her about how to access the inventory software.

He was tempted to just let her run it for him; she seemed smart and trustworthy. But he wanted to do this job right: work everything himself, make sure there were no surprises, prepare a crystal-clear presentation for when a possible buyer showed up. Toll gave him the password and showed him how to log on. She ran him through the procedures till he felt confident, then went back out front to the sales counter.

By three o'clock, he had tracked down where the profits were coming from.

The markup on the Beuchat and ScubaPro lines and the Dive-Rite cave gear was keystone. Where things got golden was the expensive high-tech merchandise—dive computers, underwater video cameras, specialized lights and housings, watches, and regulators. He was impressed as he looked over the figures.

The phone rang and he got it, still looking at the screen. "Scuba Florida," he said, then heard the double click as July picked up, too, up front. "I got it," he yelled, and heard her hang up again.

"Who's this?"

"Tiller Galloway, Scuba Florida. Can I help you?"

"Joel Kusczk, please."

"Bud's had an accident. I'm standing in for him. Did you want to book a dive?"

"A dive? No, no. Let me talk to Bud."

He always listened more closely when he caught a Hispanic accent. You couldn't help doing that, once you'd been an associate of Juan Alberto Mendieta Nuñez-Sebastiano. He said, "You a friend of his, sir? I'm sorry to tell you this. But Bud died a few weeks ago."

No response from the other end. "Hello, did you hear me? He had an accident. But we're still in business. You a caver? We're putting together a tour to Mexico, the Akumal-Tulum systems, for next month, if you're interested in seeing some very unusual formations."

"You say he's dead? Is that what you're telling me?"

No question now about the accent. That in itself meant nothing. Plenty of Cubans, Hispanics of all kinds in Florida. But that wasn't what was ringing bells in his head now. The guy wanted something, and it wasn't a guided tour of Madison Blue. He tried again. "Is there somebody else here you've dealt with? July, or Tony, or Colten—"

The line went dead.

Shit, he thought. He stared at the phone, wishing he had a call tracer. But from the sounds in the background, cars, engines, it would probably just have led to some pay phone at a 7-eleven.

"Know anything about a file called *styx.aqr*?"

"No." July swiped short brown hair out of her eyes with the back of a wrist. He watched as she skillfully fitted a new diaphragm to a used Conshelf. He liked that—she didn't just sit at

76

the desk when there were no customers; she found something else to do. No lipstick, no eye makeup. A serious girl. A no-nonsense woman. She was friendly enough; but somehow, he couldn't really say how, he got the feeling, talking to her, that he was being held off at boathook-length. "Why?" she asked, finally looking up.

"There's a file in the computer by that name."

"Inventory or personal? What's the subdirectory?"

"Business. But when I opened it, it was empty. No data."

"No idea. Sorry." She spun the reassembled regulator onto a tank, twisted the valve open. Her cheeks hollowed as she took a test breath.

"Is there a backup? Disk, or tape, or—"

"Not that I know of."

"Okay. Well, I'm taking off."

"Just a minute." She twisted a tag onto the regulator and hung it on a peg. Without facing him, she said, "Are you really going to dive Wabasso tonight with us?"

"You going, too? Yeah. That's the plan."

"I don't think you should."

"No? Why not?"

"Please don't take this the wrong way. You know a lot. But you're still not a qualified cave diver. And it's going to be a difficult dive."

He shrugged. "I've used scooters before, and done a lot of decompression time. Unless you think there's some other reason I shouldn't go?"

"No," she said. She was still not looking at him, but her expression was serious, almost sad. He waited, but she didn't say anything else.

He started out the door, then turned back and called Monica's again. This time, she answered. He said quickly, figuring he was about to be hung up on, "This is Tiller."

"Oh, hi! How's it going down there?"

"Uh . . . okay. How about you?"

"We're fine here. I just got back from taking Lunker for his shots. He's hiding under the bed."

"Are you feeling all right?"

"Sure, why shouldn't I be?" She sounded surprised.

"No reason. I just figured you'd still be mad at me."

"Oh, that. I was, last night. It wasn't a smart thing to do, Tiller. But I don't stay mad long. Hardly ever overnight." She paused, but he couldn't think of anything to say, though he was relieved she wasn't angry.

"Want to talk to Tad?"

"He there? Yeah, let me talk to him."

His son sounded distant and contemptuous. Tiller asked him where he'd been all night and he said he was camping out with Ripper.

"Who?"

"Ripper—you know, Chain Saw. You said you wouldn't be back till late, so we went over to his place and watched some videos, and finally it got so late, I just figured I'd better stay there."

"From now on, I want you home by eleven," Tiller told him, but he felt guilty; he'd promised the kid fun, had intended to spend some time with him. "Look, want to go see a guy with me?"

"I don't care."

"Be out front. I'll pick you up in a couple minutes."

The County Rescue Team was a mixed pro and volunteer group. Alan Pendleton, the diver who'd found Kusczk's body, was one of the volunteers. Pendleton's daytime contact number turned out to be a local high school. Apparently, he taught science there.

When Galloway and Tad got out of the Buick in the parking lot of the Warehouse, the humid Florida air was shimmering like boiling water. There were four or five guys and girls standing around in front, but only one who looked like a diver. Well-built, not too big, not too small, black mustache and little microbeard like Frank Zappa's. Tiller said, "Pendleton?"

"That's me." They shook hands and Galloway introduced Tad.

"How about a beer?"

Pendleton hesitated. "I can't stay too long. Got to get down to the store."

"Thought you were a teacher."

"I am. But I moonlight at a music store, too."

"Busy man. Well, I'll try to make it fast," Tiller said.

The Warehouse was much cooler than outside. Bare wooden floors, and a couple of young guys and bored-looking girls in torn jeans shoving balls around moth-eaten pool tables. The bar looked as if it had been hammered on with chairs more than once. Nobody gave them a second glance as they pulled stools up to it. He ordered a Bud and Pendleton a Silver Bullet, and a 7Up for Tad.

78

The jukebox was too loud for talk, and when the drinks came in cold bottles and cans, no glasses, Pendleton pointed his toward a back room. They followed him back into the dim, to a table in a big empty room with lightbulbs hanging from bare beams and trusswork. An empty stage stood at one end.

Tiller opened with, "They tell me you're the guy pulled Bud Kusczk out of Emerald Sink last month."

"That's right." Pendleton took a pull. "Who'd you say you were?"

"I'm looking into his death for his widow."

"You're what? A cop? Some kind of PI?"

"No. A friend of his. Commercial diver."

Pendleton's eyes slid past him to the stage. "I thought you looked like one of us bubble-blowers. How about you, Tad?"

The boy flinched. "How about me, what?"

"You a diver?"

"He's working on his basic cert."

Tad examined the ceiling, as if this was all too stupid for words. Pendleton just grinned at him, then turned to Tiller. "About Bud. Yeah, I pulled him out. It was kind of sad, because I'd seen him around CDS meetings and stuff."

"Oh, you knew him?"

"Like I said, I saw him around. But I kind of got a different slant on things than him and the other guys there."

"How's that?"

"I dive into caves, but I'm not a cave diver, if you see the difference."

"What's the difference?"

"I mean, somebody's got to go in and pull the remains out when people screw up. That's County Rescue. So I do the qualification, and I dive with these guys, but as a sport, I'm not comfortable with it. You want my opinion, I think we ought to just put grates over all the caves. Outlaw it."

"Yeah? Why?"

"Well, what good is it? I'm not saying all risk is bad, but anything you do that involves it, there ought to be some benefit. Right? If we're gonna be logical about the whole thing. If we're not, then let's just buy a revolver and one shell and play russian roulette. But cave diving, what are you actually doing? At first, a survey. You go in to locate a route; you're working through a maze, through tunnels. But once somebody does the map, what's the point in going in again?"

"To see things?"

Pendleton laughed. "To see what? There isn't a whole lot of marine life down there. There are some forms in certain sections interesting to a science guy like me, but no, not for the sights. What else?"

"I don't know. Like I said, I'm a commercial diver."

"Then you got work to do, some reason to be down there. But what is there in a cave to risk your life over? Don't get me wrong. I love to dive. But I'm more into the visuals, what you might call the spiritual effects. I like Pennekamp, the Keys, the reefs. A cave? Shit, fella, you've seen one blind crayfish, far as I'm concerned, you've seen 'em all."

"So you're saying it's dangerous and stupid."

Pendleton shrugged. "Of course, I could be prejudiced."

"Why would you be prejudiced?"

"Because I'm the guy that goes down four, five times a year to pull dead kids out. There's the family standing around waiting and hoping Junior's found an air pocket, and I'm the guy has to surface with the body bag. So you might be getting a kind of slanted view here."

Tad said suddenly, "Dad."

"What, goddamn it?"

"Can I have some money? They got pizza up front."

"Yeah, get us one. Pepperoni, green peppers." He gave Tad a twenty from the hundred Monica had loaned him. As he headed toward the bar Tiller drank off half his beer and asked Pendleton, "You want part of that?"

Pendleton checked his Seiko. "No, I got to go. Anyway, what'd you want to know about Bud?"

"Tell me how you found him. Mon told me about the campers."

"Yeah, the campers. They called us at dusk. You have to scramble when you get one of those calls. You know deep down it probably won't make any difference, but ... there was this one case when I first started on the team.

"That happened at Little River. Three brothers from Ohio, in their twenties, early thirties—they came down for a vacation. Open-water divers. But they decide they want to go cave diving. So they rent some tanks and sneak in and go down into Little River. Three guys, two flashlights. No lines. They went in to the maze area, lost sight of the opening, and got lost. Kicked up a silt-out, lots of particulate matter on the floor.

"Well, their sister, who had stayed on the surface, got worried after an hour and called nine-one-one. We found one brother in the maze and the other fifty feet from the last turn to daylight; before he died, he'd scraped on his tank with his knife: 'I love you Mom and Dad.' Not a pretty sight."

"I guess not."

"We found the last one with his head stuck up into an air pocket. He wasn't breathing, but his face was out of the water. I stuck my octopus into his mouth and did some half-assed CPR, jammed up there against the ceiling, and finally got him breathing again. Got him out stat and the emergency medical team, topside, pulled him through. Fifteen minutes later, he'd have been dead, too. So we try to move as fast as we can, consistent with our own safety.

"Anyway, Kusczk. These campers call us, say they found dive gear and no diver's come up. We got down there, team of three, half an hour after dark. You know Emerald?"

"No."

"Popular cave. A classic hourglass sink—starts sixty feet across and mushrooms out as you go down. There's an inflowing tunnel on the southwest side at sixty feet; it's about fifty feet wide and twenty feet high. The interesting stuff's on the south side, though. There's like a cave mouth—that's where you lose the daylight— and past that's what we call the Black Abyss. It plunges about two hundred and ten feet to a main tunnel that goes back nearly a mile, depths around two hundred, two hundred and ten. It connects back there with Clear Cut Sink."

Pendleton checked his watch again. "That's where I found him—back in that tunnel, a quarter mile in from the entrance— with working regulators, working gauges, and empty tanks."

"He hadn't panicked, then."

"Right, but that didn't mean he didn't drown. The coroner found water in his lungs."

Tiller nodded slowly. "What went wrong?"

"Well, we try to figure it out, put it in the report. Basically, you just try to put yourself in the guy's shoes, figure what might have gone sour and what he'd have done. It's just a guess, but there's some tight, complicated tunnels back there. Phreatic stuff—"

"What's that mean?"

"You've seen it if you've dove around here—the water-smoothed rock, kind of rounded. I figure he was back there and got confused. There's a T back there, a place where the line ties in a T, and it's easy to miss. The tie-off's back under a lip of rock.

81

If there was a visibility problem, or he wasn't feeling supersharp that day, he could have missed it going in. Not seen it."

Pendleton popped a ballpoint and drew a little map on a place mat. Tiller half-rose, squinting toward the bar, wondering where Tad had got to. He sat back down and looked at the sketch. "Then he's going around in circles back there, thinking he's on his way out?"

"Not exactly, but you've got the idea. See, he's already pushing his air supply. He had a full cave rig. Two one-oh-fours. Enough, but not really generous, considering where he was. But let's say something goes wrong—he makes a wrong turn or something. Now he's running figures in his head and he knows he's in trouble. So you've got stress added to the equation, maybe some carbon dioxide buildup. Let's say by this time, he's kicked up some silt, too. He's got to go down, get real intimate with that line now.

"Okay, so he's got it and he's turned the dive; he's following it back. Then suddenly, he hits this T he doesn't remember. You know how your perceptions narrow when things start to go wrong." Tiller nodded. "I figure that's what throws him. It's got line markers on it, but both sides of the T are marked as exits. Which way would you go?"

"If I didn't remember the T, I wouldn't know. I'd have to guess."

"Right, and he guessed wrong. That uses up still more air.

"Now he's really anxious. He figures it out at last, but by the time he gets back to the main tunnel, he knows he's not going to make it to the exit. So he pulls out his slate." Pendleton put the pen away. "You know about that? What he wrote?"

"Monica told me. 'Killer'—that was me."

"Well, then." They stared at each other. Galloway still, with part of his mind, down there with Bud; able to visualize, now that he'd been in a cave, what it must have been like. The dark pressing in at the edge of your lights; the tight, narrow passages of water-worn rock; then realizing you'd screwed up, that it was over and you were going to die. The slow creep of needles measuring the final minutes . . .

"What do you figure he was doing back there?" he asked Pandleton.

"You fellas back here ready for another?" The waitress tapped a pencil on her tray.

Pendleton scowled, checked the time again, and shook his head. Galloway hesitated, then shook his, too. The girl left. "What was

82

he doing? I don't know. There's no reason he should have been in that cave. Not alone."

"What do you mean? You said it was a popular cave."

"Yeah, because people dive it for training, or like as intermediate divers. Bud was way past that. He was in on the Wabasso Project; he was doing major exploration in Texas and Mexico. Only reason he'd have been in Emerald would have been to take a group back. And there was no group with him."

Tiller squinted into his beer. There was something else he'd wanted to ask this guy. What was it? To stall him another minute, he said, "You mentioned a coroner's report. Can I get a copy?"

"Have his wife call the county; they'll mail it to her. They don't usually send them to the relatives because it upsets people to read the details. But if she asks, she'll get a copy." Pendleton cocked his head. "Hear that?"

"What?"

"That song. Sort of the cave diver's anthem."

Tiller realized he meant the jukebox out front. It was country, or folk—with a strong beat, anyway. A male tenor, Tom Petty, George Harrison?

> Well it's all right
> Even if the sun doesn't shine
> Well it's all right
> Goin' to the end of the line. . . .

"Look, I got to get rolling. Thanks for the beer."

He remembered then what he'd wanted to ask, when he heard Pendleton was a teacher. "Hey, one more thing. This aquifer business—what can you tell me about it?"

"What, you want a lesson on aquifers?"

"Yeah. I've kind of got the general picture, but maybe I need to look into it a little more."

"Well . . . okay, but I really got to go in five more minutes." Pendleton cleared his throat. "Florida Geology one-oh-one. We start with the concept of a karst. That's a limestone region, with groundwater forming sinkholes and caves. The geological underpinning is sedimentary stone. Porous. The stone's calcium-based, limestone, bonded together with other silicates. Since ground water's slightly acidic, it gradually dissolves tunnels and caverns into the bedrock."

83

"Like around here."

"Exactly. See, the whole state's floating on one of the world's greatest aquifers. *Aqua*—'water'; *fer*—'carrier.' There are two kinds." Pendleton poured a little beer onto the table. He laid the paper coaster over it and pointed out the dark seepage. "That's an unconfined aquifer. Groundwater that's in touch vertically with the atmosphere through open springs, or permeable rock."

"What's the other kind?"

"That's if this top layer isn't permeable. It's solid, and the water's sealed down there. That's a confined aquifer."

"Which one have we got around here?"

"Mixed; but mostly, it's confined."

"Like an underground sea."

"Like an underground sea, exactly. The rock's threaded by interconnected tunnels. Some of them are hundreds of feet underground. And most of them haven't been mapped yet, because of the limitations of scuba."

"Another dumb question. Where's the water come from?"

"From the surface, from rainfall over what's called the 'recharge area.' The water flows out through rivers and wells and some upward movement into secondary aquifers. But the main way out is up through the springs, then into the rivers and out into the Gulf of Mexico. The springs occur in clusters, feeding into or flowing from an underground river. Each spring's different. Some are seasonal, the dissolved mineral content is different, and so on."

"Ever hear of Tartar Springs?"

"South of here. Part of the Styx system," said Pendleton. "That what you're talking about, right?"

"I guess. Know anything about it?"

"Not much. Never heard of anybody diving there. Look, I really got to beat it." The rescue diver got up. "Good luck with your business. And dive safe, hear?"

"Yeah, you, too," said Galloway, looking after him.

"Another beer, mister?" The girl was back.

He started to say sure, then remembered Tad. He'd been gone an awfully long time. He asked her, "Say, where's the pizza we ordered?"

"We don't serve pizza here, sir. You need to go down the street, to—"

"Wait a minute. Didn't my son order a pizza?"

"No, sir. Like I say, we don't—"

He was up then and charging out to the bar area. But of course Tad wasn't there.

Galloway stood there, clenching and unclenching his fists. *Dad,* he thought disgustedly. He was turning back to the bar for another when he remembered: Tonight he was diving at Wabasso Springs.

SEVEN

Who's this, Sco?" said the heavyset diver with the handlebar mustache, stopping in front of him.

"This here's the guy I told you about. Tiller Galloway, the oil-field diver. Tiller's got more time than all of us put together, Lamont."

"In caves?"

"Not in caves, but—"

"That's all I need to hear." Exmore smiled at him to take the edge off, but said, "We'll manage without him."

"Look, you know we need a replacement for Bud. We've already sherpa'd all the gear for three-man teams."

The hawk-nosed diver kept shaking his head. Tiller saw how it was. Exmore was some kind of god to these guys. He decided it was time to step in, make his voice heard. He told him, "Look, I'm going. So get used to it. Just tell me what to do and it'll get done. And I'll probably come out pulling one of you behind me."

That got him glances from the little group of divers and acquaintances standing in the dusking light. He stared back as Exmore searched his eyes. Finally, the mustached diver said in a quiet voice, "July, what do you think? You dove with him?"

"He's cool. Makes the right decisions."

"Okay, we'll give him his shot. But he'll be your partner. You guys vouch for him, you can bring him back." He went on, leaving them, and Tiller looked around.

Wabasso. Lights sparkled from a big old hotel above the

86

spring; it sounded like a wedding reception was just getting into the fun stage. Down here, the water was a flat dark slate, with cypresses spreading skirts of shadowy foliage motionless on the far shore. A pier on their side had two flat-bottomed boats tied up. Another rode at anchor. It looked tranquil and quiet.

He didn't feel so tranquil. According to Scovill, this was going to be a deep, long dive. Still, by commercial standards, it didn't sound too tough. If everything went as planned, they'd be out in about eight hours. There were two teams of three each: first team, Scovill, July, and himself; second team, Exmore, Skip Chappers, and Benton Ammons. The others moving about in the growing dark were helpers, spouses and friends. He had a momentary flash of anger as he remembered Tad. His son hadn't shown since disappearing with his money. He should have gotten this Chain Saw kid's number; that's where he probably was. Going to be hell to pay, the next time—

"Want to gather over here, everybody?"

He hunkered with the other divers as Exmore went over the map with a flashlight, pointing out where they'd drop their stages and scooters. Tiller studied the map intently, knowing his life and theirs might hang on remembering it.

Facing the cave entrance, which led under the rise where the lodge's windows glowed, the main tunnel went in nearly a thousand feet before curving right and then left again. A reversed S half a mile long. Meanwhile, branches led off from it on both sides. The map showed some reconnecting, others leading off into pinch-outs or else simply stopping where exploration had ended. One of those abrupt stops was a few hundred feet into what was marked as "K tunnel." Beyond that was blank.

Exmore said, "The object of tonight's dive is to push down two side tunnels that leave the main avenue about twenty-five hundred feet in. We call them K One and K Two. Benton thinks there's a possibility K One might hook right and reconnect with D tunnel. The depth looks about right, two hundred and forty feet. But maybe we'll find out tonight. I have . . . seven-fifty-five." There was a murmur as the others either confirmed or adjusted watches and computers. Tiller checked his.

Exmore went on: "Like we planned, me, Benton, and Skip will take the left-hand passage, K Two. July, Sco and . . ."

"Tiller."

"And Tiller—they'll take K One. We'll be laying line and turning the dive at the two-thirds point."

Exmore covered the gas-management plan and turn time, then finished by saying, "The important thing to remember is that nobody's ever been where we're going tonight. Play it safe, especially in the Bottleneck. There's unstable rock in there just past the breakdown room. In the new passages, go in slow. Be alert for unstable roofing, unexpected currents, silting or tannic flow. Don't get too focused. Keep looking around. Concentrate on the main tunnel, but note anything that might be a new lead. The surveyor on each team will be keeping the slate. We're not expecting a grade-five survey, just a basic stick map with your line and compass and depth gauge.

"One last thing. If things go wrong, anybody starts feeling stressed-out, turn the dive. There's nothing down there worth dying for. Anybody feels like a hero tonight, like he's gonna prove something, he better stay here." He waited, looking at each of them in turn. No one responded, so he grunted, "Okay, let's get dressed out."

Tiller and Colten and July helped one another suit up. He'd let Scovill advise him on gear this time. He was using the same twin steel main tanks as before, but this time filled with trimix, a 14 percent oxygen-helium-nitrogen mix he and Scovill had made up back at the shop. Using helium as an oxygen diluent reduced narcosis at depth, while a small amount of nitrogen counteracted the tremors and coordination problems divers sometimes got on helium-oxygen alone. They were wearing argon-inflated dry suits, since a wet suit wouldn't keep you warm enough for hours in the water. Disposable adult diapers helped keep them dry. They were each towing two stage tanks filled with trimix. Under the looming of the boat, moored out on the still blackness, were suspended more cylinders of compressed air, Nitrox, and oxygen for the last stages of decompression.

Standing there, sweating already in the heavy dry suit, all at once he started to doubt himself. Face-to-face with it, he didn't want to go into that dark water, with no way up except back through thousands of feet of black passage. He'd never been that far back, in the dark, with no bailout and no backup. Scovill was right: It really *wasn't* like punching the clock for Oceaneering or Cal Dive, unlimited gas and a couple million bucks' worth of gear and professionals on tap in case you stepped on your crank.

Too late, he realized even thinking about it had been a mistake. The dread leapt up like fire under oxygen, drying his mouth and starting his heart racing. If he hadn't faced fear a couple thousand times before, he'd have turned tail and bolted away up the bank, shedding gear as he ran. Why the hell was he doing this? Then he remembered Scovill's appraising, superior glance, the students watching enviously: "A deep-penetration push, some real challenging caving. Interested?" Call it macho stupidity if you wanted, but now he had to follow through on his mouth.

He took control of his breathing, sucked warm night air scented with flowers deep down into his gut, then let it out slowly through his nose. Again. Good.

"July tells me you're a hard-hat guy," said Exmore, mustache distinct even in the flicker of a moving flashlight.

He turned, glad to have somebody to talk to. "That's right."

"Out on the oil rigs, that kind of stuff? Couple of weeks at a time in saturation?"

"Sometimes more."

"Sounds dangerous. You wouldn't get me down there."

"Sometimes it is." He looked across the dark water. "Hey, maybe you can tell me something."

"Sure, what?"

"They paid me to do that. Paid me damn good, too. Why do you people do this? For 'fun'?"

"Not exactly," said Exmore quietly. "I guess it's just that not everybody can. And it's . . . well, kind of peaceful down there."

"You could go down thirty feet and it'd be just as peaceful."

The silhouette shrugged. "So why are you here?"

"I'm learning the business. To help a . . . friend."

The soft voice said, "We all have our reasons, then. But we aren't fools. We train hard. We're kind of anal-retentive individuals, if you want to know the truth. Four backups for every piece of gear. Overplan everything."

"But the danger's still there."

"What's life for if it's not lived at the edge?" Exmore paused. "I've looked for it other places. Done some skydiving. Done some climbing. Came close to it one night on Mount Rainier. But this *is* it."

"And what is 'it'?"

"Ever hear of a guy named Aldo Leopold? He said it the best I've ever heard it. 'Of what avail are forty freedoms without a blank spot on the map?' " The hawk-nosed silhouette turned. "Down there—that's the only blank spot left. Don't tell me you've never done anything risky."

"Of course I have. And I've heard that 'every man dies; not

every man really lives' line before. I guess I grew out of it, though. Or did enough I don't need any more."

"Or lost whatever it takes?" asked Exmore quietly. "Look, that's not a challenge. Don't let Sco talk you into some ass-cracker you're not ready for. You're not gonna be a hero. You're just gonna be dead, and probably take the rest of your team with you. Hear what I'm saying? If you want me to, I'll tell them I was the one decided you'd better not go."

He waited, and when Galloway didn't respond, he murmured, "See? You've got it, too." He touched his arm lightly, then turned away. Called into the surrounding dark, "Everybody ready to fly?"

"Let's bust the big one," Tiller said. He lurched into the water, worked the mouthpiece between his teeth, and hauled the dive scooter around into position in front of him. It was the shape of a stubby torpedo, with a shrouded prop and handles on either side to grip and steer. When he grasped the trigger handle, the prop whirred, tugging him forward off his fins and down beneath the surface. He thumbed the switch, and brilliance ignited the underwater night.

He followed Scovill's and Toll's lights down into the dark. The multiple bee song of their props droned in his ears. The scooters the cavers favored responded more quickly than the open-water DPVs—diver propulsion vehicles—he was used to; he had to concentrate to stay on course. The water was cold around his face, but the gas hissing in and out of his lungs felt good. He concentrated on that and his reluctance receded. He was back where he belonged.

Out of the darkness, beams of light appeared. They swung back and forth. They picked out an open black mouth.

The cave. Following the others, he hummed downward, clearing his ears every couple of seconds as they dropped through the lightless cold.

As Exmore had briefed, the first part of the dive would be a scooter-sprint penetration down the main tunnel, till they reached the area they'd be exploring. He clung to the handle grips, keeping the throttle down as the lights ahead disappeared, swallowed by the earth.

He was trying to clear his ears when all at once his headlight picked up the stone overjutting lip of the cave. He was too fast, too light, and too high. He ducked and rolled, a horseback rider plucking up a handkerchief, and slipped beneath it, missing rock by a couple of centimeters.

Throttled back to a creep, he rode slowly down through the vast opening in the earth, tilting his wrist-mounted light around, taking in the subterranean world he was entering.

The cave arched up massively over him, a shadowy space of flickering buff rock. The floor was nearly flat, littered with the table-sized chunks he was getting used to at entrances. As he bored in, the dark closed like heavy velvet curtains. He realized that even in the night there had been some light outside, in the basin. Now there was none, only the flicker and glow of their own, the white main lights, the yellower headlights of their machines.

The pressure leaned on his ears and he cleared them again. Time for an instrument check.

Damn, they were going down fast. The pallid inch-by screen of the wrist computer gave him almost two hundred feet, and the huge chamber was still going back and down. It arched so far above him, he couldn't see the ceiling even when he pointed his light up, just an inchoate blue glow. . . . The humming prop pulled him steadily over big flat-faced chunks of breakdown rock. Belatedly, he remembered he was supposed to be following a line. He arched his back and the scooter tipped over and headed down. The line came into view, a pale filament leading into the abyss.

At 240 feet, he made out the first depot: a huddle of eight tanks laid side by side on top of a rock shaped like Texas. He swept over them, riding a few feet above the line.

The huge open mouth of the tunnel was constricting now into a gullet. It was roughly oval, sometimes almost circular. It was leveling out, too. He couldn't tell how far it ran; all his lights gave him was that blue backglow and occasional bubbles or flecks of particulate. Scovill's and Toll's headlights rode steadily ahead. Every now and then, he caught their silhouette.

The smooth, slightly curved walls slipped past ten yards on either side—irregular, porous whitish rock, then a break to his left. Darkness swallowed his probing beam. The A tunnel. The map had showed it corkscrewing back for over a mile, through breakdown rooms and ledges and lips. No one had yet found the end.

The gas he was breathing felt slow, thick, and cold now. The metallic taste was familiar, comforting. He ran a quick systems check on himself and came up green. He felt confident and even, in the dry suit and Depend, fairly warm. Behind the steady purr of the scooter, he was doing about three knots with no more effort than it took to breathe. It was exhilarating, in a way, looking down the side passages as they slid past. Mysterious, dark. He could see why they got off on it. And he saw why they had to do their diving on tanks. You'd never get an umbilical back this far, not unless you had some kind of underwater bulldozer to drag it.

The passage eased right, in a great wide curve, and he fin-steered and rolled to turn with it. The lights ahead were getting more distant and he tucked his chest closer to the torpedo shape to kick his speed up a notch. Then he checked his stage tank. Shit, down to a thousand already. At 245 feet he was using gas eight times as fast as he did on the surface. Sucking in, blowing out eight cubic feet a minute to soar in graceful cascades behind him toward the confining rock.

He jerked his attention back, to find the others had slowed, riding now abreast of him. His mask turned from one to the other. Then he remembered the yellow suit was Scovill. His light traced a circle on a passing rock. Tiller laid his beam over it and circled okay back. They moved ahead again and he increased speed to stay closed up.

The tunnel narrowed, the overhead closing down to arch fifteen feet over the flat, rippled silt of the floor. Occasionally, a black plume blossomed slowly as July's or Scovill's prop wash brushed it. He valved a little more gas into his wings and climbed till he was sailing along just below the ceiling. Soaring through water clear as air . . . at the perimeter of moving light colors bled away to green, blue, violet, to a region where shadows lurked and writhed. He jerked his eyes back. Shit, when were they going to drop their bottles? He was almost out. Maybe he should shift to his back tanks now.

The lights ahead dipped and slowed, and he slowed, too, left hand searching for his D rings as they drifted to a halt. He hung back, admiring how smoothly Toll and Scovill did it; almost one motion, the scooter tilting up as they dropped their exhausted stage tanks, a smooth roll as they tugged fresh ones off the bottom, perfect control of buoyancy and attitude.

His turn. He unclipped the ring with one hand, holding the scooter with the other. It started to drift downward. He jerked it up, milling with his fins, and got the stage free, then took a deep breath and let the mouthpiece go. Cold pressed against his lips as he lowered the used tank.

Great, now he was floating up. He jackknifed, recontrolled the scooter, starting to curse in his head, starting to want air. His groping glove found the fresh stage tank, ran along the hose, unclipped the regulator. His teeth closed on the mouthpiece. He cleared it with a sudden quick burst of pent breath and took a tentative hit. At the same moment, his fins touched the bottom. He shoved off, and immediately a cloud of silt burst up around him.

Great, real graceful . . . Scovill and Toll were hovering, watching. He gave them an okay sign. They nodded, oriented the scooters, and headed on again.

Now the tunnel narrowed again and curved right. Smaller rounded tunnels branched off like capillaries from an artery. Into each stretched a sideline, evidence of past explorations. The floor slid past, littered with small rocks and silt. He checked his watch. It seemed like an hour, but they'd been down less than fifteen minutes.

A sunrise from behind threw his shadow against the curved walls. He swiveled his head, catching at the edge of his faceplate multiple brilliances like locomotive headlights. Team two was coming up behind him, fast.

He pulled his attention front again and sucked air so hard, his regulator squeaked. He was too light again, and headed straight for a jagged fin of rock that thrust down from the roof. He jerked the scooter down and ducked, felt his hose and the back of his tank clank and drag over the surface, then slip free. Close call. He'd better keep his attention on what was ahead of him.

Curiously, though, the near miss settled him. Or maybe it was having the other lights behind him, so he could see beyond the narrow cone of his own. The whole tunnel was filled with light now, blue and wavering, conducted along beneath the earth like some immense natural fiber optic. The last nervousness dropped away and he concentrated on the job.

At the moment, that was keeping himself centered as the tunnel curved and twisted deeper into the earth. His depth gauge passed 230, then 240. Even in the open sea, he'd be losing daylight now. It felt eerie still to be following his headlamp through the crystal fluid, pushed from behind by the second team. The tunnel sagged abruptly to 265—that was his reading even hugging the ceiling—then back to 240. Good thing they were on mixed gas; they'd be gibbering idiots here on air. His beam glittered off shimmering globules spurting up from Toll's regulator. Her faceplate flashed as she turned to check on him.

A flash flick of her wrist light, a jerk of her head to the right. The light was tinted jade. He squinted, glimpsing a black low gape before the world tumbled.

The tunnel walls rushed past in slow mo as he fought for control of the bucking beast his scooter suddenly became. It broke loose and he twisted after it, reeling in on the safety line as the dead-man switch cut power to the prop.

Green water blew in a steady stream out of the side tunnel, tugging at his mask. He got the machine pointed again, got a fresh grip, and let it pull him smoothly past the side stream, back into the dreamlike flight along a tunnel that seemed to have no end.

It was going down again, a steady descent now in a dropping curve. The ceiling came down even more, closing down relentlessly till they were riding with only eight to ten feet between rippled silt the color of cocoa and the arched ceiling.

Scovill and Toll cut their speed and he closed up, then cut back, too. They purred over a mass of fallen rock. A cuplike dome rose over it. Scovill led them around it to the right, then through a switchback out a hidden ledge at the top. He followed cautiously, committing each turn to memory. It was confusing in the fitful glares of the flickering lights. But the line stretched on, taut and reassuring, with the plastic arrows pointing back every hundred feet or so.

A restriction, depth 240. Four feet wide and silty, with the current blowing up a roiling curtain. Toll vanished ahead of him into a blast of fine black mist. He kept doggedly on after her. Was this the Bottleneck? Exmore had warned about unstable rock past here. He twisted to survey the overhead—seamed and fissured. He could imagine about ten tons of that coming down on him. No, maybe he'd better not.

Thirty, forty yards on, it widened again and rejoined a narrowed version of the main tunnel. It was headed down again. He rechecked his depth. He wasn't happy to see the needle passing three hundred.

There, ahead, a row of bottles half-embedded in black-brown silt like chocolate pudding, hoses swaying in the flow. This was where they dropped their last stage and went ahead on back tanks. He was pleasantly surprised to see a spare scooter there, too. He could feel the cold now, even through the dry suit. His feet were icy. Also, he was going to have to pee soon. Diaper or not, that would further degrade the insulation. Just hold it as long as you can, he told himself. And try to breathe slower. He was

94

using gas too fast, sucking each tank too low before the next one came into sight.

He was unhooking the last stage while this all streamed through his head, feeling around for his primary regulator, the one from his back-mounted twins. He found it and thrust it into his mouth. Took a breath, and got a little water spray with it. He purged it again and got more water, almost a mouthful. Shit, he thought, focused now. He purged it a third time, hard, pressing the button till bubbles roared out. This time, he got a good flow of dry air.

Scovill was hovering in front of him, eyes searching Galloway's. He circled his fingers and Tiller returned the signal.

A few hundred feet farther on, Toll's and Scovill's lights descended. Galloway eased off the hand throttle and coasted down to a halt behind July as she laid her scooter carefully over on its side. She drifted slowly upward and back as the current caught her. A gesture—pointing at his scooter; a wrist snap as she pointed to the floor. Then she oriented, gave a kick, and glided downward again, angling right. A hand reached out and caught a rounded knob of rock.

He looked past her into a black and lightless maw.

They were here.

The hum of props, and the narrow passage was suddenly filled with light and activity as team two slid past. He heard the bursting exhalation of bubbles as each diver passed, the clatter and rattle and jingle of gear. The last one gave him a two-fingered wave from the grip of his scooter. Exmore. Tiller popped him a jaunty salute.

The hum and clatter sank toward quiet, and he looked back again into the blackness that faced them.

K 1 had never been explored and there was no line leading in. He contemplated its open emptiness as he secured his scooter, making real sure the switch was firmly seated at OFF, then kicked slowly over to join July. He looked around for Scovill. The lead diver was already inside, his light flicking around. Then it steadied, and Galloway saw the exploring line attached to the main line. A bright yellow plastic clothespin glowed in his beam.

Scovill had briefed them on the exploration procedure. As the team leader, he'd carry the reel. July, behind him, would give him light and help route line as he laid it. Tiller would stay alert for silting or other hazards, give them light as needed, and keep the survey board. The survey board . . . he fumbled around till he felt its rectangular edge. He got the compass oriented and shot the main tunnel where K branched off, then added the first course in: 012 degrees magnetic. It was awkward. He was doing too many things at once, trying to read the compass, manipulating the lights so he could make notes, and a quarter of his skull was preoccupied again with where he was. He concentrated fiercely. Get it done and get out of here.

Scovill was out of sight now. Toll put her light on his board, then pointed to his depth gauge. He checked it and added the depth figures. Then she jerked her head toward the tunnel.

With a last look back, he followed her down.

The geology in K 1 was different from the main tunnel. He wondered if this was what they called a "chimney." It dropped fast, a narrow crack with sharp rock surfaces that caught at his gear. Below him, Toll was pulling herself downward with her hands. Her fins trailed nearly motionless. That looked like a good technique, and he imitated her, only to find he couldn't and hold the survey board, too. He finally valved the last air from his wings and just sank after her, fending off from the edges with one hand and his knees.

He crashed softly into a soot-silted floor so narrow, he could touch both walls with his elbows. Lying there, he wrote "330 feet" on his slate, then felt for the knots on the line and added "40'." As he waited for things to clear a little, he checked his gauges and watch, bringing them so close that they touched the glass of his mask; then he patted the octopus bungeed to his chest. The total silence when he wasn't exhaling didn't feel comforting now. It was oppressive, a reminder of how deep and far back they were, how many millions of tons of rock lay between him and the sky. . . . Suddenly, he got another spray of water from his regulator. He purged it again and it stopped.

All at once, he wanted overwhelmingly just to *get out of* this crack in the ground so far down, it felt like they were beneath the foundations of hell. Toll and Scovill were nuts, and here he was following them in even deeper. July's fins disappeared around a corner, kicking a swirling cloud off the rough surfaces of the rock. He stared fixedly at where they'd vanished.

He started to pant. Shit, this was worse than being pinned into a wrecked helicopter. At least then he'd had an umbilical. Finally, he forced himself to move after her.

Below them, a jumble of sharp shadows probed by an only occasionally visible light. Scovill was down there somewhere; that was where the line led. The fissure was still headed down. Would they ever stop? He caught Toll's back-turned look, her beckoning wave. He remembered he was surveying, and made a vague note on the board. Checked the depth: 336.

She grabbed a rock to pull herself forward. As she moved past and down, it came out of the wall, clacking and scraping as it fell. A cascade of rubble followed it. He waited for the landslide, staring up, but nothing else followed but an anticlimactic pebble, rolling and bouncing down slowly through the cloudy water.

Toll spied another rock jut. She reached up to wrap the line securely around the outthrust, then bent and burrowed, tanks scraping, fins working as she drove herself underneath a ledge so low and narrow, it didn't look to him as if he was going to fit.

He stared at where she'd disappeared, wanting more than he'd ever wanted anything in his life just to turn around and *get out*. The silt swirled in his light, cold and deliberate as a copperhead. This goddamn crack didn't go anywhere! Who the hell cared where it went? He'd done some dangerous diving, but he'd never been anywhere like this. *This is stupid*, his mind screamed at him.

A prickle ran up the back of his neck. He stared into the blackness, and suddenly he was ice-cold and sweating at the same time, his hands twitching.

All at once, he realized he wasn't far from losing it. And, just like everyone he'd met since he came here had told him, if he lost it down here, he'd die. The battle was internal, inside his skull. But that didn't make it any less deadly.

The thing he was fighting for control wasn't his enemy. It was his body. Its instincts had been selected for a million years to bolt for light and air when things closed down. But down here, giving way to instinct would kill him. He wasn't going to make it through this on adrenaline and panic. Mind over matter, he said to it, as if soothing a large and dangerous dog. You're right. We *are* in trouble, pal. But if I let you take over, we're both dead meat.

Slowly, the panic monster backed down. His breathing slowed. He was still scared, but he kicked a couple of times, slowly, and moved forward.

After he squeezed himself under the ledge, the cleft widened slightly into a narrow triangular tunnel. It broke left and right, the two sides fitting like teeth, as if the rock had sheared apart moments before. Ahead of him, Toll's fins opened and closed in an easy frog kick that looked ungraceful as hell but didn't stir a particle of silt. Her light looked farther away, and brown instead

97

of white. The water was growing murky. It was flowing faster, too. He squeezed through another restriction, thinking, Christ, how are we going to get back? There's no room to turn around. Was Scovill thinking about that? Was either of these Kamikaze Kavers thinking at all? He squinted ahead, only to see Toll's fins disappear into another hole. Dismay and fear were congealing just under his breastbone, as if he were carrying a set of weights there. His board scraped against stone and he remembered he was supposed to be taking notes. No idea how much line they had out now, but he checked his depth gauge and scrawled "352."

Ho-ly Christ.

When he looked up from his slate, he couldn't see either of them at all. He was squinting forward, wondering where they'd gone, when two things happened at once: A sudden blast of silt came out of the hole, and he got another dose of cold water instead of air through his regulator. He let go of the slate and fumbled his hand up, purging it violently. But each time the air stopped blasting out, he got water. The worst part of it was, he'd swallowed that first shot of it, and his throat was trying to gag and cough at the same time.

Time to get rid of this bastard. Grimly suppressing the need to cough, he tongued out the mouthpiece. His right hand found the octopus, jerked it out of its tubing loop, and thrust it between his lips.

He got air, but contaminated with the grit and mud he'd been wriggling over and dragging the secondary regulator through. As he struggled not to choke, he felt himself drifting downward, and he kicked himself up again, remembering only too late that just made things worse. He tried to swing himself around to face up. The clumsy sweep of his left arm ended suddenly as he backhanded rock and the bulb of his main light went out with a *pop*. The darkness flooded in instantly, sharp and cold as an obsidian landslide.

Struggling to breathe, he told himself, Okay. You got backups, but for right now you're alone in the dark. Let's solve the air problem first. Your primary regulator's giving you water and your backup's jammed with mud. But they're all you got, unless you want to try breathing out of your wings. Theoretically, that was possible, but he'd never heard of anybody doing it and surviving.

So that left the two regulators. They were both dicked up, but in different ways. Which did he like the most? He liked the one he had in his mouth least, so he jerked it out and tried the primary again. It fed him a heavy spray, like trying to breathe with a garden hose pointed into his teeth. But he found that if he held his head way down, he could block most of it with his tongue before it went down his windpipe.

The thought crossed his mind that it would be nice to have help, but nobody seemed to be around at the moment.

The upside was that he was diving with Neptunes, a make of regulator he'd taken apart hundreds of times in the shop.

He hung there upside down in the dark, pinning himself into the cleft with his elbows, and mentally rehearsed what he was going to do step by step in about three and a half seconds. It sounded good, so he started doing it. Ice-cold now, he told himself. Take it nice and slow, 'cause there's no margin anymore.

Step one: Get gloves off. There, they were gone, into the lightless, whirling murk.

Step two: Get his spare knife off his chest harness. It was only a two-inch blade, but it worked well enough to get the screw loose that held the faceplate of the regulator on. He stuck it under the mouthpiece and bit down on it. If he lost that screw, he could kiss his ass good-bye.

As soon as the faceplate came off, the octopus would have started blasting out air, except that he'd already reached back over his shoulder and cut the centerline tap, then closed off the air to that hose. He stripped the plunger out and felt the mud and limestone flakes stuck to it. He cleaned it off as well as he could with his fingers. Then he snapped it back into place, retrieved the screw, screwed it back together, and turned the valves back counterclockwise to full on. He spat out the Water Fountain and jammed Instant Rebuild Job in.

Air—nice and clean, and lots of it. Or at least—where was the damn gauge? No, he needed light next. His fingers found the compact solidity of the spare and it came on, bright and reassuring. The silt was clearing. He checked his gas. Still a little while to go till he could turn back on two-thirds.

It occurred to him now that he had air and light back, he couldn't see the line anymore. He didn't see any lights, either, other than his own. He'd been drifting back with the current while battling the regulators. Now he grabbed a passing knob of rock and swept his beam around.

Two openings gulped light. Silt uncoiled from both. The good news was, he'd found a larger chamber, someplace he could at least turn around in. The bad news was, he didn't know which of those two gaps he'd come out of.

He hovered there, staring at them as his mind dithered helplessly. He was getting narked now—he could feel it. You got less with trimix, but after a while you got it. He was starting to shake, too. Sight dimming. Some vertigo.

He gripped the rock, making it the anchor of his consciousness, and grimly reasoned backward. Stretching out his breathing, when he was trying to keep the water out of his lungs, he'd probably built up his carbon dioxide levels. That was the vertigo and shakiness. He took a few deep ones, flushing it out of his system as he tried to decide what to do next. He could wait, hope July and Colten came back. Not finding him, they'd follow the current and come out here. Or would they? No, more likely they'd assume he'd turned back, and they'd just follow the line on out. They wouldn't miss him till they got back to the deco station. By then, it would be too late.

Of course, he could just start swimming rapidly around, using up his gas and getting more and more panicky.

Or he could do the smart thing, the by-the-book thing, the only thing that might still save him.

He unclipped the little safety reel he'd carried that whole dive and lashed one end around the knob. He looked around one last time as it occurred to him that he was the first human being ever to see this little room, this secret chamber deep in the heart of the aquifer. He couldn't say it didn't turn him on a little. But he'd have felt better about it if he knew the way back out.

Spinning the line out, he crab-walked hand over hand into the left-hand fissure.

Two minutes later, he saw lights probing around ahead. His relief was so immense, he peed his suit a little. There they were, coming back for him. There was the line, a few feet above his head on the vertical face of the cliff; he'd passed it without seeing it.

You okay? Toll was signaling.

He hesitated. He had only one operating regulator. His main light was broken. He'd managed to lose his slate and pencil in that upside-down wildness in the dark.

Okay, he signaled back.

He finned on, after her.

*   *   *

100

After forcing themselves through fissures and cracks so narrow that they had to turn sideways, the room they emerged into looked huge in the thin beam Scovill was shining around it. It was almost ten feet across. Reddish black–crusted breakdown covered the floor. Scovill had a main light you could focus, narrow-angle or wide-angle, according to how you positioned the reflector. Tiller wanted one like it. Not nearly as much, though, as he wanted out of here. But that idea seemed to be furthest from Scovill's mind. The guy was checking his reel, then his depth. Tiller checked his, too: 360 feet.

Surely it was time to turn back. He held out his watch, then his pressure gauge. Scovill frowned at him, then pointed up.

He looked up, to an overhanging lip of terracotta rock.

Scovill swam up and disappeared over it. Toll followed, skillfully looping the line and letting it run taut. They're narked, he thought then hopelessly. Stone-dead narco-blitzed. They'll never turn back. We're doomed.

Surrendering the last hope of ever returning, he followed them.

There were two leads above the ledge, both tending upward. Scovill took the right one, swimming unhesitatingly up. Galloway followed Toll, swallowing every few seconds. Now he knew how crabs felt, heading into the trap. The lead narrowed steadily, till they were wriggling forward under parallel planes of smooth rock black and gleaming as anthracite.

Fifty yards on, the lead turned tannic and silty, with tea-stained water and drifts of black pepper in the corners. Even he could tell there was no flow, no access from above. Finally, Scovill called it, gave them the signal to back up. They pushed themselves back out single file like regimented lobsters, the reel clicking as Scovill rewound the line he'd just unspooled.

Colten hovered in front of the second lead for long seconds. Tiller was actually praying for God to intervene when he suddenly turned away. Scovill stared at his computer, then examined both their faces.

And finally, jerked his thumb upward.

July took another turn with the line around a rock knob in what Tiller was privately calling the Prayer Room, then slipped her knife through it. It was only when the cut end sank to the floor that he really believed they were heading back. They swam past him, July reaching out to squeeze his shoulder. Scovill pointed to his main light. He nodded, made a breaking gesture with his fists.

The lead diver nodded and finned on past, out of sight up the line.

After the nightmare in K 1, the main tunnel looked big enough to hangar the *Spruce Goose*. He couldn't believe he was still alive. His head felt helium-inflated. His unprotected hands were novocaine numb. He'd made enough mistakes for one day. Right now, he just wanted out.

The scooters lay where they'd left them. He secured his main tanks—he had about a sixth of his air remaining—and went to the stage bottles for the trip out. He buckled one to his harness, hands shaking so much, he could hardly get the snaps over the D rings. He glanced back, checking for the others.

And froze. Someone was hung up, fighting with his stage bottle. Its hose was snarled in the guideline. As he finned closer, he saw it was Toll.

When he gripped her shoulder, her head came up and her eyes locked on his. He didn't like this wide-eyed stare. But since he'd just been through the same thing more or less, he just squeezed her shoulder again, trying to communicate reassurance; then he started sorting out the snarl. After a moment, she added air to her wings, floating upward, and he was able to get the hose free.

He held the tank up for her, but she shook her head, pushing it away. He stared into her mask, trying to read what she wanted in her eyes. She held up her main-set pressure gauge, pointed to it, made the okay sign. He nodded and tried to give her the stage again. She refused it a second time. He gave her a questioning sign and she returned it, repeating that she was all right.

Fine, *she* was the cave diver. He shrugged and put the bottle back with the others, then headed back toward the scooters. When he looked back, she was swimming after him.

Scovill moved back toward them behind a whirring prop, checking them out. After they exchanged okay signs, Scovill circled his finger and pointed up the line in a round 'em up, move 'em out signal. Tiller checked his stage again. Helping Toll, he was already down 500 psi on the smaller bottle. But there were more tanks at the first depot. He pulled his machine off the floor and lurched into flight.

They purred along rapidly through the dark. July's light rode steadily behind him. In a few more minutes, they'd be out. He sucked gas slowly, cramming it in deep, then letting it all the way out, feeling the tension washing away as the cold water rushed past.

The narrowed walls of the Bottleneck loomed against Scovill's lights. The lead diver's prop slowed, then slowed even more, to a flicker so deliberate, it barely kept him suspended above the floor. He was threading the needle, tracking with incredible precision straight through the narrow opening. Silt whirled after him, blown down off the ceiling by his bubbles. Galloway aimed grimly, aware of his growing clumsiness. The scooter came up too fast, he overcorrected, and suddenly the prop wash was boring into the floor and he was deep in murk again. He got one hand on the line and bored relentlessly on, keeping his head down, till Scovill's lights dawned ahead. He stopped beside him, waiting for July to emerge from the black.

She didn't. He looked at his watch, which faded in and out of visibility as the cave flow moved the silt downstream past them. He looked at Scovill, then pointed back toward the restriction.

Scovill dropped his scooter, checked his gauges, then swam back upstream. Tiller followed him, stomach knotting again.

As they came out of the cloud, they caught the frantic vertical flashing of her trouble signal.

She must have brushed a loose section of line. Her scooter had eaten it, fouling itself against the overhead and pinning her against the ceiling. Galloway made a quick decision and went back on his main tanks, intending to hand her his stage. But Scovill was there before him, handing her his long hose.

Another cloud of murk obliterated sight. While Galloway was hunkered waiting for it to pass, he unsnapped the snap and got the regulator ready. She'd refused her stage at the turnback point, figuring she had enough to get back. She probably did, but had overbreathed her regulator with the stress of being fouled. Having a full one would reassure her. When the murk cleared, he worked his way under the two of them, crawling on his belly along the bottom of the tube.

Scovill was bent over the prop, working at the pale knot of tightly wrapped line. Galloway handed the regulator and then the tank past him, reaching up to her. She took the tank, but then Scovill's light shifted and he lost sight of her.

The stage bottle came back down and clanked into the rock floor. Galloway stared, then shrugged; Scovill must have given her one of his regulators. He wriggled through past them, ready to help from the other side of the restriction. Unfortunately, that kicked up so much silt, he had to stop again and wait for it to clear.

When it did, he saw her doubled up between the still-snarled scooter and the ceiling, and no stage bottles in sight. One regulator hung down from her motionless body. The other was in her mouth, but he could see dark matter falling out of it as bubbles streamed steadily up. Scovill was still head-down, preoccupied with the scooter.

Galloway lunged up and got her leg. He squeezed but got only a feeble kick.

Okay, enough dicking around. He pulled his knife and slashed the line apart savagely, then shoved the machine and the astonished Scovill aside. He climbed his way up her body and found her primary still in her mouth. But her body was bucking, convulsing. He hit the purge valve, holding it down. Gas roared out, but when he thrust his mask close, he could see it spewing out around the mouthpiece. It wasn't going into her lungs.

He grabbed the front of her harness and started swimming, kicking without regard for silt or anything else, just towing her down the passageway till he reached the breakdown room just downstream of it. Where the hell was Scovill? He didn't see his light, didn't see anything of the man.

Okay, so he was just some kind of warmed-over hard hat. What would a shit-hot cave diver do now? He didn't know. But he knew what *he* was going to do. He *wasn't* going to tow her all the way back to the entrance. By then, she'd be gone. Even if they got her breathing again, that long without oxygen, you could kiss her brain good-bye.

The cuplike dome in the ceiling suggested an answer. Maybe it was just wasting gas, maybe neither of them would make it back, but it was all he could think of just then.

He fought her limp body upward and fumbled for the stage bottle. He got the regulator off, twisted the valve to full open.

Then he let go.

The tank sank away, gas blasting and rumbling out underwater, and he shoved her upward again, then followed. Her light dangled, but enough reflected off the buff irregular walls that he saw her eyes were closed. The tank, on the floor now, kept roaring, venting upward.

When his head popped out into the air pocket, the surface was boiling, but the bubble wasn't growing. The air was sizzling away through the pockmarked rock their heads were pressed against. They didn't have long. Toll's lips were blue and slack in the dim light.

The first thing to do was to get them buoyant. He pumped air into his wings, till he didn't have to struggle to keep her head up. Then he turned her ass-toward him, got his arms around her, and Heimliched her as hard as he could through the harness and gear and dry suit. Something gave and her head jerked forward. She was vomiting again. He held her up as her arms thrashed.

When the convulsions eased off and she was breathing, gagging but breathing, he said into the back of her hood, "Better?"

". . . Yuh. Sorry."

"It's all right."

Scovill's head emerged into the bubble with them. He spat out his regulator and gasped, "I went back to the dump. Got a full stager for her."

"Good man. I was wondering what we were gonna breathe. You ready to head back, July?"

". . . Can't. Got to cough. . . ."

"Do what you gotta do, take your time. Take all the time you want." She hacked violently, as if something was still caught deep in her chest. He turned her around to face him, holding her by the upper arms. Wet hair hung out under the edge of her hood.

The rumbling below them stopped. The sizzling of outgoing air continued. The air space began shrinking at once, the water climbing up their chins toward the black rock ceiling.

"Okay, Colten, give her the stage."

She got the regulator in, gagged once, eyes bulging, but kept it in. Her glove came up, clenched, then slowly formed an okay signal.

The water rose over their masks, and they were back in the soup. He lost track of his regulator, almost panicked—he was wheezing from the effort of towing her—but traced the line from his tank and found it. Shit, they were all losing it. They had to get out of here.

The whick-whick of a prop, and Scovill pulled her away from him. Galloway whirled slowly in the dark. Then his searching hand found his last backup light. He swept the beam around the chamber. He couldn't even see the floor, just the total blackness of seething silt.

He started to swim out, then realized he didn't have the air to make it. In fact, he was almost out. His gauge was one notch above empty. His scooter was back in the tunnel. He pulled himself over the ledge and saw it lying near the Bottleneck. But when he tried it, it didn't work. He tried July's, but it was jammed so tight, the prop wouldn't turn at all.

Now he wasn't getting anything. He checked the gauge again, as if that would make a difference. He twisted the valves violently, but nothing more came.

He was hovering there, trying to resign himself to death, when the lights of the returning second team flickered at the far end of the passage. A moment later, he was hanging behind Lamont Exmore's scooter, gulping gas gratefully through a long hose, being towed rapidly toward the entrance, half a mile away.

EIGHT

The Eight Ball had been okay, the beer, but Tad wasn't sure he wanted to drink the wine. Hoyt drank a lot of wine. Hoyt was his mom's boyfriend. Tad hadn't liked Hoyt the first time he saw him. You could tell he was a creep just from listening to that Beavis and Butt-head laugh he had. "Huh-huh-huh." But his mom had dated him, then he'd started staying over, and finally she'd asked him to move into the trailer with them. From then on, things had gone to shit fast.

"You gonna just hold it?" Ripper said, across the fire from him. "If you're not going to drink it, give it here. I'll make it disappear."

"Sit on it, buttwipe," said Tad. He squinted through the bottle, then lifted it. It was sweet, like grape pop, with some lime flavor in there, too. Ripper had bought it at a Little Champ. The Arabian at the counter didn't ask for any ID. Ripper said they didn't care, they just wanted to make money.

"Give it here," the third boy said. Rafael was dark-haired, small-boned, Cuban. Tad tossed it to him across the campfire, then leaned back, looking up into the trees.

The three of them were deep in the boonies, what Ripper called the "hammocks." Ripper had a camper back here with a padlock on the door, where he kept his bikes and his arrowhead collection and stuff. The sides were rusty and there were no tires on the wheels. Tad had no idea how it had gotten back here; there was no road. But it was neat, lying by the fire listening to all the things croaking and snapping and screaming back in the jungle. Huge silent-flying moths the size of bats circled the flames, the circles growing tighter and tighter. Then at last you heard a crackle, and they were nothing but fire, drifting upward—for a little while at least. And then they'd fall, cinders. Cool.

They'd bought the beer and wine with the money his dad gave him for pizza. What was he supposed to live on, peanut butter sandwiches and milk from the fridge? He'd gone through the Mobitch's house looking for cash. No luck. There was jewelry and appliances, watches and stuff, the rifle, but he didn't know how to turn it into money. The pizza deal had come to him on the spur of the moment. Then he'd hitched over to the trailer court where Ripper lived. There was a gully back of it that led down into the swamp, out to where they could have a fire and play Megadeth tapes and hang.

Yeah, things had changed since Hoyt came along. His mom started dressing different and lost all that weight. Then she bought the pickup. She said it was for herself, but she already had a Honda. The truck was for Hoyt. But then Hoyt had changed, too. Got laid off when the shipyard closed, then got into trouble on some lottery scam. He started staying away at night, and when he did show up, there were screaming arguments.

Meanwhile, Tad had been developing a few problems of his own. He'd always had the mark, but last summer it had gotten much darker. He watched it in the mirror, wondering if it was spreading. It didn't make it easy in school. Portsmouth was a tough town; there were a lot of mean niggers, and tough white kids, too. He'd had to punch one guy out for calling him Blotch. That had gotten him suspended, and when he came back, he noticed the teachers treated him different. Like they were waiting for him to do something outrageous. So he did, and got suspended again. Why disappoint them?

Then he'd seen on television about lasers, how you could use them to remove tattoos, and fix eyes, and *bleach out birthmarks*. So he went to his mom and told her, actually begged her to take him in and get it taken off. She said, "Do you really need it?" And he said, "Yeah." Then she said, "We don't have the money. Shelly's got to have braces; it's more important for a girl to look nice. And me and Hoyt are saving for a house. Anyway," she said, "you look fine to me. It's just a little spot on your face. Maybe it will go away, that's what the doctor said when you were little." He said, "How about the payments on Hoyt's truck? Can't we use that?" And she said, "No, we need that truck more than an operation you don't have to have."

He touched his face gently. So he'd gone out and trashed her damn pickup for her. If she cared more about it than she did for him, to hell with her. Then the cop had come, and the fat son of a bitch had tried to feel his cock in the patrol car. He'd grinned and said, "Wait here. I'll be back in a minute and we'll have some fun." So when the Fag Patrol left him alone in the car, he'd jimmied the window and crawled over into the front seat, and found the guy's gun. Then he took off, and everything had just kind of gone from there. Dogs and helicopters and everything. Just like *Cops*.

Wild and woolly.

Rafael passed the bottle back over the fire. The sweet stuff tasted better this time. "So, what you guys wanna do?" Tad asked when he lowered it.

Ripper sat across from him on a log in his baggy jeans and Doc Martens and his Edge hat, face expressionless. You couldn't ever tell what he was thinking. The kid was out there, all right. He hardly ever talked, and from a couple of things he'd said, Tad wasn't sure he could even read.

"Want to go sneaking?" Ripper said suddenly, startling him.

"Sneaking? What's that?"

"I'll show you," said Ripper. He went into the trailer, and came out with a worn green pack that jingled. "Grab your bikes."

Sneaking consisted of getting on their trail bikes and going down a lot of streets that got smaller and smaller, and darker and darker, till finally they pushed the bikes under some barbed wire and rode through where it looked like they'd started to build a subdivision once but had to stop; a huge stack of big black electrical transformers with bullet holes in them and the fluttering remains of yellow plastic tape. Past that, they went down through the woods till they were actually riding in the marsh. Scummy water sprayed off the tops of the tires. Grass and bushes whipped at their legs. There were developments all around them; you could see the lights shining down through the trees. But in between were low places, wet places, wild places.

That was the way Ripper took them. It was dark, and hot, and the mosquitoes came down on them like a million staplers. At

last, they had to get off and swim in the mucky, warm black water. Rafael said, "Hey, Ripper. There aren't any gators or anything
in here, are there?"

Ripper pulled a flashlight out of the pack and shined it around.
A set of round orange eyes glowed back. "There's a little one."

"Shit, damn," Tad muttered under his breath.

At last, Ripper motioned for silence, and they pulled the bikes
up a bank into a lot of vines and kudzu. He muttered to leave
them there, and said they'd go the rest of the way on their bellies.
Tad said "Sure, right," but then he saw Ripper wasn't kidding.

They crawled like some kind of worms through some pretty
heavy brush. In the middle of it, Ripper stopped and pointed the
flashlight down. Tad looked down a slope into a little hole in the
ground, full of bubbling black water rimmed with weeds. "It's a
spring," Ripper whispered. "Lots of 'em out here in the woods. I
can smell 'em."

"Yeah?"

"Yeah. There's shark's teeth in there, and petrified bones."

Tad said, "Yeah? Neat," wanting to look for some, but Ripper
kept crawling. They went up and over a chain-link fence with the
help of a tree, then fought through more brush.

Finally, they crawled into a drainpipe. It was about as wide as
his shoulders, with six inches of stinking water in the bottom of
it, and dark and *long*. He was running sweat when they got to the
end. He'd felt good from the beer and wine, but now the high
was gone and he was starting to wonder if this was such a great
idea. There was a grate on the end. Ripper peered through it for
a while. "What are you looking for?" Tad muttered, scared there
were snakes in the dark water they were kneeling in.

"The dogs."

"Oh, great."

"Hear 'em barking? Don't show up pretty soon, they're tied up.
Then we can go in."

At last, Ripper eased the pack around and took something out.
There was a click and then a scrape as he slid it through the grate.

The electric screwdriver whirred four times. Ripper slid the
grate out very quietly and slipped out into a low pond. Tad and
Rafael slid out after him. Frogs croaked and splatted in the dark,
but he saw lights up ahead, close.

Ripper finished fitting the grate back into place and slid up
beside them. "Now reach down," he whispered.

"What for?"

"Get some of this stuff. Smear it on your face—all over."

"Yuck. Is this a leech?"

When they crawled up out of the pond, he saw they were in some guy's estate. Lights all over, a big Spanish-looking house with a tiled pool. There was a high wall behind them. They'd gone under it through the pipe. His heart started hammering. No shit, this was cool. "Don't even breathe. Just shut up an' watch," Ripper whispered, and sure enough, after a while two bitches came out of the house and stood by the pool for a second and then dove in, one after the other. One was white and one was black, and they were both naked.

Tad was astonished, but Ripper breathed into his ear, "Just watch," and so they did as the girls swam for a while. Then they got out and toweled off with the biggest, softest-looking towels he'd ever seen. Still naked. Both girls were pretty, but the white one was really beautiful. The black one had bigger tits, but the white girl had long dark hair and red lips with a faint smile that made her look really nice. He was sure he'd seen her before, maybe in the movies.

"Oh, man, I'm in love," he whispered to Ripper.

"Shut up. There's somebody coming."

"I think it's me," whispered Rafael.

A guy was coming down the steps from the house. He was kind of old. Tad figured that was why he just stopped and stood by the pool as if he was thinking about something instead of paying any attention to the girls.

But it turned out he was wrong, because after standing there rubbing the side of his face for a minute or two, the old guy came over to where the black girl was lying. Without a word, he pushed her knees apart and pulled his shorts down and started screwing her, right there in front of the other one, without even bothering to take his shirt off. Tad squatted in the hydrangeas, his mouth open. He must have made a noise without realizing it, because he felt a punch from Ripper, a harsh whisper. He half-turned. "What?"

"Shut up, shithead! He hears us, we're dead."

Just then, the dark-haired girl lifted her head, frowning toward the bushes where they crouched. He held his breath, terror wilting the lump in his jeans. But then the bald guy and the black bitch got real noisy, and she lay back down and picked up her drink and sipped it, looking up toward where the palm trees whispered against the stars.

111

After the bald guy was done, they all went back into the house. Nothing else happened, and finally Ripper made a backing-up motion with his hand and they faded back toward the pond.

He found six leeches on him when they got back to the trailer, but it was worth it. Just thinking about the girls gave him a hard-on again. He'd about decided to do something about it, say he had to take a leak and go whack off in the weeds, when Ripper muttered, rooting around inside the trailer, "Hey, Galloway, how about some reggae?"

"Some what?"

"Ganji. Weed."

"We call it grass where I come from."

"We call it that, too. There's some killer new stuff out super-cheap. . . . Wait a minute."

Rafael said, through the open door, "That was bitchin', sneaking in there and seeing those girls and stuff. That was really primo."

"There's lotsa other stuff I can show you. Learn how to go slow and keep quiet, there's lots of places to go. Went inside a prison camp once, then back out. Wasn't maximum-security, but it was a prison."

"Holy shit," said Tad. He wasn't sure he ought to believe that, but so far, every damn thing Ripper had told him had turned out to be true.

Ripper put some 2 Live Crew on the box and they smoked the grass, passing the pipe across the fire. Tad told him about the RX-7 he was going to get, with MoMo rims, but Ripper didn't say much. The kid just didn't talk.

But that was okay. Tad leaned back, sucking the sweet, acrid smoke deeper as the world started to make sense. Looking up into the trees, which were waving against the stars, just like they had back at the estate. He thought about boosting some cigarettes. It would be easy, the clerks were so stupid here. They barely spoke English.

He hadn't been here long, but he was already starting to like Florida.

NINE

When Tiller woke for the third time, the clock on the wall said 7:10. Monica was snoring softly on a couch across from him. He watched her for a while, then sat up, rubbing a sore neck. It took him a second to recognize the low furniture and subdued lighting as the waiting room of the intensive care unit, Tallahassee Memorial Hospital.

He sat up, catching sight of Tad asleep, too, in the far corner. An old black woman was the only other person in the room. She nodded soberly to Tiller as he smiled, then went back to her creased copy of the *Democrat*.

He remembered now. Out of the spring pool at Wabasso, to find it was nearly midnight. July had coughed the regulator out twice during the five-hour decompression. The paramedics had been waiting when they climbed out of the water. She'd been talking to them when she suddenly collapsed.

He and Scovill had ridden with her to TMH, taking turns holding the oxygen mask on her. As soon as they got there, the doctors took her away. An intern had lingered to explain that based on what they'd told them, she'd probably inhaled vomitus or other foreign material. They'd have to watch her closely over the next day or so to see if further intervention was needed. Then he'd taken a closer look at Tiller. "Are *you* okay, buddy?"

"I think so. Yeah."

"Realize you're bleeding?"

"Just a nosebleed. It's nothing."

113

"And your hands? Those look like knife cuts. Been in a fight?"

"Just doing some on-the-spot repairs."

"You were down there with her? Three hundred, three fifty feet?"

"Uh-huh."

"Any joint pain? Numb extremities? Tingling feelings? Nausea?"

"I know what the bends feel like, Doc. Believe me, I'd come yelling if I had 'em."

"I'd keep an eye on it if I were you."

"I'll watch him," said Scovill. When the doctor was gone, he tapped Tiller's arm. "Sure you don't want them to check you over? You look pretty wrung-out."

"I'm okay."

"Again, sorry I left you flat there in the tunnel. I thought you had a spare stage."

"That was the one I blew the air pocket with."

"I realized that halfway down the main tunnel. By then, it was too late to turn around. But I figured you'd get yourself back somehow."

"Thanks," he'd said dryly.

Now he cleared his throat, tasting blood, and across from him Monica opened her eyes. "I got here at six," she murmured, sitting up. "Colten called me. I brought Tad along, too. How are you feeling?"

"I'm okay." He dabbed his nose. " 'M I still bleeding?"

"No."

"How is she?"

"When I came in, they said she was resting quietly. They did an intubation in case there were any more problems with her breathing. Her mother and dad are in there with her. They want to see you before you leave."

He nodded. "Colten?"

"He left to get some breakfast."

Tad grunted and opened his eyes. Monica said, "Hello, Mr. Sunshine. How are you feeling?"

"All right." Galloway could see the boy hated being called that but didn't know what to do about it. He was still mad himself about being scammed for the pizza money, but that could wait. It seemed like small potatoes after what he'd just been through. He heaved himself up. "Okay, let me get this over with."

*　　*　　*

114

July didn't open her eyes while he was in the room, but her breathing sounded better. He told her parents the story out in the corridor, so as not to wake her. Her dad shook his hand, thanking him in a strained voice for saving their little girl's life. Galloway said she'd have done the same for him, that they were all a team down there.

"I don't think she should be doing that," her mother said. "She always had weak lungs, as a child. Whenever she got her feet wet, she'd get sick. I don't see why she does things like this to us."

"She's a good diver, Mrs. Toll. But sometimes too many things happen at once. That's when a buddy comes in handy." Then he excused himself, and Monica gave them her home phone in case they needed anything.

He fell asleep again in the car on the way to Killearn. Then Mon was shaking him. "I can't carry you," she said. "Come on, you need to sleep. Or would you rather have breakfast before you go upstairs?"

"I could eat something." He was suddenly ravenous; he'd burned up a lot of energy last night in the cold water.

Tad went up, leaving them together in the kitchen. Monica moved about efficiently, setting up toast and cereal. Just like an old married couple, he thought. It felt kind of nice.

"I can make decaf, if you're planning on sleeping."

"I probably ought to. But who's minding the—"

"The shop? Mark and Tony were on anyway, because of the dive. They can run things till Colten gets there." She finished setting his place and sat down opposite. "All right, what happened?"

He told her in spare sentences. She listened without a word, green eyes studying the oak tabletop. When he was done, she said softly, "You all could have died down there."

"It's dangerous, Mon. I know, everybody's been telling me that, but I didn't realize just how dangerous until I was down there, at the bottom of K One."

The coffeemaker ceased hissing and he got up, helped himself. "Want some?" She nodded and he poured a mug, set it in front of her. He looked down at her shoulders, at the smooth curve of her neck.

She said to the coffee, "Bud never talked about that part of it."

"Probably didn't want to upset you. And, look, not every dive is that hairy. Just—a lot of things went wrong on this one. And when they go wrong that far back, it's a snowball effect. Before you know it, you're in deep, deep kimchee." He sipped the coffee

115

and added a slug of cream. "Kind of like ... when Bud and I served together."

"In combat?"

"A lot of the same feelings. Yeah."

"Do you think men get ... Do you think he missed that? And looked for something to replace it?"

That was worth pondering. And not just in relation to Bud but to his own wanderings and dickups, too. "I don't know," he said finally. "Maybe. But other vets I know, they're like anybody else. Happy families. Solid citizens. It probably depends more on the individual." He looked at the ceiling. "A lot of the memories aren't so great, anyway."

She said softly, "He went there sometimes, too."

"Huh? Went where?"

"Wherever you were just then. Somewhere inside, where nobody else can follow." She closed her eyes for a moment. "Before he died, Joel got real closed in."

"Closed in?"

"That's what I call it." He examined her face from the side—the curved high forehead, hair pulled back with a barrette, green eyes looking nearly unblinking out into the garden, where hummingbirds and dragonflies darted and hovered like the iridescent life of a coral reef. "It was never easy for him to share things with me. But right before he died, he hardly talked at all."

"It doesn't mean we don't feel things—"

"It doesn't? But how would you know? Sometimes I wonder if men really do—feel things. Or if they just don't allow themselves to admit it." She glanced at him and turned the mug in her hands. Her fingers were small and pointed. "You know that when he was little his mother stabbed him?"

"What?"

"He never shared that with you, then. Not just once, four or five different times. She did it with scissors, or paring knives, whatever she had in her hand at the time. He said he probably deserved it. Can you imagine that? I don't think he knew what he was saying. Then when he was seventeen, she threatened him with a shotgun. That's when he left home and joined the Navy."

"Jeez, we're all abused, aren't we? What's your story?"

She said quietly, "My mom died when I was three. I remember the accident. I was in the backseat. It broke both my legs. She was in front, so ... when I cried for her, in the hospital, they told me she was safe in heaven. ... More toast?"

116

"No thanks. Hey. I'm sorry I asked that, about your 'story.' I shouldn't have joked about it."

"It's all right. But maybe that—his mother—was why whenever he felt threatened or stressed, he'd shut everyone else out, including me. He'd go out to the sunroom and make himself a bed on the couch. He didn't say anything; I'd just find him out there when it was time to lock the doors and turn the lights out.

"He was closed in like that the week before he died."

Tiller considered that. "Any idea why?"

"Like I say, he didn't share. I could tell something was bothering him. But I'm not a mind reader." She put her hand over her eyes. "Sometimes I wonder if it was something I did, something about us. I don't think so. But I can't help wondering. And I'll never know."

He finished his coffee and carried his plate to the sink. He stood behind her awkwardly, wanting to put his hands on her shoulders. Wanting, actually, to kiss her neck. But she didn't look up. "You can put that in the dishwasher," she said.

"I guess I'll hit the hay, then."

"Do you want me to call you? Or just sleep it off?"

"Don't let me go past noon."

But when he woke again, it was dark outside the window. He sat up suddenly, hearing the house quiet around him.

He got up and went into the bathroom and leaned on the sink. The eyes in the mirror were bloodshot. He wanted a drink. The aspirin bottle was still out, and he looked at it for a moment, touching his back gingerly. Then he shook three more onto the counter.

When he went downstairs, showered and shaved and in clean cotton Dockers and a pair of Bud's sandals, the house was deserted. Tad wasn't in his room; the bed was unmade, clothes were lying on the floor, and the black boots were gone. He said to the empty air, "Tad? Monica?"

Then he saw the flames flickering in the woods.

He followed the glow down the steps and into the garden, sandals whispering through damp grass into the dark. The pines were motionless presences between him and the stars. Fireflies searched among the azaleas. Leaves whispered like lapping waves. The flames floated like yellow-orange petals on the water of the pool.

117

She lay on the lounge chair, on the white terry-cloth wrap. A box of matches and a container of Tropicana HomeStyle were on the table. A bottle of Absolut stood on the tile beside her. She was wearing a bikini top and white shorts. He looked at her bare legs, imagining his hand sliding up the silky tanned skin.

And he stopped his mind right there. "Mon?"

She opened her eyes slowly. "Oh, you're up."

"Thought you were going to get me up at noon."

"You needed the sleep. Everything's okay at the shop. I was over there for a couple of hours." Her hand explored space, found her glass. "Would you like a drink?"

"I'll get a glass and join you. Where's Tad?"

"He went off with that Ripper boy. They went exploring on their bikes."

"Tad doesn't have a bike."

"The boy had a used one, remember? I gave Tad fifty dollars to buy it. I hope you don't mind."

"I guess not," he said, though it did irk him that the kid seemed to be a moocher, if not a thief. "Do you need anything from the house?"

She asked for ice and a fresh pack of cigarettes.

When he came back, he mixed himself a screwdriver, too, heavy on the ethanol. He pulled two chairs over to where she lay and put his feet up on the second one. "How you feeling?" she said, lighting a Salem.

"Still sore." He sat back and looked up at the moon between the trees. It glowed on the water like a cold white flame. "Anything new on July?"

"I called the hospital. She's doing fine; they expect to let her go tomorrow."

"That's good news."

She said, eyes closed, "Aside from the diving, how are you coming on the business? Are we ready to sell?"

He told her about what he'd found, and the parts that puzzled him—like the fact that all the profit seemed to come from just a few items.

She listened, nodding. He asked her, "Did you know about that?"

"I know he's sold a lot of computers and that sort of thing. The high-end equipment."

"Yeah, but who to? I don't see a lot of well-heeled customers. The people we're taking out are mostly students."

"We get a lot of Germans and Japanese here during the summer. Maybe that's who's buying them."

"Yeah, maybe," he said. He turned his head to look at her, and found her looking at him.

"You know, I'm getting used to having you here," she said softly. "You and Tad. I look forward to seeing you every evening."

He glanced away. "I sort of feel that way, too."

"Do you think that's wrong?"

"Wrong?" He felt his heart speeding up, as if he faced a constricted passage at depth. Should he take it? Should he back out? He'd never been very good at passing up challenges.

She was Bud's wife.

But Bud was dead.

He'd almost died himself last night. But he wasn't dead. He was alive. Life vibrated in his hands like an electric current.

She closed her eyes. After a moment, looking at her face in the moonlight, he leaned over and kissed her.

Her lips were cool and tasted of orange juice and cigarettes. He felt his stomach falling away, his hands shaking. After a moment, her arms came up. Her fingers settled lightly on his shoulders, but her lips didn't open. He got up, started to move onto the lounge chair, but she stopped him with an unsmiling shake of her head, a palm on his chest.

"No, Tiller. That's not where this is going."

"Why not?"

"Don't make me explain. . . . I don't *have* to explain. You can kiss me again if you want to. But I'm not going to bed with you."

He remembered Arkin then, what he'd said at the party, and felt a surge of jealousy and anger that astonished him. He stared at her cool, remote face, silvered by the distant light. "There's already somebody else in line? Is that why?"

She sat up and picked up a towel, started to turban it around her hair. She said, "I don't really know why. I like you. And I'm grateful for your help. Maybe I'm just not ready for . . . anything new yet. Can't we just leave it at that? A kiss in the moonlight?"

He didn't answer, and she said, a little wistfully, "Do you want another kiss?"

"No, that's all right. Forget it."

They sat together for a few more minutes, but somehow the magic had gone out of the evening. So presently he excused himself, then went in to see if Tad was back yet.

119

TEN

You'll hear some of the greats today," she said, pointing him toward where a steady stream of other cars and pickups were turning off. "Paul Champion played here, and Chubby Wise, and Gamble Rogers. Maybe you've heard of him. Folksinger, storyteller. He drowned trying to save some Canadians at Flagler Beach. He had a frozen spine, he couldn't really swim, but he tried to get out to them on a raft. . . . And Froggy Green, he tells stories about the old Florida railroads. There's an old-time fiddle contest, little kids five years old playing the fiddle like you wouldn't believe. That's where Aaron Eddleton won his first prize."

"Oh wow," said Tad. Tiller threw him a warning glance.

The Buick bumped over rutted grass, following the traffic that moved slowly toward the glittering fields that opened among the trees along the river. He nudged the air conditioning up a notch. It was incredibly hot, the kind of baking, brilliant day only Florida could serve up.

The dive at Wabasso had been a week ago. Since then, he'd been down twice, taking groups on guided dives through Peacock and Little River with Tony and Mark. He was more cautious, more conservative, than he'd been at first. Planning each dive as if something was sure to go wrong. So far, it hadn't, but knowing he was prepared reduced the pucker factor considerably.

Meanwhile, he and Monica had continued their uneasy orbit. He hadn't tried again to get close. But he was conscious of her presence, of the feel of her skin when their hands brushed, making

120

coffee in the morning; of the shape of her body under the robe evenings around the pool.

Tad, too, seemed to be settling in. He was halfway through his certification course. Aside from that, he spent most of his time with the Ripper kid. Tiller wasn't sure he liked that. A couple of times, he'd suspected Tad had come home stoned. But when he asked him, the boy flashed out, "You used to smuggle the stuff. What's your problem if somebody uses it?"

He hadn't really had a good comeback to that, had just stared at his son and then turned away. . . .

The truck ahead slowed for a gate. He eased off, too, and stuck out a ten-dollar bill at the uniformed Park Service woman. She passed back change, said, "Welcome to the White Springs Folk Festival. Y'all have a great old time, hear?"

The amphitheater was wall-to-wall bodies, lying on grass or sprawled on lawn chairs above the slow roll of the Suwannee, and the carillon rang out Stephen Foster tunes from time to time. Three bands were going at once within earshot, a bewildering mix to the ear; he made out bluegrass, banjo, Gaelic, hammered dulcimer, and something that sounded like a bagpipe. The high, sweet voice of a gospel singer soared clear above the musical chaos.

Stalking among the laughing, talking people, he smelled fish frying and suddenly was gripped by the unnatural certainty of déjà vu. He'd been here before, walked here before, toward some shadowy impending terror. Then he remembered. Not north Florida but south Louisiana, another sunny afternoon, another festival in the open air; he remembered Beausoleil and the Jambalaya Cajun Band, the taste of green gumbo and the heavy golden shine of an Annapolis ring from the window of a black Miata . . . and how badly it had ended, with Porch dead and Boudreaux and McCray and the grim stone killer who'd called himself Derick Winslow, all dead, dead, a thousand feet down. . . .

"What's the matter?" Monica said, beside him, and he turned his head, to see her quiet smile, her flowered dress flowing with her stride, a stray strand of red hair sticking to her forehead in the heat. And he smiled back and shook his head, because there was no point in explaining anything. She said quietly, "Bud and I came here every year. It's nice to be here with you."

They spent the afternoon drifting from stage to stage, listening and eating fried mullet spiced with flies, and hoppin' john, chicken and dumplings, coconut pie and sassafras tea set out by the New Jerusalem Baptist Church. He craned around for a beer tent. She laughed and said, "They don't sell it, but . . . come on. I have my sources."

He followed her back to the campground, and pretty soon they were sitting with a potter and her family, admiring hand-thrown stoneware and drinking Dos Equis from her husband's ice chest. "You saw all the blue glazed sets in my kitchen—Amy made those," Monica told him. He bought a huge serving plate decorated with a shell motif, thinking it might make a peace gift for Shad and Latricia.

"You going to let me have one of those?" Tad said, looking yearningly at the sweaty bottles swimming in the clear ice, the clear cold water as Frank opened the chest for another.

"One what?"

"A beer. I'll be allowed to drink in a couple years."

"That's right," Tiller told him. "In a couple years, you'll be allowed to drink."

"Oh, man. This sucks."

He ignored that and sat watching Monica talk with her friends. She was swinging one small sandaled foot, absently scratching a redbug bite on her ankle, and he wondered if it was possible—if after so long, so many disappointments, so many bad choices and wasted nights, it might be possible to come home.

They drifted again and ended up at the craft fair—sage-broom making, fiddle making, Black quilting, jewelry, rag rugs, Seminole baskets. She told him they'd had a booth there one year themselves; Bud had sold the silver jewelry he cast. But they hadn't even broken even, and he'd never tried to sell any again. Tad picked up a Cracker bullwhip from where a fellow was braiding together fine strips of leather. He held it out in front of him and looked at Tiller. Galloway cleared his throat. "You want one of those?"

"Me?"

"Yeah, you. Want one? Pick one out."

The look he got back was not at all grateful. Tad slammed the whip back on its peg and walked away. A few feet distant, he turned and yelled, "I'm sick of this, okay? This sucks. I'm gonna go back to the car."

"Do you need the keys?" said Monica.

"Don't give him the keys," Tiller muttered.

"*What?* Why ever not?"

"Never mind . . . or just give him the door key."

Looking puzzled, she gave Tad the combination to the door

lock. Tiller gave him the boxed dish to take back. The boy loped away, dirty white Reeboks flashing in the sunlight.

She turned to him. "What was that all about?"

"I don't know. I just asked him if he wanted one of those whips, and he gave me this funny look and took off."

"Tiller . . . did you do anything to him? When he was small?"

He stood in the sunlight, not breathing. Remembered a day he'd taken his belt off and strapped a small boy who was too proud to cry. He sucked a painful breath. "Shit."

"You did."

"I didn't think twice about it. Like I was on automatic."

"Did your dad beat you?"

"Well, sure, but . . . Let's not go into it, okay? I didn't get anything a billion other kids haven't had."

"That doesn't mean it's right. There's still something there that hurts, isn't there? And Tad feels the same way about you. They say no whipping is ever lost. It just gets passed on."

"Okay, I was a rotten father."

"Oh, Tiller. It's not that simple," she told him. "Like, maybe now you understand how your dad felt? When he beat you?"

"I don't know how he felt. Disappointed in me, probably."

"You said he was an admiral."

"Yeah, and there aren't many in the Coast Guard. He was a war hero. My family's been Coast Guard since before there was one, back when they called it the Lifesaving Service."

"And you were, too."

"For a while." He blew out, still not wanting to talk about it, yet wanting her to keep asking. "Not for very long."

"What happened?"

"I screwed it up . . . got into drugs."

"You're not still using, are you?"

"Not anymore. But sometimes I still want it."

She kicked a discarded beer can, and winced. "I shouldn't do that in sandals. . . . You know, you can't buy Tad's affection."

"I wasn't trying to."

"Excuse me, but you were. I've been watching the two of you circling each other like a couple of sharks. It's kind of funny and kind of sad, because you both need each other, and yet there's this . . . every time one of you reaches out, the other one bites his fingers off. Well, he doesn't want presents. He wants a father, whether he knows it or not. And you want to be his father. You *need* to be his father."

"I don't think there's much here in the way of dad material."

"You keep saying that. But you're the only one he's got. How's he doing with his diving? I see his gear drying in the shower, but I don't hear anything about it."

"Actually, he's doing good. Mark's been working with him, says he's a natural underwater. He needs work on the physics, but that and one more dive and he'll have his basic card."

"Tiller, why did you hand him off to Mark? Why didn't you teach him yourself?"

"I was busy, trying to straighten out the business end. And I'm not a qualified instructor. I just figured he could do a better job."

"That's too bad; it would have been such a great opportunity to interact. Anyway . . ." She sighed and glanced around. "Let's see what's going on over at the Marble Stage."

It was a square dancing exhibition—women in prairie skirts and boots and embroidered shirts, men in dungarees and Texas-style shirts and string ties. The band was playing "Pink Cadillac." As they got closer, Tiller made out the call. "Spin your top, dive through, square through. . . . Bow to your partner, bow to your corner, circle left, circle right. Promenade her . . . then you get her on home and you swing her. . . . All eight, circulate . . . explode, star through, touch a quarter. . . ."

"Do you like this kind of thing?"

"It's okay." He stared at something called an "ocean wave."

"When's the last time you danced?" The music stopped and the square broke, the dancers coming down off the stage, toward the audience.

"Danced?" He searched his memory but honestly couldn't say. "Years. Why?"

" 'Cause you're about to get your chance." She reached out and got a lock on his arm as an old fellow in a string tie worked his way toward them.

"What? Forget it." He tried to back up, but the crowd was solid behind them.

"All right, a volunteer," the fellow said, grinning ear to ear. "Don't be shy, mister. It's a lot of fun, and good exercise. Something a husband and wife can do."

She grinned at him. He muttered, "Shit" under his breath, then followed her tugging hand up the steps. Before he knew it, he was in a square, half the dancers costumed, the others civilians like him and Monica. "We'll start 'er slow," crooned the caller, and signaled the band.

124

He had to concentrate at first, staring at the others and figuring where to put his feet and hands. He felt huge and ungainly, like a dancing bear, and he could hear the assholes down in the audience laughing at him.

But he kept grimly on, and after a while he found you could do the call without thinking about it. And every few seconds, her flushed happy face came around like a carousel to meet him, the press of her hand, the feel of her waist under his arm as he swung her in a do-si-do. Then a blur of faces, one after the other, faces, hands, glowing cheeks, gusts of perfume.

> I talked to the man in the moon
> I said sir, is she coming back soon?
> Left allemande that corner, dosado your own
> Left allemande and weave—this is what he said
> I don't know a thing about love
> Swing the lady 'round and promenade
> I just watch from the sky, will love grow, will it die
> I don't know a thing about love.

The set ended, and the audience gave them a hand as they trooped offstage. He raised his clasped hands in a victory sign.

"There, that wasn't such a torture, was it?"

"It wasn't so bad. Don't try to get me in a club, though."

"Everybody enjoys dancing. I've seen people in wheelchairs dance. If you could forget your worries and let go once in a while, maybe you wouldn't need to—"

"To what?"

"To—nothing. Forget it." She rubbed her face. "I didn't bring any sunscreen. Am I getting a burn?"

"Yeah, on the nose."

"I burn so fast. Are you about ready to go?"

Tad was sitting in the car, thinking again about the walled estate, the girls, the pool. He wondered when Ripper would take them back. Maybe next time, they could take a camera. He thought about that for a while, then jerked awake. It was goddamn hot. How long were they going to stay at this hick circus?

He was trying to figure out the CD player when a guy in a straw Smokey Bear hat leaned in the window. Just the sight of him peeking in, shading his eyes with his hand, gave him a major flashback. He stared up, hand frozen on the power button.

125

"Having trouble, son?"

"No. Just trying to play a disc."

"Trying to play a disc. This your car, son?"

"No. It belongs to, uh, my dad."

"What's in the box?"

"A blue dish he bought for a friend of his."

"A blue dish. Did I see a screwdriver as I came up? Are you taking that tape deck out?"

Tad squinted up at him. Dressed like a cop, a gold name tag, gold badge. He felt himself tensing up. The pricks were always in your face. "No. I told you, this is my dad's car."

"Where is your dad, son?"

"He's up at the festival."

"Up at the festival." The guy straightened, adjusted his belt. "Well, you see, unfortunately I happen to know whose car this is. Out of the car. Hands on the hood, please."

As soon as he came out, he saw Tad bent over the car, an officer in a green uniform standing over him. "Oh, crap," he muttered, breaking into a sprint.

"What's the problem, Officer?"

The man turned from Tad, still holding him down over the hood with a hand on the small of his back. "Excuse me, sir?"

"That's my son. What's the goddamn problem?"

"Don't curse at me, buddy. You gonna tell me this is your car?"

"No, it's hers." He jerked his hand over his shoulder.

The guy took his hand off Tad, then let him up. "I thought this was Bud's car, with the Tallahassee sticker and the DAN decals. That makes you Galloway. Right?"

"That's right."

"Sorry," the guy said offhandedly to Tad. He dusted his hands, then offered one to Tiller. "Bob Ferebie, Florida Park Service."

Tiller didn't shake it, just turned and looked for Monica. There she was, coming from the Porta Potti. He waved till she spotted them, then turned back. "Yeah, everything's okay here, and that's my son, so how about moving along."

"Well, not quite so fast," said Ferebie. He was leaning on the hood. "I'd heard you took over for Bud. Been meaning to call you. But now we ran into each other, maybe you could spare a minute."

"We're trying to enjoy ourselves, friend. Here's a card. How about you call me at the office Monday."

"How about not," said Ferebie. He went over to his truck and opened the passenger-side door. "Get in," he said.

Tiller looked at him for a second. He said to Tad, "Sit in the car. Wait for me." Then he got into the truck.

"What the hell is this?"

"Mr. Galloway, maybe you didn't catch my name. I said I was Bob Ferebie."

"So what?"

"I'm the manager of the Styx River State Preserve."

"Yeah? So?"

"So, I determine access to that and other state land."

"You're an important guy, huh? Who goes around scaring fifteen-year-olds."

"A lot of your diving takes place on state property, Mr. Galloway."

Tiller glanced out the windshield, to see Monica watching them from the car. He waved to reassure her, made a "just a minute" gesture. "Okay, let me see if I'm starting to get a picture out of this. You're telling me you control my access to Peacock Springs, Manatee Springs, the other diving sites on state land?"

"That's right. Peacock, Manatee, Wakulla, Rainbow River, Ichetucknee."

"We don't have a legal right to access public land?"

"You're a for-profit user. You have rights, but we decide if you get to exercise them."

"And you're asking for what?"

"For a consideration, for making those dive sites available to your business."

"I think I'm getting it now."

"Good," said Ferebie. "But let me make sure everything is perfectly clear to you. The Park Service is responsible for proper use of those springs. You don't maintain good relations with us, we start finding safety violations. We've got to make sure precautions are observed. Then there's rowdy behavior, parking infractions, environmental infractions, littering—you get the idea. They sound minor, but two or three of them and we can suspend Scuba Florida from diving on Park Service land."

"Which effectively shuts me down."

"Which shuts you down, exactly. And there's not gonna be any public outcry. The public thinks of these as killer springs. You're just some guy trying to make money on a bunch of nuts with death wishes. But on the other hand—I don't want to come on all

127

negative—on the other hand, we can be a lot of help. Deconflicting schedules, arranging special access to remote sites, making sure you don't get some fly-by-night coming in, starting up competition for you. And we're still acquiring. Pretty soon, we're gonna protect every divable spring in Florida. Bud understood all this," Ferebie said. "I understand he had an accident. You come in from outside; you didn't know. I understand that. But now that you're on our field, you play by our rules."

Tiller stared out the window. They were always there, the men with their hands out. Pay off, or they'd wreck everything you'd built. If it wasn't the mob, or the Colombians, it was the government. He said slowly, "How much was he paying you?"

"Thousand a month."

He figured everybody always tried to jack over new guys. "No way. Best I can do is five hundred."

"This isn't a dealing situation."

"Every situation is a dealing situation."

"Not if the other guy holds your balls. Look, I'm not the only one involved here. I can maybe do eight hundred."

"Seven, I write you a check right now."

"A check! What kind of dumb ass do you think I am?"

"If you want cash, I need time to come up with it. We're trying to sell the business; the accounts have got to balance. I'm not sure how I'd cover that."

"You don't put it in the *accounts,* Mr. Galloway. But I promise you, if I don't see the cash in a week, you won't have a business to sell. And I want an envelope on the first of every month after that, you want to keep operating on state land."

Tiller didn't say anything, and after a minute Ferebie opened the door. The ranger gave Monica a barely noticeable tip of his hat, then turned back toward the park.

"Who was that? What did he want?"

"Says his name's Ferebie. He says he knows you. You don't know him?"

"No . . . I don't remember him, but I meet lots of people at the hospice, and the library board, and—what did he want?"

"Nothing, wanted to talk about Bud." He thought about telling her more, then decided it could wait. She glanced at him, frowning; then she started the car, her face clouded.

That night, they were sitting together downstairs, on the sofa, watching a tape on the big screen, with the lights off and her cat,

Lunker, lying on her lap. Its blue eyes regarded him sleepily from between half-closed lids. When the credits rolled, she picked the cat up and put it down on the carpet, then snuggled into his arms without a word, as if they did this every night. Then they kissed, and this time, after a moment of hesitation, her lips opened under his.

Her breasts pressed softly against him, but he didn't reach for them. He wasn't going to embarrass himself again.

When they broke for air, she sighed, then turned away and groped on the end table. The remote clicked and the screen winked out. Her lighter flared and he sat back, watching the moon sailing higher through the open window behind her. Moths batted softly against the screen. He listened to the tick of the overhead fan as the blades went round and round.

"I like that," she murmured. "Don't get the wrong idea, I do like it."

"I like it, too."

"It's not that I don't want to . . . make love to you, Tiller. It just doesn't feel right. Not yet. Maybe not ever . . . and maybe it will. . . . I just mean, it's too easy just to jump into bed. Easier than it is to think if it's the best thing for both of us or not. Do you have any idea what I'm saying? How about you? Would it feel right to you?"

He thought about saying he both wanted to and didn't, felt like riding her slim hips till she arched and shuddered like a cat, and like apologizing to Bud's shade for even thinking about it. No, that was probably one of those things that was better left unsaid.

She chuckled. The cigarette glowed and faded in the dark. Her hand moved slowly across his stomach, then down to his crossed legs. He closed his eyes, tracing its progress by its warmth. When it reached the cuff of his shorts, her fingers hesitated, then moved under them. Her fingernails left glowing trails on his skin, made each hair prickle and stand upright.

Shit, he couldn't take much more of this. "Uh . . . you sure this wouldn't be easier upstairs?"

"No. . . ."

"Then maybe you'd better stop doing that."

She took her hand away immediately and stretched. Murmured, "I'm sorry, I don't mean to be so equivocal. Just that before I do something, I want to be sure. Look, I had a good time today. The best I've had since . . . well, for a long time."

"So did I."

"I don't know how you feel about this. Maybe it's the wrong time to bring it up."

"What?"

"There's nothing that says we absolutely have to sell the business. If you wanted to . . . it might be that you could just keep on running it."

He didn't answer, and she hesitated, then went on in a whisper like dead leaves stirring in an October wind. "I like Tad. I wanted kids, but Bud and I could never have any. I don't mean that if anything *does* happen between us, there's some kind of string attached. There wouldn't be. But . . . *if* it did, and if you wanted to, you could stay."

The cat stared at them, crouched in the shadows. He stroked her hair, contemplating the hovering flame of the moon beyond the window. Bud's business, his house, his wife—it would be like taking his place. Like stepping up to take point after another guy went down ahead of you. But Monica was attractive. She seemed like a nice person. True, he'd only known her a short time. But both Tad and he could use a home.

"Look, don't say anything, all right? You don't have to answer now. I know you guys need time to think about this complicated emotional stuff."

"I don't think I can. Answer now, I mean."

"Then don't. Just think about it. We both will. All right?" She touched his lips lightly, then laughed and leaned over to stub the cigarette out. "Good night."

Her shadow swayed between him and the moon. He watched her slim, straight form mount the steps. He felt a dark tunnel opening ahead, luring him deeper and deeper as he inhaled steadily, breath after breath, the narcotic, flower-perfumed air of the Florida night.

ELEVEN

Hands in his pockets, standing beside Scovill, he surveyed the sales counter two weeks later. Today, chocolate cake was the centerpiece instead of the newest dive computer, along with a carafe of cappuccino from Val's Place and frozen yogurt in reserve in the office fridge. Napkins and plates from the latest Disney movie. And a big computer-printed banner that read WEL-COME BACK JULY. WE MISSED YOU.

"Here she comes." Mark backpedaled from the window, and the next moment July Toll was holding her hands over her mouth like an overwhelmed child. "For *me*? Oh wow, this is so great! I could kiss every one of you!" But the first one she got her lips on was Tad, who stuck his hands deep into his pockets and leaned back into a rack of wet suits that promptly gave way behind him.

Toll looked thinner and paler. She told them about the aspiration pneumonia and how she wouldn't be able to dive for a few more weeks, till the doctor was sure her lungs could tolerate the dry breathing mixes. "But basically I'm okay, and real glad to be back with you guys again," she finished, smiling around at them all—Scovill, Tiller, Mark, Tony, Monica, Tad, and two regular customers who'd come in during the party.

"All right, everybody, we'd better get back to work," Tiller said at last. Scovill swept them back to their places, and the customers moved up to ask about some new kind of underwater communications gear.

*　　*　　*

131

He was sitting at the computer, finishing an order, when the phone rang. He picked it up absently. "Scuba Florida, how can I help you?"

"Till? That you?"

"Shad? *Shad!* How the hell are you?" He saved the file, swung his chair around, and put his feet up. "I picked something up for you and Latricia at White Springs. Haven't gotten it in the mail yet, but—"

"Well, I hadn't heard from you, so I thought I'd call."

He was glad to hear the familiar home accent, but he felt guilty that he'd been here almost a month and hadn't called Aydlett, hadn't even dropped him a bimbos-in-Florida postcard.

"So, how you like cave diving? Been down yet?"

"Oh yeah, quite a few times. It's hairy, pal. Remember when we were groping around inside that wreck, down in The Abacos? Worse than that. But I think I'm getting the hang of it."

"You'll never get me down in one of them holes."

"I hear ya. It's not my idea of fun, either. Latricia okay?"

"Oh yeah, and we got some news. Gonna be a new little Aydlett in the family."

He whooped, and congratulated Shad. If it was a boy, his partner said, they'd name him Clifton.

"After Captain Cliff."

"Yeah, kind of in memory, you know . . . you know how those names keep on around here."

"Sure do. That's great! I've got some news, too."

"Yeah? What?"

"A woman. The one who owns the shop, the one who sent the telegram. Name's Monica. It's early, but . . . this might be for real."

"Till, that's good to hear. But does that mean—what, that means you stay there? Or would she come up here?"

"The business is doing good, Shad. It's a nice part of the country." He weighed his words, but when he said them, they sounded right. "I'm thinking about settling down here."

"The Banks not be the same without you, man."

"Well, time marches on. You, a daddy? That is *great.*"

"Reminds me, how you doing with Tad?"

"We're getting along. No major news items there."

"Now look, what I said about not wantin' never to dive them caves—"

"Want to try it? Make sure you don't throw a chance away. This could be our break."

"You don't want me down there, Till. Anyway, this might not be the right time, with Latricia and all."

"Like I said, you decide," Galloway told him. "I ever have a job to offer, Shad, you'll always have head-of-the-line privileges."

He hung up and stared at the screen, grinning to himself. Shad, a father. He'd have to see that to believe it. Then he got back to work on the orders.

July brought the morning mail in around ten. He told her she looked great, that it was good to have her back. She closed the door and his smile faded. "Sit down," he said, pushing the chair toward her.

"Thanks. Look, I had some time to think, there in the hospital."

He nodded, waiting.

"And I . . . I don't know if I want to do the deep exploration stuff anymore. It's just too risky, Tiller. I have things I want to do with my life. Diving's not my only dream, like it is for Lamont and Mary Ellen and people like them."

"You sure? You always struck me as a champ, July. You can dive rings around me down there." He searched for words. "Look, I've felt that way sometimes after a job where somebody got a bad hit. It goes away. Just take it easy, get all recovered—"

"I don't think we're talking about the same thing."

"No?"

"Joel wasn't the only one, Tiller. Just the closest to home. Dave Stern last year, in Texas. Jennifer Schieff-Sanders, drowned in a sump in West Virginia. There're two or three go every year. I guess I'm just losing my taste for the idea of getting to know people, then suddenly having to say good-bye forever." She took a deep breath. "I don't think it's wimping out. I'd go back into Wabasso in a second if somebody needed help. Maybe it's the idea of it as a business. I'm not comfortable anymore with the idea of teaching people to do something that's eventually going to kill some of them."

"You could say that about a lot of sports. Flight training, sport parachuting. Hell, driver's ed, even. Look, you don't have to take the problems of the planet on your shoulders, July. They want to go into caves, they're gonna go whether we train them or not. If they come to us, at least they're gonna know what to do when the snakes come out of the basket. Right?"

She thought about that. "I don't know."

"Look, I remember how it was back when you didn't have to

133

go through this qualification stuff. You just strapped a tank on and jumped in," he told her. "Maybe that's why I don't care for all this C-card bullshit, but when you look at the number of people who used to die in these springs, they're pretty horrendous. Good instructors save lives." He came around the desk, put a hand on her shoulder. And for a second, God help him, he felt fatherly. "You're a great diver and you've invested a lot of time and skill into getting where you are. You're doing something a lot of folks only get to dream about. Plus, we need you. So don't toss it before you think about what I said."

When she left, he looked at the open door for a second, blankly, wondering if he'd convinced her.

The mail lay where she'd left it and he shuffled through it, dropping most of it straight into the trash can. Bills, flyers, a couple of letters from overseas, foreign divers requesting information or wanting to make reservations, and a long bulky white envelope. He stared at this last, then realized what it was. It was addressed "Attention: Monica Kusczk," but he tore it open anyway.

It was the coroner's report on Bud. He started to read it, but immediately the phone rang. Somebody wanted to talk to Mark about his regulator free-flowing. He went to the door and yelled, "Daughtrey, phone," then leaned into the retail area. "July, how about getting the phone for a while? Got something important I gotta read."

With the door closed and the phone off, it was easier to concentrate. He propped his feet up again and started going through it line by line.

According to the report, the subject, a Caucasian male, had been recovered from a depth of three hundred feet in a freshwater cave. No signs of violence. No injuries. The coroner's finding was death by drowning. There was a description of the water found in the lungs.

He read it through, having a little trouble with the medical language but getting the gist of it. Then he frowned and went back to the sentence he'd noticed. It said the subject had died without any air in his tanks.

He didn't know what was wrong with the sentence, but it dragged a fingernail across his mind. He decided to take it apart. Subject—no problem there. Died—well, he *had* died. Without air in his tanks? He tried to imagine a way you could die *with* air in your tanks, your regulator in your mouth, then have the rest of

134

your air bleed off somehow. He couldn't, unless there'd been some kind of gear failure. But if what killed Bud was a regulator problem, a free-flow or some other kind of failure, he would have gone to his octopus; next, to his buddy tank; and if by some amazing and horrible coincidence *that* didn't work either, he'd have done what Tiller had when July got into trouble: bypass the regulator and use air direct from the tank, either by forming a bubble or by sipping it breath by breath straight from the cylinder valve. It wasn't easy—it took iron self-control—but that's what a diver as experienced as Bud would have done.

Okay, so *without any* was okay. What about the next word—*air*?

Yeah. That was what was wrong.

Bud had died without air in his tanks?

Then something was rotten in north Florida.

Because Bud shouldn't have had any air in his tanks. Not where they'd found him. It was too deep. Bud wouldn't have been in there on air. He'd have been using a mixture, most likely trimix.

It might sound like a niggling difference, that Pendleton and the coroner had put down *air* instead of *gas*, but he'd noticed cave divers didn't use the words interchangeably. That made sense, since taking a hit off the wrong one at three hundred–plus feet could kill you within seconds. The most dangerous, the pure oxygen bottles, often had special covers you had to unsnap to get to the regulator, for the same reason: Grabbing the wrong one in a moment of confusion or absentmindedness could be fatal.

Was it a mistake? He went out into the corridor and found Montagnino in the shop. He was squatted over a scooter, thoughtfully screwing the cap back on his inhaler. Tiller said, "Sniffles, you're gonna OD on those one of these days."

"Better than having my head back up and explode."

"Hey, you know what happened to Bud's stuff?"

"What stuff?"

"His gear. What he was wearing when he died."

"Oh, yeah. The regulator and wings and that, they're in the blue milk crate back by the compressor."

"What about the tanks?"

"They were regular rental tanks." Montagnino started to go back to the scooter, then said, "No, wait, I lied. Those were his own. Two one-twenty-ones and a single eighty. Right over there, second rack, with the scuzzy-looking valves on them."

"Rigged for what? Trimix?"

"I think just for air. Why?"

135

"What about his suit? Where's his suit?"

"Mon buried him in it." Montagnino reached for the inhaler again.

"*What?* You shitting me?"

"No, that's what she said to do. That's how he was laid out at Bevis-Colonial. It was the way he'd of wanted it, Tiller."

Galloway grunted. He started to leave, but instead, he halted in front of the plywood stowage racks. He looked at the dull steel cylinders, the ones Bud had been wearing when he died.

Mute witnesses. But . . . could he make them talk?

"Need something?"

"Yeah, you charged them since then?"

"No, just stuck them up there. Actually, I only got them in last week. They were over in Mon's garage and she called me to come and get them; she didn't want 'em around there anymore. They're in pretty bad shape, need some work before we can rent 'em out."

Tiller reached for a regulator and gauge set. He spun it on and cracked the gate valve. Two hundred and fifty pounds. Here at atmospheric, there were a few breaths left in the big tanks. He took one, getting the creeps again as he thought how much Bud could have used it. It tasted okay.

Montagnino was watching him. He hoisted the tanks to his shoulders and carried them to the back and put them on the analyzer. It came out 21/79 oxygen/nitrogen.

Plain old compressed air.

He got the wings and regulator out of the milk crate and carried everything back to his office. He propped the tanks against the filing cabinet, noting what Montagnino had pointed out: how worn and corroded the valves looked. When he squatted down, he saw it was because there was no chroming left. He was looking at the base brass itself. Funny, didn't seem like the way Bud Kusczk would keep his equipment. He'd always had the most squared-away gear in the squad; the lieutenant was always pointing him out as the good example while the rest of them tried to keep from rolling their eyes.

He closed the door again and swept the other mail and everything else off his desktop and laid out Bud's other gear, the wings and harness assembly, the regulators and gauges and the reel. He looked at them for a while.

The chrome was gone off the outside of the regulator, looked as if it was eaten off, just like it had been eaten off the tank valves. Most of the rings and snaps were stainless. But one clip on the harness had a whitish growth he could just barely chip off with his thumbnail. Underneath, it seemed to be marine bronze. The line reel had the same kind of corrosion as the clip.

It looked old, but it wasn't. It looked as if it had been recovered from the bottom after lying in salt water for a year. But he knew it hadn't.

He stared at the wall for a time, then got a clean Styrofoam cup out of the drawer. He upended the wing and harness assembly and depressed the purge button on the BC mouthpiece, holding the black rubberized nylon upside down until a few drops trickled out. You always ended up with a little water in your wings after a dive. It got in through the power inflator and the mouth inflator assembly, or maybe a few drops leaked in around the dump valve diaphragm. There might be pinholes in the nylon itself, if it had been around a few years. He ended up with a couple of tablespoons in the bottom of the cup. Cupping his hands around his nose, he bent to whiff it in.

Along with the musty smell of rubber, he got an unmistakable tang of sulfur. A few tiny grains of black sand lay beneath a quarter inch of brownish water.

He sat back down and resumed his former feet-up thinking position. After a while, he picked up the coroner's report again and flipped to where it had mentioned the fluid in Bud's lungs. Then he got up and squinted at one of the charts on the wall, the one labeled WATER QUALITY OF FLORIDA SPRINGS.

No doubt about it.

Maybe they'd found Bud in the Black Abyss. But he hadn't died there.

The chart said that, like most of the other clear blue north Florida springs, Emerald Sink was a calcium-magnesium bicarbonate spring. The water was fresh-tasting and clear and chemically slightly basic.

While the coroner's report had clearly stated that when the subject's lungs were emptied, the resulting frothy fluid was brownish.

Just like the stuff in the cup.

He was examining this in his head when the phone beeped and a voice said, "Tiller, your son's here, and he's got something to show you."

"Yeah? I'll be right out."

Tad was standing by the counter, showing July something in a plastic sleeve. Tiller saw halfway across the room what it was.

137

His son saw him and for the first time since they'd come to Florida, there wasn't a sneer or a detached look on his face. He said, "Hey, Dad, come look at this."

He examined the card. It was just like thousands of others that got issued every year to beginning divers, aside from reading "Theodore L. Galloway." "You passed the written exam, huh?"

"The repeat-dive calculations were tricky, but Mark said I did good."

Tad was leaning against the counter, halfway back into his "I don't care" shell, like a threatened turtle. Tiller studied him. Then he did something he didn't really feel comfortable doing.

Tad looked astonished as Galloway got his arm around him. They hugged stiffly, and after a moment his son's arm came up, too, gave him a sort of halfway-back grip. Tiller stood awkwardly in the hug, feeling how fake it was, then patted him on the back and let go. Shit, the kid was gonna be as big as he was pretty soon. He cleared his throat of a sudden thickness. "Yeah, good going. I know people took that course three times before they passed it."

"It wasn't that hard." Tad rubbed his mouth in a gesture that was oddly evocative of somebody. After a moment, Tiller realized it was himself.

July was smiling at them. He cleared his throat again and jerked his thumb over his shoulder. "Come on down the office. Got something I want to talk to you about."

He closed the door behind them and stood for a moment looking at his son. Yeah, he was gonna be big.

"So, what did I do now?"

"Huh?"

"You got me back here to rip me a new asshole, just wondered what I did."

"Shit, Tad, I just didn't want to share our business with everybody in the shop." He looked at the chart again, remembered what Mon had said; that he should have taught Tad to dive himself, that it would have been a great way to work on the relationship. Well, maybe it wasn't too late. "So. You're a qualified diver now. That's good, because I was thinking of driving down tomorrow morning and taking a look at some property Bud owns down in Crane County. Want to come?"

"Me?"

"Yeah, you. You don't have to spend every day roamin' the woods with that goddamn Ripper." He held up his hand. "Look,

I know he's your friend. Just don't get the idea you can drop out of school like him. What the hell do you guys actually do?''

"Just stuff. Tube the rivers. We went down the Itchetucknee last week.''

"What else?''

Tad shrugged. He sure as hell wasn't going to tell his dad what they really did, which was drink a little, smoke a little, and go sneaking. They'd been into two more private estates, and though they hadn't seen anything quite as interesting as that first time, it was a charge invading places you weren't supposed to be. For his part, he'd filled in Ripper and Rafael on the fine points of boosting cigarettes. "I don't know what you got against him. He's okay. He knows the springs and the rivers and stuff like the back of his hand.''

"Maybe. Anyway, sit down. Let me tell you what we got going here.''

Tad sat. Keeping his voice low, Tiller told him what he thought about Bud's death. The boy went still, listening. When Tiller was done, Tad said, "Sulfur, huh?''

"That's right. There aren't that many sulfur springs in Florida. But one of them's the one Bud was trying to develop—Tartar Springs. So how about you come along with me, back me up while I check it out?''

Of course he only shrugged, but Tiller could swear the kid looked almost pleased.

TWELVE

The next morning, they saw the first signs not far south of Perry. He had a map, too, a pencil sketch Mark had drawn for them. They turned off Route 19 into flat land dotted with pine woods and horse farms with names like Oak Springs and Elysian Fields. As they rocked across a 1930s concrete bridge, another sign, half-hidden in undergrowth, reassured them: ONLY 3 MORE MILES. TARTAR GROTTOES.

"Holy smoke," said Tiller, braking a few minutes later. They stared up at the billboard. A grossly obese Santa Claus was wrestling an alligator. Beneath it, huge sun-faded letters read TARTAR GROTTOES. HOME OF THE WRESTLING HALL OF FAME. 628-POUND SANTA CLAUS. ALLIGATOR PIT. BOTTOMLESS CAVERN. A PLACE FOR FAMILY FUN. SEE IT ALL $2. And below it, tacked on more recently, a FOR SALE sign with a Tallahassee number.

"Bizarro," said Tad.

Off the paved road, a sand path disappeared away into dappled forest sunlight. Tiller put the van back into gear and bumped and rocked along to the gate. It was locked. "I hope this works," he said, looking past it as he got out Bud's key ring. "Or we're gonna be humping those tanks in a long way."

The padlock was well oiled, to his surprise, and opened with an efficient click the third key he tried. He swung the gate back as Tad shifted to the driver's seat, then followed him on foot as the boy drove swaying and bouncing down the rutted sand road till it emerged from the woods.

140

Three plywood-sided sheds looked down into a pear-shaped pit, a sunken gap in the forest. Tiller caught up as Tad parked. He was already sweating. He noticed again the eerie silence that seemed always to surround these springs. The only sounds were a crow's croak and the sawing of the cicadas, the rustle and chatter of squirrels chasing one another through the oaks. The black unreflecting surface of the river was visible through the trees, broad and flat and nearly motionless, as if solidified by the heat. That had to be the Styx.

"Lock it?"

"I don't think we need to. You can start pulling shit out while I look around."

"Jeez, did you bring enough tanks?"

"Just take the ones behind the seats. The rest of those are spares from last night's class."

The first shed had a rudimentary patio, a plank deck with a corrugated fiberglass sunshade. Another FOR SALE sign was stapled beside the door. White plastic lawn chairs stood around a table, its masonite top warped with humidity. Next door, a gear shack had a Mako compressor, racks of worn wet suits, and a NO SMOKING—OXYGEN placard. Another cabin seemed to be a retail store. None of the keys fit the door, but he could make out a dusty counter inside, littered with a jumble of cardboard boxes.

At the far end of the clearing was an abandoned trailer on concrete blocks and a two-toilet shack with R-14 insulation on the walls, the ground visible through the floor. Palmetto bugs froze as he stepped in, then darted for cover.

He read faded clippings stapled to the insulation as he urinated. They were dated five years before, about the auction of the caves. The museum and underground zoo had been an attraction back in the fifties, when families driving south spent their money at a succession of penny-ante roadside tourist traps before there was a Disney World. The last item said a Tallahassee businessman named Joel Kusczk had purchased the site. The clipping said that up to now, divers had avoided Tartar Springs because of its poor visibility and a deadly reputation—thirteen people had died there over the years—but that Mr. Kusczk planned to map the system and build facilities to attract advanced divers and wet-cave spelunkers.

The toilet flushed, and somewhere a pump hummed to life. He looked into the trees when he came out and saw the power line.

He headed down toward the pit, to find Tad emerging from its mouth. "Hey, it's neat down there. Bats and stuff. We're gonna need lights, though."

"Oh yeah? Did you find the spring?"

"It's down there. Stinks like a wet fart, too."

He could smell it as he started down the worn brick stairs, as the sliced-open limestone rose on either side. Not like rotten eggs, more like burned gunpowder. Not a reassuring smell. The stairs, slick with condensation and mold, accompanied a rusty pipe handrail down one flight, then zigged left into darkness. Glass panels set into the walls held unidentifiable blackened things. He stopped at the boundary of darkness, then felt for the handrail and continued down, feeling for each step before he trusted his weight to it. The sound of rushing waters grew. He halted again when he felt a cool sulfurous breath on his face. Things rustled and peeped, skittering away from him into the sheltering dark.

A flash of light, boots clattering down the steps. "Watch it; it's slippery," he called. "Hold the rail."

The dive light's beam illuminated only a narrow slice of the cave, but still he could see it wasn't very large. His side had been "improved," with a cracked concrete floor and stairs leading down into the black water, their corners crumbling, so that the pebbles of the aggregate showed. Impenetrable blackness ate the beam on either hand, the stream rushing out of darkness into darkness. There was no sign of the alligators, or Santa Claus, or the Wrestling Hall of Fame. The water stank. He went to one knee and dipped up a handful. It was cool, sixty-eight or seventy degrees. He rinsed his mouth with a sip, then spat out the nasty taste. He didn't see any guidelines, or any light switches, or any easier way into the water than down the steps.

"So, you gonna check it out?"

He glanced up to Tad's quizzical stare. "Might as well, now we're here."

"Am I coming in, too?"

"Oh, no. No way. You're not anywhere near qualified for this."

"Neither are you."

He grinned. "Let it go, all right? I'm going to need you here as safety guy, and to hand me my tanks." He straightened and dusted his hands, looking around. "Okay, let's start hauling that gear down here."

An hour later, he stood knee-deep in the rushing water, bent under the usual 150 pounds of twin cylinders, cave gear, reels, and lights. He'd rigged out with air, figuring it shouldn't be a deep dive. A scooter lay on the bottom step, its headlight making the swirling water glow like smoky amber. He couldn't leave it on long—the headlight would suck too much juice from the battery— but he figured he'd start with it on and see what developed.

He said to Tad, above him, "Okay, we clear on what you're doing?"

"Yeah, stand around and hold my dick."

"That's right. You get bored, you're gonna suit up and come in, yes or no?"

"No," said Tad sullenly.

"That's right. When I get back, we'll get you dressed out and do a little cavern practice. Get you down where it's dark and show you what it feels like. All right?"

The boy brightened. Tiller regarded him a moment longer, then sealed his mask. He held his arms up and Tad lowered the stage bottle. He clipped it off, tucked the regulator into his mouth, and did a last check. Good air.

Giving Tad a wave, he half-stepped, half-fell down into the rushing black.

Alone in the dark, with only his light for company. Sure murky down here. It turned the beam brown and blunted it only a few feet out from his hand. The water chilled his skin under the wet suit. He could taste sulfur with every breath.

He decided to go upstream first, make it easier coming back. He aimed the scooter carefully downward. And kept going. The stream was deeper than he expected—maybe twenty-five, thirty feet. There, there was the bottom, smooth dark stone sliding by. A lot of water going through here. White catfish materialized from the black, then veered away, barbels dangling from gaping mouths.

A rectangular paleness loomed up. He throttled back, hooking a hand over its edge as he looked the square over. A rigging platform, where divers could adjust their gear and get comfortable before they went on. You saw them at commercial diving sites, like Blue Grotto and Vortex. Ought to be a guideline nearby. . . . His light searched out and a sturdy nylon rope glowed back at him. It led away and down, into the black.

The scooter hummed, pulling him along. He couldn't see far, so he kept his eyes straight ahead, remembering nearly creaming himself on the roof at Wabasso. Gradually, it got so murky that

143

he lost the guiderope. He angled closer to the bottom but couldn't pick it up again. Better take it slow; he was going too fast for the visibility.

Fifty-five feet. The ceiling was coming down. He could see it now at the edge of his light. Finally, it arched down and met the floor right in front of him.

Shoot, he thought. He swerved, purring along the seamless meeting of blackened rock, a kitchen roach searching for an escape crack.

There, a black gap, and the blast of cold flow in his face. He could see right away he wasn't going to get the scooter in there. He checked his depth: sixty feet.

He fired up his main light, shut the scooter down, and parked it on the bottom. Then he got down on his belly and pulled himself hand over hand between the narrow lips of rock.

It was nearly impossible to make headway. All the volume of water flowing through the cavern was blasting out of this narrow slit, maybe twenty-three or -four inches high and fifteen feet wide. To make things tougher, the floor was covered with little rounded rocks like marbles. He tried to crab-crawl in, but his fingers just slid backward, raking through the pebbles with a faint musical rattle.

He rested, reevaluating the situation, and decided he wasn't going to make it in without reducing his drag. That meant leaving the stage bottle and proceeding on his main tanks. He still had independent air, from the split manifold. He clipped the stager to the guideline, switched to his main regulator, got a solid breath, and went back in.

This time, he tried it on his back, fly-walking, but the ceiling was smooth limestone coated with some kind of brown shit, slippery as hell; he got maybe five feet in, pushing as hard as he could with his fins and dragging with his fingers, before his fingertips slid off the slick stone and the current bulled him backward again. Then he turned his head at the wrong time and scraped his mask off. It whirled away into blackness and he was blind.

He knew he should have worn it under his hood. Into the old kit bag . . . he got his fingers on his pouch, got the spare mask. It didn't fit great. It was a cheap one that had been lying around the shop; it was uncomfortable and leaked. But as long as he cleared it every couple of minutes, he could see again.

By now, he was puffing. He fought for a couple more minutes, telling himself that if Bud could get through here, he could, too, before realizing he was building up CO_2. Finally, he gave up and hauled himself in hand over hand along the guideline. It was inelegant, not good caving practice, but it got him through the restriction with only a couple of tank bangs.

He unbent himself from the line and swam forward again, into a room beyond. The flow was less buffeting here and he rested, holding to a pinnacle, aiming his light about. It was maybe as big as a walk-in closet. The walls were covered with fluffy fungoid stuff that looked as if it belonged on the inside of a septic tank. It was nasty to look at, and when he touched it gingerly, his hand sank in and disappeared. Soft, like slimy drowned hair. When he pulled his hand out, the stuff came apart, blowing murk and detritus into the room. It was raining down now from above him, too. His exhalation bubbles were knocking it off the roof.

He snorted the mask clear of an inch of brown water and crud and pulled himself grimly past a branch leading left and through another narrowing tube for about twenty yards, the slimy stuff oozing away under his hands and the rock under that soft and crumbly, too. He couldn't actually see anything now; his light head was just a generalized brown glow in the murk. It was like crawling up a whale's lower intestine. Gonna be one fine diver's haven, Bud, he told Kusczk. You stumbled on a goddamn gold mine here, boy.

Look, Killer, some divers like a challenge.

Oh, they'll love this one, Bud. No shit. And after five dives, they'll be certified to work for Roto-Rooter.

Past another pinch-off to the left, the restriction opened out some. He grabbed rock and waited, letting the water clear as he examined yet another growth on the wall. This one looked like a pus blister, yellow in the center and brown all around. He felt no temptation to touch it. The softness of the limestone here worried him. For the most part, the guideline lay flaccid on the floor, but occasionally it was tied off around a protruding knob or handy rock. White plastic line arrows pointed the way back to the entrance. Trouble was, the knobs it was tied off on felt about as durable as stale cheese. For a second, he wondered exactly what was in this water, then shook his head angrily, concentrating.

He blew snot and scum out of his mask and pushed on through a northeast curve into a section that pinched up from below with a lot of amorphous breakdown matter, not rock as much as pulverized limestone mixed with powdery particles. The ceiling was a hollow bowl with filmy streamers fluttering off it. The passage

145

split here, the larger tunnel going right and down. The guideline didn't; it went left and up into a smaller tunnel. He followed it as that passage narrowed. His depth gauge was up to forty feet when it curved back down again and intercepted two passages, one broad and low, the other almost perfectly round. The guideline led into the right one, the round one.

He paused there for an air check, bumping his gauge against the computer, switching to his octopus and right tank to balance his consumption. Then he ran a diver check. Was it time to turn back? He could feel the insidious assurance of safety that was the most dangerous effect of nitrogen. Finally, he decided to push on another hundred feet. The guideline kept going, so there must be something up there.

Then he thought, Who are you kidding? Even as he slid into the round tunnel, shuffle-kicking himself along with fins held high, he thought, This is stupid. Kusczk had obviously bought this property thinking he could develop it into a dive site. He'd seen the receipts in the files for the materials that went into the buildings. But the buildings were half-finished, the store never opened. Bud had made a bad investment, that was all. The best thing he could do was help Mon unload it. Actually, the topside location wasn't bad. Along the river and all. Maybe they could subdivide. Styx Estates. No, that was his brother thinking. He'd just sell, get out from under and concentrate on running the business.

The tunnel necked down again and zigged left, his compass telling him he was going north now, and did a string-of-pearls number with little chambers with narrow wiggle holes between them and worm-bored little passages leading off too small to get into. The flow was very strong in the restrictions. He pulled himself forward like a stubborn crab. The rock was harder now under his hands, gritty and black. He could feel the differences in the limestone layers as he tunneled his way gradually down.

Passing eighty feet again. The guideline wove through a triple split, faked left, then took the center passage. That led to another chamber, the biggest yet, with a high conical roof that looked as if it might have been sinkhole-connected to the surface at one time. It felt huge, and he floated free in the center, consciously relaxing himself. His initial anxiety was dissipating, blowing away in the stream of pressurized nitrogen pumping through his lungs.

He left the high chamber and bored on, following the line as the passage branched again. Fingerlike side channels splayed off

146

into the darkness. The line tended right, dropping steadily along what seemed to be two parallel tunnels connected at intervals by cross branches. The water gradually turned darker, from murky ginger ale to root beer, and his light outlined rough, bubbly brick-colored walls, fissured and split.

He remembered the river. That might be where the dark stuff was coming from, the tannic acid from the cypresses along the river bleeding down. Remembering the way Devil's Ear and Eye opened under the Santa Fe, he wondered if there might be an access somewhere here, too, a path up. He cut his light, searching above him with craned-up neck, but made out nothing but the instantaneous and absolute black.

Depth: 105.

He halted suddenly as a rockfall loomed in his light. The reddish stuff was tumbled in chunks, with the now-familiar cavity arched above it. The interesting thing was that the guideline was buried under the breakdown. That meant the fall was recent. He pulled a couple chunks out experimentally. Silt clouded the water, then blew past him. He took a couple more out and pushed them back under his body, making room for his shoulders.

Wriggling like an eel entering a drowned body, he forced himself up into the narrow gap he'd created. Rocks scraped and clattered away. A hint of doubt—Should I be doing this?—was answered by the calm comfort that pervaded his mind now. Nothing was going to happen. Why had he ever bothered to doubt or worry? Everything was going to be fine.

A section of the roof against his back shuddered, then sagged gently. He shoved back and suddenly had a moment of clarity. He was a quarter mile in and nearly a hundred feet down in an unfamiliar cave. He had no buddy and no qualified backup, and he didn't even have all that much air in his tanks anymore. He hadn't been switching back and forth, and now one tank was almost empty, while the other still had 2,800 psi. Yeah, everything was going to be okay, but maybe it was time to go back.

Instead, he pushed ahead. No line now, but he figured he knew where it was. Maybe it would have been smart to clip a jump reel to the main line . . . but it was too late now. He clawed on, and the ceiling rock shuddered, vibrated, but held. Good, a little more room around him . . . still more.

His beam licked out into clearer water, and he saw the line again.

Only this time, it wasn't the same line. This was yellow. A dif-

147

ferent lot, a different batch? He didn't see any arrows. He decided to give it a brief checkout. Just to be sure he didn't get disoriented, he dug into his pouch and snapped one of his own markers onto it, the plastic dart pointing back toward the breakdown he'd just wriggled through.

Ninety-five feet, and the computer was telling him he didn't have much longer before he was into a decompression requirement. The line bent downward; then the walls opened out. His fins dragged; he was getting heavy. He triggered a burst of air into his wings, then hovered in the center of a swirling mist of silt.

Gradually, he made out veined, fissured walls that gave back a strange deep scarlet to his beam. The Red Room, he thought. He pirouetted, hanging in emptiness like a spacewalking astronaut, and his beam swept around and picked up the yellow line, still leading down into an interstellar black.

He plunged after it, wriggling down headfirst into what quickly turned from a cleft into a narrow tube. As soon as he was fitted into it, he regretted it, but by then it was too late to turn around. It closed in tight as sausage skin around meat. So he kept going down, jerking his jaw to clear his ears. How the hell deep did this go? Maybe he ought to stop. Back out while he still could. But the line kept going down, and he thought again, If Bud could get down this, so can I.

He was thinking that when suddenly his light showed nothing below. He blinked and shook his head, cleared his mask, and looked again. Still nothing. With a grinding shriek of steel against stone, he left the tube and dropped free, working his fins slowly to arrest his descent.

His beam lanced out, and he stopped breathing.

Below and ahead and around him stretched a massive emptiness huger than any cave he'd ever seen before. His beam lanced downward but touched nothing, as if he were dangling a silver thread down into the Grand Canyon. He stared around, unable to believe what he was seeing. It was enormous.

He was still dropping slowly. Now he caught faint shapes in the distance, out toward where the yellow line disappeared, zigzagging along the ceiling. It slowly penetrated his numbed mind that the water was incredibly clear, and noticeably colder on his face than the murky stuff permeating the labyrinthine passages above. He exhaled, still sinking, and checked his depth gauge as the bottom, at last, came into view far below his wavering fins:

148

170 feet. . . . That distant rocky bottom had to be 250, maybe even more. Maybe even three hundred, clear as the water was.

It was an enormous reservoir, a huge subterranean lake of clear, sweet water, millions, maybe billions of gallons of it.

He glanced at his computer and sucked air in dismay. He was deep into decompression. He had to go back . . . but the yellow line still stretched ahead. . . . Decompression didn't matter. Neither did air. He was going to find out what lay at its end.

But even as he decided this, the little cold intelligence that observed at the deepest layer of his mind was taking over. It shouldered aside the nitrogen-drunken Galloway who no longer cared about air or life. It forced him back along the line, back maggot-wriggling up into the vertical chimney. Back through the Red Room, air swelling in his chest as he ascended. Breathe, breathe, vent the increasing volume that inflated his lungs. . . . The relief valve on his wings farted great gushes of air. Back into the chambered room, and there was his own line marker. Ten feet past it, the yellow line disappeared into the breakdown.

He stared at the mass of tumbled rock and crumbled junk with groggy dismay. Had he really come through that? Apparently he had. But now, which way was *back*?

He chuckled into his regulator. Did he need this thing in his mouth, anyway?

The little cold intelligence said yes, he did, and that he didn't have enough air left to waste lolling around. It pushed him up and into the breakdown.

Into an interstice so narrow, he wheezed his lungs empty as he squeezed between two flat rocks, one fallen, one trembling suspended from the ceiling. Silt closed in again, sealing itself over his mask like a brown close-pressed palm. He kicked hard as his tank scratched and donged along the ceiling. Rocks clattered down. He smiled around his mouthpiece. He felt happy and light, omnipotent and clever. Almost out. Downstream the rest of the way. A quick swim back, hang for half an hour's decompression, then catch a sandwich with Tad—

The rock above him shifted, made a grating noise, and came slowly down out of the roof, laying itself gently down on his back. He tried to scuttle back out from under it, but he couldn't. He tried going ahead, with a little better success. The rock sagged down and split apart behind him with a clacking rustle. The black silt puffed out and cut his visibility to zero. He sucked a slow breath, the blade edge of alarm dulled by the many martinis' glow

149

of depth. He still had rock pressing against his stomach, down on his back, and had his elbows jammed into it on either side. He didn't have the line for a visual reference anymore, and he couldn't reach it, buried as it was a couple of feet under him.

Maybe this hadn't been such a hot idea, crawling into a fresh, unstabilized fall. Next time, he'd lay a jump line. Still, he knew the way back. All he had to do was swap ends like a worm in a straw and go back the way he'd come.

Not a problem. Not for Killer Tiller Galloway, cave fighter extraordinaire.

He elbow-wriggled his way up to what felt like the crest of the breakdown pile and got a little room there, enough to snake himself around in a circle like a dog preparing for sleep. Headed back now. If he could get past that chunk that had sagged, pick up the line again, he'd be okay. He just hoped nothing else went wrong. His mask was getting annoying, digging into his nose like a blade, leaking steadily. But he was still getting air, no nasty blasts of water or anything else untoward. Just find the friggin' line again, okay?

But wait a minute. He'd been going out when the rock came down. So that now, was he headed out, or back into the cave again?

Take it easy. Just breathe nice and slow and deep, and try to concentrate. Burn through that nitrogen haze.

He'd realized as soon as he turned back that things weren't going to be that easy going out. Now he was going downstream, and every particle of murk and silt he stirred up was moving right along with him. And the goddamn mask was flooding again! The pain drilled through the fuzzy numbness that was spreading over his face. He was suddenly sick of clearing it every two minutes. Didn't need it anyway, too murky to see. He could feel his way back along the line. Screw it! He pulled it off and let it go.

He slid back into the slit, fingers searching out like desperate blind anemones. They groped along rock, rock, soft breakdown . . . pushed. . . . The softness gave way suddenly and he dug forward and down, bending his body like a ferret entering a snake hole. He felt the edge of the collapsed chunk and twisted his body around it. Past it . . . his outstretched fingers brushed a thin, flexible smoothness . . . the line! He got a handful and pulled, but there was too much slack to get a purchase. Still, he had it back. Just that made him grin. Home safe.

He was stretched out like that, full length and half-twisted onto his back, kicking hard against the rock above him to drive himself the last couple of feet out into the tunnel again, when the ceiling gave another grating sound and a second chunk, this one the size of a refrigerator, detached itself and settled, clamping like soft jaws, right down over his hip and legs.

Tad stood by the black hollow sibilance of the underground river, playing with his flashlight. He flicked it on and off, then finally left it off.

He sat in the dark, thinking. And gradually, he forgot where he was, and what he was doing.

He was a little kid again.

He remembered back when they'd all lived together, his mom, his dad, and himself. It was in a trailer, down in Louisiana. He remembered it at first as a happy time. There was a pond his mother would take him to, and they'd play in the pond. Once, he saw a huge snake, and he tried to tell her about it, but she didn't understand what he was trying to say. And his father carrying him, and once putting his helmet over his head. The huge space inside smelled like rubber and metal and his dad. Sometimes he was afraid of his father, because he got mad sometimes, threw things, shouted. When that happened, Tad figured he'd been bad, and he tried harder to be good. But mostly, he loved his dad. He was strong and he brought him toys. He told stories about playing tricks on the tenders, and sometimes his dad's friends came over, Top Cat and Hacky and Uncle Otis and Jaxon Man. Them drinking beer out of the cut-down drum filled with ice, and him going from man to man, asking for sips till he was so dizzy, he staggered. And they all laughed, and he staggered even more, happy to be noticed, to have his father smiling down at him and grabbing him and wazing his head good with his knuckles.

Then he remembered his father and mother arguing. How he'd crouch in his room, with fear stuck in his stomach like a heavy stone.

He remembered later, seeing his father from a distance, with the woman his mother called "that coonass bitch." Staring at them across the parking lot, his father arguing with a big black-bearded man on a motorcycle. Them shouting, then his father suddenly spinning and kicking the guy so hard that the motorcycle went down, and the man, too, his face surprised. His father drawing a gun in a motion so fast, he never saw it, just that the gun was there, pointing down at the bearded man lying helpless on the road. The woman touching his shoulder and laughing. His father

151

holding the gun steady, the guy begging and finally crying. And finally his father tucking it away with a disgusted look, kicking the motorcycle's tire, turning to go. Then he caught sight of them, of his wife and his son, and Tad had waved and yelled, "Daddy, Daddy," but his father had looked through them as if they weren't there anymore.

The son of a bitch . . .

He was brought back a long time later by something rustling, up on the steps. He got up and went quietly after it to see what it was. He went all the way up to the top and stood looking through the trees toward the river. He wished he had some music, something to play some tunes. There was a player in the van . . .

It occurred to him that his father had been down an awful long time.

He went down the steps again and stood uncertainly by the subterranean stream, shining the flashlight down into it.

Tiller lay exhausted, sucking air hard through the narrowed straw of the regulator.

He'd tried everything he could think of to worm out from under the collapsed ceiling. Tried to twist and corkscrew his way out. But every time he moved, the rock came down a little more, shifting to bite down just ahead of his knee and again just before the swell of bone and flesh at his ankle. He'd exhausted himself struggling, and for a time outstripped the ability of the regulator to deliver air. Almost choked, sucking on the rubber mouthpiece.

Now he lay full length on his back in the dark, turned slightly to his right. Rock pressed down into his face and up under his back. He had about five inches of turbid water between his unmasked face and the down-pressing stone. He'd slammed his unprotected nose and forehead into it during his struggles, until his eyes were swollen almost shut. His arms were extended back of his head, gripping the line. He'd taken up slack till he got resistance, but he knew all he was doing was tightening the knot downstream. The cold water flowed steadily around him, fluttering the surgical-rubber bungees on his harness. If only the pressure would build up enough to spit him out . . . but it wasn't going to. The flow would search out other ways around him, through fissures and parallel channels.

He lowered his left hand, still holding the line with his right, and groped across his chest until he found the console. He brought it to his face, and then found, of course, that he couldn't read it. Shit, how had he gotten so narked that he'd let his mask go? . . . And that had been the spare; he didn't have another. Now he couldn't read his computer or his gauges. He'd know he was at the end of his air only when the regulator started closing down. The next breath would come harder—he'd have to fight to suck it out of the tank—and the one after that wouldn't come at all. There couldn't be much left. He'd been past the one-third point when he turned back. He'd used a lot more since then, fighting to get free.

Even if he could get loose somehow, get this crushing weight off his hips and legs, he probably didn't have enough to get back.

Strange as it seemed, the knowledge calmed him. He turned the light off again and relaxed, lying back in the dark. Here at last, death. He stared into the black behind swollen eyelids, searching for the peace that was supposed to come.

Then his body contorted, convulsed, fighting against the jaws of the trap until he could get no more breath, until a bloody red flamed behind his eyes and he had to sag back, concentrating all his attention into stopping his panic-stricken body from blowing out the mouthpiece and trying to claw its way up and out through a hundred feet of solid rock.

He must have blacked out then, because he had a confused dream. He was back aboard his father's sailboat, he was sick, and his father was looking for him. He was buried somewhere. He was buried under the sails. They'd tumbled down in the forward berth and the heavy, damp, wet cotton was pressing down on him. He cried weakly for his father, but there was something in his mouth. He got his fingers on it and was about to take it out when he came back.

And then he realized he had his mouthpiece in his hand. He was a hundred feet down, and his legs were pinned fast, and he'd been about to take it out and yell for his dad.

But his father was dead; he'd shot himself when they told him the verdict. . . .

He stared into the dark. He'd really dicked up his life. His family first—his dad and Ellie and Tad—then the people who tried to love him after that. Nicolette . . . well, she'd been pretty far gone when he met her. . . . Bernie, she'd wanted to stay, but he'd told her he'd never change. . . . Shad . . . and his cousin Jack, dead off Hatteras because of his greed . . .

Rocks clicked and scratched down off the ceiling behind him.

He heard a far-off rumble. Great, the whole tunnel was going to collapse. Well, it wouldn't make any difference to him. He just hoped they had the sense not to send anybody down this hellhole after his body. It would probably be Pendleton; he was County Rescue. Well, Pendleton had told him. He couldn't say he hadn't been warned about caves.

He noticed it was getting hard to breathe. The diaphragm clacked and wheezed. Not much longer . . .

What could he say or do here at the end? Not a goddamn thing. If he could talk, he'd say plenty . . . like Bud, scratching on a slate. . . . What a dickup—he couldn't even do that. Who would he write to anyway? Everybody left hated him. His brother, his stepmother, Tad, Ellie—they all hated his guts, and no wonder. If only he could say how sorry he was. He'd read someplace where you were supposed to see somebody surrounded by light. . . . He didn't feel any presences. This far down, he was a hell of a lot closer to the guy with the horns than anybody else.

The regulator chattered as he sucked harder, dragging the last air out of it. He held each breath as long as he could, then trickled it out a molecule at a time. In a few more seconds, he wasn't going to have any more, ever again.

A fist rammed itself up the line and jammed his knuckles painfully. He grabbed it instantly, fastening himself to it so hard, it instantly reversed itself and fought to get away. He heard the bubble and squeak of a regulator not three feet from his ears, saw, through the dark, the probing cone of a flashlight beam.

That little shit, he thought, consumed instantly with rage like nitrated paper. I told him not to come down here.

The hand came back and explored through the soft crumbled rock up to his shoulder. It felt his harness. Then the fingers dug themselves suddenly and painfully into his right eye. He writhed away, lungs pumping desperately to pull the last tablespoonful of air from his all-but-empty tanks.

Rocks slid away from behind his head and he sagged backward, feeling as if his neck was going to break. The line jerked out of his hands. He grabbed for it, but got nothing but the rotten rock and sand. Then he felt arms thrusting in past him, felt a body worming in along his. He opened his swollen eyes to the inchoate milling of murky cold water and the biting scratch of grit and rock.

Tad was fighting and digging his way in headfirst along his side. His mask slammed Tiller's right hand. To his horror, Tiller

154

felt the rock that pinned him tilt and sag, starting to slide toward the new disturbance. He tried to push his son back, make him retreat. But Tad evaded his hand and ducked down, burrowing on. The water carried the scratching scrape of gloves clawing out rock. Pebbles clacked and bubbles roared.

He took another breath, but nothing came. His lungs strained uselessly. His hand clawed at the valves on his back, twisted them all the way left, all the way right.

Nothing. Out of air.

Tad's body was pressed against him now, full length, as if they were strange lovers covered by black sheets. Now his hand burrowed desperately toward his son. The fingertips brushed the front of his harness . . . not far enough. He strained forward, dying, and his fingertips touched the octopus on his son's chest. He felt Tad react, pulling away. Galloway's rigid tongue ejected the useless mouthpiece from his lips. His jaw gaped helplessly, grit, sulfur, and water flooding into it in a dark tide. His fingers strained toward the round disk that he just couldn't pull any closer. . . . Then Tad seemed to understand and slid backward, giving him slack, and Tiller got the regulator and got the mouthpiece between his teeth and purged it and sucked, blew, sucked, blew. The cold wind filled him and he sagged back, eyes rolling open and unseeing deep beneath the earth.

Beside him, Tad hesitated, hearing his dad groan as he pulled air through the spare regulator. Tad was shaking, so scared that he'd already had to piss in the suit.

He'd gotten worried, it had seemed so long, and finally he'd decided to suit up and go down and see what it was like. He'd swum around a while, feeling adventurous in the dark, shining the light here and there and chasing the fish. Then he'd seen the tank, and the line going into the cleft. He'd looked at his watch then and known that something was wrong.

So he'd gone on in. He hadn't gotten very far before he realized he wasn't ready for this; there was no way out if you screwed up or got scared. But he was afraid to go back, too. So he'd just kept going, through places that got narrower and narrower, and he'd gotten more and more scared. But he made himself keep on. . . .

And then he'd reached the rockfall, and heard the scraping and bubbling from up ahead.

Now he lay listening to his father breathe and wondered what in the hell he was going to do next. If only he'd thought to bring the other tank, the one outside that first crack, he could leave it with his father and go for help. But all he had was the one tank he'd come with himself. And he had to leave soon, or there wouldn't be enough for him to get back on, especially with two of them breathing on it.

His dad seemed to be caught in a cave-in. Tad had tried to free him by going in headfirst along his leg. There was a huge rock—he could feel it—lying right across his father's lap and legs. Way too heavy to lift. Then Tiller had gone after his spare, and just about pulled it out by the roots. Tad got his light around and checked his tank gauge. Had to hold it real close to read it in the black-brown murk. Was horrified to see it had less than 1,000 psi.

He had to get out of here. But he couldn't leave his dad without anything to breathe.

He lay there for a couple of seconds, thinking hard.

Finally, he backed up till his face was right next to his dad's. He felt around the harness, finally reaching what he wanted: the mouthpiece you used to inflate it if the power inflator didn't work. He tapped it against his father's face, then grabbed the regulator and tugged at it gently.

He felt his father's head nod under his hands. He gave him a quick hug and let go, backing off a few inches, though they were still bound by the umbilical of the octopus whip.

Galloway didn't understand what was going on. He was dazed, pretty far out of it from the nitrogen, he figured, and from the CO_2 buildup, and from the cold. He didn't understand why Tad wanted him to inflate his wings. But he was willing to go along. So he set to work. Without air in his tanks, there was no way to power-inflate. So he had to take a breath off Tad's octopus, remove it from his mouth, replace it with the inflator mouthpiece, and breathe out. Then replace it with the regulator, get another breath, blow it into the wings.

Gradually, the bladders grew rigid, straining against his chest and his harness. He half-twisted his head. Okay, that was done. What—

Without warning, the regulator was jerked suddenly from his mouth. He strangled, swallowing water. His flailing hands banged into rock, groped backward, but found nothing but the soft, treacherous giving of sand. His hands reached after his son, but they felt nothing but rock. They came back and roved aimlessly about his chest. They fastened on the inflator mouth-

156

piece, then put it between his lips, out of despair more than hope.

He lay totally motionless, breathing slowly from the few swallows of air in his wings.

Tad swam back as fast as he could, pulling himself along the line, kicking up huge clouds of silt that traveled with him and blotted out everything from sight. His light dragged in the silt, bounced off the rock.

He figured he had about five minutes, maybe less, before Tiller ran out of air.

He moved as quickly as he could through the reticulation of parallel tunnels, through the big chamber, through the string of rooms connected with tiny entrances. His valves clanged on rock as he shoved himself through. Then finning fast through the round passage, rising now, feeling something ease off his heart as he lifted past forty feet. Then into the restrictions, one after the other, and again visibility vanished. The powdery stone kicked up like a white storm in the already-murky water. Sucking desperately for air, he blundered into the soft shit on the walls and knocked it down; he slammed into stone every time the line was tied off. He bit down on his mouthpiece and kept going until he slithered through the last tight gut and felt the hard flat pressdown of the lips, the bubbling, rattling pebbles beneath his hands. He slacked his grip on the line and the current grabbed him and shoved him through and he was out in the underground stream. He swept his light around, desperately searching the shadows. There was the stage tank. He grabbed it and, before he could think any more, turned round and grabbed the line again and started pulling himself back in, against the current, back to his dad.

Tiller was sliding into the dark, rebreathing the air in the wings over and over as its carbon dioxide level rose. It was rising over him like a dark tide, advancing on him like a moving wall of black ice. Red flickers lightninged over it, outlining its face in scarlet fire. He'd given up on getting himself free by now. He no longer struggled against the pinioning stone. Just lay motionless, panting more and more deeply as the level of his blood oxygen dropped.

When Tad reached him again, his fading consciousness did not even register that his son was there. Tad's hand found his mouth, jerked out the mouthpiece, clumsily and roughly tucking in another.

Fresh oxygen-laden air burst into his lungs, stripping away the

157

black. When he could move, his astonished hand searched down the hose. It met smooth cylindrical steel: the stage tank, nestled against his head.

For a moment, he was grateful beyond anything he'd ever felt. Then he was enraged. Nothing had changed. He was still trapped. He'd already gone past the hard part. Now he'd have to do it all over again when the stage bottle ran out. Why couldn't the kid just let him go? . . . He reached back, groping for Tad, but to his surprise, he was gone again.

His revived mind ran over it all once more, asked whether there was any way out at all. . . . He had the knife. Was it time to start sawing off his leg? . . . But the rock held both legs. He'd die of loss of blood long before he got free. From the one time he'd seen an emergency amputation, it wasn't that easy to get a leg off, either. He was pretty sure it was beyond him.

He was trapped here, that was all, and if Tad had bought him a reprieve, all it meant was that he had a little more time to think.

He lay on his back, shivering uncontrollably with the cold that filled him now as if he were just a thin skin over a core of ice. He breathed shallowly, listening with regret and avarice to every bubble that trickled out of his lips and sailed out and up to percolate away into the rock above.

But where the hell was Tad?

Thirteen

Tad stood bent at the van's rear doors, pulling things out and throwing them to the ground. Finally, he saw what he needed. He grabbed it and was slamming the doors when the green truck turned out of the woods and drove slowly up to the edge of the pit.

When it stopped, the driver rolled down the window and whistled as if to a dog. Tad stood still, watching him. The Park Service officer was in the same green uniform he'd worn when the bastard had hassled him at the park. But now a scoped rifle was racked in the pickup's back window.

"Gate was unlocked," Ferebie called. "Doin' some diving?" Tad nodded wordlessly.

"Where's your dad, boy?"

"He's down there. I have to take him some more air."

"What, he in trouble? I need to call for help?"

For a moment, he wondered if it was what he ought to do—get some other divers. . . . Then he looked at Ferebie's casual, arrogant slump and knew exactly what his dad would say.

"We'll take care of it ourselves," he said. "Look, I got to go, all right? You gonna be here when he comes up?"

"Nah, I got to go over to Steinhatchee an' help look for a panther tore some woman up. But you tell him I'm still looking for something from him. All right?"

"For what?"

"Just tell him that I'm still looking for something from him. But

159

I'm not going to wait much longer. Or the only place he's going to be able to dive is in that smelly shithole he's got here." Ferebie jerked his head toward the pit, then rolled up the window. The engine snorted, and the truck backed, turned, and headed in a plume of dust past the sheds and down the road and into the woods, back toward the highway.

As soon as it was out of sight, Tad turned and ran for the steps, sweat and water squishing in the booties of his wet suit.

Tiller lay with open eyes in the darkness, staring up through water that had finally become almost clear. His primary light had faded to a dull, unilluminating spark and then to black, but he'd pulled out his backup. If he switched it on, he could see the granular fissured rock above his face. He was used to being without a mask now. It seemed kind of appropriate, to die without being able to see clearly.

Because that was pretty much the way he'd spent his life.

No, don't go through all that again. There was no point torturing himself anymore. He'd already gone out once thinking this was it, the end. So in a way, this was kind of an afterlife already. Not that he could do anything different . . . just lie here . . . but he didn't want to think anymore. Besides, he was cold. Couldn't feel anything below his navel; the steady pressure of the rock had cut off all the blood to his legs. Even if he got out . . .

But he wasn't going to get out.

He lay motionless on his back and let the air bleed slowly into his lungs from the stage tank. Held it for a few seconds, milking every molecule of oxygen he could, then let it trickle away. Had to stop thinking about that, too, about where he was and how soon the end would come. Think about something else, anything else. . . .

Such as what in the hell Bud had been doing back here. He could see how at first Kusczk might have thought the place had some appeal, at least to advanced divers. That would have been the right approach, market it as the cavers' hell, the toughest mother there was, the way they pushed roller coasters. But there had to be something at the end, some reward. Otherwise, who would come back, or send his buddies? He had his suspicions about cave divers, but he didn't think they were actual masochists. Diving Tartar Springs was like diving a damn sewer system, and dangerous to boot: a killer cave, just like they said. . . . Your liability premiums alone would eat up whatever you got from admission fees.

He was still thinking about that when he heard again the scrape and rumble of an approaching diver. Tad again? He hoped not. God, he hoped not. . . . Couldn't the kid leave him in peace to die?

Tad was shuddering, gulping air so hard, his regulator felt as if it was going to stop dead. The second time back through the tunnel had been almost more than he could take. This third trip was a nightmare, and he sobbed into his regulator as he made himself go on, deeper and deeper. Once, he lost track of the line. It was buried under the silt, which they'd stirred up so much that there were long passages where he couldn't see anything at all beyond his faceplate except the brown milling murk, glowing from his light. He groped frantically around for it, hearing a strange high whine growing in his throat, convinced he was lost, that he was never going to make it out.

But at last, he found it again. He forced himself to keep going, and finally he made it back to the breakdown, where his father lay on his back with his hands outstretched. That was what he saw first: the hands, sticking out from the soft sand and muck as if his dad was buried, which he was.

This was his last chance to get him out, and he wasn't sure it would work.

He grabbed one of the hands and after a moment it squeezed back. He was still alive, then. He let go and started digging.

The stuff was sand and silt, but with rocks buried in it, like Chunky Monkey ice cream. When he hit one, he pulled it back under his chest and wormed himself a couple more inches forward into where it had been. At first, his head was beside his dad's, under the same rock surface, only facing down, of course. But gradually, he worked his way in till he was level with his father's chest, and then his waist. That was the way he'd tried to get him out at first, but he hadn't been able to budge the chunk of rock that pressed down on his father.

Halfway there, he felt something soft in the dirt and rock. He was about to push it back, too, when his fingers recognized it. A mask. He thrust it under his chin, holding it, and kept digging.

Finally, he got to the biggest rock. He touched it lightly, with his fingers held above his head. If it gave way now, it would pin him headfirst. Then he heard bubbles rumbling from behind him—his dad breathing—and knew this was going to be it. He couldn't come back here again. Even if he could, his father would be dead by then.

He began digging, scooping dirt and stones back from underneath it and flinging them back under his body like a frenzied dog. He hoped there wasn't more getting ready to fall off the ceiling. He heard a groan from his father as the rock sagged another inch. Shit, it was lying right on the back of his neck. God, he wanted out of here, *out of here* . . . but he made himself stay and scoop the last armload of broken rock out, leaving a gap the size of a football under the rock plate.

Then he twisted backward, fumbling at his waist. He unclipped the heavy chunk of steel he'd dragged in, after leaving his weight belt back on the steps.

He fumbled the jack from the van into position and groped again in his harness for the steel rod that formed the handle. He pushed his face close to feel it into the socket, then shoved the jack awkwardly in, hoping he was putting it where it would do some good.

Then he started cranking, working the handle up and down. The clank of the ratchet came through the water as clearly as if it were inside his own head.

Beside him, he felt his father's hand groping around. It felt the lever, then ran up it to the jack. He pushed it away impatiently. The old bastard had to stay out of it. If he got his glove or fingers caught in the jack, that was it. Hard enough as it was, with his head and shoulders stuck into this crack, trying to work the damn bar up and down.

The jack stopped; he couldn't move the handle anymore. He stopped, too, puzzled, and thrust both hands in to feel it. The rack was at full extension. The bottom plate was just hanging in the sand. It had driven itself down into the soft bottom without lifting the rock up at all.

Shit, Tad thought. Now what?

He was lying there at a loss when a piece of rock came down and slammed off the side of his skull so hard, he saw the Fourth of July. He scrabbled back, thinking it had come down off the ceiling, that the rest of it was collapsing on them, but then the same chunk slammed down again and he glimpsed his dad's glove powering it. For a second, he didn't understand. Then he did, and he grabbed the flat rock out of his father's hand and wriggled forward again, feeling for the jack, thrusting the flat chunk of breakdown under the base plate.

The ratchet rattled again, and this time he felt it bite down, felt the increased effort it took to rack the handle as it strained against the overlying weight. He lay out full length, putting all his strength into it. Great bursts of air tore from his regulator.

The rock stirred. He cranked on, fearing he'd come to full extension on the jack and still not move the rock enough to help.

Galloway felt it move, too. An oh so slight lessening of the terrible pressure on his legs. He couldn't believe it. He hadn't thought of the jack, in the van. But Tad had. He still didn't think it would be enough, but . . . He stretched backward as far as he could, got a double-handed grip on the line, and pulled with every ounce of freezing, numbed, oxygen-starved muscle he could command.

The jack creaked again, and the rock plate grated and came up another centimeter or so. Tiller hauled again, hearing muscle fibers snap, bones crack in his back.

Something gave way under his shoulders, and he slid a few inches backward and down in a sibilant shower of stones and sand. His thighs scraped the bottom of the rock. He felt it teetering on the jack. Now or never; it could slip any second. He gathered another armful of rope and hauled again, with a last desperate grunting effort. His son let go of the jack and grabbed him and hauled, too, and he came backward and out as the jack tilted over and the rock dropped out of the ceiling and rumbled down onto his fins. He kicked fiercely and felt the strap snap as one tore off, but he didn't care. He was free.

Tad backed away down the tunnel, still hauling on his dad's shoulders. The water was black, full of swirling sand. Rock grit scratched at his mask like a hungry kitten. Mask, yeah. . . . He untangled the one he'd found and felt around for his dad's hand and put it into his palm and closed it over the strap.

Tiller didn't recognize it for a moment. He was preoccupied with his legs. He couldn't move them very well. Couldn't feel much, either. . . . He fitted the mask on clumsily and cleared it. He found his spare light and flicked it on, illuminating a roiling murk that had another glow deep in it somewhere: Tad's.

And something else, white, smooth, triangular . . . something that had been covered by the fallen rock up till now, till he'd slid back over it and uncovered it. . . .

It was one of Bud's line arrows. He fingered it, puzzled, then ran his hand back along the thinner line it was snapped onto and felt the knot where it joined the main guideline.

It was a side line, leading off to the right.

Tad was pulling on his manifold, tugging him back toward the entrance. Galloway kicked experimentally. His legs worked, but he still couldn't feel them. He had to get out. There couldn't be much air left in the stage. Tad had to be close to empty, too. But instead of finning after his son, he doubled himself, sliding his glove out along the thinner line. From a jump reel, it felt like.

He had to get out now. He knew that. Could he be thinking wrong from the fatigue, the CO_2 buildup, narcosis, hypothermia? He paused, then edged out another couple of feet.

Blackness ahead. An opening?

He felt something grab his one remaining fin: Tad's hand. He kicked it away and burrowed forward.

The rocks and sand fell away, and he bored forward through them into open space. His light reached out through the murky dark water along the jump line.

There was another passage beyond the fall, narrow, heading upward. He started to enter it; then an old reflex froze him. His eyes centered in the darkness, and very slowly, he brought the light up. Then he ran it over to the side of the tunnel, along a faint glint, all but invisible in the dark water.

His light and his eye followed it to a piece of white plastic pipe wedged into the rock.

He hung there motionless for several seconds, staring at it, wondering if he was still stuck, still hallucinating. But he didn't seem to be.

He was looking at a simple but very dangerous booby trap. The glint was monofilament line, fishing line, tied off on one side of the passage and run slantwise where a diver would cross. The item inside the pipe—he gingerly shone his light down into it— was a fragmentation grenade.

A diver coming down the tunnel would hit the line, and before he felt much of a tug, would pull the grenade out of the pipe. Then the spoon would fly off, igniting the fuze.

Simple but effective. He'd seen them before, set just like this. In Vietnam.

There wasn't a doubt in his mind that Bud had set it. And made sure it was waterproof, too.

Tad came up beside him and Galloway grabbed him in a bear

hug, immobilizing him. He stared into his son's eyes through the faceplate. Pointed to the glint, then to the grenade. He mimed it coming out, mimed an explosion with his hands.

Tad looked from him back to it. Slowly, he nodded, then jerked his thumb backward over his shoulder. Held up his air gauge.

Galloway hung there, staring toward where the tunnel led away into shadows their lights couldn't penetrate. The tea-stained water ebbed steadily past their faces. He felt his belly quivering. He had to leave. But people didn't set things up like this unless they were protecting something. What had Bud been protecting? Curiosity and fear struggled.

At last, curiosity won. Dropping to the floor, turning on his back, he slid beneath the deadly shine of the trip wire. He glanced back once, to see Tad hovering on the far side of it, watching him. He tapped his watch; held up five fingers; jerked his thumb toward the surface. Tad nodded.

He swim-limped awkwardly down the tunnel, towing the stage bottle after him. The space was oval now and about four feet wide, gradually tending upward. He checked his depth: sixty. The flow was a dark breeze in his face. The rock walls were smooth and dark as melted pitch. The jump line lay on the floor, slack, apparently unattached to anything. Or perhaps whatever it was made fast to at the downstream end had given way in the breakdown.

Then he saw light.

It was so unexpected, he didn't believe it. He put his hand over his spare, masking its beam, to make sure. There it was, a faint radiance ahead. He swam a little faster, sweeping his eyes from side to side. Where there was one booby trap, there might be more.

The ceiling lifted above his head, and he followed the line up into it.

Without any warning, his head broke the surface.

Suddenly, he had the mouthpiece out and was breathing air, real air—fetid and sulfurous but real, and as much of it as he could cram into his aching lungs. The crevice he was in stretched far above his head. Up there were little cracks of white light. They didn't look large enough for anything larger than a mouse, but it was sunlight and this was air he was breathing. He was in a syphon, a pocket beneath the ground. So he had to be on the far side of the river now.

He swept the light around and saw behind him where there

165

had once been another passage, cut by the flow back when the water table was higher. Now it was air-filled. He grabbed the lip and hauled himself up into it and looked around the chamber. It was narrow and high, and dim in the faint light falling from above. He was sitting on damp sand, and as his eyes adapted, he saw that he wasn't the first one here.

The litter of plastic Baggies, the twist ties and broken rubber bands and empty cardboard circles from rolls of electrical tape, the row of rusted and probably empty tanks against the far wall—they all told the story, if you knew the language.

It was a drug cache.

Or rather, it had been once, because now the plastic wrappings were empty and the twist ties that littered the sand were rusty red. Either Bud or somebody else had cleaned it out, probably a long time ago. He looked at the tanks, thinking, Yeah, and maybe they're booby-trapped, too. Better leave them alone.

He remembered Tad; his son was waiting; he had to get back before his five minutes ran out. But at the same time, he felt a menace here. Maybe it was the grenade that made his gut so tight. Or maybe it was the memory of when he'd smuggled the same stuff himself. Or maybe it was just that he'd expected to be dead by now and hadn't come to terms with the fact he was still breathing. But his head was definitely someplace else.

Back in the Rung Sat Special Zone . . . remembering the sullen villagers, the low hootches, the caches for weapons and ammo and rice the VC used to dig under the pigpens, where they thought the Americans would be too fastidious to investigate. . . .

Pulling out his knife, he slid it into the mud floor. Probing carefully with it, the way he'd once used a bayonet to search for buried mines.

There was something down there. It wasn't more sand, and it wasn't rock, either. He laid the knife aside and scraped the damp, sticky earth away with his hands, noticing only then how bloody and torn they were.

It came up reluctantly, and he dipped up water and dribbled it over it to get some of the mud off. His light revealed heavy green canvas, a rusty steel hasp, a rusty padlock, sealing the mouth of an Army-style duffel bag.

He had to leave. He was putting Tad at risk with every second he spent here. But he couldn't leave without finding out what Bud had thought was so valuable, so important, that he'd hidden it all

166

the way back here and set at least one deadly trap to protect it. He looked around. Reached out for a rock. Then put the padlock on it and smashed it a couple of times with his stage tank, grunting as he lifted it. The lock broke on the third blow and he unhooked it, tore the bag open, and shone the light in.

The next moment, cursing in disbelief, he was hauling out handfuls of gear.

He'd expected drugs, cash, something valuable . . . but the duffel was filled with diving equipment. Then he looked again. The diving lights had broken lenses, missing bulbs; the masks were cracked; the weights were on frayed belts with broken buckles. The regulator housings were stripped, the valves corroded and missing parts. It was filled with *junk*. He stared at it lying on the mud, and felt like clutching his head and screaming. Then he saw something else deep inside and thrust his hand in again. More weights, the plastic-coated kind . . . and lying amid them, a waterproof Ziploc with something small and flat in it.

He held it up to the faint light, squinting; approximately a three-by-three object, light, square, wrapped and taped tightly in black plastic.

It was long past time to go. He was shaking with hypothermia; he was going to have to decompress when he got back to the entrance. He was asking for the bends right now just sitting here. He looked up at the daylight, unwilling to leave it behind. But he had to; he couldn't get up those sheer walls. Then he looked at the useless gear. What in the hell had been in Bud's head, to hide and bury worthless shit like this?

Finally, he shoved everything except the square packet back into the duffel, snapped it shut, and scooped the muck back over it. He unzipped his wet suit and tucked the flat package next to his chest. Then he peered at his pressure gauge. He'd have to skip-breathe, stretch it like he'd never stretched air before if he was going to make it.

Thrusting the regulator back into his mouth, he slid into the black pool at his feet.

With unutterable relief, Tad saw the probing star of his father's light at the far end of the passage. He'd watched the hand of his watch go around seven times, had been on the edge of turning and bolting. But now his dad was coming back.

As soon as he came into sight, Tad pointed at the trip wire, just to make sure he remembered. Then he turned and finned downward again. It was quite a distance to the entrance, but the flow was behind them.

Tiller, following his son, was breathing as slowly as he'd ever breathed, holding each breath, counting five, releasing it slowly. As he swam, he tried not to think about how much he needed air. Instead, he mused about what he'd just discovered.

Kusczk had used the caves beneath Tartar Springs as the perfect hiding place. It was a terrific cache. Safe from police or sniffer dogs. No casual passerby could stumble over it. But then someone had killed him, and presumably *they* had taken whatever had been in there and replaced it with useless junk as some sort of laborious joke. Unless somehow it had served as ballast; most of it was solid metal, valve housings and weights and such.

Why?

And what had Bud originally hidden there?

He puzzled over it as they moved with controlled haste through the underground maze, passing under the river, then slowly drawing closer to the subterranean stream that passed through the Tartar Caves.

But abstemious as he was, he ran out of air in the final narrow passage before the lips. He thrashed after Tad, trying to reach him, but the boy's fins snipped like black scissors just out of reach. With only one fin, he couldn't catch him. So he set his teeth and held his breath and swallowed again and again and at last shot, scraping, through the entrance. He slammed his head on the overhead, but a moment later burst up into black air. A few seconds later he was hauling himself up the slick, slimy concrete steps on all fours, trying not to vomit with relief and reaction.

Tad ran him back another tank from the van and he went right back in and spent an hour doing his thirty-foot, twenty-foot, and ten-foot deco stops. Tad loaded their gear, too; Tiller was too weak to help much. When they got back to the highway, he pulled the van into a Texaco. He left Tad pumping gas while he got an icy Hires out of a machine and drank it, then fumbled quarters in for another. When the sugar kicked in and he felt a little less shaky, he went over to a phone booth, shielding the ear away from the phone against the roar of passing traffic. Then he tapped in the number he'd copied off the FOR SALE sign back at the grotto.

Five rings, six. Shoot, maybe no one was there, it was almost lunchtime . . . A male voice answered on the seventh ring, impatient and hoarse. "Arkin and Laughton. Tim Arkin here."

He almost hung up, hearing the voice of the attorney he'd knocked into the river at the Apalachee Lodge. But he held on. "Uh . . . hi. I'm calling about the Tartar Springs property. Understand you're representing that? It still for sale?"

"Thanks for your interest, but we've accepted an offer on that property already. A few things to work out before the closing, but I think it'll go through. So thanks for your—"

"You have? The sign's still up, out here at the property."

"Sorry, that should have been taken down. . . . Say, haven't we met? To whom am I speaking?"

He hesitated again. "Tiller Galloway."

The voice sharpened. "Mr. *Galloway*. I thought I recognized that voice."

Tiller cleared his throat. "Look, maybe I overreacted the other night—"

"Think so? Do you know how close you came to crushing my larynx?"

"But you got to admit, cap'n, you let your mouth get away with you. So I don't figure I got anything to apologize for, except hitting you in the throat when I was aiming at your jaw. You want a rematch, be happy to fix it up."

"We don't all operate on your level, Galloway. We thought about an assault charge very seriously over here. It's only because Monica asked me to that I finally decided to overlook it."

"Who's buying the property, Arkin?"

"A private buyer."

"Who?"

"That's privileged."

"Must be real privileged if you're not even bothering to follow up a possible backup offer."

"It is. A very special buyer. One who will turn around and transfer it to the state to become part of the Styx River Water-Management System, preserving the natural beauty and unique ecology of the river and its springs for everyone who loves wild Florida."

Tiller held the phone, thinking.

Bud had bought the property, hoping to develop it for divers. He hadn't wanted to sell it. *Monica* hated it. She'd wanted to sell it. And now it was being sold. And maybe it was unfair, but whenever he heard a lawyer talk about anything the way Arkin was talking about preserving the springs, he got suspicious.

"Hello? Galloway, you there?"

He hung up slowly and turned to look toward where Tad stood by the van, transfixed by two teenaged girls in totally inadequate white shorts who were walking toward a Corvette.

He didn't want to think the thought that had surfaced in his mind like some scaly creature rising from black depths.

He touched the flat square through the fabric of his pocket—the package he'd found in the duffel. When he'd stripped the Baggie and the taped black plastic off, he found the flat wafer of a computer microdisk underneath. There were still a couple of layers of transparent wrapping to go, but he could read the label. STYX.AQR, BACKUP. The same file name he'd found in Bud's computer, but the contents of the file had been deleted from his hard drive.

Maybe now there would be some answers.

FOURTEEN

They didn't break any speed records driving back north. He still had the shakes, and his back felt as if someone had done acupuncture on it with a cold chisel and maul. They stopped for dinner in Waukeenah, fried ham and greens and corn bread, and it was after dark when they got back to Tallahassee. Then Tad asked to be dropped at Ripper's; they were going to catch a movie. Tiller had no choice but to agree, not after what Tad had done for him that day.

With mixed feelings, he watched the boy stroll off toward a mobile home ringed with rusty cars and recumbent washing machines. He'd been having a lot of those feelings since becoming a dad again. But Tad had done damned good down there when the going got tough, risking his life for a father who was, after all, still half a stranger. So that Tiller, alive when he hadn't expected to be, pulled in to the driveway of Monica's house feeling better than he had in a long time. He didn't see the Land Rover in the drive or the garage. She must be out. Okay, fine, he didn't feel like facing her right now, given what he was starting to suspect. He let himself in with his key. Then froze, there in the hallway.

The hall carpet had been torn up and flung against the wall. Through the french doors to the living room, he saw that every book and tape and CD had been torn out of the racks of the entertainment center. Sofa and chair cushions had been ripped apart, spilling their guts and joining the piles of knickknacks and pictures that littered the floor.

171

He ducked instinctively, fading toward the wall, and stepped out of his shoes. He slipped silently down the hall.

The dining room looked as if it had taken a ninety-degree roll in a storm; broken plates, smashed glass in the beautiful Queen Anne hutch, the table upended and the leaves torn out. Through the door to the kitchen, he saw that every box of cereal or crackers, every bottle of sauce or spice had been ripped out of the cupboards. The open refrigerator's light shone like a cold beacon. The compressor throbbed, curling white frost smoke out into the air.

He hunched, listening to the house. Nothing . . . but he couldn't be sure. At first, he didn't see how they'd gotten in. Then he did: the slashed screen back in the sunroom. Anger curled his fingers. The bastards couldn't just come in and take what they could sell. They had to destroy everything, ruin everything.

He looked around for a weapon, then remembered Bud's rifle, upstairs, in the closet of Tad's room. He slid around the corner to the back stairs—carpeted, shadowy. He paused, listening to the house. Nothing but the steady *om* of air conditioning. Shit, he thought, they must have heard me drive in. Either they were already gone . . . or they were waiting, listening, just as he waited and listened.

He eased himself onto the first step and paused again, then went softly on up the narrow back staircase. The carpeting muted his stockinged footsteps to a whisper. The throb of the fridge faded behind him. He turned the corner and stood at the upstairs landing. Listening again, he heard only the sigh of air through ductwork and out the registers. The distant mechanical grumble of the air handler. Tad's bedroom door was five steps down the hall. He still didn't hear anything. Maybe they were already gone.

He was standing there, tensing himself for the dash, when the pistol barrel jammed itself up under his jaw. He could tell it was a barrel because it was steel-cold. He could hear its owner breathing, though he couldn't turn his head.

"So, Mr. Galloway, we meet at last."

"Yeah?" he grunted.

"You thieving asshole. I think I shoot you here, leave your brains all over this pretty carpet."

The voice was almost familiar . . . almost. Then it wasn't. But it didn't seem to belong to who he'd expected: a street punk, a burglar.

"Where is it?"

"Uh . . ."

The barrel jammed in tighter, right under his ear. He swallowed, then finally managed to say, "Hey, if you want to tell me what you're looking for, maybe I—"

The barrel left his throat, but he had no time for appreciation before it came down on his head so hard that he dropped to his hands and knees, blinking at strobes popping inside his head. His reflexes started to roll him down the staircase, but he caught them. All the guy had to do was step around the corner, aim down, and put a bullet into him as he rolled. So he just stayed hunkered, blinking at expensive huaraches of Italian braided leather. The bare toes inside them were dark and gnarled. He listened to labored breathing above him.

Suddenly, he placed the voice. It was the guy who'd called the office at Scuba Florida, the one who'd asked for Bud.

He grunted, "You called me at the office—when I told you he was dead."

"You remember."

"I remember that. I remember you wouldn't tell me what you wanted."

"Where's the safe?"

"Uh, the safe . . . I don't know if there's a safe here—"

His body convulsed as a sandal slammed up under his breastbone. It was never a good sign when the son of a bitch who was working you over knew exactly where to kick people. When he got a little breath back, he pushed himself shakily off the carpet. "Hey . . . mind if I get up? If we're gonna have a long conversation?"

"We're not having any conversations. All we going to do, you are going to tell me where the safe is. Then we are going to open it."

"Sure, great, but I got to tell you up front, I don't know if there's a safe or where it is, all right?"

He felt the barrel pressed against the back of his neck. "You are sure of that," the voice said.

"No," he said, sweat wringing out suddenly over his whole body. "Wait. Okay, you win. One safe, coming up."

The muzzle left his neck and the sandals moved back. "Get up."

He hesitated, then hoisted himself. Funny, he knew his back should feel like hell, but right now it didn't hurt at all. The magic of endorphins. He was sure using air fast, though. He sucked a deep one, risking a quick glance at the man who stood in the darkened hall.

173

He was dressed casually in rather baggy pleated linen slacks and a too-large pale green silk shirt with a little sailboat embroidered on the breast. Plenty of room in that outfit to conceal the big stainless Ruger automatic he was holding at waist level, pointed at Galloway's navel. He called it as a .40, plenty of gun to take a man down with one hit. Anybody in Florida could get a concealed-carry permit, but he doubted this guy had bothered to fill out the forms. He stared at the shadowed face. Dark hair, brown eyes, and a stiff little goatee beard. Gold glittered at both ears and at the vee of the shirt, and there was more on the hand with the gun.

"Okay, show it to me. Upstairs or downstairs?"

"Upstairs."

"Which room?"

"Uh, this next one. To the left."

Which was Tad's room. Not much of a chance. He needed a distraction. But where was it going to come from? The gun waved, though, and he had to move. He sidled down the hall, half-turned at the door. "So, you knew Bud?"

"I knew him."

"Close friends?"

"Shut up. Show me the safe."

He wished he could. Hell of it was, there might even be one somewhere in the house. But if this lad, who looked like a pro, couldn't find it, Tiller doubted he could come up with it simply by guessing.

Tad's room was a mess—clothes all over, backpack a gaping frog mouth on the floor, spewing batteries and Oh! Henry wrappers; plates under the bed, underwear flung against the wall. It smelled rank. . . . He jerked his head back to where he was, with an armed thug behind him and about five seconds left to figure out some way to get through this alive. Behind him, the guy said, sounding suspicious, "Why here? The safe, it's usually in the master bedroom."

"Fooled you, didn't it?"

"All right. So where is it?"

He pointed to the louvered doors of the closet. "Uh, one thing."

"Open it."

"I said, one thing. You know where Bud and I met?"

"I don't give a shit. Open the safe or I'll blow you away right now and open it myself."

"I don't think you want to try that. Bud and I were in Vietnam together—"

"So what? *Open the safe!*"

He turned, getting angry himself. "Look, *cholo*, you want to kill us both, just keep yelling like that, all right? I'm trying to save both our lives here."

"What are you talking about?"

"Bud was a SEAL. We were in Vietnam together. Monica showed me where the safe is, but she hasn't opened it yet. She's afraid to. See, he liked to set booby traps."

"Booby traps?"

"Little surprises that blow up when somebody tries to screw with them. You know, wires, explosives, shit like that. Get the picture? Now, you want me to open this thing. And by God I'm going to try. But what I'm tryin' to get across to you is, once I open this closet door, if I touch the wrong thing, if I guess wrong—"

The gun didn't waver, nor did the eyes. For a second he was afraid the bastard wasn't going to buy it. But then he took a step back, then another, till he was out in the hallway again, pointing the gun through the open door.

"Okay," he said. "Now open it."

Tiller nodded. He stared at the wall switch to the left of the closet, bit his lips as if psyching himself up. Then he reached out slowly, hesitated, and clicked it on.

Light shone through the louvers.

He bent at the knees and unlatched the door and eased it open, very slowly. Ran his eyes and then his fingers up the shelves, making a production out of it.

Inside, the stock and trigger guard of the SKS came into view.

He reached out very slowly, then withdrew his hand. He said over his shoulder, "Oh, boy. There's a wire here."

"A wire?"

"I don't see what it's connected to. The safe's here, but the wire disappears inside it."

"Open the safe."

"I'm getting to that, okay? Look, you want to come in here, do this yourself?"

No answer, so he took that as a no. He turned back to the closet, to the rifle. Tad must have put it back just the way he found it. It was hanging from a top shelf by its front sight, back behind some woman's coats. The closet smelled of mothballs and the murky liquid in the Damp Rid canister on the floor. He ran his hand through his hair and it came out wet. He didn't have to fake being nervous. If this didn't work, he was dead. He wiped his palm on his shorts and rubbed his mouth, then reached out slowly.

"Grenade!" he yelled, and dropped. With the same movement, he yanked the rifle down, slammed the action closed, and rolled, coming up to face the open hallway door. Just as he'd hoped, it outlined emptiness. He crouched as a second went by, then another.

Like an emerging moon, the guy's face showed at one corner of the jamb. Tiller swayed the front sight a quarter inch, till the post, inside its round protective hood, rested where his heart would be behind the wall.

"April fool," he said. "*Nada grenada*. Let's have the gun."

"You lose," said the guy, and running his eye down the jamb, Tiller saw the pistol pointed straight at him.

They stood there for a couple of beats. Finally, he said, "So."

"Is there a safe there? There is no safe."

"I told you, I don't know where it is. You decided not to believe me."

"I can shoot you."

"And I can shoot you. Or, we can just part as friends," Tiller said. "Unless you want to talk about it first. 'Cause if you had some business with Bud, like you said . . . well, I'd like to know more about it."

The automatic was rock-steady, braced against the jamb. "What the hell you want to know?"

"Who I'm dealing with, for starters."

The guy still had just his face visible. The rest of his body was behind the wall. But Tiller figured the full-metal-jacketed rifle bullet would go through plasterboard, even a couple inches of wood, no problem. On the other hand, he himself was pretty much out in the open. At nine feet, neither of them was likely to miss. It was kind of a mutual assured destruction situation. Well, it was still better than it had been two minutes before. And like the NRA was always saying, an armed society was a polite society.

The guy said reluctantly, "I'm Sergio Dugan."

"Tiller Galloway. Now, what's your business with Bud?"

"Business."

"Drug business?"

"What other kind is there?"

Tiller considered asking him if he worked for Nuñez, then decided not to. If they hadn't made the connection between the Galloway who was taking over Scuba Florida and Galloway the former smuggler, he sure as hell wasn't going to outline it in yellow Hi-Liter for them. And they might well not have made the connection. The lower on the feeding chain you were, the faster the turnover. The cops took the street dealers; the bosses ruled for decades. This Dugan probably had been a thirteen-year-old running errands in the streets of Medellín when Galloway had been running boatloads out of the Golfo Triste. There was no reason he should recognize his name.

Another point on his side was what he'd been reading in the papers. The Colombian government was finally starting to move against the head traffickers. Nuñez and the other lords were fighting for their freedom, even their lives. By the same token, that meant they needed to keep the lawyers, money, and guns coming.

So if Dugan was a distributor, on whatever level, his overwhelming priority would be to reestablish whatever connection Bud's death had broken.

"Your move," Tiller told him. "Tell me what you want."

"Kusczk had my money. I want it back."

"Oh yeah? How much?"

"How much? A mil and a half."

"A million and a—that's a lot to trust a guy for. What was he doing for you?"

"Hell with that. Give me the cash, I let you live. You got a gun on me now? Great. You gonna walk around with it the rest of your life?"

"Maybe."

Dugan turned his head and spat on the carpet. "It costs me a thousand to have you made. Hire a local, a lot less. Don't think 'cause you got a gun on me now you walk. You go around the corner, we pop you tomorrow. And the woman. And the kid. Or maybe we pop them first, show you we mean business."

Tiller didn't bother doubting him. He'd seen how the Organization worked first hand. Compared to the Colombians, the Mafia was a widows' and orphans' benevolent society. He'd been alcohol-bombed by a thug just like this. He'd seen the bodies, guys who got a silenced .22 in the back of the head. These days, they favored submachine guns in parking lots. Less subtle, but the principle was the same.

He had to deal. There was no other way.

177

"So. You understand me?" Dugan asked him. Galloway nodded. He swallowed.

"I think we can do business," he said.

Dugan hoisted the pistol, dropped the hammer. He lifted his shirt and tucked it into his slacks. For the first time, he smiled. It made his goatee twitch. Tiller watched it, fascinated.

"Let's go downstairs," he said.

They sat in the trashed sunroom, on wicker chairs they'd set back up. Dugan held a glass of scotch, Tiller a much-needed straight bourbon. The rifle leaned in the corner. He felt better with it in reach. He lifted his glass to Dugan. The other just stared at him. Tiller drank it all, fast. He needed it to fill up the hole that was left when every hope he'd ever had of getting free of people like this forever had dropped away. The alcohol burned its way down and he poured himself another, right away.

"To business," he said.

"No, not to business. Not yet. First I need the million and a half."

Very briefly, he remembered the damp canvas bag that lay buried at the end of the Tartar Springs cave. Had it once held what Dugan was talking about? He had a nagging suspicion it had. If he was right about that, whoever had killed Bud had it now.

He thought briefly of telling Dugan this. There were three problems with doing that, though. The first was Dugan had no reason to believe him. He'd never seen the cache or the duffel, and unless he was a world-class cave diver, he never would. The second was that if he told what he knew, and Dugan found out who had the money before he did, he wouldn't need Lyle Galloway anymore. Not a good situation to be in. And the third reason was that he just plain didn't feel like telling the son of a bitch anything.

It was risky. But he didn't seem to have a better game plan at the moment than to play for time and hope he found Bud's killer and this missing cash before everything went to shit.

So now he said, "Look, I told you I don't know anything about any money Kusczk had. All I know about is his diving business, okay? That's what I'm running and that's all I know about."

"You take over his business?"

"Yeah."

"All right, fine. Then you're on the hook for what he owed me."

"I can't work with you on that basis, Mr. Dugan. Sorry."

"It's a simple choice. You do business with us or you don't. It don't make any difference to me which one you pick."

"I already told you, I think we can do business. But you have to tell me exactly what we got going here if I'm gonna be any good to you. You got to trust me a little bit. But I'll tell you one thing: I'm not going to start out that far in the goddamn hole."

"You work for me, that's how you start."

"Well . . . look. Tell me what I'm getting into here."

"I give it to Bud. He moves it. He pays off the people he needs to. I don't know who, probably the county sheriff, the cops—"

"I know about the Park Service. The guy came to me with his hand out."

"The Park Service?" Dugan looked blank.

"Well, never mind. Who else?"

"I told you, whoever he had to. Then he moved what he had to move."

"I get it, but look, I don't know what his distribution was. I don't know who he sold to or how."

Dugan took a drink. He looked at Tiller over the glass. Then he set it down on the Mexican tile.

"I'll be right back," he said.

Galloway stood by the door, waiting. He didn't see where Dugan had gone, but he was back in no more than four or five minutes. He carried a black sample case, the kind you carried files in. Tiller held the door for him. Dugan put the case on the floor, unlocked it.

"There it is," he said. "Move it. And you live. Otherwise—well, we talked about that."

He'd expected cocaine, the plastic-wrapped bricks. His stomach had been churning, the bad old excitement rising. He stared down instead at what it really held.

A solid block of money.

Dugan's voice came in like a badly tuned channel. He was saying, "The problem is not distribution. We have an excellent distribution system. The problem is getting money out of the country. It used to be easy. We would fly the product in, and the flight back, we would fly cash out. A small plane carries three hundred and fifty kilos; you take back five or six million dollars. Or we would just take it to a bank and wire it to Panama. But now there's air interdiction, we can't fly so easy. And the funds transfer—the federals monitor that now. The banks report all large transactions.

The product still comes in. I won't tell you how, but it comes. Because of the interdiction, the price actually goes up. We can't lose; the less there is on the market, the more we charge on the street. But now we got the problem—how do we get our profits out?

"Kusczk handled that for us. He cleaned the money up and shipped it out of the country. It went into overseas accounts and then back to Cali. I will write down on this catalog the number and bank of the final account it goes into. For this, Kusczk received a fee. He kept one-tenth of the cash and passed through the other nine-tenths. You take over, you get the same cut."

Galloway swallowed, staring at the rows of Andy Jacksons and Ben Franklins. It was clear now. All too clear.

Bud had been in the business, all right. But not as a distributor, like he'd thought, seeing the remnants scattered around the cache.

He'd been handling the cash side.

"Uh, do you know . . . do you know how he got it out of the country?"

"No, I don't," said Dugan. "He never told me, and that was smart, that was right. It must be very good. The monthly gross, it is hundreds of pounds of bills. But you'd better find out." He stood, dusting his slacks, and Tiller caught for just a moment the print of the automatic through silk. Then he reached down into the case again and held out a pad.

Galloway stared at it. "What the hell's this?"

"What does it look like? It's a receipt."

"You want a *receipt*?"

"That's right," said Dugan. "Both our *cojones* are on the line for this money. You cover me, I cover you, enough to get you some time to earn it back. Understand, *compadre*?"

He was about to sign it when he saw the amount. He said slowly, "There's not two million dollars here."

"That's right. That's only five hundred thou."

"You're asking me to sign for everything he was into you for, too. That ain't right."

"No, it ain't right," said Dugan. "And, you know? There's not much about this business that is. But you are inheriting it. You are taking over a going operation. That's your buy-in, that. Or do you not like this business opportunity I am offering you?"

Galloway took a deep breath, then signed it, noticing how his palms left dark prints on the cheap pulp paper of the dime-store

Rediform sales book. He waited till Dugan tore off his copy and handed it to him. "Uh, two more questions."

"No more questions."

"What's the throughput gonna be on this? I mean, how much is there gonna be coming through a month, a year? I got to know, to plan how to do it."

"Bud put through forty-nine million, three hundred and fifty thousand dollars last year," Dugan told him. "We need to do at least that much this year, and I hope more. Ten percent of what you move is yours. So if you work hard, you see you can pay back this amount you owe very quickly. After that, you are making money."

"One other thing."

"What?"

"Bud. I think—he didn't die by accident. Somebody killed him."

"Yes?" Dugan's head came up. "Who?"

"I don't know. I was wondering if it was you."

The goateed man laughed. "We did not kill Mr. Kusczk. We needed Mr. Kusczk. That should be obvious to you. No other questions? Well, I will be going now."

"Uh, where can I get in touch?"

"You don't. I get in touch with you. *Hasta luego—compadre.*"

Galloway stood motionless as Dugan let himself out, into the whispering night. Then he sat down, all at once, beside the case. His legs were that weak. Shit, that had been close. He was surprised the guy had talked, even faced with a rifle. They usually didn't; they just killed you.

He looked at the case. Acting on its own, his hand picked up a sheaf of bills, held it to the light, ran a thumbnail along the edge.

Cash—a lot of it. Wrung from every drug deal in Florida. The payoff from all the misery and crime coke and crack and Colombian heroin caused. In the eyes of the law, it was their equivalent.

If he got caught with it, that meant money laundering, tax evasion, trafficking, currency smuggling, and racketeering charges. As a repeat offender, he'd die in prison. And the government would seize everything Monica owned.

But if he didn't move it, and more behind it, Dugan or his employees would kill him. Those weren't empty threats, about killing Tad and Monica, too.

He didn't want this. He'd taken five years in prison and kept his mouth shut. He'd never flipped or even let himself think of it; he'd kept his part of the bargain: silence or death. But he wanted out, he wanted *out*. He'd told Nuñez that to his face. "What is it gonna *take* to get these assholes off my back?" he muttered.

Slowly, he snapped the case shut and hefted it, then glanced back inside the house. He'd better get busy picking up. He didn't want Monica seeing this, wondering why the place was a wreck.

In the garden, a shadow stood motionless amid the trees. From out here in the darkness, everything, every movement and gesture, had been visible through the full-length windows of the sunroom.

Tad Galloway stood in silence, thinking about what he'd just seen.

FIFTEEN

H ey, everybody. Morning, July."

"Oh . . . hi." But the second she said it, lifting her face from something lying on the counter, he felt disaster in the air. Like the *Challenger,* or Oklahoma City. The faces of the other divers reading over her shoulder only confirmed it. He set the case down and said, "What is it?"

Without a word, she held up the front page of the *Democrat,* and there was a picture of Lamont Exmore in a red sweatshirt. He was looking up at the camera from a dock, an array of tanks and diving gear at his feet. His smile was gentle and reflective. The headline said, CAVE DIVER MISSING IN CHINA.

"Oh, shit. He's dead?"

Toll lifted her head, and he saw that she was crying. Daughtrey and Montagnino weren't far from it. Scovill looked hornet-angry, cheeks flushed. He said, "They're not sure yet, but it looks like it. He was exploring a totally new cave; no one had ever been in it before. A deep shaft—two hundred meters, but the bottom sloped down. . . ."

"What happened?"

"Who knows. The paper says he was on heliair. He had Billy Borden on safety at three hundred feet. He thought he saw some twitching just before Lamont went out of sight. But a lot of stuff that comes out right after an accident, it turns out to be wrong, specially in the papers. They haven't . . . they haven't found the body yet."

183

July said, "He took it too far, once too often. It had to happen. He knew it was going to happen someday."

"What are you talking about?" said Montagnino. "He always dove safe; he was always in control."

"He wasn't this time, was he?"

"Wait a minute," said Tiller. "All of you, just calm down. This is bad news, but, you know, he knew the risk. He accepted it."

July screamed, actually showing her teeth at them. "You bastards are so cold. 'He knew the risk.' If it could kill him, it can kill anybody. I don't want to work here anymore."

They all stared at the door after it slammed shut behind her. At last, Daughtrey cleared his throat. "She'll be back. All her gear's still here, and we got Germans flying in this afternoon for the grand tour—"

"Maybe," Tiller said. He looked at the paper again. "Look, you guys think we should close?"

"It might be better," said Montagnino.

"How about our Germans?"

"They're cave divers. They've heard of Exmore. They'll understand."

"Colten?"

"Tony's right. It's the best thing to do. Nobody's going to feel like diving till after the funeral."

"You guys know the community better than I do. Okay, let's start calling people." He left them standing there and headed for the back. Before he got there, he remembered the case and turned back for it. Scovill said as he bent for it, "Oh, yeah—here."

"What's this?"

"Don't know. Just came in Federal Express."

He carried it and the case back into the office and shut the door, then fell into his chair with a grunt. Too bad about Exmore, but he was just as happy not to dive today. Every muscle he owned had shrieked in pain when he got up. It had taken six aspirin and half a tumbler of vodka even to get into the car and get down here.

And he still didn't know where Tad had gone.

He sat there for a while, alternately wishing he'd brought the rest of the bottle of Stoli and feeling glad he hadn't, and finally flipped the computer on. Then he remembered the FedEx package.

It was from South Africa, a guy asking for information about the operation. He'd heard it was for sale from a diver who'd come through one of the Orlando–North Florida package tours. Tiller made a note to send him a flyer. It sounded like a long shot. Still, it was a nibble, the first they'd had.

The machine was booted up by now, the screen waiting, and he took the microdisk out of his pocket and got a knife out of the desk. He slit the last wrappings open. He held it up to the light as if he could read the magnetic data through the case, but of course he couldn't. He popped it in and did a directory. There was only one file on it. He tried the word-processing program. It came up smooth and he sat back, looking at:

THE TARTAR SPRINGS/STYX RIVER AQUIFER SYSTEM
by Joel "Bud" Kusczk, NSS # 38740

He read it, occasionally reaching out to scroll down another page. It seemed to be an article Bud had been writing for *Underwater Speleology*. Kusczk hadn't spell-checked it yet. Occasionally, the sentences were confusing. But it kept him reading.

The first thing he realized was that Bud had done a lot more exploration than the guidelines he'd found. He must have been diving and surveying out there for years. The article described miles of labyrinthine twistings beneath the karst limestone of Crane County. There were long stretches of dry caves, apparently flooded till only quite recently in geological time. (Tiller remembered the cache syphon.) It interlocked with other cave systems, other springs, though Tartar itself was the only sulfur spring; they were apparently rare. The article described some unique flora and fauna, including colonies of anaerobic bacteria. There were no pictures with the text file, but he figured these had to be the things on the cave walls that looked like giant pus blisters.

He had to admire how Bud had brought out the mystery and attraction of penetrating the caves. The way he described them, they were unique on the planet, a fascinating challenge to the experienced caver. Hell, he almost wanted to go and see them—that is, if he hadn't already.

He settled his feet on the desk and scrolled down. Now things got technical. He skimmed the geology, picking up only that Tartar was just one element in a much larger and more complicated watercourse. Other springs, some submerged and some not, contributed to an immense underground flow that emerged from the underlying aquifer of northwest Florida and made its way toward the Gulf. As he read, he got the impression of a gigantic underground river, an immense sea, and at last Bud used that expression:

> The Styx system . . . constitutes one of the most extensive underwater cave systems yet discovered. It taps a tremendous and unexplored class-one artesian aquifer, a concentration of freshwater huge as the "sunless sea" Coleridge imagined in "Kubla Khan," shortly after reading traveler and naturalist William Bartram's description of the Florida springs:
>
> > *In Xanadu did Kubla Khan*
> > *A stately pleasure-dome decree:*
> > *Where Alph, the sacred river, ran*
> > *Through caverns measureless to man*
> > *Down to a sunless sea.*
>
> Its existence has profound implications for understanding of groundwater flow and environmental protection in the entire four-county drainage area. Long lost in darkness, it is only now gradually being brought to light, to become a destination for cave divers from around the world.

That was how the article closed. He stared at the last page. Hell, he hadn't known old Bud had that kind of stuff in him. Except for that last part, about becoming a destination. Surely he'd understood the hellhole that was Tartar had no possibilities for development. But of course by then he'd bought it, built buildings, sunk cash into it. Hope blinded a man to reality.

Then he noticed that the last page wasn't the last page. There was more. He hit "page down" again and got a screen of references, mostly on the sulfur bacteria and on hydrology and geology of karst plains. He hit the key again, then leaned back, taking a breath. It was as if Bud were speaking from the grave, the words leaping off the screen. Miscapitalized and run together, as if they'd been hastily typed in and never edited.

> since completing this articlel ast year i've learned some more interesting stuff about this system. for one thing, the tartar river—the stream in the park, where the alligator tank was—flows the opposite direction it originally flowed. i found that out by accedent, talking to a

186

geezer who used to run the wrestling hall of fame there.
at first I thought he was crazy; then I found the original
survey, back in 1908. when they discovered the caves.
and he was right. it used to flow south, and now it flows
north.

what could reverse the course of an underground
stream??

Galloway frowned. He scrolled down again.

she second thing i realized is that the dry tunnels in the
thirty to sixty foot depth range have been submerged
more recently than I'd thought. the collapse features are
in such soft limestone that they can't be very old. finally,
in the clavo, i came on the remains of troglobitic crayfish
in fairly well-preserved condition. I realized it had happened not just within historic time but within the last
five to ten years—it's hard to be sure in that sulfur environment. but they couldn't have been very old. they
looked like they'd died just yesterday.

?? which would mean that the water table is dropping
??

need to rewrite this article and get it in to the magazine

Will look into this more next month. Follow the passage—not clavo passage but the white passage—the
flow heads that way now—see why.

Sitting in his office, Galloway pondered the words of a dead
man. *Clavo*—that sounded familiar, but he couldn't remember
what it meant. Spanish? Latin? He wished he had the map the
article kept referring to. But whoever had erased the data file from
Bud's hard disk must have rifled the paper files, too.

But he was starting to get the picture.

Bud hadn't died because of an accident, or even because he was
involved with drugs. He'd died because he'd stumbled on a massive theft. And what was being stolen? He didn't think there was
any question about that.

Water.

Fresh water, in overdeveloped, overpopulated Florida, was
nearly impossible to get in any quantity. There were millions of

gallons in the Styx system. But the artesian flow led not to the river, as it once had. Instead, it led north—backward—to what could only be a massive diversion.

Where was it going? There were no cities there. Nothing but a scatter of crossroads towns, then empty scrubland, swamp, and stunted forest. He slid open the file drawer, found the *Welcome to Crane County* brochure the chamber of commerce put out. It had a map, a few sentences on each of the attractions, and a list of the major employers in the county: the Naxahatchee State Hospital; St. George Paper, a big pulp mill outside Abaton; and Florida Foliage, a division of General Sugar.

General Sugar. He remembered the writer's description of Billy Holder's connection to General Sugar and then one guy saying, "the stuff they stock in nurseries, to decorate bank lobbies. Ship a few thousand tons of that north every year, you got a good income."

An operation like that, they'd need water—a *lot* of water.

The phone rang. What fresh hell . . . He glanced at the door, then picked it up. "Yeah."

"Outside call, Till."

"Who is it?"

"I don't know. Somebody from Virginia."

"Put them on. . . . Scuba Florida, Galloway speaking. Can I help you?"

"Mr. Lyle Galloway the Third?"

He hesitated. "Speaking."

"This is Officer Hugo Walman, with the Portsmouth Police Department. We're doing a missing persons investigation on your son. Can we talk for a few minutes?"

He sat up. "Missing? Tad's missing?" Then he had the good sense to shut up and listen.

"We have a report from his mother. It took us a while to find you, Mr. Galloway. Do you make it a habit just to drop out of sight?"

"People who know me know where I am."

"I see. Well, I'm sorry to tell you this, sir, if this is the first you've heard of it. But your son's been reported to us as missing, and we've been trying to—"

"Officer, let me solve your problem for you. There's obviously been some kind of miscommunication. Tad's here; he's been with me the whole time. My understanding when he showed up on my doorstep was that his mother knew he was coming down to spend some time with me."

"Unfortunately, that's not the case. He vanished without telling her where he was going. Am I right in assuming that you don't talk to your wife?"

"Ex-wife. No, we don't talk much."

"You didn't think to have your son call his mother?"

He felt guilty. "No . . . but I've had a lot on my mind."

"You're a parent, Mr. Galloway. Maybe not what we'd call an active one, a participating one, but you're the kid's dad. How would you feel if you didn't know where he was?"

"Uh, pretty bad, I guess." He didn't feel like admitting he didn't know where Tad was now. "But he's here with me in Tallahassee. So you can tell Ellie—"

"Mr. Galloway, you better call your wife yourself. We'll tell her the boy's been located, but you need to talk to her. She's upset, and I can't blame her."

He said he understood. The cop gave him the number, and he typed it in the middle of Kusczk's article, on the screen. Then he hung up and sat immobile, his whole thinking process derailed. Shit, he didn't want to talk to Ellie.

A knock, and Scovill stuck his head in. "Till, getting ready to close up. I told everybody we'd reopen after the funeral."

"Let's do it. I feel bad about Exmore, too. Shit, I dove with him. Hey, did July come back?"

"Not yet. Look, you want to close the store, that's fine, but I have a Nitrox class coming in tonight and—"

"That's your call. You want to hold it, go ahead. But put a sign on the door to say we're closed, and tell our people they can go home. I'll call them in a day or two, let them know when we'll reopen."

Scovill disappeared. Galloway waited till the door was closed, then punched the button again to repower the monitor. He'd blanked it instinctively when the door opened. This file was more dangerous than pure oxygen at depth. It had already killed one guy and it could kill anybody else who knew about it. As the screen came back, he suddenly remembered what *clavo* meant. It was a smuggling term—what they called the compartment in a boat or a plane, the secret compartment where you hid your drugs or your money or whatever else you had to hide.

He hit the page down button once more.

tim wants to know if i'm interested in listing tartar
springs for sale. connection???

have to document all this somehow. maybe the best
thing to do, find out more. then see a lawyer, find out
who to notify. can't be arkin, though. maybe Mon can
suggest something, from when she worked at legislature

He paged down again, but the screen didn't move.

That had been the last thing Bud wrote. Except, of course, for
the words on his slate.

He leaned back, wishing again he had a drink. But he had to
think this through, forget Ellie and Tad and Dugan and the rest
of his own problems, at least long enough to get a handle on this.

He'd already figured out Bud had been murdered, and that
most likely it had happened at Tartar. How did this tie in? Or did
it? After all, nobody knew about Bud's suspicions.

Or, wait—somebody did. Whoever had deleted the file from his
hard disk, and gone through the drawers. The only thing they'd
missed was the backup, hidden deep in the caves.

Sitting there, leaning back, he felt suddenly icy. His eyes re-
tracing the phosphor-glowing words:

Maybe *Mon* can suggest something . . .

Bud must have told her. But unknown to her husband, she was
involved with Arkin. And Arkin worked for Holder. Was the
pudgy, silent little man capable of killing, to protect his interests?
All Tiller could say to that was, he'd known men to do it before.

The phone again. "Yeah," he snapped, annoyed at all the in-
terruptions.

"Tiller, I got a Walter Richter calling from Orlando, the head of
the German team. He wants to talk to you about the cancellation.
They really want to dive Alachua and Ginnie."

"I'll take it." He talked to the guy, promised him they'd be back
in business as soon as the funeral was over. Told him to take a
day off, go to Disney World. He gave him another 10 percent off
and finally got him off the phone.

He sighed, then went to the door, went back, took the disk out
of the machine. Should make another copy. He'd do that tomorrow. Meanwhile, he'd keep the original with Dugan's money.
Only one thing to keep his eye on then, instead of two.

"Mark, you still here? I'm taking off. Where's Scovill?"

"He went over to Gainesville; he knows Exmore's family. Hey, that yours?"

"What?"

"That case. Looks nice. Where'd you get it?"

"Thanks. . . . Oh, over at some store in the mall. Okay, we'll be giving you a call."

"So long," said Daughtrey, looking after him.

Galloway stood outside, looking at the white blaze that covered half the sky. Another hot day. But where the hell was Tad? And he still had to call Ellie. He threw the case into the trunk, and another weight sagged down onto his chest. How was he going to move half a million bucks out of the country? How in the *hell* had Bud moved almost fifty mil a year? He hadn't seen anything in the accounts that would mask that kind of movement. The unexplained profit, he knew where that had come from now. It wasn't from selling dive computers. It was Bud's cut of the outgoing money. But he hadn't seen anything that would explain his technique.

He hunched over the wheel, face crimped with worry. Finally, he turned the ignition on, listened to the motor grind and then start. It was nice to do that without having to sweat whether it was going to be his last instant on earth.

Enjoy the feeling while you got it, he told himself grimly. Because if you dick this up, you'll never know which day is going to be your last. Only that it's coming soon.

He called Ellie from Monica's, and it was so much fun, he had to have a second large vodka after. Tad showed up around five and said he'd spent the night with Ripper, said he'd told Monica about it. Monica looked at Tiller, shook her head silently no. He thought about calling the kid on it, then let it go. Tad went on upstairs, and Mon called after him, "We're having dinner at six. You might want to take a shower." His reply was too muffled to make out.

She was making steak and broccoli, and Tiller wandered into the kitchen halfway through the preparations and volunteered for the salad. He chopped and peeled as she moved purposefully about, talking about her work at the hospice. He mumbled something occasionally, looking at her back as she stood by the counter and reached up to get plates down from the cupboards. Her lifted arms lifted her breasts, too, and he ran his eyes down her slim, strong body.

191

They ate outside by the pool, with fireflies drifting past them in the gloom. Tad wolfed his food and got up. "You want to be excused?" Tiller asked him.

"Uh-huh."

"Say 'Excuse me, please.' "

"Whatever you say." The boy's face was remote; even when he was looking right at him, it was as if he wasn't looking at him. What the hell was wrong now? He'd thought they were closer after Tartar Springs. Now it was back to square one, Tad was as much a stranger as he'd been that day he turned up at the marina.

"Oh, hey. Wait," he called to his retreating back. The boy turned silently. "Your mom—I called your mom today."

"What'd she have to say?"

"She didn't know where you were. Actually, she had the cops looking for you. I thought you said you told her you were coming down to spend some time with me."

"I forgot."

"Look, we got to have this out. You can't just say whatever will make people happy, whatever will make the trouble go away."

"No," said the boy. "I ought to be just like you, right? Mister Honesty."

"What the shit's got into you?"

"Nothing. I just thought I had a dad."

"You *have* got a dad. And I want some respect when you talk to him."

Tad looked up into the tops of the trees. "Sure you got time for it?" he said. Then, surprising them all, he just took to his heels. His sneakers flashed in the night; the slap, slap of departing footsteps echoed back along the path. Then he was gone.

Tiller sat looking after him. Finally, he shook his head and blew out. "I have no idea what that was all about," he told Monica.

"He's angry at you."

"That much, I got. But I don't know what for. I thought we were getting along."

"Me, too. But that mark of his—on his face—"

"What about it?"

"At his age, that's got to be hard for him. That may be what's eating him. It probably has nothing to do with you."

"You think so? Well . . . maybe."

She sighed and reached across for his hand. "I heard about Lamont. Hallie must be inconsolable. I tried to call, but her phone was busy all afternoon. I thought, I've just been through it, so I

192

might be able to help. Joel, and now Lamont. They were so much alike."

"Bud and Exmore? I don't think they were alike. Other than both being divers."

"They were both so gentle."

He couldn't say anything to that. It was a word he'd never have used to describe Bud Kusczk. But then again, he hadn't been married to him, and, too, it had been twenty years since he'd seen the guy.

But maybe there were things Bud hadn't known about her, either.

She got up and stood by the pool. He looked past her at the smooth blue surface of the lighted water. At first, it just looked flat. But then, as he looked closer, he saw the bewildering complexity beneath that sapphire glow: whirlpools and eddies and upcurrents churning and remixing in a dance too endless and bewildering even to begin to understand. She moved to the left and disappeared from his field of view; then her hands came around him from the back, and he felt her breath against his neck.

"How about dessert?"

"Dessert?"

"The no-calorie kind," she whispered, and licked his ear.

That was how it happened. As suddenly, and as unexpectedly, as that.

Afterward, he lay on his back in her bedroom for a long time, watching the fan blades circle like mechanical vultures above them. Maybe Shad was right about him; that when he got fixated on something, everything else fell away. For the last hour of sweaty striving over and then under and then over her again, he hadn't thought of a thing but the ecstatic oblivion she teased and teased him with, then suddenly forced out of him, so that now he was left squeezed empty as a buddy bottle after an emergency ascent. He lay naked, the warm wind stirring the hairs on his thighs and chest. It felt like insects walking over him. His heart and his breathing slowed and his mind drifted toward dream.

"That was nice," she murmured, beside him.

"Uh-huh."

"I've been wanting to do that for a long time. But now we did, I still don't know if we should have. What do you think?"

Instead of answering, he roused himself and got up, easing out of bed.

"Where are you going?"

"Get a drink. Want one?"

"Please. A short gin and tonic."

"Done," he said, though he'd planned on sitting downstairs and thinking this all through over a glass of Jack Daniel's. As he felt his way through the darkened house, a sudden movement at his feet made him start. A shadow trotted across the floor: the cat. Tiller swallowed, remembering stalking Dugan through these same hallways.

His sex-induced relaxation ebbed. A sense of impending doom clenched his stomach. Surely she couldn't really have been involved in Bud's death. If he even suspected it was possible, what was he doing sleeping with her? He was thinking with his little head instead of his big one. What the hell was he going to do?

When he passed her the ice-tinkling glass, she was sitting up, propped against one of the huge pillows. She said, "What are you worrying about?"

"What?"

"I can tell you're worried. Are you going to do like Bud, and close yourself off?"

He tilted the glass back and didn't answer. He didn't get back into bed, either. Just stood in the dark, looking down into the backyard. She had left the flambeaux burning, and their long, flickering flames made the shadows of the bushes and the lawn furniture writhe like tormented spirits.

"Well?"

He said, "Were you sleeping with Tim Arkin?"

It came out harsher and flatter than he'd intended, and the silence got twice as still. At last, she sighed. He heard her glass click as she set it down. "How did you know about Tim?"

"Is it true?"

"It's true. But it was years ago. It was a . . . troubled time in our marriage. Bud and I both had problems. That's not an excuse, I know, but the fault was not all on my side."

"What are you saying?"

"Just that your friend wasn't perfect, either."

"So, what are you saying? That he was sleeping around, so you did, too?"

She turned, and the dim light that came through the windows outlined her breasts and upper body. "It wasn't that cold-blooded. But he went over the fence first. No, we didn't have the perfect

194

marriage. But we kept it going. We got past that bad place. The last couple years, they were good years. I thought the rough part was behind us." A pause, during which he heard her breathing. "Or did you think I was perfect? I'm sorry to disappoint you."

He said, too harshly, "Anyone else I should know about?"

"I don't understand what you mean."

"Who else were you sleeping with? Scovill?"

"No."

"So the thing with Arkin was over?"

"That's what I said. And if you don't mind, I don't feel like talking about this anymore."

He sat down on the bed, wondering how far he could push without showing how much he knew. "Okay, then maybe we should talk about the business instead. Straighten out a couple things."

"If you want."

"There's some things I don't understand. There's more income than I can account for."

"Well, I've told you I don't know that much about it. Did you talk to Dorothea? The accountant?"

"Yeah. She wasn't much help. Look, these foreign investments Bud had—"

"What foreign investments?"

"There's income listed from them in his tax returns. You know anything about them?"

She said slowly, "I know he had some money invested in the Bahamas."

"What's that?"

"There are saltwater caves under Grand Bahama Island. Bud knew the man who discovered them. They're one of the most beautiful cave systems in the world. He saw right away it was going to be a popular location. He bought part of a dive shop there. Some local people run it."

"How often did he go there?"

"He took groups out a couple of times a year, sometimes more often. . . . You could ask Colten or July; they went."

"Did you?"

"Sometimes."

"Uh-huh . . . how about Mexico? Did he have any investments there?"

"The same kind of thing, but I'm not sure he actually had any money in it. It's like, we advertise and book the tours, take the divers in, but you need to have local facilities for air, gear rental, and so forth."

"Right," he muttered, thinking hard.

"Tiller, have you found out what Bud was involved in?"

He flinched. "Huh? Oh . . . I don't know. What were you—"

"I mean what had him so closed in before he died."

He shook his head, forgetting she probably couldn't see him, and they sat in the dark, together yet apart. Then finally, she said, "Well, I'm going to get some sleep," and turned over. He sat there, still thinking, occasionally taking a bite of the bourbon. No diving tomorrow. He could relax.

What was he going to do?

Or was he going to do anything?

Because looking at it stone-cold, he shouldn't do a thing. All he had to do was stay with the situation. He'd get a cut of the business when it sold. Or, if he really wanted to get into serious cash flow, he could just . . . take over.

Take over not just a diving business but a functioning piece of the Organization, too, complete with local protection. Ten percent of 50 million a year . . . tax-free. Vistas of endless profit paraded themselves through his mind. Yet still he sat, sipping and looking down into the garden. He had the link to the overseas banks now: Freeport and Mexico. Bud had obviously used the diving trips to smuggle money out. He still didn't know exactly how—you couldn't just throw hundreds of pounds of cash into trash bags and carry it through customs—but he'd figure it out eventually.

But the woman lying next to him, the woman he'd just made love with, might have set Bud up to be killed.

Could he stay here, suspecting that?

What if she decided to do it again?

He thought he heard something out in the hallway. He looked out, but nothing moved in the shadows. He went back into the bedroom, groped for the glass.

Okay, but what were his alternatives? Short of bailing out, calling it too dangerous and just getting on a plane back to Carolina. He didn't want to do that. He still had his obligation to Bud. And Mon . . . could he be wrong, suspecting her? He'd been wrong a hell of a lot of times before, especially about women.

For just a moment, he thought, unaccountably, neither of himself nor of Kusczk, but of a man he'd met only once and barely knew. What final image had imprinted itself on Lamont Exmore's brain as he fell away into that Chinese abyss? Had he desired that fatal meeting, however unconsciously? Or had his long tango with death been, as simply as he'd said it was, a celebration of life?

He got into bed at last, but couldn't relax. He lay there for a long time, listening to her soft, regular breathing, before at last he closed his eyes, too.

SIXTEEN

Tad crouched motionless on the upstairs landing, looking at the door to the room his father was sleeping in with the Kusczk woman—finally. He'd been wondering what was taking them so long to get it on. . . . He waited for a long time, until he heard snoring. Then he moved. He put his sneakers carefully on the carpet. The bedroom door grew closer. He remembered sliding like this beneath the earth. Just like it, dark and still, except he had all the air he needed now.

He eased it in through his open mouth and nudged the door open.

A faint light came through the blinds, enough to make out the bed, the square darknesses of pictures on the walls, the chair, the sofa, the dressing table. His father's snore sawed at his ears. How could she stand it, lying next to him? He stood motionless, looking around the room from the corners of his eyes.

He sank slowly to his knees, putting his hands out till his fingers sank into the carpet.

He'd caught some z's early, knowing he and Ripper were going out that night. So now he was alert. And his heart was going *wham, wham, wham*. He paused, one hand lifted like a deliberating cat. Was this smart? Then he thought again of everything he needed. Yeah, it was risky. But it was a hell of a lot more worthwhile than kyping Camels from the local 7-Eleven.

The dark blotch off to his right, under the table—that must be it. He crept toward it, pausing every few feet to listen to the min-

198

gled breathing from the bed. Monica muttered something and turned over. He waited, then went on.

Finally, he put out his hand, very slowly, so as not to knock it over accidentally. His outstretched fingers explored the snaps of the locks, then curled around the handle.

Lifting the sample case slowly and noiselessly from the floor, despite it being heavier than he'd expected, he lifted his body at the same time into a cramped crouch.

He waited for some reaction from the humped forms on the bed, some interruption of the steady breathing. But it went on, slow and regular. He smiled sardonically at himself. What had he expected? The old bastard wasn't Spider-Man. He couldn't see in the dark or get telepathic warnings.

A step at a time, he eased himself out of the room. In the hallway, he breathed more freely. He eased his way down the stairs and went into the kitchen. He reconnoitered the windows, then set the case on the breakfast bar and popped the door of the microwave. The bulb glowed on behind its protective grille. In its light, he tested the latches. They were locked. He spun the little brass dials back to 000—they came from the factory that way—and, guess what, both of them snapped open when he pushed the buttons.

"Holy shit," he whispered, looking down.

He hadn't known what was in it, only that after the bearded guy and his dad had talked in the sunroom, the guy had given it to him. And that Tiller hadn't let it more than a couple of feet from him since.

In the pale square of light from the microwave, he lifted first one stack of bills, then another. Then he took them out and arranged them in a line along the speckled Corian surface. He unsnapped the rubber band on one and leafed through it. His hands were shaking. Five hundred-dollar bills, fifty tens: a thousand. The next pack was fifties and twenties, a thousand again. He dug his fingers deep into the case, estimating the number of packs.

He was looking at $500,000. He grabbed the case and hugged it. Then he sobered, glancing quickly around the kitchen. He had to get it into something else, something that wouldn't look out of place for a kid tooling along on a bike. His pack? A trash bag? Maybe the box the Pepsi cans came in—nobody would think of looking in there. Even put some full cans in on top of it, so if anybody looked—

The door creaked, and he froze. It opened an inch or two. He

199

grimaced, searching his mind for some explanation he could offer when his dad flicked the light on. He couldn't think of any. Then he relaxed as a shadow edged through the half-open door. "Shit, Lunker, you little bastard," he muttered.

He got the soft-drink box out of the trash and held it, ready to sweep the cash in. But his hand stopped. He took a deep breath and shut the door of the microwave. There was a click and he stood in darkness again.

"Shit," he muttered. His hand rested on the stacked piles of soft paper. It wasn't trembling now; it was still. But another kind of struggle was going on in his head.

"Shit," he muttered again. He tried once more to sweep it into the box, but his hand wouldn't move.

Sweat was dripping from his armpits, running down his ribs under the T-shirt.

With this much cash, he could go anywhere he wanted. Buy a fast car. Go to California. Get his face fixed, with the lasers.

But he remembered the way the guy with the goatee had looked when he was talking to his dad.

Finally, he whispered "Shit, goddamn it," and tore a paper towel off the roll. He got a pencil out of the drawer with the batteries and the lightbulbs and wrote on it, big jagged letters. Then he pushed the money back into the case—not stacking it, just pushing it back in so the packets bent and crumpled. He put the paper towel on top of it, forced the lid down, and locked it, spun numbers into the dials. Hating himself the whole time. He'd never have a chance like this again. Half a million goddamn bucks!

He left it sitting just inside the bedroom door.

When he got to the trailer, Ripper and Rafael were sitting on the log by the fire. They looked up as he laid the bike down in some leaves. "Where you been?" Ripper said.

"Sorry, got held up. Where we going tonight?"

"Someplace you like," said Ripper. He got up, tall and lean in his baggy jeans and heavy boots and his Edge hat. Rafael, slight and brown in his black jeans and T-shirt, got up, too. "You ready?"

"Sure."

They went a different way than they had the first time, and it wasn't until they were almost there that he suspected where they were headed. They didn't go through the abandoned project, and they didn't go through the marsh. He didn't know whether it was because Chain Saw had been testing them the first time or if he'd found an easier way. But it wasn't till they came to a long wall with a guarded security gate, the lights shining down the road, that he figured they were going back to the place they'd seen the girls.

Ripper motioned them silently to hide their bikes behind some posts set into the ground to look like a dock. They kept low, glancing toward the gate. They could see a guy's head in there, but it was bent; he was reading something. Little TV screens flickered behind him.

Ripper muttered, "Rafe, you first, you're the lightest. Then Tad."

"What we gonna do, Chain Saw?"

"Throw him over the wall. Then he pulls us up."

Rafael disappeared silently, propelled by both their arms locked under his running shoes. They crouched again, waiting, and after a while words floated down. "I dragged a table over. Come on."

On the far side of the wall, it was so dark that you couldn't really see anything. Ripper hesitated a second after they jumped down from the lawn table. He looked around, then loped off. Tad followed, wondering if Ripper had actually reasoned out where he was going or if he just knew, like an animal. They ran through bushes and leapt over fences, weaved between trees. Once, a security light flashed on, outlining them, some kind of motion sensor. They froze, but nothing else happened, so after a minute they ran on, past the corner of a big house with a long row of windows. The light stayed on behind them for a while and then went out.

They scaled another wall, and suddenly there it was: the big Spanish house, the pool glowing with drowned light. They lay full length in soft black soil under some hydrangea bushes, peering out. Then Tad smelled dog piss on the leaves.

"What about the dogs?" he whispered into Ripper's ear.

Ripper didn't answer, just took Tad's hand and pressed it against his leg. Tad started to jerk it away, thought maybe he was getting queer, but then he felt something in Ripper's pocket.

"Pepper spray," Ripper whispered. "Dog Mace. That'll cool them long enough for us to get out—if they're around."

Tad put his head down till it rested on the dirt. An hour ago, he'd been running his hands through major money; now he was where some bastard had every right to shoot them. Maybe it was the very silence of the huge house and the waiting tranquillity of the blue water that made him so spooked.

"You guys wanna go for a swim?"

"Rupert, you're nuts," the Cuban kid muttered.

Tad turned his head. *Rupert?*

Ripper crab-crawled down the line of shrubbery, keeping his head down till he got opposite the pool. Tad hesitated, then followed him. The dirt felt cool. Crickets spurted away, making dry noises as they crashed through the leaves. He remembered the movie, where the guy got shot in the swimming pool. The guy with the gun had just stepped out onto a balcony—shit, there was a balcony overlooking the pool here, too.

A light came on back inside the house. Tad froze. He lifted his head, trying to see into the windows. He hoped the girls were still here, especially the one with the long dark hair and the secret smile. But what if they'd just been staying here that one night?

"Ripper, no," Rafael called out behind him, and Tad jerked his head around and saw Ripper out of the bushes, halfway to the pool. He scuttled along, dragging his arms like an ape. He was grinning. "Come on," he said. "You don't come in, you guys don't have a hair on your ass."

Tad shook his head in resignation. He didn't want to do this. But he wasn't going to let Ripper crow about how none of them had any balls but him.

Lunging out of the hydrangeas, he forced his unwilling legs toward the pool.

Just then, doors slid back, up on the balcony, and two heads appeared, accompanied by a sudden flood of light and music. Two men lingered in the doorway, then approached the railing.

When he heard the music, Tad altered his course instantly, diving for the cover of a stuccoed enclosure, then swinging himself over into it. Inside, a green-painted pump and filter equipment hummed to itself. The top of the enclosure was open, but he had cover if he stayed low.

But Ripper was still out in the open. Tad squeezed his eyes shut, waiting for the yelling to start.

It didn't. He opened them again, found a sizable gap where one of the pipes went through the box, and pressed his eye to it. He swept his gaze around the pool. Where had Ripper got to? Then he saw him. He was lying under one of the lounge chairs, pressed full length against the patterned tile. The men above couldn't see him; all they could see was the chair. It was the same chair the black girl had been lying in when the bald man pulled his shorts down and started doing her.

Ripper caught his eye, and smiled back at Tad across the forty feet separating them.

The music faded, cut off by the sound of a closing door, and the voices floated down. They must have thought they were alone. They were speaking Spanish.

"*¿Lo has visto? ¿Dónde crecen las plantas?*"

"*Tres F's es muy impresionante. No hay duda tiene la capacidad de hacer lo que promete, y mas.*"

The voices fell. Tad hugged his knees. The sharp edge of the pump foundation dug into his side. He felt like an idiot. Why had they come here, anyway? Just to see those girls again? Shit. If there was something they could steal, it would make sense.

Then he remembered that when he could have taken something that mattered—enough to make him rich—he'd let his damn conscience screw him. Maybe this was payback. He hadn't taken it when he could, so now he'd suffer.

The music came again, and when he looked up, the balcony was empty. The accent lights glowed around the pool. Moths hammered softly on their globes. He breathed out and rose warily. A motion in the hydrangeas: the gleam of Rafael's eyes, the flicker of his hand in a beckoning gesture.

Ripper was sliding out from under the lounge chair when the ground-floor door opened and the men came out onto the terrace that led down to the pool.

The first to move out into the light was the bald-headed man. Tad, crouched again, saw that although before he'd thought the guy was old, he hadn't realized just how old. Now he saw the chest hair was white and his left cheekbone was sunken, as if the bone under it had been removed. He had feral arched eyebrows that were black in the center, where they met at his nose, and white as snow at the outer tips. He didn't have shorts on this time, but long white slacks and white shoes. No shirt, but white shoes. He held his hands locked behind him, explaining something in a low voice as he came down the steps, directly toward the chair beneath which Ripper, like a startled hermit crab, had instantly pulled himself.

Tad, folded as small as he could make himself, applied his eye to another gap where a power cable led out.

Into the field of view came the second man. Tad froze, and not just because the guy had a gun in his hands.

He wore a loose shirt, baggy slacks, an oversized suit jacket, no tie, braided sandals. He had close-cropped dark hair, dark eyes, and a small black beard, stiff and glossy as the bristles of a cheap paintbrush.

It was the guy he'd seen at Monica's, the one who'd handed the case to his father.

He was holding his gun out butt-first, as if trying to surrender it, or hand it over. Or as if demonstrating his willingness to use it in the other's service. The older man pushed it away. He said a few words in impatient Spanish. The younger bowed his head, then slid the gun back into his waistband.

Tad watched, unable to breathe. They were still headed for the lounge chair. Ripper's eyes, snapped wide, were staring at Tad. He made a quick inquiring motion, *where are they?* Tad shook his head desperately, put his finger through the hole, and pointed straight down, signaling Ripper to stay put.

The bald man turned, calling back to the house. Tad couldn't see the person who he was calling to, but a moment later all the lights came on. Not just the accent lights and the underwater ones but also high-powered security lights among the trees. He blinked and ducked his head; he'd been looking right at one when it buzzed and flickered and suddenly popped into eye-searing radiance.

The older man went straight to the lounge chair and let his weight down slowly onto it. Tad stared at the shadow that was Ripper, inches from the old man's shoes. The guy with the gun stood above him. They talked in low voices. Tad caught only fragments of words, parts of phrases.

"*No, tenemos razones para pensar que los poderosos locales son todos amigos suyos.*"

"*¿Cuándo?*"

"*Ocurriré el veinte, dijo el.*"

Something stirred in the bushes and both men stiffened, turning. Tad tensed, too. All they had to do was look down and they'd see Ripper. He couldn't believe they couldn't *smell* Ripper.

"*¿Qué era eses ruido?*"

"A squirrel, I think," the man with the goatee said—in English, for some reason.

The older man stretched, then rose. He stood there searching his trouser pockets for something. Tad stared, unable to draw

204

breath. He could see Ripper's head not six inches from the man's feet. Then, to his horror, he saw Ripper's hand creeping toward the old guy's ankle. "Ripper, *no*," he whispered, so scared, he felt like he was going to puke.

The bald man found what he was searching for at last. He offered a cigar to the one with the goatee. The younger one shook his head, murmuring, "*Gracias, señor, no.*"

As they stepped away from the chair, Ripper snatched at the old guy's pant leg. Tad didn't think he was actually trying to get it; he was just showing off. But Tad still felt weak.

The two strolled once around the verge of the pool, looking down into the wavering depths, then went up the steps and through the french doors into the house. A few seconds later, the security lights died.

But at the same moment, not far away, they heard a deep growling and barking.

Tad jumped for the top of the equipment enclosure and swung himself over it, landing lightly on the tile. Ripper was fighting himself out from under the lounge, legs jerking like a stepped-on spider. Rafael yelled softly from the bushes, "Dogs!"

"Let's get out of here," Ripper muttered. "Them freakin' dogs is the meanest—"

The three brown-and-black pit bulls came out of the trees at full run. They didn't bark now, just ran toward them across the manicured lawn in a spooky silence. Tad cast a despairing glance toward the wall. They'd never make it, not before the dogs got them. He could hear them panting now.

"Get back of me," Ripper said, pulling something out of his trousers, and Tad remembered the pepper gas. He and Rafael scrambled back. Ripper flipped up a little lid and aimed as the first dog got within jumping range.

The spray hit its open jaws and the dog choked and rolled, pawing frantically at its head. Ripper nuked the others as they came in range, too. They circled away, choking and whining. Foam dripped from their muzzles. Then they started to bark. It was weak at first, but it got louder fast. Tad looked again toward the wall, a long way away. Lights were coming on again in the house.

Then he remembered how they'd come in the first time.

The dogs were recovering. They growled and snarled, circling in again. More lights came on in the house, then more, all of them, buzzing and popping on all around the compound.

Voices yelled in excited Spanish.

Tad grabbed Ripper and pulled him toward the pond. Rafael splashed in after them, shaking a rake handle he'd found at the dogs. Tad fumbled at the grille over the drain tunnel, cursing, close to crying. The lead pit bull, the biggest, followed them down the slope, splashing into the pond. Ripper hosed it again with the pepper spray. The dog jumped back, but then the canister hissed empty.

"Oh shit," Ripper said.

The grille came off in Tad's hands. He grabbed Rafael and shoved him in. Ripper reared back and threw the empty canister at the lead dog. It dodged and came right for Tad, jaws open, long yellow teeth eager for his throat.

Without taking time to think, he slammed the heavy grille down on its slavering muzzle. It yelped and backed off, but the other animals were snapping at Ripper. Then he and Ripper were both in the tunnel and he was fitting the grille back into place while the dogs tried to bite his fingers off. Ripper was jabbing them with the blade of a knife through the holes. Tad couldn't get the screws in, so he just sort of hung it there. Then they turned and crawled back into the fetid dark as fast as they could go, the roaring of the dogs echoing hollowly in the confined tube.

They were deep in the marsh, maybe half a mile away, before they stopped to rest. They collapsed against trees, with their feet in the slime and sawgrass, and sucked air. Tad's knees were quivering so violently, he could barely stand. When the dogs had attacked, he'd thought they were going to die.

Rafael coughed in the dark. "Rafe, you okay?"

"I'm . . . all right."

"That was too stinking close. Were those pit bulls?"

"That's what they were, all right," grunted Ripper. "Man, I thought pepper gas worked on dogs."

"It did—till it ran out," Tad said. "Hey, Rafe—"

"What?"

"Those guys, they were speaking Spanish, right?"

Rafael kept coughing. It sounded like he'd gotten a whiff of the gas, too. Tad heard him wheeze as he inhaled. "Yes, that was Español."

"You speak that, don't you?"

"Sure, I understood it."

"What were they talking about?"

"Nothing much. Just talking about somewhere they grow a lot of plants. A place called *Tres F's*—Three F's."

"What were they saying about it?"

"That it was like a big deal, a big business, you know. Oh, and they said something's happening there on the twentieth."

"Who were those guys? Did you catch their names?"

The boy gave him a strange look. "No, they didn't use their names."

"We better keep going," said Ripper, tottering over to them. "What do you guys think? Do I take you exciting places, show you fun stuff?"

"Yeah, Chain Saw," said Tad, wiping the sticky muck from his face. "Oh, yeah."

SEVENTEEN

The grassy lot in front of the church was parked full when they got there. Tony Montagnino met them at the door. He ushered them up the aisle and people shoved over to make room. It had been a while since Tiller had been in a church. He wondered if he ought to kneel. Monica didn't, so he just sat beside her, glancing around.

It reminded him of the church on Hatteras his stepmother had taken him to, back when he was little: white walls, a simple lectern, mahogany-stained pine pews. There wasn't a choir or anything ornate or expensive. Whoever worshiped here, they didn't put much stock in show.

The minister came out, not in robes but in a plain black suit. "Please join me in a moment of prayer," he said, and the service began.

It went along as simply and plainly as the furnishings. Tiller couldn't tell how well the minister had known Exmore, but the lesson he chose seemed appropriate. It was from Job:

> Surely there is a mine for silver,
> and a place for gold which they refine. . . .
>
> But where shall wisdom be found?
> And where is the place of understanding?
>
> Man does not know the way to it,
> and it is not found in the land of the living.

The deep says, "It is not in me,"
and the sea says, "It is not with me."

It cannot be gotten for gold,
and silver cannot be weighed as its price.

There was complete silence when a young man came up from the congregation. He stood in the pulpit, head bowed. To Tiller's surprise, it was none other than Colten Scovill.

He started the memorial quietly, asking them each to recall something of Lamont Exmore. One by one, men and women stood up and told of old times and old friends. Most were divers, but there were family members and business associates, too. Then he asked for a show of hands, of those whose lives Exmore had saved. And a full two dozen rose and hovered beneath the lofty ceiling before they slowly drifted down again like flakes of dislodged rock falling to rest on a sandy floor. One of them was Tiller's, as he remembered his deliverance at the end of that horrendous Wabasso Springs exploration push.

Scovill said, "Every one of us here has a vivid memory of Lamont. Will time erase those pictures we have of him? Will we forget someday we ever knew a man with a mustache and a shy smile?

"I don't think so.

"But Lamont would not have wanted us to look back. He never looked back, not at his childhood, not at the medical career he gave up, the sacrifices he made in order to dive. He grieved for the friends he lost, but no one ever spent less time in the past. He always looked ahead, to the next cave, the next challenge.

"Lamont brought something new to the world of cave diving. Before he tackled it, it was a suicidal, kamikaze-type sport. Dozens died every year. And then he and five or six others decided to turn it into a science. They set up the two-thirds rule. They started training programs. Then, after they laid that guideline down for others to come after them, they started exploring in earnest. Stage diving—Lamont was there on the first stage dives. The first to use a scooter in a Florida cave. And in the last couple of years, he was testing rebreathers, a technology that's opening up miles of new passages too far in for us to reach now.

"I'm not going to tell you all the records he held. I'm not going to talk about how many miles of beautiful caves he opened up in Florida and Texas and Mexico, and the Blue Holes in the Gulf and

Andros Island. If you're a caver, you know about them, and you know that what he did will make his name live forever in the annals of exploration.

"No, what I want to talk about is his spirit, and how it's always going to be out there leading us on. Not in any sense of unsafe diving. But in the grandest, Mount Everest sense of exploration. You've heard the prayer: 'It's better to light one candle than to curse the darkness.' Lamont Exmore lit that candle, and he carried it into the darkness, and darkness vanished wherever he went. That is what he bequeathed to us: personal bravery combined with personal responsibility. Lamont would have been a master and a leader wherever he went in life. We were fortunate he came to us.

"And as he always ended a conversation, so let me finish this brief memorial: 'Y'all dive safe now, hear?' "

Scovill bent his head, and after a moment the minister stepped up. "Will you join me in hymn number one hundred and seventy-six," he said, and the hush was broken by the shuffle of feet, a collective sigh.

When the service was over, Tiller stood outside, blinking in the near-noon sunlight. Around the church, the fields stretched away till they met distant forest. A few clouds glowed in the west. He stood beside Monica, nodding as divers he knew filed past. They looked strange in suits. July joined them. She looked wrung-out. "Too many funerals," she said to Monica.

"I know what you mean, honey."

"Did you talk to Hallie? She's still in there—"

"No. I called yesterday. We're going to have lunch in a couple of days, once things quiet down."

Then Ferebie was tipping his uniform hat. "Hello, Mon."

"Oh . . . hello."

"Tiller, how's it going? Nice service, huh?"

"Yeah," said Galloway. He didn't want to talk to the ranger, but Ferebie caught his arm. "Hold on. You want to talk here, or over by my truck?"

"Excuse me," he said to Monica, and she turned her head slightly from July and gave him a sad half smile.

Back to earth, he thought as he followed the loping stride of the Park Service officer. Halfway to his truck, Ferebie looked back. "Your son tell you I was looking for you?"

"What?"

"Out at Tartar. I saw your van out there, stopped by to talk. He seemed kind of hinky. Anything wrong?"

"No, nothing. I guess he forgot to tell me."

"Well, here's the problem." Ferebie handed him a piece of paper. It was a letter, on official state stationery. The subject line read "Denial of Access to Facilities." Galloway scanned it, then handed it back. "No, you get to keep that," the ranger said. "It's like a writ; you got to serve it personally. And I just did."

"Is this legal? You can just bar us from state parks like this."

"Is it legal? Take it to your lawyer, ask him. Who is that? Tim Arkin? He'll tell you. You can fight it if you want. There's a state board you can appeal to. But that'd be the expensive way of dealing with the situation."

Tiller sighed. He looked back toward where Monica was talking to people on the steps. "You want to come over to the car?"

"Delighted."

He'd put the sample case in the trunk, and he shielded its contents from Ferebie as he set the dials and unsnapped it. Then he gaped down at the message, scrawled on a paper towel.

DAD YOU OUGHT TO KEEP A BETTER EYE ON THIS SHIT.

"What's the matter? Goose step on your grave?"

"Uh, nothing ... just remembered something else I gotta do. Uh, how much did you say you wanted?"

Ferebie held up ten fingers.

"Wait. I remember now. Seven, that's what we decided on."

"That was as of the first of each month. Now there's a late fee."

Tiller gave up and picked up one of the bundles. He stripped the rubber band off and crumpled the bills, just so Ferebie didn't get the idea he carried a lot of cash around. He locked the case and then the trunk. How in the hell had Tad gotten into it? He glanced around, making sure no one was pointing any cameras at them. He was tempted to just drop it on the ground and walk away. Instead, he folded it up in the denial of access and handed it over. The ranger nodded in a satisfied way.

"Count it. A grand even."

"I trust you. But next time, save some money; make it the first of the month."

"Look, I got a couple questions."

"At your service. See, it pays to maintain good relations."

"You're the manager of the Styx River Preserve, you said. What do you know about Billy Holder's operation?"

"Triple F's right next door to us. What you wantin' to know?"

"Where he gets his water."

"His water? Artesian wells, I suppose. Why?"

"Is he one of your victims, too?"

Ferebie grinned. "I maintain professional confidentiality about the identity of my friends. But I'll tell you this. Billy Holder runs that business by the book, right down the line. He's got all the right permits from the Department of Environmental Protection. He's part of the big picture got everybody down here so excited."

"What big picture?"

"The second phase of the Styx River Preserve. I can send you a plan outline, if you want. Might be interesting."

"Sure, but how about a thumbnail sketch?"

Ferebie looked back toward the church. "There's eight thousand acres of land downriver of the present preserve that's still undeveloped. It's held by a company called St. George Paper. They just clear-cut, and it's a good time to make them an offer. Well, it's gonna be made. Not by the state, but by the Heritage Conservancy."

"Oh yeah? Wait a minute. Blanche Holder, right?"

"She's active in it."

"Why do I wonder where they get the cash to buy all this land?"

"That's the best part." Ferebie touched his cap brim as an older couple—Exmore's parents, relatives?—went past. "You've heard of the wetlands conservation program? Where if you develop a piece of land that's classified as wetlands, you got to create new wetlands someplace else? To replace your natural filters, your wildlife habitat?"

"I've heard of it."

"Well, we just got a law where instead of your developers and landfill owners trying to develop their own marshes, they can donate money to a nonprofit—like the Conservancy—and they get what you call a wetlands credit, so much an acre for every acre of wetlands they destroy. That's where the funding for this phase two acquisition is gonna come from. The St. George buy will make us the second-biggest natural preserve in Florida, after the Everglades."

"What about Holder? Is he selling, too?"

"No, far as I know, old Billy's staying where he is."

"Let me ask you this. What if you found out he was violating some environmental regulation or other?"

"Who, Billy? Why should he? He gets all the waivers he needs from the DEP."

"Oh, he pays them off, too?"

Ferebie squinted. "He puts out his share of contributions. And you know who his dad was."

"Whose dad?"

"Billy's. You mean you don't? Ever hear of Hiram C. Holder?"

"Oh, the coach? He coached the Forty-Niners or something—"

"It was the Chargers, and that was real late in his career. He was the Seminoles coach for about twenty years. Florida State U. So you mention Billy Holder to anybody in Tallahassee, they know who you're talking about."

"And the Conservancy, they wouldn't be the ones to warn, or complain to."

"No, it all works out pretty well," said Ferebie.

He tried a feint. "I understand Tartar's going to be part of the preserve, too."

"Tartar?" The ranger looked puzzled. "I heard it was for sale, but I didn't hear that. But I'd be glad to have it; that'd be the last puzzle piece of the river system. Anything else I can do you for?"

Tiller shook his head, and Ferebie tapped his Smokey Bear hat and drifted off. Tiller looked after him, leaning against the hot metal of the trunk.

Speaking of puzzle pieces, he'd pretty much put them together already, but hearing it from Ferebie's point of view made him more confident about his suspicions being right.

Holder, the Park Service, and the Conservancy were trying to remold the entire Styx River spring and basin system into a vast new state preserve. Ferebie was in because it built his little kingdom. Holder was in for the water. Blanche ran interference for her husband, shielding him on the environmental front with her smoke-and-mirrors "conservancy." Holder's PAC contributions and his old-boy connections from his father's coaching days bought off the state Department of Environmental Protection.

It would be set up as a victory for the environment. But what it really meant was that the "preserve" would monopolize all the fresh water in the Styx basin for Holder's floral and greenery empire.

He leaned there for a while, thinking, then pushed himself off the trunk and headed back toward the church.

When he got there, Monica was holding Timothy Arkin's hand, as if they'd just shaken. She released it as he came up. The attorney smiled down at him, frosty and remote.

"Now, you remember what I told you," she said. "We all have to work together. So let's shake hands and forget about it. Both of you."

Arkin looked as if he'd been ordered to grab a turd, but he extended his hand. Galloway looked at Monica. "Do it," she said.

He did. Then he wiped his hand on his slacks. On Bud's slacks, he remembered. Bud, who'd died somewhere else than where they'd found him.

"Hey, do you dive?" he asked Arkin.

"I've done a little snorkeling. When I was young and foolish."

"We're taking a German party out this afternoon. Want to come along, take a dip in the basin?"

"Thanks, but I've got to go back to the office. Monica, nice to see you." Arkin nodded, moving off. Cars were trickling out of the lot, the divers' faces sober.

"I don't want to hear it, and I don't want to see that expression, either," Monica told him.

"What expression?"

"I know what you're thinking. I told you, it's over between Tim and me. It's been over for a long time."

"Does he know that?"

"Yes, and he knows I'm seeing you. So I want both of you to stop being ridiculous."

Scovill came out of the church with Tony and Mark. Monica complimented him on his eulogy. He said, "I wrote it last night. I figured, keep it short."

"Yeah, you did good," Tiller told him. "What time are we scheduled to meet Richter?"

"Who? Oh . . . they're gonna be at the spring at two."

"Excuse me," Tiller told her. "Got to go make a paycheck."

Three hours later, he floated at the entrance to the White Room, counting the Germans as they came out one by one. Their lights probed away into the darkness as each picked up the guideline, and moved toward the Big Room. He counted five, gave Scovill an okay sign as he came out. Scovill returned the signal and swung in after them. Montagnino waited ahead, his video camera floods sweeping away the darkness like sparkling brooms.

214

During the van trip to Ginnie, Scovill had filled him in on a call he'd taken the day before, while the shop was closed; as the manager, he had call forwarding from the store number to his home. It had been from South Africa, notifying them a Victor Fabricante would be arriving in a couple of days to look at the operation. Tiller remembered the Federal Express inquiry. "That's good," he said.

"That means he'll be here tomorrow."

"Okay. No problem."

"If he makes an offer, we need to talk. About my share," Scovill told him. Tiller said sure, then added it was too early to worry about that. Let the guy come and look around, see if he was in earnest or just wanted a way to write off a dive trip. Africa was a long way away.

The Germans were good divers, competent and methodical, just like Germans were supposed to be. They wore their equipment differently, mainly side-mounted, and they moved as if awed by the space and visibility. Richter had said they didn't have very good diving in Europe. The caves were tighter, the flow more violent, and the heavy silt meant visibility was always poor, especially on the way out. That was why they'd come to Florida, and Ginnie would be only the first of five systems they were going to explore, each of gradually increasing difficulty.

He followed their slowly moving fins out into the Big Room. Now their lights, which had seemed bright in narrow passages like the Cornflakes, were tiny, distant illuminations, flickering here and there like roving fireflies. Far beneath the earth, he felt the massive lift of the stone ribs of the planet above his head, felt the dark pressing silent and soft against his chest.

Tiller was the only guy on a scooter, sort of an extra safety measure in case anything went wrong. Or maybe, he thought, more like the only lazy diver. As he hummed along, half his brain absorbed in the dive, the other half pondered what he should do about the larger situation.

He knew one thing already. He didn't know where Monica stood, but he wasn't on the same side as Holder and Ferebie and Arkin. He wanted no part of them or their crooked deals.

But why not? What was it to him if they found a way to beat the system? Wouldn't he do the same, if he could?

But even as that cynical voice in his head asked the question, he knew the answer.

It was a wordless answer made of rock and water and time. The caves were beautiful as a dream. The clear water was like a heavier, colder air, enriched with just enough intoxication to make his blood throb and his heart lift and sing.

He'd seen what happened when the moneymen had their way. He'd seen every leaf and sand grain of Hatteras Island assessed and tagged and sold away. Tad would never know empty beaches echoing with storm surf, the heart-stopping thunder of ponies' hooves through miles of woods along the Sound. No one ever would again. They'd been sliced up and paved over and sold by the foot like so much lumber. The herds were gone forever, cleared from the land for miles of trailers and ticky-tacky cottages nail-gunned together from particleboard, time-shares and shopping malls, mini-golf courses and waterslides, leaving only a few remnants penned for tourists to gawk at. The beauty of empty dawns, sanderlings skittering along the beach like windup toys, the trawlers putting out before sunrise, moving through Oregon Inlet in a long parade like a fleet going to sea—life would never be that simple and that beautiful again.

You couldn't blame it all on outsiders, either. His brother had been first in line to grab the pie, chop it up, and sell it off.

The Germans were pumping steadily along the line, out of the Big Room and up, following Scovill's flickering fins into the Pillar Room. Twisted, eroded verticals clawed down from the overhead. A brown velvet carpet of clay silt covered the floor. Mercury clouds of bubbles burst from their regulators, spreading and cascading across the pockmarked limestone as if each sphere of air were searching desperately for escape. Scovill threaded the pillars, then led them out again, angling east into the long tunnel that led to the Hinkel.

Maybe he'd just seen too many bastards making money out of ruining things for everybody else. His brother, Nuñez, the bastards in the Bahamas, Shattuck and Boudreaux in Louisiana. A glance at the gauges—time to shift to the right tank. . . . Maybe it was futile. There were too many of them. They understood how to work together. They knew how to keep secrets. Maybe even thinking of taking them on was another piece of the same stupidity that had ended him up in prison.

But if nobody spoke out, they'd run everything.

Well, so what? What was that to him?

Then he remembered Tad. Did he want his son to live in that kind of future? It made a difference how you looked at things, when you had a kid.

But what could he do about it? He could try to get Bud's case reopened. Try to persuade the cops it had been murder instead of an accident. But if Ferebie was right about how far Holder's tentacles penetrated the state, he couldn't expect much from a new investigation.

And what would reopening the case do to Monica? She was just getting back on an even keel. He still had to think about her, and not just out of loyalty to Bud. But there was the nagging question of whether she'd had anything to do with Kusczk's death. So far, he hadn't been able to figure a way to find out. And until he could, every impulse toward her was accompanied with a revulsion away. Not only that, now he had Arkin to worry about. She'd admitted to an affair with him. She saw him nearly every day, apparently. Was it really just legal matters, and selling Tartar Springs? And didn't that give Arkin another reason to kill Bud?

What it all came down to was that he didn't believe in anything Arkin and Holder had their hands in. It wasn't for the public's benefit; it wasn't for Monica; it wasn't for anybody's enrichment but their own. He'd love to pitch a wrench into their well-oiled little machine. But how?

Purring slowly along in the dark, he came to no clear answer.

They had dinner early, since it was Monica's night on duty at the hospice. After she kissed him and left, he sat in the living room watching the news. He channel-surfed, watched part of a movie, five minutes of a new show, then clicked it off. He sat in the dark for a while, then got up and went to the bar.

He was sitting with the bottle and a cooler of ice by the pool when Tad came out of the house. He came down the path, hesitated as he saw his dad, then came out of the trees and stood unspeaking at the deep end, hands in his pockets, looking into the water. Tiller watched him, trying again to match the chubby toddler he remembered with this tall, angry boy. How much of that change was his fault? How much was just bad luck, from the disfiguring birthmark to the fact his mother didn't have any more judgment about men than his father had about women? He started to top off his drink, then didn't. He was drinking way too much. He decided he'd better ease off, do without for a week and let his system clear.

Tad came closer, like a deer warily edging out of the forest, and perched on one of the lounge chairs. But he still didn't speak.

Finally, Tiller cleared his throat. "I found your note. In the case."

"Yeah?"

"How'd you get in there, anyway?"

"Took it when you weren't looking. The lock was shit."

"When wasn't I looking?"

"When you were asleep."

"You still taking other people's things? Didn't we have a talk about that?"

"I brung it back," Tad said. He was thinking, and that's what I get for it. Should have kept it, just took off.

"Thanks for that, anyway." He looked at the boy's expressionless face. The mark looked different with the tan the kid was getting. Not as noticeable, though you still couldn't miss it. Shit, Mon was right, if he'd had something like that at Tad's age, when just a zit could ruin your day, he'd be carrying around a chip the size of the *Monitor*, too.

"Look, if you got something to say, spit it out. Don't make me dig for it, because I'm not going to. And don't act so goddamn sullen."

Tad said, face averted, "I seen the guy give it to you."

"Guy? What guy?"

"The guy with the beard."

Tiller passed a hand over his hair. "What? When did you see that?"

"When he gave it to you. Saw it from out here. All the windows were lit."

"Okay, so you saw him. Now what?"

"I counted it, too," Tad said, not looking at him. "Where'd it come from? What are you doing with it? Who *is* that guy?"

Tiller thought, Great. Now let's see how you're going to explain this. He thought for a couple of seconds, but there didn't seem to be any plausible alternative to the truth.

First, though, he ought to lay in some of the background. "Okay, let's have this out," he said. "It's about time we talked about some of this man-to-man. Tad, you know why I left your mom?"

"What's that got to do with the money?"

"You'll see. Why did I leave you and Ellie?"

"Because you didn't like us. You and Mom were always arguing and—"

"Whoa. Wait a minute. It wasn't because I didn't *like* you."

"You said we got on your nerves. You were fed up with us."

"Maybe I said that, but it was the coke talking, not me. I was high just about every time I wasn't actually blowing bubbles. Then I had to get more, and the company was cutting back on my hours. There wasn't enough for what I had to have and for you and your mom, too. So I had to get rid of you . . . had to throw everything else overboard. I had to have what I had to have, right then, and screw everybody who got between me and it."

"Uh huh," said Tad. "How about the Cajun bitch? Nicole?"

"Nicolette. She was using, too. It was easier to be around people who used. Your mom wouldn't. I tried to turn her on, but she said no. I thought she was too uptight to have a good time. So I found somebody who wasn't. That wasn't your mom's fault, or yours. It was mine. All mine. Damn it, I admit that. I was totally in the wrong, all right? And, goddamn it, I'm sorry. I'm sorry for dropping the ball back then. I know it dicked your life up, and I—"

Sitting with his hands on his knees like a patient old man, Tad said, "So where'd all that money come from?"

"I'm getting to that, okay? That's how I got into moving drugs. First, I sold to the other guys in the crew. Then when the company let me go, I got in with the Steinberg organization, and then from there to a guy named—"

"The Baptist."

"How'd you know that? Anyway, you're right. . . . Señor Juan Alberto Mendieta Nuñez-Sebastiano. I ran drugs for him. Did okay at first. But the last cruise, the Coast Guard was waiting, when I got to Hampton Roads. Somebody burned me."

"Who?"

"I don't know. I'll find out someday. Anyway, I did my time and kept my mouth shut. I knew that was the only way I was ever going to make my release date alive."

"Is that when my grandfather shot himself?"

"That's right," Tiller said, tasting the bitterness that never went away. "The paper called him, said it was a conviction, asked if he had a comment. He said he didn't. Then he hung up and went into the next room and picked up a gun."

He took a deep breath, let it out. His son's averted face was expressionless. He couldn't tell if he judged or sympathized. But he'd told him. In years to come, he could think about it and maybe understand a little. . . . He decided to finish up, get it over with. "Since then, I've been trying to go straight. Only it isn't that

219

easy to walk away. Nuñez tried to get me back into the business once, in the Bahamas. It didn't work out too well for either side."

"Then what about the *money?*" Tad muttered.

"That's what I'm trying to tell you. . . . I found out Bud was mixed up in the same thing. Only not smuggling, but money laundering—getting the profits out of the country. The guy you saw, the one with the goatee, he gave the cash to Bud. Kuszck handled it from there, got it down south, to the Bahamas and Mexico."

"How'd he do that?"

"A good damn question. But *that's* where the money came from. Okay? Dugan expects me to do the same thing, or else his thugs light up you and Mon. He'll do it, too. But so far, I don't know how."

"Was it cash or something else? When he sent it out of the country?"

"I guess it could be anything, but we've got to start with cash." Something else occurred to him, and he added, "Look, I don't want you in this, okay? We're not talking about busting up a truck here. I'll tell you about it, but if you're ever questioned, you don't know anything about what I was—"

"Dugan. That's his name?"

He started to feel apprehensive. It was one thing to fill Tad in on ancient history, but getting him involved with the cartel could end up getting him killed. "Forget his name. Shit! I didn't mean to mention it, okay? Maybe I shouldn't have told you any of this. The less you know about these animals, the safer you are."

"I want to know. I want to help you."

"Yeah? Well, thanks, but about the only way you could help is if you can figure out a way to get a hell of a lot of money overseas without using a bank or alerting the feds or customs."

"I'll think about it," said Tad. "What about the old bald guy?"

Now it was his turn to stare at the pool. He tried to think who the boy meant, but he couldn't come up with anyone. A diver? One of the buzzards at Blanche's party? Finally, he said, "What bald guy?"

"He's kind of tall, and real old, but he can still screw. His face looks like—one side of it is gone under the skin. Kind of sunken down, like the bone's gone or something."

"I don't know who you're talking about. Where'd you see him? In town?"

Tad sat hunched and silent. Finally, he muttered, "I got something to tell you, too."

He told his dad about going sneaking with Ripper and Rafael. He told him about getting into the estate the first time and seeing the bald guy and the girls. Then he said, "And last night, we went back, and we saw him again—it must be his place. A big house and all. But there was somebody else with him. I saw him real clear. I was only about twenty feet away. It was the same guy who gave you the case."

Tiller started. "What, you're saying . . . Dugan was there?"

"That's right."

"You're sure?"

"Yeah. And they were talking and we were real close. Rafael, he understands Spanish. So later, when we got away, I asked him what they said."

"What did they say?"

"They were talking about the place where they grow the plants. About FFF."

Tiller sat immobile, epoxied to his chair. After a moment, he reached out and poured himself another shot of bourbon. "Want a drink?" he said.

"A drink? Sure."

Then Tiller remembered, but he'd already said it, so he just added, "Just a sip." He passed Tad the bottle. The boy upended it. "Hey, that's enough."

Tad was coughing. It burned, not like the wine coolers or the beer. He passed it back. "Tastes like shit."

"Uh-huh . . . You *sure* he said FFF?"

"That's what Rafael said he said."

"What did they say about it?"

"Said it was a big operation, there were lots of . . . capacities. Something like that."

Tiller rubbed his mouth. A connection between Holder and Dugan? It raised interesting possibilities. But who was the man with the sunken face? "Did he seem like a South American, a Latin? The older guy?"

"They were both talking Spanish. Dugan used English once, but the bald guy never did."

"What else did they say? Did your friend Rafael overhear anything else?"

"Just that something's gonna go down out there on the twentieth."

"Something? Like what?"

Tad shrugged, and Tiller mulled that over, too. Yeah, this could make life interesting. A thread, a line leading into the dark. But how to follow it? "Uh, you sneak out to this place, this villa, very often?"

"No. We were only there twice, and the second time the dogs almost ate us. Pit bulls." Tad shivered, remembering the feel of the smooth wet teeth on his fingers as he fought to get the grating closed, the pepper gas burning in his eyes and nose. "I'm not going back there again. Why?"

"I'd like to figure out what's going on. Who this guy is, what's his relation to Dugan and the Funny Fern Farm."

"Well, how about if we just go out there and look?"

Tiller frowned. "You just said you wouldn't."

"Not there. I mean, go out to this other place, the one they were talking about. See what's going on. Maybe we could even get in," said Tad, thinking he'd learned a couple of things from Ripper, maybe he could use them now. Maybe Ripper would like to come.

Galloway thought about that. From what Ferebie had told him, he had a pretty good idea of where Holder's operation was. Northwest of Tartar Springs. Maybe Tad was right: Maybe they could get inside, find out . . . whatever they could find out. Do a little SEAL-type recon.

"You want to go take a look?" said his son, standing up. For the first time in the whole conversation, he looked directly at Tiller, directly down at him.

Tiller frowned up, not in anger, but in a sudden mute questioning; at this stranger, yet blood of his blood; at the child he'd abandoned, the adolescent who stole and lied, the young man who'd saved his life. He looked for a long while at all three together, the mystery of all these in the one person of his son.

"Okay," he said, grateful to whatever or whoever had given him this moment. Capping the bottle, he got up.

EIGHTEEN

A few hours later, Tad lay beneath a dripping screen of palmettos, watching as the shadow that was his dad melted imperceptibly away toward the lights ahead. "Hey, he's good," Ripper whispered beside him.

He nodded silently. Yeah, his dad seemed to pick up sneaking pretty quick. In the dark pants and heavy dark shirt, black gunk smeared on his face, you couldn't see him three feet away in the hammocks. He blended with the trees and he stayed so still between movements that you doubted he was still there.

Behind them, Rafael muffled a sneeze. "Goddamn rain."

"Shut up," Tad told him. "He's almost to the road."

"Well, let's follow him," Ripper whispered.

Tad reached out to grab him—Tiller had been emphatic that only one of them went in close to scout—but the tall kid was already sliding away beneath the nodding bladelike leaves. Tad saw how it was. Ripper was jealous. "Chain Saw!" he hissed.

"What?"

"Come back here."

"Take it easy. Be right back."

Then they were both gone. He debated going after them, but he didn't see the point. It wasn't that he was afraid. It was just a plant nursery, after all. He'd been a lot more afraid when the pit bulls were trying to kill them, and he'd done all right then. But

223

his dad was right: The fewer guys went in, the less chance they had of being seen.

He decided to stay put. Staring into the dark, he listened to the rain tap and rustle in the leaves just like someone sneaking up behind them.

Twenty yards up, Tiller lay full length against the warm, moist ground, letting the ants crawl over his hands and then his face. Their tickling progress and occasional fiery bite, the smell of wet earth, the creaking, chirping din of the jungle at night was all too familiar. All too tuned to memory and instincts he'd almost forgotten he had, except in dream.

It was just like the Rung Sat. And as he wormed ahead, stopping to raise his head to check out where the trees ended, his senses seemed to open out, relays snapping shut to light up circuits unenergized so many years, he'd forgotten they existed. His sense perimeters expanded to take in the hum of insects and the coarse-hair touch of mossy branches and the soggy crepitation of leaf mold as he slid his weight forward. Things scuttled and slithered away from him. Lizards? Tarantulas? They sounded big. His pupils widened, alert for the glint of wire in the faint gray bleed of light reflected off the low clouds, for the flash of light off equipment, for the slightest motion. Yeah, rain was good. Gave you aural cover. Lulled sentries. They figured if they didn't want to go out in bad weather, neither did anyone else.

Wrong.

Only thing missing was that his hands felt empty. They missed his Ithaca, or the M16/XM-148 he'd called "Lady Samantha" for some reason he'd forgotten years ago. But funny, he remembered why now, pulling it out as if it was all tied to one string and once he found the first loop, everything else came sliding out. In the rain-hissing dark, he remembered Sam So Shy from Hatteras High and the night out on the beach under Avon Pier, the world outside the windows forgotten until the incoming tide hissed around the wheels. . . . Shit, he'd stolen cars himself when he was Tad's age; he'd forgotten that . . . let it go. Focus on the now. But his hands felt empty without a weapon and his back felt light without sixty pounds of pack, fins, C rats, ammo, flares, smoke, grenades, water, compass, first-aid kit, Ka-Bar, spare belt for the M60, H harness, UDT life jacket, prisoner-handling kit, all the shit 'n' gear they took on their RP&B missions, deep where they should never have—No, don't slip back into all that—

224

His heart gave a lurch, and his arm stopped halfway through the creep forward.

The beams probed above him, lighting up the boles of the trees. Holding himself rigid-still, he squeezed his lids shut, seeing the red of his own blood as the glare neared. The motor sound came late, muffled by the rain. Not all the advantage was on his side. He lowered himself slowly into the sticky, slippery soil, feeling it squeeze between his splayed fingers, slightly gritty, like warm toothpaste. Then the lights moved past him and on, and the motor noise with it. He glanced at his watch, noting the time. He was raising himself again when he heard somebody behind him.

He tensed, the possibilities racing through his mind. He'd told the boys specifically not to follow him. He snaked his hand out, found a bush, and shook it, giving his pursuer a fix on his line of advance. Then rolled off silently to the side, into the embrace of a tree bole. The sounds came closer. The guy behind him was good, but not as good as he had to be. When he came abreast, Tiller tossed a clump of mud past him. A silhouette head lifted, searching for the sound.

Galloway landed on his back, slamming his head to the rear with a chokehold. But even as he ground the guy's chest into the mud, he felt who it was. He held the grip for a second, just to get the message across, then gave him enough slack for a breath. "Totally quiet," he whispered. "Ripper?"

"Yeah?"

"You on my team or not?"

"Yeah. But—"

"No buts. You're on my team, you follow my orders. Hear me?"

The kid muttered an assent and he let him go. He whispered, "Now get on back there and hold our rear. I don't want to see you again until I whistle."

"Okay," Ripper whispered. "But I just wanted to tell you. If I were you, I'd make a little more noise crawling around in here, or you're gonna step right on a coral snake."

Thirty yards on, Tiller came out onto the road. He crouched in the brush, alert for other vehicles or foot patrols, and surveyed it, taking his time.

The night sky was overcast, but there were lights inside the fence. They lit it and the road, even though they also were shining directly into his eyes. He shaded them and examined the barrier patiently, looking for cover that would let him work his way closer. Finally, he spotted it. He waited for a gust of rain, sprinted across the road, and crouched again on the far side of what seemed to be an electrical distribution box.

The fence was good quality, heavy plastic-coated chain link about ten feet high. He checked the road again—dark and silent—and the grounds on the far side. No movement. The box hummed to itself. He wondered if the fence was electrified. But there didn't seem to be any insulators on the posts, and he couldn't see any warning placards. Dark though it was, he should see their outlines if they were here.

He decided it probably wasn't electrified, and slapped it with the back of his hand to make sure. Nada. He set his toes into the fence and hauled himself up it. At the top, his extended hand stung and he cursed, jerking it back from razor-sharp concertina wire.

Interesting. To keep intruders out? Or to keep the poinsettias in?

A distant glow warned him the vehicle was coming back. He dropped from the wire and huddled behind the box. The head-lights came into view a long way away, maybe a mile, and grew slowly. The fence was straight and very long, and for the first time he started to appreciate how large this operation was. The lights neared. He couldn't see much behind them, but as the pickup passed, spraying water and with the wipers whipping back and forth, he caught a glimpse of its extended cab, two shad-owy figures inside. Then it was gone, taillights bleeding red into the falling mist.

He checked his watch again and saw fifteen minutes had gone by between the two passes. If they were driving at twenty-five and hadn't stopped during the circuit, their perimeter was some-thing over six miles.

He looked at the fence again, then stood up and peered through it. A cleared space of maybe a hundred yards lay inside, then just blue-white lights and low buildings beyond that, too far to make out details.

He dropped again and considered his options. He wished now he'd brought a night-vision device, line, bolt cutters. . . . Well, he'd just do a quick recon and see what he could see without all the gadgetry.

But there was sure a lot of razor wire and guards here for a plant nursery.

He went back into the woods, and as soon as he put his hand

on the first tree to steady himself, a scorpion stung him. He cursed, snatching his hand back, but it was already burning. He gave a low whistle. Several minutes later, three shadows detached themselves from the woods. "Come on out onto the road," he called.

Standing with them on the sand, trying to ignore the throbbing in the web of his hand, he explained the layout to them, then the plan. "Rafael and I, we'll go to the right. Ripper, Tad, y'all go left along the fence. Got your watches? Go for fifteen minutes, running pace, but one you can keep up. Then turn around and head back. We'll join up again right here. Just make sure it's us you join up with."

Ripper and Tad jogged off. Tiller and the Cuban kid, Rafael, started running to the right, on the far side of the road. He didn't know if there were motion sensors, patrols with night-vision scopes. So this was a risk, but they were still outside the boundary fence. He jogged along, listening to the kid start to pant behind him. A good way to show him the downside of smoking cigarettes.

They jogged for about half a mile before he slowed to a walk. Rafael was wheezing, but he'd kept up without complaint. Tiller's hand was throbbing good now, pain shooting up his wrist. He walked for a hundred paces, noting red lights beyond the fence, the rounded bulk of a water tower blacker than the sky. Then he started jogging again. Another half mile, then he'd turn around and head back.

White floods came into sight, tiny and distant at first, but growing brighter. He figured that was where the main road hit the farm. He muttered to Rafael, "Back into the woods," and they detoured back into cover and crept ahead till they could observe the lit area.

It was the main entrance. Sliding gates and a lot of lights. Razor wire coiled on top of the gates, too. A glass booth for the guard, the kind you saw at the entrances to shipping terminals, industrial plants. The gate was open, though, and as they crouched, watching, they saw headlights emerge and swing onto an exit road.

The trucks rumbled through, one after the other. One, two, three, four, five.

Bingo, he thought.

They were huge eighteen-wheelers with the Florida Foliage Factory name and logo billboarded on their sides.

It occurred to him suddenly that with a shipping organization like this, you had ready-made distribution throughout the country. Holder could put anything he liked in those trucks. It didn't have to be potted plants.

Snorting and roaring, the trucks drew gradually away down the road. He looked longingly at the open gate but didn't approach it. He nudged Rafael. "Let's fade back," he whispered.

"It's friggin' huge," said Ripper in an excited, hoarse whisper. "We must of gone two miles. Nothing all that ways but the fence and once a power line going in."

"We found the gate," said Rafael.

"Did you go in?"

"No. There were guards."

Tad said, "We can make some noise, fake them out—"

Ripper said, grinning, "Do y'all want to go inside?"

"What do you mean?"

"I mean, you want to go *inside*? Bet I can find a way in, you want to go. You might get torn up a little—"

"No," said Galloway. "We've seen enough. It's time to go home and try to get some sleep."

When they got back to the car, his whole arm was on fire, but there wasn't as much swelling as he'd expected. Maybe it hadn't been a scorpion. Ripper examined his hand and said there were lots of other things that stung in the hammocks, velvet ants, caterpillars, assassin bugs; unless he started vomiting, the best thing was ice and aspirin. When they got back to the highway, they stopped at an all-night Chevron for ice. Tad drove while Tiller held his hand down into the plastic bag.

The house was dark when they pulled in, after dropping the other two boys off at Ripper's. "There's Mom's car," Tad observed.

At least he wasn't calling her names. Tiller said, "Yeah."

"What time is it?"

"It says there on the dashboard. See the little numbers? Read it yourself. It's easy."

Tad didn't respond.

When he let them in with the spare key, his son went upstairs without saying good night. Tiller stood in the kitchen, examining his hand. The ice seemed to be working; the swelling was going down. He wanted a drink, then remembered he was cutting down.

228

He compromised on a short one, gulped it—he was tired—and went up, too, looking forward to a hot shower and removing the ticks he could feel crawling around under his clothes.

When he slid into bed, he could tell she was awake even before she murmured, "Where were you?"

"Out."

"Was Tad with you?"

"Yeah."

"Are you going to tell me where you went?"

"I told you, just out." He put his hand on her hip. It felt warm. "I just took a shower."

"I heard you in there. That's what woke me up."

"Sorry. How are you doing?"

"What do you mean by that?"

"Forget it," he told her. He'd meant something like, How about rubbing your tits against my manly chest? But the tone of her voice told him it wasn't going to happen tonight. "Just making conversation. See you in the morning, okay?"

She didn't answer. He got his pillows fixed, the extra one under his legs so that his back wouldn't hurt in the morning.

He hadn't meant to bring it up this way, but he didn't know where in the selling process she was—the closing on the property could be tomorrow. He turned his head. "Look, can I ask you something? Before you go to sleep."

Her voice was muffled. "What?"

"You said Tartar was on the market. Have you got a buyer yet?"

"I think so. Tim says we do."

"Are you sure you want to sell?"

"Yes. Why shouldn't I be?"

"I went out there a few days ago. Have you ever been there?"

"Too many times. It's a cesspool. I told Joel anybody who wanted to pay money to go there and dive could go to the bus station toilet, turn the light off, put their head into the commode, and start flushing it as fast as they can. They'd get exactly the same thrill."

He couldn't help smiling in the dark, both at her description of the place and from what he was about to tell her. "Well, I found out something. You're right. It's pretty . . . unpleasant. But only in the upper passages. It's not all like that."

She shifted, not turning over but at least turning her head toward him. "What are you trying to say?"

229

"Down below those narrow tunnels and all that sulfur smell, there's another system. It's huge, beautiful, it's clear, and the caves are amazing."

"Oh, really? I'm glad."

"Bud must have died just after he found that out. That's why he never told you."

"I'm gradually gathering that Bud never told me a lot of things."

He let that one go by. "Well, what I'm telling you now is that he was right about Tartar. We've got—*you've* got a major diving attraction there. It'll take development—"

"Someone else will have to do it."

He stared toward where she lay, then reached out for the light. When it came on, she sat up, looking angry.

"Did you understand what I said?" he asked her. "I'm telling you there's no reason now to go through with the sale. Bud did the tough stuff—the exploring, the surveying. I found the caves he discovered. They're fantastic and huge and they're going to make us money."

"I've already made a deal, Tiller. With the Conservancy. They've already put down a good-faith deposit with Tim."

"Is it final? Have you closed on it yet?"

"No. But I'm not going to go back on it. Blanche is my friend, and so is Billy."

"You might not think that if you knew everything they were up to."

"What do you mean?"

He almost told her, but stopped himself in time. He was getting a creepy sense, not of déjà vu exactly, but as if this had happened already, only not to him but to someone else.

Yeah, this was exactly how it would have happened. Late at night, in bed; Bud, excited, telling her about the springs and the river and finally what he suspected about Holder's plans. And she turning around and telling Arkin.

Then some still-shadowy somebody had killed her husband, and rigged it to look like an accident.

So he couldn't tell her everything. He didn't want it to happen again, to him. But he had to give her the chance to back out, just in case he was wrong about her. So he tried again. "Look, all I'm saying is, why do we have to do it right now? You asked me down here to help you with the business. This is business advice I'm giving you. Put the sale on hold. Let me see how extensive these

230

caves are. Let me put together something we can take to the bank, get a development loan. Or if you still want to sell, take it to a commercial real estate company, get a realistic appraisal—"

"I told you why. We're past that. It's all arranged. Tartar Springs is the last piece of property they need to take the Styx from its sources down to the sea. It'll be the greatest natural preserve in north Florida. That will be Bud's memorial. And it will stay that way forever."

"You think so?"

"Of course," she said simply.

"Is it really for Bud? Or for nature? Or is it for Arkin?"

"I won't even answer that." She turned over. "I'm going to sleep. Your jealousy was cute—at first. Then it made me angry. Now it's just pathetic."

"I guess that's a good-enough answer," he told her. He got up and stood beside the bed, but she didn't move or say anything. So he picked up the pillow and took it down the stairs.

The sunroom was cool now, the windows open. He turned the fan on and watched the blades going around for a while, cursing her and all women with her. Then he got up and built another drink and carried it back to the sofa.

That had been his last chance. Now, staring into the dark, he finally admitted to himself that he was really going to do what he'd sworn he'd never do.

NINETEEN

When he got to the shop the next morning, still carrying the locked case, customers were three-deep at the counter. Mark gave him a wave. Tiller nodded a greeting to him and to Scovill, who was fitting two women for wet suits. Business was suddenly good. That was terrific. Fabricante was due in today. He hoped the store looked just like this when he walked in.

"Colt, Mark. You guys need help out here?"

"Think we got it covered, thanks," Scovill said. Tiller smiled a welcome at the women, not bad-looking but very pale, obviously from somewhere up north. One smiled back. He told Scovill, "We got a possible buyer coming in this morning at ten. Make sure everything's squared away; get the trash put out back and so forth." The manager nodded.

In the office, he settled in behind his desk. When he touched the keyboard the monitor powered on immediately and he saw that the machine had only been resting and that he'd left styx.aqr on. Not smart. . . . He got a fresh disk and made a backup of Bud's article and comments. He put this into the case along with the money. He slid the original into a padded envelope, addressed it to Shad, and dropped it in the outgoing tray. He made sure the file was closed and turned the computer off. Then he peeled the edge of the Band-Aid up and suddenly jerked it off his hand. He examined the red patch beneath. The swelling was almost gone, the pain faded to an ache.

He picked up the phone. The moment was here, the one he'd postponed minute by minute since waking up. The moment he'd sworn years ago would never come, no matter how dark things got. He took a couple of deep breaths, then lowered the handset slowly back to its cradle.

Better think it through again, make damn sure. Was this the smart thing to do? Probably not. Okay, then, was it right? By one code it was. By another, it wasn't. He didn't like what Holder and Arkin and no doubt other associated fat-cat local assholes were doing. But they had the state government, the Park Service, and the local media in their pockets. He was pretty well convinced by now there was only one way of stopping them.

Still, why did *he* have to do it?

Well, first, because nobody else knew what was going on out at Styx. Bud had, but now Bud was dead. Buried in his goddamned dry suit, for Christ's sake.

Maybe that was really what it was about, deep down. If anybody was ever going to pay for that, for Bud's murder, it was up to him.

It would be dangerous. But if he did it right, maybe he could pull it off without absolutely tattooing a bull's-eye on his chest.

Montagnino came past the door, lugging two 80's by the valves. Tiller called, "Hey, Sniffles, call me when this Fabricante shows up, okay?"

"Will do."

"Uh, you heard from July? She call in or anything?"

"No, she hasn't called yet." Montagnino waited a second, then picked the tanks up again and went on back toward the air banks.

Tiller got up and closed the door and regarded the phone again. Finally, he picked it up and placed it against his head with pretty much the same feeling as if it had been a revolver.

The long-distance operator came on. He said, "Hi. Area code for Miami, please."

"That will be a three-oh-five area code."

He dialed 305-555-1212 and asked for the Miami DEA office. Would it be any good disguising his voice? No, don't be melodramatic. He was starting to sweat, though. He reached out and turned the desk fan on. Better.

"Drug Enforcement Administration, Miami Office," a woman answered in a Cuban accent.

"Hi. Is there an Alan Zeno still assigned there?"

"Hold please. I'll connect you with Mr. Zeno's office."

Last chance to hang up. He kneaded his legs, consciously relaxing his calves.

"Mr. Zeno's office."

"Hey, is Al in?"

He was told Mr. Zeno was not in at the moment; he was in the field. If he'd give his number and name, the secretary would pass it along to him when he checked in. He ran his hand through his hair. Finally, he said, "It's a sensitive matter."

"Well, if you want him to contact you . . ."

Finally, he gave her the office number and his name. "But tell him not to identify himself if someone else answers the phone," he added.

"Yes, sir, I'll make a note of that."

After he hung up, he had to get up and walk around the office. Shit, maybe this was a bad idea. He didn't have a lot of confidence in the DEA. He remembered the first time he and Zeno had met, on an Aerocoach twin-engine from Fort Lauderdale to Treasure Cay. Remembered a Star of David gleaming in chest hair under an open-throated guayabera, gold-rimmed aviator frames, a Miami tan. Tiller'd taken him for a vacationing dentist at first. Then they'd run into each other again at the party at Bayou Serene, rubbing shoulders with ex-Presidents and prime ministers, finance consultants, ambassadors, investment bankers. Then the whole business with Troy Christian and the wreck had gone down. . . .

Mark was at the door. "Hey, Till, your man's here."

Victor Fabricante turned out to be a lean, handsome blond in his forties, with styled hair and an accent that sounded Australian. After they shook hands and talked about his flight in, Tiller said, "How did you hear about our business being available?"

"Didn't I mention that in my letter? Some mates of mine came here to do some diving. They happened to tell me you were thinking of selling. I've been thinking of emigrating, you see. The whole process is much simplified if you have business interests, money invested in the States."

"Is that right? So this would be a double good deal for you."

"Something like that, but that doesn't mean I want to buy something that's going to go wheels-up—"

"Course not. You're a diver, right? What, open-water? Cave diving's kind of a different proposition. Well, let's start with our facilities here. This is only one of three locations . . ."

*   *   *

After the basic tour, he turned Fabricante over to Scovill, after building up the manager with a couple of compliments. Colten had been giving the South African a fish-eye stare since he'd arrived. Tiller figured he'd better include Scovill in the process. Then he sat in the office for a while, but he couldn't keep his mind on the billing. Finally, he went out and looked at the compressor, decided it needed a filter change, and started tearing it down. That helped.

He was sitting on the floor, surrounded by parts, when Montagnino found him. "Oh, here you are. Call for you." He held out the cordless.

"Who is it?"

"Says it's the termite inspector, he's returning your call."

"The termite inspector?" He put the phone to his ear, said, "You must have the wrong number, pal, I didn't—"

"Galloway, buddy," said a half-familiar voice. "Good to hear from you."

He swallowed and told Montagnino, "Tony, let me take this on my office extension, okay? Give me a second to get back there; then hang up."

He nodded and Tiller went back, trying to slow down his heart rate. He closed the door, picked up the phone, waited for the hang-up click. "Okay, we're private."

"You know, I always figured I'd hear from you again. Don't know how—just some feeling you develop—but my beeper from God just said, Al, baby, you and this guy have got a future together. And now here you are giving me a call. Where the hell are you? And who, exactly, is squeezing your nuts hard enough for you to remember old Al?"

He remembered now how he'd never felt comfortable talking to Zeno. He didn't sound or act like you expected a law-enforcement guy to act, more like an incompetent Hollywood agent, or a bad stand-up comic. He talked way too much, which wasn't exactly a confidence builder. But that wasn't the real reason he made Tiller feel hinky. It was like the feeling he got sometimes talking to women, that there was some other conversation going on underneath the one you thought you were having. "Well, I just wanted to stay in touch. You gave me a card, remember?"

"And I saw you drop it in the carp pond. The way that big guy went for it, I should try them for bonefish. Anyway, it's nice to hear from you. You still with Don Juan?"

"No. No! I haven't heard from him in a long time."

"He's got himself in some trouble down there; they're finally mustering some political will. But just between you, me, and *USA Today*, I think he'll get out of it clean. They called me the other day for some background. You might have seen the quote . . . The other guys, I don't know about, but he's got too many irons—financial, weapons deals, venture capital. I just don't think they're going to let him go down the chute. . . . I've got a lot of respect for Señor Nuñez. I don't know of anybody else who's lasted near this long, especially with the new gang from Cali eating their brunch these days. Manderell, Escobar, Orejuela—they come and go, speaking of *cocaína*. Just a joke. But I'd love to take him down. That offer I made stands. Helping us get him, that'd make us overlook a lot of things. Do another trip . . . set him up where we can get at him—see where I'm coming from?"

Tiller wiped sweat from his hair. He'd known two people associated with the Combine who'd been suspected of being *chivatos*. One had died in her hot tub, without a mark on her. His FBI handlers had found the other one in his laundry room—with his wife, mother, three children, and their maid. All shot in the back of the head.

"Uh, . . . Al, listen, because I'm going to say this just once: I'm not going to give you Nuñez-Sebastiano."

"Then what have we got to talk about?"

"First of all, are we taping?"

"We tape everything, *compadre*. You know that from the movies. But I can turn it off if you want. Click, it's off. Now let's talk about what you are going to do for us and what we can do for you."

Tiller's hands were wet on the phone now. "This is anonymous. Okay?"

"Sure, but we got to give you a CI number, all that stuff, give you a code name."

A CI was a confidential informant. "You're not listening, Al. I don't want to become a CI. I don't want a number or to be officially or unofficially in your system in any way, and I don't want anything in return for what I'm gonna tell you. Understand me?"

"Then what's the point? How can I go to bat for you when you take a fall? You ought to know by now you can't walk some kind of line between us and them. You're either theirs or ours, and it sounds like to me you're ready to join the saved. Look, CI status is close-hold. We're not gonna come up to you on the street and kiss you on the cheek. . . ."

He wondered once again why whenever you got around drugs it was like swimming past an inflow; you had to kick like hell or you'd just get sucked down and down into the dark and nobody would ever see you again. . . . "I'm hanging up now unless you promise me my name is out of the loop. This is an anonymous tip. That's all."

The agent sighed. "All right . . . but if you're anonymous, we can't use it as evidence."

"That's your problem. Go in and find the evidence."

"Okay, but you still got to have a code name."

"Why?"

"How else do we keep you anonymous? How about—you know the stuff they put on surfboards? I'm doing a little surfing these days. Actually, I just got back from two weeks in Costa Rica. Landed at San José, picked up a rental car, drove down to Guanacaste Province. Paraíso; Playa Negra, Playa del Coco, Witch's Rock, Ollie's Point, down by the border. Fantastic surf there. Ever been to Costa Rica?" Galloway didn't answer. "We'll call you Dr. Zog, after that stuff they put on surfboards. Dr. Zog's Sex Wax. Okay, Doc, what you want to tell Uncle Al?"

Tiller grimaced. He checked the door and turned the fan up till the moving air roared in the mouthpiece. He muttered, "I want to tell you about a guy named Billy Holder."

"Holder . . . rings a bell, but not Notre Dame. . . . He a player?"

Tiller told him who Holder was. He told him about FFF and about the trucks and how easy it would be to distribute cocaine in them.

Zeno listened, not interrupting, but when Tiller was done, he said, "Who exactly is this Holder again?"

"I told you, he runs a foliage company. Only there's a hell of a lot of guys around it with machine guns."

"A BMIF? Big man in Florida?"

"Yeah. His dad coached the Seminoles for about a hundred years."

"I don't know . . . might be snarly. . . . What's your interest in this, Tiller? I mean, Doctor?"

"I don't have an interest."

"Then why are you calling me? I mean, not to impugn your motives as a citizen, but the last time we talked, you were distinctly unforthcoming. And I know you and Don Sebastiano have the relationship—"

"No, no, *no*—"

"Okay, *had* the relationship at one point. . . . Oh, wait a minute. . . . Did he order you to rat on this Holder guy? He's a competitor, maybe?"

"Shit, no. I'm not involved with him anymore. I keep telling you that!"

"Then why are you calling me?"

He said unwillingly, "It's personal."

"Uh-huh. Woman? Money? He run over your dog?"

"I think he killed a friend of mine, had him killed. He's got the local power structure nailed. This is the only way I can see getting justice done."

"Uh-huh, interesting concept . . . thinking of us for justice. . . . Hey, can you hold? I got another call coming in—"

"No. Let's finish this up. If you don't want to pursue it, fine. I'll talk to somebody else. Maybe the FBI."

"Well, wait a minute. You don't want to go to those guys. . . . Matter of fact, some of what you're saying might interlock with some movement data customs has been putting out. Traffic's up through Florida the last year or so. It was moving into the Bahamas, then shifted to Mexico; now we're seeing the Florida connection picking up again. Port of Miami, Lauderdale, containerized cargo; hell, we got go-fast boats off-loading coke right into the Keys again. As if they know exactly where the Coast Guard's gonna be that night. We know there's a distribution network downstream of that, but we don't know how or who. Ever heard of a guy named Carlos Díaz-Báez?"

"No." It crossed his mind that might be Dugan's real name. But he wasn't going to blow Dugan. Anyway, all he knew about Dugan was the money laundering, and not really much about that. Still, there was the connection with Holder through this mysterious bald guy. Tenuous, but it was conceivable that if everything worked out, Zeno might shoot Dugan off his back along with the Holder operation. He didn't have any moral problem with that. He'd made it plain to Dugan from the start that he didn't want to be involved.

But finally Zeno said, "It's interesting, but it's not enough—that you suspect this Holder might be moving product. I mean, we can't initiate action against a U.S. citizen on that basis. Find out more, maybe I can help you out. Otherwise, I just can't commit the resources. Understand what I'm saying?"

"Hold on now, just—"

"And I don't think that if you go to some other agency, you're

238

going to get a different answer. Have you tried the local sheriff, the Highway Patrol? I know you said he's got connections, but he can't literally have everybody on the payroll. Murder's a serious charge, but basically it's not a *federal* crime, see what I mean? Love to do business but . . . so. You got my number? Obviously. Stay in touch. Got another call. . . . Sayonara, Doc."

The line sighed like distant wind. Tiller lowered the handset and stared at the blurred disc of the fan blades.

He'd taken the risk and struck out. He eyed the wall, wondering if he could put his fist through it and, if so, how many little bones he'd break.

A knock. He yelled, "Come in."

"It's an interesting setup. Your lad Scovill seems sharp as a tack. Can we chat about it?"

He cleared his throat, pointed to a folding chair. Fabricante sat forward, legs spread, the attitude of a man ready to get down to business. Tiller forced his attention back. If it was useless, if he couldn't get anyone to move against Holder, maybe it was time to get realistic. Help Monica sell. Give Dugan back his money somehow, at the point of a gun, if that was what it took, and head back to Hatteras with his sales commission. The only other alternative was to take out Holder himself, and he drew the line at that. Not because he had any ethical problem lighting up whoever had wasted Bud. Just that he wasn't absolutely certain that Holder was the right guy to kill.

If he only had some way to find out. . . . He remembered Fabricante, blinked and cleared his throat, found the South African staring at him. "Yeah," he said, pulling the presentation folder out and sliding it around so Fabricante could see it. "Start with the three-year income summary. Here's our balance sheet as of this month. Notice the bottom line. Nice, huh? All CPA-certified. We're looking at a chunk of change soon from sale of some property. That will go to the principals, but it'll actually improve the profit picture, since there'll be no more capital investment, taxes going out there. . . ."

Scovill came in when Fabricante left, taking with him copies of the prospectus and Xeroxes of the last three tax returns. He said he wanted to study them and talk it over on the phone with his attorney in Capetown. The manager closed the door and leaned against it. Tiller glanced up, noted his folded arms.

"You're gaining some muscle mass," he told him.

"Been doing some weight work. This Fabricante, he seems interested."

"He does, doesn't he?"

"He know I'm part owner?"

"I told him, and it's in the documentation. You're covered, Colt. Relax."

"How does that work? If he makes an offer."

"However you want it to. Do you want to sell him your twenty percent? Or do you want to hang on to it, partner with him?"

Scovill looked into the distance. Finally, he said, "I've been here six years."

"Ready to move on? Take the bucks and run?"

"I've had offers. Now that Bud's gone . . ."

"Those times come," Tiller told him. "Okay, we'll proceed on that basis. I'll keep you informed when and if he comes in with an offer, and we'll need your signature on the sale. You get twenty percent of net proceeds, less selling expenses, title-transfer fees, et cetera cetera cetera."

"How much is Monica paying you?"

"Why do you need to know?"

"I owe you a cut, too. For handling it."

Galloway shrugged. "You can talk to her about that. Whatever the two of you think is fair."

"We'll miss you around here."

"Don't get your hopes up; he hasn't made an offer yet." But Scovill was holding out his hand. Tiller stood and took it, then winced. "Hell."

"Didn't mean to hurt you."

"It's not you; it's the hand. Something bit me while I was . . . cleaning out the garage."

He sat again after Scovill left, feeling deflated and vaguely sad. As if it was coming to an end, not with a bang, but with a whimper. His dreams of moving here, getting together with Monica were drifting away. Scovill was right: Fabricante seemed interested. . . . Maybe it was time to start thinking about what he was going to do back in Hatteras. He'd have enough for a down payment on a used boat. Oddly enough, the prospect didn't thrill him. In a way, it was nice not having a boat to worry about. If that wasn't blasphemy for a Hatteras man. And now he had Tad to consider. . . . He sat thinking about it until it was time for the afternoon class.

*　　*　　*

He was standing in front of the shop after they locked up that night, having just slammed the Buick's trunk shut on the case, when a pearl-colored Infiniti with tinted windows rolled up beside him. The window hummed down, revealing a tan leather interior and Sergio Dugan, in a linen jacket and sunglasses. "Get in," he said.

"I was headed home."

The passenger side door unlocked. Tiller hesitated, then walked around and let himself in.

Dugan backed out and slid out onto Gaines. He turned east, then left again at Monroe, and drove past the building with the striped awnings Tiller remembered Monica telling him was the old capitol. Tiller studied his profile, the stiff little goatee, the gold and jet earrings. Left again at Tennessee, a six-lane strip of bars and restaurants and trendy shops. He pulled into the lot in front of Rubyfruit Books and turned the engine off.

"I haven't got word back that the shipment has arrived."

"Uh . . . we need to talk about that."

"It is extremely urgent, *extremely* urgent that it get there soon. Do you understand? Has it gone out yet?" Dugan asked him.

Just looking at the set of the guy's face, Tiller realized his half-formed idea of giving him his money back wasn't going to work. He said, "Uh . . . no. But it will. Very soon. In fact, it's en route now."

"There are problems?"

"Problems? No, no problems."

"You found out how Bud transferred the funds?"

"Uh . . . yeah," he half-lied. "Not exactly all the details yet, but I found out where it—"

"Good," said Dugan. He reached into the back. To his horror and dismay, Tiller found himself with another case, identical to the first, on his lap.

"Hold on," he said. "I can't take on any more. Why don't we hold off, not push this—"

"Push it," said Dugan. He reached down to adjust what Galloway assumed was the automatic, under his shirt. "Have you taken your cut out of the first shipment?"

He remembered paying Ferebie out of the first case. "I took a grand out."

"Forty-nine more are yours. Out of this—another forty." He reached over and patted the case on Tiller's lap. "Four hundred thousand, not quite as much as the first, but next week we'll have

241

more. We need to keep it moving. *¿Comprende?* I don't want to hear arguments! *Más que idiota.* Do you need some lesson in how serious I am?"

"No. But it's not that simple."

"Kusczk managed it. You're as smart as he was. No?"

Dugan peered at him over the sunglasses, and Galloway knew suddenly just from that glimpse of his eyes that he wasn't just a distributor and financier. Now he understood the hair-trigger temper, the erratic reasoning. Shit, he'd been there. Dugan was under pressure. But being a user, too, made him not just dangerous but unpredictable, too.

Galloway tucked his hands under his armpits, feeling how wet the cloth was there. Trying to choose his words was like stepping out into a minefield. "Look, I'm on your side, pal, but I keep telling you, I'm still learning his system, okay? And I'm not a goddamn bank. If you keep giving me cash, I can't be responsible for it. Shit, I'm still—" He was about to say he was still carrying the first shipment around with him, but then he remembered he'd said it was already en route. He finished, "I'm still getting the bugs worked out."

"Do you need help?"

"No. I'll do it, but I need more time. Here, take this back—"

"You keep it. I trust you."

"Why do you trust me so much?"

"Because you know I'll pop your son." Dugan leaned back against the leather. His eyes followed two women going into the bookstore. "And your *marinova.* And then, we cut your legs and your arms off, and then *te voy a castrar,* and finally, your head. No, I think I can trust you with any amount of money I choose."

Galloway felt as if there wasn't enough air inside the car. He slowly slid his hands out from under his armpits, staring at the man sprawled in the driver's seat.

He was debating whether it might not be the smartest move to take this guy out right now, right here, in this dark corner of a parking lot. He was feeling more and more certain that it was going to come down to that eventually, him versus Dugan. Why wait? The Colombian's window was closed. A short blow to the head would bounce his skull off it. That wouldn't kill him, but it would stun him, keep his hand off his gun. His sight narrowed to the hollow of Dugan's neck. The skin there was thin. Under it was the carotid and the windpipe. Get two fingers in there and

242

he'd be dead in fifteen seconds. He didn't enjoy doing things like that and he'd hoped never to again, but maybe that was the only way out of this deepening well of shit. Snuff this *dinky dau* bastard and leave him and the money here, make sure to wipe every part of the car he'd touched—

Dugan lifted his hand, signaling to someone behind them. Tiller slid his eyes to the rearview and saw the other car, against the curb on the far side of the street, one of the men in it raising his hand, too. He eased his breath out, dropping his hands again to rest in his lap.

"Any questions?" the Colombian said.

"No—yes. Where's all this cash coming from? No, forget that. I know the answer. But how much more's there going to be? How often can I expect deliveries? If I can do some advance planning, this would all work out easier."

"The less you know, the safer we all are. The law enforcement here does not yet accept our pay . . . at least directly. They are not yet entirely part of our team. They are not very alert, but you can't entirely forget they are there."

"Yeah, what about that? What do I do in case somebody comes around? Cops, feds, the DEA—"

"Just hide the money and stay calm," Dugan told him. "It will not happen. But if it does, we will warn you in advance."

"In advance?" He looked at the car behind them again. Black Lincoln, not the latest model. Its lights were out and he couldn't see the plates. "How can you—"

"Never mind how. I'm just telling you, if there is to be a move against us, we will get at least twenty-four hours' notice."

"Well, good. But another thing. The dive business, I've got a guy thinking about buying it. If he does, I'll be out of here, back to—where I live. I'm only here temporarily."

"I like you where you are," said Dugan. "Buy the business yourself. I can advance you the money. But you don't want to leave Florida. No, I don't think you want to leave Florida now."

"Great," Tiller said, rubbing his face. He looked down at the case, then opened it. He touched a couple of stacks. All hundreds this time. He cursed himself silently, cursed Dugan, cursed the whole damned business. How had he gotten back into it? Was it a flaw in himself, that he just couldn't seem to stay clear of this shit?

"So do not worry about that, or anything else," Dugan told him. He patted his shoulder with a manicured hand laden with gold, truculence transmuted into benevolence now by the unpredictable alchemy of cocaine. "You are part of our family now. You will be protected. Remain loyal and we will make you rich and happy."

He said, "That's a relief, Sergio. Believe me, that's a real relief."

TWENTY

He sat in a meeting hall the next night, nursing a paper cup of coffee as an earnest-looking guy with fuzzy gray sideburns clicked slides through a projector. The local Speleological Society "grotto"—chapter—had invited a biospeleology expert as the keynote speaker, and to everyone's dismay, he was into the second hour of his presentation and still going strong. The cavers around him were talking in whispers about Exmore's death and what it was going to do to cave diving. Galloway looked across the darkened room and yawned. Then his mind returned to his problems.

Since Zeno had killed his last hope of outside help, he'd accepted that he'd have to solve things on his own. He didn't want to. He was no Mack Bolan, no John Rambo, charging in and wiping out his enemies alone. It was a nice fantasy and he'd even indulged in it for a few minutes, but he knew from bitter experience how that would end in real life: with one dead good guy and not very many bad ones on the ground. What he really needed was something that would take them all down at once, tie them all together and then sink them: Holder, Ferebie, Arkin, Dugan, everyone in the whole stinking conspiracy.

He thought about how to do that as the speaker droned on about *Horologion speokoites* and the chances of its rediscovery in the West Virginia deep caves.

If he couldn't manage Holder and Company, at the very least he had to take out Dugan. If he had to kill the man to pry him

245

off his back, so be it. It wouldn't be easy. He was armed, he was suspicious, and he had bodyguards. He'd have to find out more about him: where he lived, who he did business with, when and where he went without his thugs. That would be dangerous, just as the hit would be dangerous.

That meant he was going to have to send Tad back to his mom.

And Monica? He'd have to cut that off, too. Actually, it felt dead already between them. Maybe it was time to find a room out in town.

It might be even simpler just to leave. He still wanted to find out who'd killed Bud. But it seemed less important the deeper he was sucked into the mess—no, hell, the *messes*—Kusczk had left behind. Wouldn't it be simpler all around just to vanish? At some point, he was going to have to get out. Why not now? Explain the situation to Tad. Tell him they were headed back to Hatteras. Tell Monica he was sorry but that it wasn't working out. Scovill could handle the shop. The manager would be happier without Tiller Galloway on his ass. If Fabricante came in with an offer, let her chum Arkin handle the negotiating.

Maybe it was time to let go. Who the hell did he think he was? The avenging angel? The hold of old times only went so far.

"And in conclusion, the future of these unique and wonderful cave creatures is up to us. Thank you."

He clapped gratefully as the lights came up. The old guy peered around, astonished, as if he'd never been applauded before. The chairman rose, and after a few more remarks, the meeting broke up. He stood by the door, seeing familiar faces here and there.

Then one detached itself from the crowd and July Toll took his arm. "Tiller."

"July! Where have you been? We called but just got your answering machine."

"That's because I haven't been here. I'm saying my good-byes tonight. I'm leaving town."

"Leaving? Where are you headed?"

"The Yucatán. Actually, Cozumel. A resort diving operation called Dive Paradise. They run tours out of the big hotels, vacationers, dive groups. Reef trips, dolphin adventures, feed Charlie the Grouper."

"Sounds great."

"No, it sounds stupid and . . . cowardly. But that's still where I'm going." She eyed him straight and he hesitated, then had to nod.

"I know it wasn't a spur of the moment thing. Actually, I'm thinking about getting out of here myself."

"If you want to come down and visit, once I've got a place to stay—"

"I might do that someday." He knew he wouldn't, but he figured she knew that, too. They looked back at the dispersing cavers. "How about a farewell drink?"

"I don't know. It's late. . . . I've got a couple of beers left in my truck from the last road trip."

"Deal."

He climbed into her Ranger and she handed him an Old Milwaukee from an electric cooler. He popped it and drank in silence. Then noticed she wasn't. "You're not drinking?"

"None for me, thanks. So what did you want to say?"

"What did I want to say? Oh, just good luck, I guess, and good diving."

She looked out the window and he had a sudden suspicion that maybe she'd expected him to ask her to stay . . . that maybe she— no, that was silly; he'd never thought of her that way. But why hadn't he? She was no model, she was a little heavy, and her complexion wasn't perfect, but she was attractive enough. . . . all he could come up with was that distance, that private reserve she wore as effectively as a chador.

"Don't you want to know why I'm leaving?"

"I guess so. Yeah."

"Because I'm sick of wondering who's going to be the next one of my friends to die. I got into diving because it seemed like fun. This doesn't feel like fun anymore. It's, like, obsessive. Guys like Lamont and Joel, the best divers there are. I don't know if you knew about Bud and me—"

He stopped the beer can in midair. "What about you and Bud?"

"We were lovers."

"No. No, I didn't know that."

"Does it surprise you?"

He thought about Monica and Arkin, and Monica saying the fault was not all on her side, that his friend Bud wasn't perfect, either. He cleared his throat, not looking at her. "Nothing surprises me anymore, July."

"Well, that's part of it. And now that I'm leaving, I guess it doesn't hurt to tell you the last of it. I'd like to be able to tell somebody. There was a child."

"A *child*?"

"Or there could have been. When I found out, I confronted him. I didn't tell him that. I just said I was sick of waiting, that he had to decide about us. He told me he wasn't ready to leave Monica yet, that he had to have more time. By then it was three years, and I knew it was more of his bullshit. So I . . . terminated the pregnancy. He never knew about it."

"I'm sorry."

"I don't know if he'd really have left her. He said so, but who knows?"

"I always thought his word was good—back when I knew him."

"I've noticed there are guys who are honest to other guys but not so honest with women."

"You have a point there."

"But anyway, you see where I'm coming from. Then he died, and Lamont, and—it's not about when I got into trouble, there in Wabasso. I've been down since then."

"I don't think you lost your nerve, if that's what you mean."

"It just seems . . . pointless. So I said my good-byes tonight. I'm not a cave diver anymore. I'll just take the tourists out and show them the reef at thirty feet, and hitch rides on sea turtles, and lose ten pounds." She wiped her eyes, and he realized she was crying.

On the spur of the moment, he said, "You know, I don't think Bud's death was an accident."

She wiped her cheeks and didn't respond.

"Did you hear me?"

"What?"

"I said, I think he was murdered. He didn't die in Emerald Sink, that's for certain."

Toll looked at him, and all at once he felt his back stiffen. *She* could have killed Kusczk. She was a skilled cave diver; she wasn't big, but she was strong. It might have taken her a while, but she could have gotten a body out of Tartar and into a truck . . . maybe into *this* truck. . . . And she had a motive, too. A damn good one.

"You think someone murdered him?"

He took a breath, plunged on, although he reminded himself there had to be limits on what he told her. He explained about the autopsy and what he'd concluded. She nodded soberly. "That's right, you always have a little water left in your wings. . . . So who do you think killed him?"

"You don't seem upset."

"What do you want, hysterics? I don't do those. Anyway, just

248

because he died in Tartar and they found him at Emerald, that doesn't necessarily mean he was murdered. All it means is that someone moved the body."

"Why else would they do that, unless they'd killed him?"

She pursed her lips, and he finished the beer while she thought about it. Finally, she said, "The only thing I can think of is a landowner trying to avoid liability, being sued—"

"But he owned Tartar."

"Right, so that's out. What do the cops think?"

"I haven't told them."

"What? Why not?"

"I have good reasons not to until I can tell them exactly who it was, with some proof stapled to it. But let me ask you this. Who might have wanted Bud dead? I have some suspicions, but let's hear yours."

"Maybe you'd better ask Blanche about that."

"Who?"

"Blanche Holder. It wasn't Monica he was holding out for after all. It was Blanche."

Galloway ran his hand over his hair. Here was a labyrinth more tangled than the karst caves, level beneath level. "Wait. I'm getting confused here."

"I don't know why. It's perfectly simple. Bud took whatever he could get, where and when he could. From me, from other women—remember Gloria, you met her on your first dive? Then I found out he was seeing Blanche, too. Look, I'm sorry to have to tell you this about your old army buddy, but actually he was a real bastard. Monica kept forgiving him, but I think even Mon was getting fed up. Anyway, I had it out with him. Told him I'd had enough, that I didn't want him touching me again. I was through playing his games."

"You said he was waiting for Blanche—"

"That's right. After we had our discussion, he said he was sorry for what he'd put me through, but if he ever did leave Mon, it was Blanche he really belonged with. She was going to leave Billy. He told me more, but I didn't want to hear it. I just wanted to blot it all out. If I'd had a gun or a power head right then—well, you wouldn't have had to wonder who did it. I was mad enough." She turned her face to him and he saw it was hard and shining as polished agate. "So it's not entirely because he died in a cave that I'm leaving. That's part of it, but not all of it. I want to go away and forget this whole mess, if I can. I want to meet some-

249

body who's honest enough that when he says he loves me, I can believe it. I can build something on it."

"I wish I could apologize for Bud. If he'd lived, I'm sure he'd have realized it someday, that he didn't treat you very well."

"It's a nice thought. Anyway, I'm leaving tomorrow." She held out her hand. "Good-bye, Tiller. If there's anything else, you can write care of Dive Paradise. The address is in the magazines."

When he got back to Killearn, Tad was watching television. Tiller told him that things were getting too dangerous here. He was sending him back to Virginia, to his mom. He watched his son's face turn white, watched him turn back into a stranger. He moved out of Monica's room, too. She tried to talk to him when she saw him making his bed on the sunporch, but he cut her off. And after that, the house was quiet in the deepening night.

TWENTY-ONE

The next day was the nineteenth, the day, when he and Shad had owned a business, he'd always tried to get a start on bills. He went in early and had them lined up on his desk—power, Yellow Pages, phone, insurance, the cable bill, the monthly payables from the suppliers—when he heard someone let himself in the front door and click the display-area lights on. He yelled, "Hey, Colt? Why do we have cable here?"

Scovill stuck his head in. "For the TV. We play tapes on it, for the gear classes."

"I understand the VCR, but why do we have cable?"

"Bud got it two, three years back. Sometimes there are things we tape, National Geographic specials and the Discovery Channel, stuff about diving. So it's a business expense. But mostly it's for the winter, when things get slow."

Tiller grunted, considered canceling it, then thought, It's a morale thing. Let the staff have it. He typed in the amount and the printer hummed. He stuffed it into the envelope, then picked up the next one.

By ten, he was done. He carried the stamped mail out and said hi to Montagnino, who was manning the counter, with his feet up, reading *DeepTech Journal*. He mulled this over on the walk to the mailbox and when he came back said, "Tony, how are you at display work?"

"Window displays? July did those."

"Well, she's not gonna be doing 'em anymore. Let's get those

251

palm trees out of there. Ditto with the fishnets, and the babes in the color-coordinated skin suits."

"What do you want?"

"This is a goddamn cave divers' store. Let's get some technical-looking shit out there. Neutralites, those new OMS backplate systems, maybe put a Superlite out. Some crusty old stalactites or something, some of those fossil sand dollars—"

"No stalactites," said Scovill from where he was slicing open the day's UPS shipments like a seer searching for signs in their entrails. "Take nothing but pictures. Leave nothing but bubbles."

"Okay, then Nitrox tanks, computers, dive reels—you know what I'm talking about. I want people to look in that window and think, Shit, this is some hard-core deep-diving kind of place. Let's go in here and sign up for something dangerous. You find a skull, we'll put it out there with a mask on it."

"You'll lose some customers," Montagnino said. "Not everybody likes that."

"Tough. They can go down the street to Powder Puff Skindivers, with the heated pool." He stared Montagnino down till he put the magazine away.

He didn't know why he felt this way, charged, on a buzz. But it was satisfying kicking everybody into activity. Or maybe he was just asserting what little power he still had over his environment. He made another circuit of the store, then went back into the repair area and checked the ledger. He pulled a ripped Viking suit off the rack, patched the tear, then started replacing the neck seals.

The phone rang. Scovill yelled, "Tiller! For you."

He muttered, "Shit." He yanked the portable out of the manager's hand. "Galloway."

"Hey, Doctor."

It was Zeno. After the shock of recognition, he went down the hall and ended up in the bathroom, door closed, holding the remote close to his ear. He looked at the faucet, then turned it on.

Sitting on the commode, he murmured, "What do *you* want?"

"Well, we're here. Pretty fast flight. Look, we need to get together. Like, as soon as we can. Got a car?"

"Wait. Wait. What are you talking about? Where are you?"

"Here, in Tallahassee." The DEA agent said something to somebody on his end of the line, then came back on. "Look, how about—no—somebody suggested the Junior Museum. Know where that is?"

252

"No, I don't."

"They tell me it's east of the airport, on Orange Avenue. That help? Anyway, find out and meet me there. By the panther's cage. Eleven—that give you enough time?"

"I don't get it. Last time we talked, you didn't have the time of day—"

"And we were on the phone, and it was a cold call, and I had to check some things out before I made any commitments. But mostly, I wanted to keep this close-hold. Y'unnerstand me? Funny things been happening. We plan a raid, real weird, somehow everybody seems to know we're coming. I'm not saying we're penetrated, but this time we're gonna move fast and quiet. Real fast and real quiet. You haven't told anybody you talked to me?"

"Jesus, no. You think I'm nuts?"

"I don't know very much about you at all, Mr. Galloway. Just what I read on your rap sheet, that you're a former player, and talking to you for twelve minutes a couple years ago. So we're taking each other on faith, right? Eleven, the panther cage. Be there. Alone."

Tiller sat holding the phone, feeling angry and confused and, for some reason, stupid. He turned the faucet off, then turned it on again and washed his hands. He flushed the toilet and started to go out into the shop, to ask Scovill or Montagnino where the kids' museum was. Then he remembered: close-hold. He went back into his office and took out the city map.

The Junior Museum was called the Tallahassee Museum of History and Natural Science now. He paid his admission and went through the visitor center and out into the Animal Natural Habitat. He'd expected a cage, since Zeno had said "cage," but there didn't seem to be any. Just woods and winding sand paths and here and there fences so you couldn't get too close to the animals—alligators, foxes, red wolves. Finally, he found a sign that said FLORIDA PANTHER, and stood peering into the woods. It was hot and still. He wiped sweat out of his eyes.

"Dr. Zog, I presume."

He turned from contemplating the empty forest.

Alan Zeno had aged. Or maybe it was just that he looked older in a window-plaid suit than he had in a guayabera. He was still Miami-tanned, though, and still wore those same contour-ground glasses in gold aviator frames. "Thanks for coming," he said, shaking hands. "And thanks for the call. That took guts, to take that first step back."

He didn't say anything, looked at the other suits. Zeno introduced them. "J. T. Jager, Bureau of Alcohol, Tobacco and Firearms; Nelson Gionet, Customs Service; Hugo de las Heras, U.S. Marshal's Service. We also got guys coming in from the FBI and, everybody's favorite, the IRS. You see we got an interagency thing going. That's the big concept these days. It sort of grew out of the old—"

Tiller interrupted him. "Look, I told you I don't want to get involved with you. I came out here to tell you that. You want to act on what I told you, do it. Good luck, but leave me out."

He started to leave, but the massed suits blocked his way. He looked past them to a posse of second graders trooping past. One kid glanced their way, but his eyes slid off like they were coated with Armor All: grown-ups. De las Heras said, "Hang, mister. You don't turn the federal government off like some telephone solicitor, wants to sell you ballpoint pens made by the blind. See what Al's got to say."

"You like raccoons?" Zeno asked him. "Clever little thieves. I love 'em. Let's go look at the raccoons."

"I like it here," said Galloway. He turned and looked between the trees and thought he saw a flash of something tan. When he looked again, it was gone. He put his back to the fence and rammed his hands into his pockets. Sweat ran down his back, under his shirt. His eyes roamed the passing kids, looking for a Dugan, for a bald old man, for a Holder.

Zeno said, "So. Here's the big picture as it appears at this point in time. We checked out the guy you mentioned and, lo and behold, there are other people who from time to time have voiced their suspicions to us re the selfsame guy. We routed the inquiries to the local cops, but they always came back squeaky."

"He's got connections."

"Yeah, his dad. The Seminoles are kind of a secular religion around this part of the state. J. T. here, he's an FSU grad. He used to play second string for old Hiram C., back when Ron Hester was playing." The ATF agent grinned.

"You still in touch with your teammates?" Galloway asked him.

"Every day," said Jager, showing incisors.

He saw that Jager was set up to be the bad cop. At the same time, he heard something behind him, a purring rumble like a distant gravel tipple. He glanced back but didn't see anything.

"Anyway, that gave your story credibility. So we set up a flight. And provided a couple more details get worked out, we're going in."

Tiller asked what he meant. "He means we're going in," said de las Heras. He had a large, flat, hard face that looked like it belonged in a 1930s labor mural. "If the property's being used to process and ship drugs, we can seize-and-forfeit—federal prosecutor, federal charges, federal court. We don't have to do anything through the state."

"The other interesting thing," Zeno told him, "is that this fella Holder is a pillar of the local GOP. It's not going to help the current governor if one of his chums goes down."

"Yeah, he's a conservative Republican. But what difference does that make?"

"You're absolutely right. What difference does it make? None at all. We're strictly nonpartisan. But just between you and me, it means we got the green light for this a lot faster."

Tiller started to say something but stopped at a sudden warning grimace from Gionet. All four men stared past him. "Uh . . . better not make any sudden moves," said Zeno.

He caught it then, the back-alley stink of cat piss. He eased himself slowly off the mesh and looked back. Flat yellow eyes stared right into his from a sloped skull. The panther's hide was tawny, its neck and shoulders speckled with white spots. Its tail brushed the leaves. *Whish. Whish.*

"Nice animal. First time I ever see one."

"They're endangered. Only a few of 'em left."

He could sympathize. He turned his back to the open pathway, wishing he had a thicket to creep into like the cat. "You're talking some kind of raid."

"Now you're getting it."

"But there's a problem," said Zeno. "A sticky little wicket called probable cause. See, we've got an anticipatory warrant, based on your statements and some other corroborating evidence. But the search is only authorized on condition we confirm there are drugs on the premises before we go in."

"Isn't that what you're doing the raid to find out?"

"Hell, no. What if we came up empty? No, the point of the raid's to gather evidence of what we already know is there. We don't do the raid and then say, Hey, Judge, we sure are sorry! There really isn't any product here," the ATF guy told him. "There's been some criticism from certain quarters of recent actions. Saying we're 'overzealous.' So we need to confirm there's like drugs there, or automatic weapons, like you told Al."

"Overzealous," Galloway said. "You mean like when you shot the guy's daughters in Montana? The supremacist. Chouquette?"

"He killed his daughters. Not us."

"That's not what the papers say."

"The papers lie," said Jager. "Anyway, what do you care about some stinking Nazi? You one, too?"

"Cool off, boys." Zeno slid in, put an arm around Tiller's shoulders. "Bottom line, we need you, Galloway. We got lawyers, we got snipers, but you got something right now we ain't got that we need bad. So let's see how we can help each other out."

Tiller pushed the arm off. "Let me restate my position. You got an anonymous tip. I'm going to deny giving it to you. And I'm not going to help with any raid. That's what you get paid to do."

"You want to be paid? That what I'm hearing?"

"No! What you're hearing is that I'm not gonna be one of your official stooges."

He started to walk away again, and this time, smoothly but with irresistible force, he found himself pressed back till the wire mesh imprinted itself on his back and the ammoniacal cat stink burned his eyes. He'd never been literally surrounded by a wall of feds before. Jager had his hand inside his suit coat. Tiller leaned back, intensely conscious of the rumbling growl behind him. Between a rock and a hard place. The devil and the deep blue sea. The stink of annoyed panther and the stink of mean cop.

"Well, unfortunately, it doesn't seem to be possible to do it without you," said Zeno. "And we're very eager. One thing we hope to find is some link to a guy named Díaz-Báez. I think I mentioned his name to you. He's a Caleño *pesco gordo*. A big fish. In charge of U.S. distribution for the Cali cartel. We know he's in Florida right now checking on the cell heads for the home office. If we can find an operating cell, maybe we can luck out and find a lead to him, too."

"Don't know him."

"You sure? Anyway, that's the plan."

"No, it's not. I'm not helping you."

"You haven't even heard it yet. Are you listening?"

"No."

Zeno said, "You said you know Holder. We want you to use that. Penetrate the farm for us. Once you confirm the shit's present, you notify us. We move in and arrest everybody, take them and the evidence into custody and let the courts straighten it all out."

"Excuse me," said a new voice. The suits turned, to face a black security guard. "Is there a problem here, gentlemen?"

"Yeah," said Tiller. "Help. Rogue cops, assaulting a citizen."

"Go away," said de las Heras, holding out a badge. The guard looked at it, then at Galloway. Zeno and Jager flipped open badges, too. The guard went away, then turned and called back, "Don't feed the panther."

Jager laughed.

Tiller said, "That's the stupidest plan I've ever heard. I met the guy just once, at a goddamn charity event. He's not gonna let me in. Why don't you just stop one of the trucks?"

"That wouldn't work," said Gionet. He hadn't said anything up to now. "We stop a truck, find a few hundred kilos, the driver goes to prison, but everybody else walks. It doesn't take long to destroy evidence. We want to prove continuing criminal enterprise. All you need to do is go in, find it, and give us the high sign. We take it from there."

He thought about it, standing there waiting for fangs in his ass. Boxed in, goddamn it, they were boxing him in again. Just the way Dugan had. Different species, but the same kind of predators.

But what Zeno and his fellow baboons didn't know was that he didn't really think there were drugs at FFF. Dugan and his friends could distribute cocaine without trucks. They could do it in the glove compartments of cars going up US 95. But if the feds went in, he could get the water diversion on the record, blow the Styx operation apart that way.

It wasn't the way he'd wanted to play it. But maybe it was the best he could hope for. Rip it open and let the pus spatter all over Florida.

But the next minute, he thought, Would it really go that way? Because it never did. Not when you were dealing with cops. He could trust them as far as he could trust Dugan, except that Dugan represented a far more effective and seamless organization. He said, "You make a good case, but—no thanks. You can't do it without me, you'll just have to fold up your tents and go home."

"J. T., read him his rights," said Zeno, sighing.

Jager took his hand out of his jacket. Instead of a .38, it held a folded document with a legal blue cover. "We took the precaution of swearing out a subpoena."

"What for?"

"A grand jury."

"So what? I'm not going to show up."

"That's called failure to respond."

"So jail me."

"Oh, no, we probably wouldn't ever get to," said Jager. "See, the thing you got to bear in mind is, subpoenaed individuals, that becomes public record. Even guys we call as friendly witnesses."

He stood immobile. "You bastards," he muttered.

"But we don't want to do that," Zeno announced. "That's not the way we like to operate. You want to be anonymous? You will be Mr. Nobody. All record of your involvement will disappear. The four of us will suffer collective amnesia regarding your existence. All you have to do for us is go in and confirm presence. Then we go do the stuff that goes into the newspapers. We all get what we want. Except the bad guys."

Galloway stood defenseless. He understood now that there was no way out. His name on a friendly-witness subpoena would be a death contract as far as the Cartel was concerned. Like a cornered king on a chessboard, he had no other moves than to try to stay alive as long as possible.

"Look, I told you I knew Holder, but there's no way they're going to let me just walk in there. And if I did, how in the hell am I gonna be anonymous?"

"Then get in some other way," said Zeno. "Cut through the fence. Use your imagination. You're a free agent. We're not."

"I *told* you, the place is wired with concertina. The perimeter is patrolled. I wouldn't be surprised if they have motion sensors in there."

"You're supposed to be some kind of hot special forces–type guy," Jager sneered. "Medals and all. You figure out how."

He stood immobile, looking down at the ground.

"What's wrong?" said Zeno.

"Nothing . . . just a minute. Lemme think." He rubbed his mouth, considering. He tried to remember how the labyrinth beneath Tartar Springs ran, how the Big Cave tended, what Bud must have seen to reach the conclusions he'd reached about Holder and his plans for the Styx.

He said slowly, "Yeah, there might be another way in. When were you thinking about doing this?"

"Attaboy." Zeno hugged him. Taken by surprise, Tiller pushed him away violently. "When? I'll tell you when. Just as soon as we can set it up. Like how about tonight?"

TWENTY-TWO

At 1:00 A.M. the next morning, he sat with his legs immersed in the black chill of the alligator pool at Tartar Springs. Flashlights from back by the steps traced light across the curving black roof. From outside, radios crackled and motors revved.

"Want your tanks now?"

He flinched and nodded, lifting his arms as Tad helped him on with the backplate and tanks. He clicked the harness snaps together and looked down into the dark water. Fear filled him like the worthless stuffing of a cheap doll.

It was like the feeling before a mission, but worse. At least back then, he'd known his buddies, known he could depend on them to get him or at least his body back. He didn't have that kind of confidence in his current partners. Since the ultimatum at the museum, there had been three increasingly confusing and acrimonious meetings. There were more people and the shouting got louder at each one. Somebody new was in charge, a senior executive type everybody addressed as sir. He hadn't spoken to Galloway at all. He talked about him to Zeno and Jager as if he wasn't standing there, or as if he were a draft horse or a sheepdog that would do its job on command. The last meeting had been at midnight, in the classroom shack here at Tartar Park. Tiller had left them there, still arguing.

He thought with resigned dread that they'd keep arguing right up to the moment he got his ass solidly into a crack. Then they'd decide to call the whole thing off.

Tad leaned close and whispered, "They're all over there by the steps. You want it now?"

"Just toss it in. I'll get it on the bottom."

Tad glanced back, then bent. The plastic-wrapped bundle slid from under his jacket and disappeared into the water.

As the echoes of the splash died away, footsteps, flashlights, and voices approached from the entrance. The first to come into view was Jager. Galloway stared at him in the backwash of the lights. He had on body armor, black nylon tactical gear, night-vision goggles, a holstered pistol, and a black ball cap with ATF on it in gold. His black tactical jacket read POLICE U.S. AGENT in huge white letters.

"What the hell are you supposed to be?" Tiller asked him.

"What I am. A peace officer." Jager bent, clapped a heavy hand in a fingerless shooting glove down on his shoulder. "You sure when you come up, you're gonna be inside that fence?"

"No, I'm not sure. But I think I will."

Jager reminded him again to call the minute he was inside the compound, then he went over the backup plan with the flare. Tiller hoped the little radio worked; he didn't cotton to the flare idea at all. But he'd already made his objections during the meetings and they'd all been overruled. So now he just sat like a resting seal, breathing deep and slow to keep himself from shrieking in front of Tad, and waited.

More footsteps again, echoing off the curving overhead. He glanced up at Zeno and the executive type.

"Incredible, this smell . . . rather hard to breathe, isn't it? He's been briefed?"

"Oh, yes."

"He understands this is completely voluntary on his part? That we're making no promises of any sort?"

"He wanted it that way," said Zeno quickly, covering Galloway's incredulous laugh.

"Excuse me?"

"Nothing, nothing. . . . Tiller, you ready?"

He wished Zeno would stop using his goddamn name. He kept remembering what Dugan had said about getting twenty-four hours' notice before any police action. All some mole had to do was sneak off and make a phone call and he'd get a bullet in the head the second he stuck his head out of the water. The dry suit seemed to be getting tighter and tighter. He wished they'd just let him go.

"I asked you if you were ready."

"Yeah. Yeah, I'm ready, Al. Look, about Tad—"

"We'll take care of his son," said Sir loftily. "You can assure him of that, Alan."

Tiller twisted his neck, looking up at him. He said to Zeno, "Look, I don't like this 'this little piggy' shit."

"Little piggies?" said Zeno.

"Yeah, all this 'we, we, we, all the way home' shit. You got eight different agencies here. *Who* exactly is going to take care of him? And what does that mean? I don't make it through this, I want him watched, protected, and taken back to his mom in Portsmouth, Virginia."

Sir frowned. "Aw, Dad," said Tad. But Tiller went on, figuring this might be the last thing he ever got to say, "I want you to do it, Al. Personally. You sign up for that?"

"Okay, okay. I'll make sure of it."

"And you make sure he does." He stared up at the FBI honcho, who averted his eyes as if addressing him directly violated some taboo. But at last, he nodded.

Tiller turned to Tad. "Okay, the stages first, then the scooter. Take it slow and don't let them hit the rocks." He pulled his mask up, fitted it, and tucked his regulator into his mouth. The first breath of heliox in his lungs, he slid downward into the black.

Familiar tastes, familiar smells. The sulfur reek of the water, the taste of rubber. He was breathing heliox rather than trimix or air. He'd specified the expensive helium-oxygen mix because he didn't have to worry about narcosis, because he was used to it from the oil fields, and because the feds were paying for it. They'd supplied all the tanks and equipment. He didn't know where from; all he knew was that he hadn't had to go back to Scuba Florida and that all the gear was slightly unfamiliar. But he was used to that; commercial divers dove a lot of different rigs. So that as he sank bubbling toward the bottom of the subterranean river, cupped by the darkness, he felt for a moment almost confident that he might actually get into FFF this way. Then he hit the inflator valve and rose again toward the surface.

Tad swung out the first stage bottle, struggling with its weight. Jager stepped out of the dark to lend a hand. New steel 125's, supercharged to 20 percent over normal rating. Four of them. He wouldn't have to worry about what to breathe for a long time.

261

When he had them clipped to his harness, Tad bent again and the scooter came into view, a brand-new AquaZepp, silver-colored casing gleaming in the flashlights Jager and Zeno held focused on it.

The last few minutes, the last few details. His free hand patted here and there, checking console, computer, wings, compass. His legs sculled slowly, holding him above the surface. At last, his hand lifted in farewell. His son waved back. The others simply watched as the black water rose slowly, obliterating his final view of the world that knew light.

The dark covered him and filled him, and the cool dry gas he inhaled was like breathing the darkness itself. He didn't turn on his lights right away, just let his slight negative bouyancy take him downward. The bottom came up against his fins. He groped over the smooth stone till his hand hit the hard length of the package. Under the plastic, he felt the tube of the barrel and the smooth curves of the stock.

The upshot of meeting number two had been that the feds wanted him unarmed. Sir said (not to him) that this gave him deniability in case he was captured. He suspected the real reason was some kind of interagency rule about civilian auxiliaries not being armed.

He'd been overruled, but overruled or not, he wasn't going in naked. He'd demanded some sleep, and got permission to go back to Monica's for a few hours. Tad had been there, thank God, and after he explained what was going down, his son helped him disassemble and wrap Kusczk's rifle for submerged carry. He didn't have the right lubricants, so he used lots of silicone spray and hope. He sealed the ammo in a Ziploc bag. If they gave him enough time to drain and reassemble once he got inside, at least he wouldn't be helpless.

Something bumped him in the dark. He hoped it was a catfish. He got everything redistributed—had to be three hundred pounds of gear, with the stages—then wrestled the scooter around.

He pressed the switch and the light leapt to life, illuminating a murky brown world filled with fleeing eels. The prop cut on and he let it tug him up off the bottom into a clumsy parody of flight.

The square pale glow of the rigging platform loomed from the dark like a collapsed billboard. It swept slowly past. . . . The motor whined, but he was moving awful slow. . . . He was really dressed in drag, towing all these bottles. Breathing now off the first stage tank. His air plan was simple. He was going to use each tank up and drop them one by one. It wasn't good cave-diving procedure, but he didn't want to have to carry them all through the whole dive. That meant more risk if one of them failed, sheared a valve or something. But if there really was an exit to FFF, as he suspected, he wouldn't be coming back this way at all. The feds would extract him at the other end, after the raid was over.

He dipped the nose, and there was the guideline glowing back from the bottom.

It got murkier fast, the beam blunting down till it was about six inches long and he was boring along in a brown ball of trapped inchoate light, like a bug trapped in dirty amber. He lost the guide rope, picked it up again. Ceiling should be coming down now . . . His back mounts scraped and he eased off the throttle as the black gap of the Lips parted, blowing cold water into his face.

He wasn't going to get in there hand over hand this time, not dragging the shit he was carrying. It was the scooter or nothing. He aimed it into the narrowing slit of rock and tucked his head and forced his breath out, all of it, till his lungs ached, empty. The scooter whined and thudded, digging him deeper and deeper into the cleft. The water blasted out around him, tugging at his hoses, at the tanks he dragged. His belly scraped over the pebbles. The bottom crept past, hesitated, then crept a few more inches. Then it stopped.

He started drifting backward, expelled by the immense confined pressure of the murky flow, even though the prop was whining at full speed.

He turned on his side and shot his elbows out. This locked him against the slick stone above and the sliding, clattering pebbles below. His backward drift stopped. He lay there in the coffin-narrow dark, sucking deep breaths of helium-oxygen and thinking calming thoughts. This would have been a nightmare six months ago, sixty feet down and jammed into a crack so small, he filled it with his torso. It was where he'd lost his mask, last time he went in.

He let go of the hand throttle and the scooter's whine stopped. He twisted and thrust an arm out, finally wrapped a glove around a chunk of solid rock. His left hand unclipped one of the stage tanks from his harness and with some further twisting and grunting into his regulator he finally got it pushed ahead of him past the restriction. A few minutes later, he was able to follow it into the first room.

He stopped here, grabbed a pinnacle, and caught up on his breathing, glancing around at the walls. The fluffy stuff rained softly down from the roof. It caressed his mask with soft, disgusting fingers, blowing past him like a current of hairy shit. He checked his watch, holding it an inch from his faceplate. He had two hours to get to where he was going. So far, he was about on schedule.

He kicked himself into motion again, pulling himself down the left branch and through the restricted tube. He felt like a mite burrowing into someone's ear canal. About the same scenery, probably. The crumbling rock felt slimy under his hands. He debated shutting off his light, decided to leave it on. Keep the stress level down.

Past the next pinch-off, things got more comfortable. The tunnel walls opened out and the water cleared a bit. He let the scooter do the work, settling in for the long pull. The guideline stretched along the floor, drifted over there and there. As he passed over, the prop wash blew it clear. What with the scooter, and the narrowness, and his clumsiness at being overloaded, he knew he was leaving silted-out passage behind him. But if everything went as planned, he wouldn't be coming out this way.

Ninety feet. This time, he felt a lot more alert than the last, diving on air. No nitrogen equaled no narcosis. On the other hand, now he had nothing to counteract the fear.

He shook that off and pushed on northeast by his compass into the pinched-up section with all the breakdown. Filmy streamers fluttered from the overhead. This was where the passage split, the main tunnel running right and down. He leaned left, following the whirring disk of the prop up into the smaller branch. The walls whipped by. There was less flow in this side tunnel. Forty feet, and he curved back down like the top of a roller coaster. Another choice of two passages. Jesus, he thought, they all look alike. A guy would have a hell of a time finding his way back if he lost the guideline.

Maybe it was as simple as that, what had happened to Bud. He'd lost the guideline in the murk, searched around as his air ran low, then found it again. Was on his way back when he ran out of air.

But then, who had moved him? That faceless blank wall of question barred his way again.

He paused for a gear and computer check. He pressed the purge on his primary, clipped to his chest, and was reassured by a snorting roar of bubbles. Just to make sure it was there. Keep that stress level down.

Now the passage was wide and he tucked his head, pushing his speed up. Then thought, What am I doing? He throttled back. No sense getting there early; Zeno and his posse weren't going to be in jump-off position before 4:30.

The tunnel necked again and turned left. Yeah, here was the string of pearls. He cut the scooter and wriggled through the first passage, then the next, pushing the silvery torpedo-shape through the restrictions ahead of him. His light caught startled pale crustaceans peering from the worm holes in the black rock. He struggled grimly past them, realized he was growing lighter as he used gas. He valved a little out and felt himself settle back into neutral buoyancy. Better.

Eighty feet again. Damn nice to be on heliox. Sport divers hardly ever used it because it was so expensive, you were dumping costly helium with each breath, but you could go deep and long. Only trouble was, helium was a light gas. It didn't insulate; it sucked the warmth out of your breath and body. That was why he shivered now, feeling the first knife edge of cold.

Triple Split. He lost the guideline for a second before catching one of Bud's line arrows in the center passage. He triggered the scooter again, whirred through it, then came to High Chamber. The conical roof stretched up out of sight in the murky water. It felt smaller than it had the first time and he didn't stop to admire it or relax, just kept on. The faithful horse of the DPV hummed steadily. His breath clicked and roared in his ears, slow and deliberate. He had plenty of gas, but after so many years of working underwater, his brain took over automatically when he thought about other things and slowed his breathing. He bored steadily on, following the golden cone of the scooter's headlight. He was using the battery power fast, but again, he was figuring this as a one-way trip. Past side channels shooting out into the darkness, filled with melted darkness, crammed with solidified darkness. There was 60 million years of it down here.

The line curved right and he remembered the parallel tunnels, the occasional cross branches tying them together. The water was darkening now. The walls were turning reddish brown, cracked and frangible. He shuddered, anticipating what lay ahead. The river was above, broad and slow and turbulent, not eager for the sea.

Depth: 105.

And here he was, and he felt the icy touch of fear sharp and clear as he let go of the handle and the massy assemblage of metal and flesh and gas he was the heart of gradually lost way through the water. The tumbled rocks loomed up, the ones he'd lain pinned beneath. The guideline disappeared, buried beneath the breakdown. He moved in slowly, staying off the floor. There was the gap he'd caught himself in. To the right, and he'd come out at Bud's little cache room. To the left, and he'd drop into the abyss—if, of course, the ceiling didn't let go again.

He swallowed, fighting back the panic that kept pushing up from his stomach. Shit, shit, shit. I know it's scary, he told the frightened kid deep inside him. I don't like it, either. But we'll take it slow.

He found himself sucking hard on his regulator and realized his first stage had picked just then to run out. Okay, it had lasted pretty long. He felt around for the second stage, got his hand on the regulator. He thrust the mouthpiece out with his tongue, replaced it with the new one. His hands crept over his harness like crabs, unclipping the exhausted tank and dropping it to land with a slow, grating clank. A flower of silt with black curling petals bloomed, wilted, drifted downstream. The new mouthpiece felt strange. He chewed it, getting comfortable. The old pacifier routine. He got his jump reel free and tied the end off where the guideline vanished.

Then he grabbed himself by the balls and pushed his unwilling body up and into the restriction.

Soft rock against his belly, closing in . . . the silt puffing up, suddenly snuffing out all sight, even the existence of his lights. His tank valves slammed against the ceiling. The muffled bell toll made his heart lurch. If another chunk came down, he wasn't going to wait to suffocate like last time. He'd just have a goddamn heart attack and get it over with. His outstretched hands burrowed into the cheesy mass, shoving aside rock, scooping out fluffy detritus. Was he imagining it, or was there more than last time? Was the damn ceiling still letting go, dropping pieces of itself down into the tunnel?

He clawed on like a crazed crayfish. Only slowly did he realize he wasn't going anywhere. Something was caught, stage, tanks, the scooter he was dragging. . . . He bit his mouthpiece and closed his eyes, fighting the trapped terror that surged suddenly up from his belly. In, two, three, four; out, two, three, four . . .

Gradually, the terror loosened its grip and he was able to half-turn, groping back along his body with one gloved hand till it found where his last stage bottle was hooked on a projecting tooth of rock.

A few minutes later, he was through and looking down into the cleft that led to the Red Room. He tied off the jump reel and unsheathed his knife, cut the line, then restowed the reel. Might need it again later. He checked everything—depth, gas—made sure he hadn't lost or scraped off or damaged any gear crawling through the Trap. Then he cleared his ears and started down.

He dropped out of the Tube heavy and let the weight take him down clear of the ceiling. Then he sent a shot of gas hissing into his wings. He braked and stabilized thirty feet below the roof.

He searched it with his light for a moment, watching his bubbles gushing upward. This deep, even bubbles acted different, exploding as they emerged from the regulator into a myriad of tiny swirling spheres that glittered like glass beads in his beam, whirling upward through the crystalline water.

He lowered his light, sweeping it across the faraway floor. The room had so little in it to clue the eye to scale that only gradually did its true size impress itself on his brain. He realized now that his first estimate of it, huge though it had been, was too modest. Stones he'd taken for man-sized were actually as big as cars. He'd never imagined a space this huge could exist underground. It was like being slowly lowered into the Superdome on a cable woven of silver bubbles.

All at once, he found himself grinning around the rubber clamped in his teeth, which was feeding him the thick, cold pressurized gas that sustained his life like a candle flicker in this immense, eternal dark. It wasn't a nitrogen elation, not this time. It was awe. After all his labyrinthine gropings, he'd found his way to a central beauty so sheer and stark and dangerous to man that God had hidden it away since the beginning of time. He was only the second person ever to see it. What must Bud have felt, to be the first! He understood now what Exmore and the other cavers had meant. He felt as if he hovered in the slowly pulsing, inmost heart of creation itself.

267

He cocked his wrist to see the depth digits winking out, reforming: 265, 270.

He was going too deep for his dive plan. Building up that debt to decompression. He was also using gas too fast. The awe retreated, washed away by fear. He pulled the scooter around in front of him, squeezed the grip, and headed back up toward the ceiling.

There was Bud's yellow line, zigzagging off into the inky distance. He tucked his head and extended his arms and let the whirring propeller pull him along for minute after minute, trying to ignore the shivering that was beginning along the outside of his thighs. The ceiling swept by, but the cave stretched on and on. It must have taken Bud weeks to explore this—weeks of surveying and staging gear—because he'd done it all himself. If only he'd recovered a map, or notes . . . but it was all gone, erased or stolen. All he had now were the yellow line, appearing from the blackness minute by minute as he whirred ahead, and his faith.

Then he saw the line lift, leading upward along the roof as the great cave fissioned into huge subsidiary tunnels, each pooled and choked with darkness so endless, his searching beam made no impression at all. He aimed the scooter upward and followed it. Passing 160. Passing 150, 140, 130. The walls closed to a vertical-sided tunnel. He kept boring on, blinking through the tempered glass walls of his mask.

A discarded tank, red paint peeling off, slid past on the floor.

At seventy feet, with the tunnel still tending upward, he decided it was time to start thinking about decompression. He cut the scooter off, set the bezel on his watch at zero, and pulled the heliox table from his pouch. Hovering against the ceiling, squinting at it, he went over his depths and times and gas supply. His max depth had been 270, but he'd been there only a couple of seconds. Calling it 170, where the ceiling was when he came down out of the Tube, and calling his bottom time twenty minutes, his first decompression stop would be for seven minutes at sixty feet. It was also nearly time to drop the second stage. He was breathing about as slowly as was safe, but now he was starting to wonder if this was going to work out. The main cave had been much longer than he'd expected. The line was tending toward the surface now, but if it didn't lead to a way up soon, he'd have to either turn back or run the risk of running out of breathing mix before he got back to Tartar. As it was, he was crowding the margins already.

He'd have to decide soon. Looking first at his computer and then at his pressure gauge, he ran some numbers through his head and down the slate. Finally, he decided to go on and do the next stop, ten minutes at fifty feet, then decide whether to go on or head back.

When he looked up from his slate, he saw that he was drifting, not back, but forward. Curious. He frowned ahead, seeing where the line disappeared as it rose around a blind corner. The propeller whined again, and the scooter's headlight penetrated the passage beyond.

He stared at a perfectly round light-colored opening. Only when he rode closer did he recognize the light, smooth material as metal, and the tunnel itself not as a cave passage but as artificial. By that time, it was too late. Together with his scooter and all his gear and the clear water around him, he was being sucked smoothly and remorselessly up into it.

He tried to grab a rock outcropping as it sailed by, but his grasping glove just missed it. He groaned into his regulator, sucking gas fast, kicking viciously, trying too late to reorient the scooter. None of it made any difference to the escalator. The steadily accelerating current sucked him smoothly and silently up into the mouth of the seven-foot pipe.

He tumbled, slamming and rolling against the unyielding walls. Pain knifed into his sinuses; his ears fizzed and farted. His tanks rattled and scraped along the steel walls. His hands dragged in helpless and futile resistance against their smooth, curved featurelessness. Lights flickered like a jarful of lightning bugs as the scooter rattled and banged, swept upward, too, but more slowly, following him, till a particularly hard slam was followed by an eye-searing flash and then darkness. His shoulders and then his head blasted into unyielding metal. He gave up fighting, trying instead to ride the flow. No light, no light . . . couldn't make out his depth gauge in the battering vibration of confined water. . . . He was passing all his so carefully plotted decompression stops.

Then he stopped worrying about that as a roar began ahead. The image of whirling blades imprinted itself on the screen of darkness. His arms shot out again, but again they dragged uselessly against unyielding steel.

Suddenly, every piece of equipment was being torn off him; pressure was squeezing him from all sides; a roar hammered at his aching eardrums. Something hard and light struck him squarely between his eyes.

Twisting and flapping like a gaffed shark, he was suddenly thrown bodily out into a turbulent and roaring blackness. He grabbed for a regulator, but his hand swept empty water. Both fins were gone. His tanks were hanging by one harness strap. His mask was gone. His main light was gone, too, torn off by whatever he'd just passed through.

At last, his groping, stinging hands dug out a spare light and clicked it on. He pried his eyes open, to see low-arched concrete slipping serenely by inches above his head. But his eyes were above the surface of the water.

Air? He parted lips and pulled in a wary throatful. It seemed breathable, dank but a reasonable approximation of a normal atmosphere, and he sucked and sobbed it as he spun, feet dragging against a smooth bottom, whirled steadily through the dark toward a destination and a fate he could no longer even guess. Then, *bam*, suddenly he was pinned against what felt like iron bars stretched across the passage.

The water immediately crested up, submerging his face as it rushed around the temporary dam his body made. He groped blindly with one arm, reaching above himself. He'd expected a grating along here, something to block out any debris. If this was it, there had to be some way to access it for cleaning.

His fingers found a clamp and he inched his way up against the terrible pressure of the roaring water. Still no air. His straining lips reached up to within an inch of the arched ceiling before he found some. His fingers explored whatever was holding the scuttle closed. It felt like the underside of a dogging lever. His fingers tore on it, but it didn't move.

He hammered it with his fist, starting to panic. He was sucking air and water together, starting to cough, starting to strangle. A hammer, something heavy. . . . He didn't have any tools but his knife. . . . He recollected the light in his other hand. Bracing himself awkwardly, head cocked back, he swung again and again until the corner of it struck fair and the scuttle popped open and he blinked and gaped and shoved his head and shoulders through, coughing and retching as he hung half in, half out of an immense pipe that ran through a shadowy alley inside a closed space echoing with the steady throb of large electric motors.

He dragged an arm across his mouth, blinking at a headache so sudden and blinding, jagged skeins of lightning interrupted his vision. Rapid ascents were bad news—not just because of the bends but also pneumothorax, barotrauma, blown-out eardrums. Something had popped; he tasted blood coppery and slick on his tongue. But there was no way to go back down. He'd just have to take his chances.

A door at the far end of the building opened. A light came on down there. It silhouetted a man with a billed cap and a hip holster. Tiller's end was still in shadow, but the man immediately turned and began walking toward him.

Galloway suddenly realized that one of the many pieces of equipment stripped off him while he played pinball up the pipe had been the rifle. He dragged himself the rest of the way out of the scuttle, lowered it cautiously, and rolled as silently as he could off the top of the pipeline and into the shadows beneath some large piece of equipment beside the shed wall. The steps kept pacing closer. Another overhead light glared on inside its cage, pulling into existence pumps and green-painted pipes and large handwheels on feeder lines that split off from the central duct and ran out the sides of the building through gaps stuffed with rat wire.

The man came on, reaching out every few paces to click on another overhead light. He was wearing a security guard's uniform and heavy boots. He looked around carefully as he came. Galloway figured the guy had heard the hammering as he tried to knock the dogs free. The man advanced another few steps and turned on another light.

Then he stopped. He regarded the top of the pipeline, then stepped up and swung his body up. He reached out, then frowned. Tiller could see his face plainly.

The guard lifted his hand and examined the water on it. One hand went to his hip as he looked to the side, down along the floor, at the still-wet footprints leading to—

Galloway hit him with a full-body block, not as hard as he wanted to, but as hard as he could. But the guy wasn't ready for it and the impact knocked him flying off the elevated pipe. He crashed down to the concrete floor on the far side, still struggling with the holster. Galloway slid his legs over the top of the pipe and came down off the walkway with both feet. The guy grunted and quit struggling. Galloway finished the fight with a kick to the head, then bent.

The holster held not a gun, but a walkie-talkie. He stared at it, then whacked it against the floor till pieces snapped off and flew.

He breathed out, looking back along the now-illuminated perspective of the pipe shed. He didn't know how long the guard would be out, or if anyone else knew he was coming in here. He bent again and went through pockets, finding a folding knife, coins, a wallet, a batch of keys. He took the keys. He tore some wires free from a silent pump, got the guard's hands and feet secured, and shoved him back under the pipe for a little nap on company time.

Time for his first report. He unzipped the dry suit. He experienced a moment of horror as his fingers groped emptily under his armpit, but then they found the little pack and he pulled it out and stripped the plastic off and pulled out the antenna. He hit the transmit button and the red LED came on. He put his mouth close and murmured, "I'm inside."

He got a crackling "Roger" from a voice he didn't recognize. The sound quality was lousy, but it worked. He was relieved; not many things did after going as deep as he'd just been. They asked something else, but he didn't answer, just put it on mute. He looked at the security guard's clothes for a moment, then decided he liked the black dry suit better.

Okay, they wanted him to find some coke. The problem was, he didn't expect any. He was going to have to find something that looked as if it had coke concealed in it. Or at least a guy with a submachine gun—that would make Jager happy. Then call the feds and tell them to come on in. He had what he wanted, the pipeline. Rip the cover off that, and he was pretty sure the whole Conservancy–Park Service–Holder cabal would unravel. Another good thing to find would be some oxygen. If he could get hold of that, he'd lessen the chances of decompression sickness from that fast ascent.

The door stood half-open. He'd clicked each overhead light off as he passed it, returning the pipe alley to shadows, and as he stepped out into the open night, it was a transition from darkness to darkness. The air smelled of mowed grass and the fecund scent of damp earth. He stood immobile, searching the compound with the edges of his sight.

He'd come out inside the wire, all right, but he didn't recognize where he was. He oriented to north with his wrist compass. The gate had been at the south end. He decided to head that way and see what there was to see. The turf was soft and springy under his booties. It was 3:30. Hard to believe he'd slipped beneath the surface at Tartar only a couple of hours ago. It felt more like three days.

He stood there for a moment, debating whether it would be wiser just to stay where he was and call in the raid. That had been his original plan. Roaming around was likely to get him shot. No, he'd just call them in, let them go through their drill, then lead them to the water diversion. Rather than coming up with empty hands, he figured Zeno and Jager and the FBI agent would be happy to prosecute on that.

Only now he couldn't just sit tight. He was sweating. His back was starting to hurt and his skin itched. Christ, he thought. Where in the hell would they keep oxygen around here? The only place he could think of was in an infirmary.

Distant spaced lights, most likely the perimeter fence. Between him and them were more long, low buildings. He ran bent over, trying for quiet more than speed. But fifty yards on, he ran full tilt into a heavy pipe a few inches above ground level. He suppressed a yell, huddled over what felt like a broken shin. When he resumed his jog, it was much slower and with a limp.

The shadow of the next building grew slowly as he made up on it. When he reached it, he crouched beside it, catching his breath. He unzipped the dry suit a little more. Report in? He touched the radio lightly. Maybe in a minute or two. He searched the darkness for movement. Nothing but the distant security lights, and the even more distant whine of a light truck—the perimeter patrol.

He edged along the wall until his fingers found a window. There didn't seem to be any way to open it, so he slid on, feeling nothing but smooth metal, a *long* stretch of smooth metal wall. What the hell? . . . His outstretched foot touched a stoop. His outstretched hands found the outline of a door.

The second key he tried clicked the bolt back. Maybe things were working his way at last. He eased the door open, slipped inside, pulled it shut behind him.

Black velvet darkness. He advanced a step, hands out, and was stopped by a yielding wall or stiff curtain of heavy black cloth. He stopped, puzzled. Then understood, and stepped around the light barrier.

He blinked and shielded his eyes, squinting into a hot white blaze like full noon.

The foliage stood in eerie motionlessness, but the murmur of water was everywhere, trickling and echoing under the long roof. Condensation dripped from glass panels. The tropical air felt as if he could grab a handful and wring it like a wet towel. It wasn't just damp; it was heavy, loaded with dank nitrogenous smells reminiscent of compost and manure, yet at the same time strangely inorganic, almost sterile. He lifted his head, squinting anew as his sight met the ranked glare of hundreds of arc-purple Gro-Lites.

He shuffled forward and found himself standing in a couple of inches of warm water at the edge of a raised white vinyl trough. Two feet wide and a foot deep, it was filled with what looked like bone chips. Bending closer, he saw it was crushed limestone, permeated with a slowly flowing fluid that looked milky but that also had a scarlet tinge as if of blood. Each plant stood with its roots in the fluid, its stalk held upright by a spindly plastic framework. Their tops were higher than he stood. The waste fluid that covered the floor seemed to be oozing from small holes along the bottoms of the troughs. Beyond it, separated by only a few inches, was another plastic trough, also filled with closely spaced plants, and beyond that, another, another, farther than he could see. . . . The strange motionlessness, the close heat, the absence of the hum of insects or the sigh of wind made the scene weird and dreamlike. A forest of nightmare, nature shorn of all naturalness and reduced to mass production.

Then he noticed, all at once, what the plants were.

They weren't ficus or poinsettias or forsythias.

At first glance, they looked like a decorative bamboo, with their long spearlike leaves. But they weren't bamboo, either.

He walked slowly along the murmuring troughs. Again it was dreamlike, as he looked down long rows of tall reedy bushes, long aisles that disappeared as if on a turning wheel, as if he was passing cornfields in a speeding car. Acre after acre of them, and still the far end of the building only gradually grew nearer. Every fifty meters, more PVC piping branched in and fanned out to manifolds. At the head of each trough, transparent vertical cylinders held white and red fluids in suspension. Metering devices peed a thin stream that blended with the crystalline water, turning it the hue of milky blood. Fertilizers, pesticides . . . as the used solution trickled slowly out onto the concrete, it gathered around grates and was carried away. He reached out slowly to turn a long, hairy leaf, to touch one of the tiny greenish flowers.

274

It wasn't the kind he knew. The leaves were different. And all the plants were female.

He rubbed his chin, understanding now why Billy Holder needed millions of gallons of pure, unaccounted-for artesian water.

He was looking at a couple of square miles of what was obviously high-yield, genetically altered *Cannabis sativa*.

Under the screen of a huge potted-plant nursery, the guy was actually running a gigantic, ultramodern hydroponic marijuana-production facility.

He moved in awed wonder through a futuristic environment. Automatic machines ministered to these plants. All they had to do was grow, and distil their hallucinogenic nectar. He'd heard about the high-yield grass that was lighting kids up all over the Southeast. So cheap that user statistics were skyrocketing again, after years of decline. So potent, one hit had the same effect a whole reefer once had, when he'd been in the same sorry business.

He recalled suddenly that he didn't have a lot of time to stroll around with his jaw hanging open. The pain was lancing into his knees. The sweat was rolling off him, and it wasn't just from the heat. His only chance of avoiding permanent paralysis or even death was to get the feds in here as quickly as he could. He pulled out the radio, extended the antenna, and stepped into the plants, till he was screened by a motionless, sweet-smelling forest of green.

Zeno answered instantly. "Damn, Doc, where the hell you been? We been calling you since you reported in."

"Never mind that. I can confirm what you wanted to confirm. You can start the raid."

"Say again?"

He repeated it. "What exactly you got there?" the DEA agent asked him. "And where are you?"

Tiller told him that he was in some kind of production facility for drugs. He didn't say what kind. Zeno must have held the mike open as he decided what to answer, because he could hear excited discussion. He cut in. "Look, they might have scanners. I want to sign off and move. Over."

"Okay, find yourself a safe place till dawn."

He stood there appalled amid the whispering waters. Pressed transmit, whispered, "*Dawn?* What the hell do you mean, dawn? I thought you were coming in as soon as I called."

"The plan's been refined. The helos can't go in at night. It's only an hour or so more till first light."

"Shit, yeah, but—I need help. I ascended too fast. You wait till then, I'm gonna be in Bends City."

"Sorry, buddy. Everything's set for dawn. Just sit tight and we'll take care of you then."

Zeno signed off. Galloway crouched amid the spooky greenery, feeling his skin start to crawl around on his bones. No use asking why the feds hadn't bothered to check with the pilots before they set up H-hour. He had to do something, and fast. For one thing, he had to get out of this heat. Gas came out of a warm solution faster than a cold one. He unzipped his dry suit farther, wishing he'd dressed in something other than a garish pair of Bud's swimming trunks with a large-size Depend underneath.

Outside again, and still full dark, despite his hopeful glance eastward. He was still sweating and itching, but the distant chorus of crickets and tree frogs was reassuring after the rigid rows of immured plants nourished by pumps and chemicals and ultraviolet-rich artificial light. He cursed softly as each step stabbed a sharpened wire under his kneecaps. Had to find oxygen. . . . But now that he knew what Holder was growing here, he was even less eager to go prowling around. The law around open-forest marijuana patches was "shoot on sight." He had no doubt the same rule held within the razor-wired fences of Holder's private empire.

Finally, he stripped the dry suit off, grunting each time he had to bend his joints, and stuffed it under the open foundation. He ditched the diaper, too, but kept the booties. Bare-chested, the radio and his dive knife in the pockets of his trunks, he scuttled across another open space and fetched up against a second building, where he leaned, breathing harshly and rubbing sweat out of his eyes. Now his back was starting up in earnest. He put his hands to his hips and stretched, but it didn't help. He remembered what the Oceaneering doc in Bayou City had said about how bubbles accumulated at the sites of old injuries. Shit, much worse and he wasn't going to be able to move at all, just lie in the grass and mew like a hurt kitten.

A door, a key, a quick peep inside. The hot air was the same. The same lights glared down. But instead of marijuana, rows of decorative palms stood in clay pots; instead of star-shaped leaves, the festive green of poinsettias covered the floors. Pallets of dusty sacks—fertilizer, lime?—were stacked near a forklift. He retreated again into the night and slid along the building to its end and looked past it.

To the gate. There it stood, floodlighted and with two guards in the same semimilitary uniform as the one he'd hosed. They were standing casually with slung guns. He ducked back and dropped, then edged his head out again near ground level. He scanned the entrance area. A large truck park, furrowed ground and ripped-up asphalt to his right; an eighteen-wheeler with lights off and engine running. Another shed building stood beyond that. To his left, above the distant trees, glowed the steady-burning red lights of the water tower he remembered from the reconnoiter.

A radio spoke inside the guard shack—too far off for him to make out what it said, but it got the guards' attention. They moved to each side of the gate. A moment later, with a hum and clash of motors and gears, it began to roll open. He lay on the ground, grass tickling his cheek, watching it gradually widen. He wondered what his chances were of getting across the two hundred yards of open lot to it and into the darkness beyond without catching a bullet in the back. He didn't come up with a reassuring percentage.

What caught his eye then was the building across the lot, to his left. There were windows, and lights shone in them. It wasn't a production shed.

He figured it had to be the office. If there was a dispensary, that was where it was going to be.

Back behind the poinsettia building, he limped along through tall, cool grass brushing his calves. Something rustled away through it, something big, a canebrake rattler or maybe even a middling-sized gator. He was gonna be in great shape by dawn. Every muscle in his back was cramping tight with sympathetic pain. The bends were nothing to screw with. He knew guys with permanent paralysis, bone necrosis, brain infarcts. And that was only the beginning of a long list of nasties.

A yearning glance back toward the east. Was that the faintest hint of dawn above the shadowy crests of the sabal palms?

Finally, he reached the lighted building. He crouched there, panting against a propane tank behind it. His shaking hands riffled through the keys, dropped them, tried one after the other. At last, a bolt snicked open.

A narrow hallway, a dim night-light . . . photocopy and fax machines, bathroom, storeroom . . .

A door with a red cross. He jerked it open and flipped the light on. A moment later, his hands closed on a green cylinder.

He sucked in the cold, vivifying gas, then tucked the tank under the arm that held the mask against his face as he rummaged through the cabinets. Aspirin! He bolted a quarter of a handful and lifted the mask for a chaser of tap water. Then he settled himself on a leatherette-covered examining table. He couldn't stay here. But every minute he could spend on pure oxygen would let more helium bleed safely out of his bloodstream. Paper crackled as he sank back onto the table. Gradually, his racing heart slowed.

Half an hour later, he sat up again, recalled from an exhausted nap by the sound of voices not far away. He couldn't tell if it was the massive overdose of aspirin, the oxygen, or both, but his back felt better and the itching was gone. Maybe he wouldn't spend the rest of his life in a wheelchair.

Then steps paced down the hallway. They passed outside the dispensary, then hesitated. He glanced around, but there was nowhere to hide. Then he heard a door close. A pause, then the hiss of a urinal flushing.

When the steps passed again and all was quiet, he let himself out into the hallway and then out the back door, moving into the dark.

Only it wasn't dark anymore. The sky was charcoal gray and the outlines of the trees and buildings and power wires above him were crisp cutouts of black. He felt naked, revealed. He stuck his head around the corner, looking toward the gate.

It was still open. He stared, concentrated as a hunting panther, at the guards. He was much closer to them here than he'd been behind the poinsettia shed.

The sudden rapid knock of distant machine-gun fire tensed his legs, almost started him running just from reflex. He recognized it in the next instant as an early-rising woodpecker, at work out in the woods. He wavered between laughter and a sob.

At last, he decided he just might make it if he started running when both men had their backs to him.

He was crouching for the dash when lights wheeled in off the road. The guards straightened. They approached the vehicle, peered in, and then stepped back, waving it on.

It was a Land Rover. He stopped breathing as he watched it cross the lot and crunch to a halt in front of the office.

Monica Kusczk was wearing high brown leather boots. Her long hair fell loosely over a dark plum car coat. She looked both worried and anticipatory, and to his surprise, she was wearing glasses. He didn't even know she needed them.

He couldn't figure it. What the hell was she doing here? Then the only possible answer occurred to him.

The closing must be going down today. She was going to sign, transfer Tartar and everything beneath it to Holder's front organization. He edged out a bit, saw that hers was only the latest in a nest of cars that had arrived while he'd snoozed in the dispensary. One was a silver Infiniti. Another was a white van with blue lettering that spelled out SCUBA FLORIDA.

He pulled back behind the propane tank and considered his options as coldly as he could. Dawn was almost on him. Should he call off the assault? On the other hand, wasn't this what he'd prayed for, some way of trapping everyone at once, then letting the courts sift out the good from the bad? Like the joke they'd told each other in Vietnam, about killing them all and letting God sort them out. Never really funny, but at the time it had had a certain grim appeal.

Forget the dead past. Think about now. He could see men moving around back by the long sheds. Sooner or later, one of them was going to look up and notice a half-naked guy in loud bathing trunks lurking behind the office. He couldn't stay out here, not in the growing light.

At last, he eased the back door open again. His heart hammered as he tiptoed down the slick green tile and laid his ear against the door. Distinct voices came from the far side. He looked at both sides of the hallway. The bathroom, dispensary, photocopy room—and one other door, stainless steel, with a small rectangular window.

He pushed through it and found himself in a tight, efficiently designed galley that looked as if it belonged aboard a boat. Stainless counters, stainless cupboards, stainless-steel stove. Tureens and pans gleamed above his head. A sliding serving door topped a counter that led, obviously, to the meeting room on the far side.

Reaching up, he got a heavy chopping knife. He inserted the tip under the serving door and levered it up a hair at a time, lowering his eye till it hovered level with the gradually opening slit.

He could see them all in the narrow strip of image. All of them, sitting together at last around a polished table: Monica, Blanche and Billy Holder, and, sitting with them, Arkin, Dugan, and a balding older man. As Tiller watched, the bald guy turned his

279

head, presenting the far side of his face. It was caved in, sucked dry from beneath. . . . He noticed another man, slim, blond, with his back to the window. He couldn't see well enough to identify who it was. But beside the slim man sat Ferebie, relaxed into his chair, hands locked behind his head.

Yeah, the whole cast was here . . . plus at least a dozen spear-carriers: stocky men with closed faces, standing against the walls. Like the old paintings of medieval conferences, the bravos with halberds and bows all standing around locking eyeballs, there to keep their royal masters from dirking one another. The weaponry here was concealed, but he could see it was there, hidden under billowy windbreakers, baggy trousers, readily accessible in carry bags and pouches, each handy to its owner's reach.

He knew then he had to call off the attack. Zeno and Company weren't prepared for something like this. But instead of leaving, he pried the stainless slab up another millimeter, till words squeezed through.

Arkin's words: "I know we all have other commitments today, so let's move on to business. We're here to finalize a very significant occasion in the progress of the Styx River Preserve. Now, usually a ceremony like this would take place at Apalachee Lodge, with media representatives, community leaders, local celebrities . . . but it is in the interest of all parties concerned that the transfer of Tartar Park to the Heritage Conservancy should take place in private. However, I want to emphasize how essential to the future of our wild community this event is."

The bald man said something in Spanish. Arkin inclined his head. "You're right, sir. So we'll make it short. An informal closing . . . I have the documents with me." He reached under the table. As the briefcase came up, Galloway watched the men around the walls straighten, watched hands edge toward pockets and belts. The attorney unsnapped the locks and laid out three documents before Monica. She adjusted her glasses and leaned forward.

A pen scratched and she sat back. Across the table, a perfectly coiffed Blanche Holder stood, angular and pale and emerald-eyed, from her place beside her husband. "Blanche Holder will accept for the Conservancy," Arkin said.

In the kitchen, Galloway suddenly realized he could see daylight through the window behind them. He let the door slide closed, started to put the knife back, then changed his mind and thrust it into his shorts. He eased the door open and stepped silently out into the hallway.

He was halfway down it when the bathroom door opened and a man stepped out, one hand working to fasten his fly. They stared at each other face-to-face, the other's dark eyes early-morning sleepy for a moment, then widening.

Five seconds later, Tiller was bending over him, jerking a pistol out from under his jacket and trying not to groan too loudly from the knee he'd gotten in his crotch. But the Colombian was in worse shape. Tiller dragged him into the dispensary and set the bloody knife neatly on the sink. He started to leave, then decided to see what else was under the loose shirt.

The guy was wearing a ballistic vest. He decided that might come in useful, and on second thought, he took his shirt, too. He closed the door softly, glancing toward the meeting room. If somebody else had to whiz . . . but no one did, and a moment later he was outside again. Crouched beside the propane tank, he extended the antenna.

"All, this is Dr. Zog. You got to call off the assault."

"Jager, over. Say again."

"This is Galloway. Scrub the assault, Jager. There's way too much firepower here for your guys to take."

"What? What the hell are you—Negative, can't comply. It's going in."

"Turn them around. You want illegal guns? You got 'em, in spades. And some innocent civilians, too."

"We'll watch for them." Jager's confident, hard voice cut through his protest. "Just take cover, wiseass. We'll see you after the caps stop popping."

He glanced at the silver drum he sheltered next to. Propane? Not a good place to be once bullets started flying. Like they were gonna start flying as soon as the feds tried to come through that fence. Shit, shit, shit. Monica was in there. How was he going to get her out? How was he going to get *himself* out?

He watched the light of day snap on behind the trees, shooting its rays up into hazy high clouds. Watched the fence turn a tarnished platinum in the new-minted light.

Far off, yet growing swiftly closer, a sound began that stirred the hair on the back of his neck. It was one he'd heard before, and never without the adrenaline starting to pump. He stared at the treetops, waiting for them to come into sight.

He listened with a sinking heart to the whock and flutter, the pulsing drone of helicopters coming in for a low-altitude attack.

TWENTY-THREE

He never saw who fired the first shots—whether they came from the black helicopters that lifted suddenly over the tree line, or from one of the gate guards, or from the black-clad line that appeared suddenly from the forest, advancing across the road. As he dived for cover, rolling downhill into a long ditch behind the office, all he knew was that it was hitting the fan at last.

It might even have worked if the helos had arrived after the gate team jumped off, or if they'd stormed the entrance without warning, just a dark tide too sudden to resist. But instead, to his horror, he heard an electronic crackle, then the echoing screech of a bullhorn set too high, feedback generating an enormous reptilian scream like a dying archaeopteryx.

No, he thought, hugging the ground, half-submerged in the stinking milky water that paved the bottom of the ditch. No *talking*, Al—

The bullhorn stopped screeching. It cleared its throat and squawked, "This is Alan Zeno of the Drug Enforcement Agency. This is a police raid. This is a federal raid by armed agents of the federal government. Lay down your weapons now. Do not initiate fire or we will use lethal force." It paused, then repeated it in Spanish.

Galloway seized his head in despair.

Because, of course, the gate guards, now warned and alerted, simply started firing as soon as they saw men emerging from the woods. As soon as they did, the doors to the office and to the idling eighteen-wheeler slammed open. From each and all of them spilled out heavily armed men. FFF guards, Dugan's Colombians, and the bald guy's bodyguards, all pulling out H&Ks and Uzis and Glocks. The snap and pop of the opening shots built rapidly to a clattering roar as the automatic weapons started firing.

Powerless to help, he watched the advancing line of men in black jackets marked ATF and FBI and DEA waver, then keep coming. They were brave, he gave them that. Not one turned back. But they hadn't expected fire this heavy. They weren't armed as a SWAT team. Most were carrying pistols. They began falling even as they crossed the road. Then they all went down, hitting the deck, laying down a spatter of return fire. Rounds punched through the thin metal of the guard shack. The gate guards sagged and sprawled, and the feds shifted their fire to the rough line that was forming behind cars and Dumpsters and stacks of palleted peat. Bullets hummed and whirred over his head. But it was too late. They'd given away the element of surprise, they'd come in too lightly armed, and now it was all turning to shit.

Then the rising beat of engines above him obliterated every other thought. Jerking his head around and up, he saw the first black machine flared out, starting to settle. And saw, too, what its pilot couldn't see from above, against the still-shadowy ground: the power line, feeding electricity for all those banks of lighting, all those pumps.

He stood upright in the ditch, frantically giving him the wave-off. But either the pilot didn't understand or the gunner took him for a hostile. Bullets whacked into the damp ground around him, and Tiller dropped back into the shallow cover of the drainage canal, seeing what was going to happen, powerless to prevent it.

The hazy circle of the descending helo's blades merged with the power line, the rotating airfoils contacting it one after the other with four spaced cracks like rifle shots. The unsuspended fuselage floated in midair for a long instant. Then it lurched, yawed, and dropped with steadily gathering velocity twenty yards straight down through the roof of the poinsettia shed.

The blast sent up a balloon of orange fire and sent glass shards hissing across the compound. He made love to the dirt as they scythed above him. From behind the cars, Holder's guards fired rapidly. Some of them had tracers. The second helicopter pulled up, showing U.S. CUSTOMS markings. It hovered uncertainly, absorbing several more rounds, then slid sideways off toward the trees and vanished.

The firing slackened as both sides reloaded. He saw Dugan and the bald man crouched behind cover. He didn't see Arkin or Holder. In the growing light, four or five motionless forms dotted the outer road. None of the feds had even made it inside the fence.

The bullhorn again: "This is Alan Zeno of the Drug Enforcement Agency. You are surrounded by agents of the federal government. Continued resistance is futile. Throw down your weapons and come out with your hands up."

From where Tiller lay, concealed by the culvert, he could hear talking behind the barricade. Most of it was in Spanish, but it didn't sound like anyone was ready to give up. They were laughing and boasting like a soccer team after a goal. It sounded as if they were digging in for a long siege.

He didn't see what they had to laugh about. Granted, they'd just creamed the opening assault in what was shaping up rapidly to be the biggest disaster for the feds since Waco. But the cops were still out there, and Holder's people—he knew now it was bigger than that, but he still thought of them all as Holder's—were still inside the fence. Zeno would be on his cellular, screaming for backup. Federal marshals, FBI SWAT teams. And state, local cops—once shots had been fired, even Holder's pull couldn't stop them coming to the assistance of federal officers in a firefight. They could even get the military, Special Forces and Rangers, SEALS and Air Force Special Ops guys from Tampa and Jacksonville and Georgia. Shit, in two or three hours, there were going to be armored choppers coming in, paratroopers falling out of the sky.

They had to know that: that if they didn't get out, they'd either die or have to surrender. And that if they were going to break out, they had to do it fast, before the cavalry arrived.

Then he saw Monica.

She was standing just outside the office, held by two of the bodyguard types in loose jackets. Her face was so pale, it looked like mime makeup. And he knew—his guts told him as he lay in the mud watching—that it wasn't going to be the breakout.

They were going to bargain with her life.

He was trying to think of something he could do, when a shot crack-boomed from the woods. One of the thugs holding her stag-

284

gered back. He looked surprised. Then he looked dead. The last thing he did in his life was fall.

The bald man, in a surprising access of strength, pulled her back behind the makeshift barricade as the others unleashed a roar of fire into the woods. Galloway couldn't see what they were aiming at. He doubted they could, either. The police marksman had scored a clean kill.

Zeno was clamping down an iron bowl over the compound. From here on in, anyone moving around inside it, leaving cover, had a life expectancy measured in seconds.

The downside was, that included him. From five or six hundred yards, the distance the sniper was working from, they couldn't tell him from one of the baddies. But he couldn't signal his identity without giving himself away to some other armed and just as dangerous people at considerably closer range.

Without waiting to think any longer, he scrambled up out of the ditch into a three-second zigzagging dash. He dropped again, heart slamming, behind a concrete and metal ramp that had apparently been used for loading the trucks.

Crouching there, he pulled out the weapon he'd taken from the man in the hallway: a 9mm Browning. Not the most modern pistol around, but the thick-butt magazine was stuffed with fourteen rounds of unpleasant-looking hollow-points. And he'd used one before. The SEALs had carried silenced Brownings. He slapped it back in and racked the slide, then glanced back at the farm, reviewing its layout in his head, trying to figure some way he could get to her without getting himself blown away.

Yeah, he'd been here before . . . the crackle of fire, the suck of mud, the smell of powder and fuel and things burning. Trouble was, he'd seen a lot of guys die since then, guys who thought they were too tough and fast and smart ever to go. Till they caught an AK round, that is, or made a mistake six hundred feet under the Gulf of Mexico, or pushed a strung-out buyer with a knife too far.

He shoved that out of his head and thought terrain. Terrain dictated tactics. The ground here was flat, except for the ditches and ponds, so that meant the buildings. The truck lot, office, truck service facilities, and the warehouse were conveniently grouped inside the gate. Service roads ran inside the fence, not coincidentally giving both a field of observation of anyone examining it and a field of fire if they tried to scale it. Turnoffs led to the ends of the growing sheds. He'd counted three sheds between the pump house and the transportation area. The water tower was east of the pump house.

He popped his head up for a quarter of a second to verify it, noting the column of smoke and fuel flame climbing above the poinsettia shed. He also saw in the morning light that the drainage ditch led in a straight line east to a little triangular pond. Something about the pond . . . He waited thirty seconds, then popped his head out at another corner of the loading stand. The other ditches led there, too, but he didn't see any outlet.

The bullet came out of nowhere, preceded by no sound, exploding a fist-sized chunk out of the concrete lip of the loading dock beside his head. Only then did the *crack-boom* of the supersonic round arrive. Ears ringing, he ducked back, wiping glass-sharp gravel and sticky asphalt off his palms. The sniper had his range. A half minute of angle and he'd be dead.

He had to decide what to do, and fast. The old man was pushing Dugan and Monica toward her Land Rover. Once they slammed the doors and started moving, there were only two things that could happen. Jager and the rest of the feds would start shooting, and everybody in the car would die. Or Dugan and Baldy would make it out of here. But once gone, they wouldn't need Mon anymore.

He had to get closer. But that meant giving the marksman another chance. He ran his hands back over his hair, sucking in air, then set his feet in a sprinter's start.

He broke out from behind the loading dock, already at full speed. The sniper must have been looking somewhere else, because it took him a couple of seconds to get onto him. The bullet hissed behind him as he slid home behind some pallets of fertilizer. Another miss. His luck was great today. He hoped it held just a few minutes more.

Two Colombians looked up at his arrival, startled. He gave them a sketchy salute, lying beside them. *"Buenos días,"* he said.

"¡No es un buen día! ¿Quién diablos eres?"

Instead of answering, he glanced over the top of the pallet, popped the gun over it, and pumped off two quick shots in the direction of the woods. This seemed to satisfy them, and they resumed firing, too.

He fired again, then slapped the closest on the shoulder and pointed to the red car. He made pumping motions with his arms. The guy frowned, then nodded. He said something to his pal.

They stood and fired rapidly into the woods, covering him as he lurched up and headed across the open lot. He kept expecting a bullet, but none came.

He crashed into the knot of men behind the Land Rover, knocking several down. They whirled, struggling to aim at him, but they were too close together. Before they could react to the new threat, he had his arm around the bald man's neck and the muzzle of his automatic snugged tight under his jaw.

Dugan stared at him. "Galloway. ¡*Mierda*! What are you doing here?"

"Hi, Sergio. Just passing through. Let Mrs. Kusczk go or I shoot your boss."

"Sorry, he's not my boss. You lose."

"He's these guys' boss." Tiller nodded at the other bodyguards. He had about six guns pointed at him. If this didn't take, he wouldn't suffer long. "Tell them to let her go."

"*Haz lo que te dice*," said the old man. Dugan stiffened, then snapped off Spanish. They averted their barrels reluctantly.

"Now shove her over here. Hi, Mon."

"Tiller," she said, face white. Her hands were locked over her shoulder purse, fingers digging into the leather.

"Where are you going with her?" said Dugan. "Not that I care, but you will not get very far. Or do you have an understanding with these *federales*?"

"I don't have any understanding with anybody. Just trying to get her out of here. Mon, you okay?"

"I'm all right, but I don't—Who is that out there? They say they're police, but—"

"They're cops, all right. Mostly DEA, but a lot of the rest of the alphabet, too. You haven't been keeping very good company."

"My God, Blanche is in there, and Billy and Tim and—"

"They made this bed, they're gonna have to talk their way out of it. Us, we're gonna back out of here and find someplace safe. You with me?"

She nodded, still clutching the handbag as if it were a life preserver. He edged backward, keeping the old man on the tips of his toes, the Browning jammed into his neck. The guards stared icily, fingers rubbing their guns.

Now, what to do with Baldy? The safest thing was just to give him back to his guards. When they had twenty yards between them, Galloway gave him a hard shove, figuring he'd serve as cover while he and Mon went the other way. "Run. Run!"

Instead, the bald skull suddenly exploded. It was that sudden, one moment a back-turned scowl and the next an instantaneous sphere of red mist, out of which a horribly disfigured but still vertical corpse reeled, arms and legs jerking guidanceless as a hatcheted chicken before it toppled over onto the grass.

Tiller gaped. So did the bodyguards. All except one. Reacting more quickly than the others, he jerked his gun up and snapped off a round—not at the distant sniper who'd just bagged their boss, but at Tiller.

He felt the blow to his stomach; then, without any intervening time, he was on his back, looking up at the sky. He couldn't breathe. He couldn't even really think about what had happened; it was as if his brain had been paralyzed along with his body.

"Tiller, come on!"

He couldn't speak, or move. He just lay there, still gripping the pistol. "Stay back," he grunted. "Stay there—"

But instead, she was above him, seizing his shoulders. He couldn't believe those slim arms were pulling him across the grass. He tried to help, managed to get up on hands and knees. Red hair flashed in the morning sun as she shoved him the last couple of feet to cover behind the office building. He stumbled and fell forward.

Behind and above him came a sound like an ax hitting a tree, a hard, heavy thud. He knew what it was before he turned, screaming, *"No!"*

He dragged her back, staring at the red horror that single round had made of her chest. The distant sniper must have meant it for him. Surely he wouldn't have targeted an unarmed woman. . . . She was bleeding too fast to last long. All he could do was gather her up into his arms.

He remembered then that he was hit, too. But his searching fingers touched disintegrated cotton, then ragged but still-intact Kevlar. The ballistic vest. He'd forgotten he had it on.

She was coughing, eyes wide. He felt her pulse: weak and fast. The pop and crackle of shooting had lessened. It wasn't over, just a lull. He watched the fence, wondering what Zeno and Jager would try next.

She tried to say something then, and he bent his ear to her lips. "What?"

"We could have loved each other," she whispered. "Couldn't we?"

Even through his shock, he knew there was only one thing he could say to that. But instead, he muttered, "Why did you do it? Why'd you have to sell out to Holder and them?"

"For us."

"For *us*?"

"Who else wanted Tartar? Bud had it on the market for years; he never got an offer. They'd come in and smell it and leave." She gasped for breath. "Then when he died, and . . . you came . . . I just wanted to sell it. The springs, the business . . . then you'd never have to go into a cave again." She blinked slowly. "Am I going to die?"

"No. We'll get you to a hospital. A few more minutes. Can you hold on?"

She didn't answer, just groped for her chest. He tried to stop her, but her hand pushed his away. When her fingers found the wound, she closed her eyes.

He muttered, "Did you know Bud was laundering drug money?"

"Not Bud," she whispered. "He had his problems, but he'd never . . ."

"Did you know about any of his other women? July? Gloria? Blanche?"

"I knew there were others once. But he changed. We got past the bad part."

Cradling her in his arms, he realized she was innocent. She'd never cared about money, never cared about insurance or profits or what she could get out of the land. If she had a fault, it was that she trusted too much, and forgave too easily. But was that a fault? Was it a greater one than his own rage and greed and paranoia?

She whispered, so low he had to bend close to hear: "Why couldn't you trust me? I never . . . I would have . . . It's getting dark, isn't it? Like it's waiting for me. Do you want to kiss me?"

He felt her breath come one last time, warm and bubbling with salty blood. Then her lips went still under his.

When he lifted his face, she was dead.

He sat with her body heavy in his arms, staring down at her closed eyelids. From the distant woods, the bullhorn spoke again. He didn't hear. His ears registered it, but his brain was occupied with something else: with his own blindness and stupidity.

He should have handled the sale, with Arkin. *He* should have made it his business to help, to find out what she really knew. If he'd trusted her, shared his suspicions and asked for advice, she might have canceled the sale. Instead, he'd kept it all to himself. Narrowed his sights to one thing: revenge for Bud. And even at the end, he hadn't been able to say the words he should have said.

It was what Shad had warned him about, and Bernice, and everybody he'd ever gotten close to. He understood it now, as if he were reading the words through deep, clear water.

Because of that suspicion, that separation, he'd killed her as surely as whoever had pulled the trigger.

He sat rocking her body as if it could still comfort her, looking out over the field and listening to the crackling as the poinsettia shed burned. Across the road, the bodies lay on the gravel, and others huddled like crumpled tissues on the hardstand of the truck lot.

Suddenly, he felt like destroying them all—those who killed to defend their profits, and those who killed to impose their idea of order. He didn't in that moment of rage see any distinction, any more than a man takes sides in a war between red and black ants.

He laid her gently down in the long grass. Bent again, to press his lips against a cooling cheek. Whispered, "I'm sorry, Mon. I'm sorry."

Then he picked up the gun.

His charge caught the men behind the first barricade by surprise, their backs to him. Ten yards away, he dropped to one knee and fired two-handed, the automatic kicking with each round. Men spun and cried out, clutching at where his bullets struck them, then falling. Submachine guns chopped holes, perforated asphalt with instantaneous dotted lines. When they were all down, he sprinted forward again toward the others, hearing but not bothering to bow beneath the hiss that passed swiftly by his head. The crack of the marksman's rifle was lost in the rapid blast of his automatic as he squeezed round after round into the mass of bodies behind the cars.

Then they were firing back. Bullets hummed past in the bright air. One tore through the meat of his thigh, but he didn't react or flinch. He just swung his locked hands and pumped round after round into the muzzle flashes—until they stopped.

The last figure still standing reeled out of his sights, fell across the hood of an Infiniti, and slid slowly down to the ground. He looked down at a stiff little goatee, slicked-back hair, bloodshot eyes that held his for an astonished moment before they slowly froze.

His ears rang. The world staggered with vertigo. He held the smoking, empty gun pressed to his torn thigh and looked around in sudden silence. Everyone behind the cars was dead. But there were only five bodies. It was a rear guard. Where were the rest? And why wasn't the marksman firing at him, standing alone on the hardstand, completely and carelessly exposed? He spread his arms and tilted his head back, lifting his face to the hard and empty sky. An offering. Let the invisible sniper who had killed her take him, too.

The marksman didn't fire. Tiller didn't know why. Maybe Zeno had finally gotten the message to him that there were friendlies in the compound. Or maybe he was just taking a coffee break. Whatever the reason, the clear and still-brightening blue stayed arched above his head. Air kept pumping in and out of his lungs. He was still alive.

Then he saw why.

The thin white mist moved slowly toward him, filtering through the fence. Another ferret round popped, gushing up smoke; then another.

Gas.

Watching that gauzy curtain walk closer, its pace that of a sauntering man in the light breeze that had risen with sunrise, he realized Al Zeno wasn't going to wait for reinforcements. That was a sign of failure. He was going to try another assault.

He tossed the empty gun away and began trotting downwind, wondering with the part of his brain that still worked, even when all higher functions were numbed, whether now might be the time just to go. Just drop into that ditch and crawl and crawl until he left the gate area far behind. No, that would put him in enfilade, a perfect target for the marksman.

Only the gas and smoke would blind his aim. Wouldn't it?

Meanwhile, the oncoming gas drove him on, pushing him along downwind like a pilotless boat. When the leading edge reached him, it stung immediately in his unprotected eyes, as if freshly cut onions had been pressed to them. CS, same stuff they'd used in Vietnam. It would get worse. Much worse. He limped faster, but the mist streamed inexorably past. He wiped streaming tears off his face. He began coughing.

But as he faded back toward the ditch, he glimpsed a dark figure within the approaching cloud. Someone else had figured it the same way he had . . . only this figure advanced deliberately, as if the burning atmosphere didn't affect it. Tiller wiped his eyes, staring.

Colten Scovill came plodding out of the white haze. Galloway saw the mask first, then the regulator tucked into his mouth. No wonder the gas didn't affect him. He was breathing from his little Spare Air, which must have been in the shop van. Tiller blinked and knuckled more tears away, but the gas just burned deeper into his eyes. He half-raised his hand as the younger diver came on.

Then he saw the bangstick. Scovill carried it down by his side, a short metal shaft with a surgical-rubber sling on the haft. It was capped with a power head.

He knew what was in that stainless tube. A twelve-gauge shotgun shell, set to fire on impact.

He turned and limped into a hobbling run. The silence was eerie behind him, broken only by the occasional pop of another CS cartridge. Arkin and the Holders and the remaining crooks must be holed up in the office building, trying to seal out the gas. That sounded like a losing game to him.

When he looked back, Scovill was running quietly behind him. The little air cylinder didn't seem to slow him down. His slim legs flashed rapidly over the grass.

Tiller came to the ditch again and slanted instinctively down into it. Maybe it was his SEAL training. When you were in danger, you retreated to the water, used it to hide you and conceal you and take you away. Only this was shallow, useless as cover. The mud sucked at his legs.

He ran as hard as he could, till his heart was close to bursting. When he looked back, Scovill had gained on him.

His vision was dissolving in a blur of tears. The gas burned in his chest now, a fiery tide rising in his lungs. But if he stopped running, Scovill would be on him with the power head. He labored on, swinging his arms to keep his leaden legs plowing through the water.

There, ahead, a triangular patch of white—he pulled an arm across nearly useless eyes—the settling pond. That wasn't any good . . . or was it? He still didn't see any outlet ditch. But you couldn't settle water without an outlet. . . . He glanced back. The other was keeping pace now, not closing in anymore. Waiting for him to tire? Waiting for him to fall?

He yelled hoarsely, "Colt! What the hell?"

292

The other man didn't answer. He just kept loping along, holding the bangstick like a short spear in his right hand. Was he grinning under the mouthpiece? Were his eyes creased with mirth behind clear tempered glass?

He understood suddenly that he wasn't going to outrun the younger diver. Scovill was lighter and faster and he wasn't breathing air that was half tear gas. If he got his hands on him, Tiller felt confident he could tear his arms off. But Scovill seemed to know that. That was why he was letting him run, until he couldn't anymore. Now, loping along, he caught Galloway's next look back. He waved, flip, sarcastic, then made a gun with his finger and pointed it.

Going to get you, Tiller.

The drainage ditch deepened, its bottom plunging to its intersection with the others at the pond. The pale surface was flat and motionless. He couldn't tell how deep it was. He couldn't even see very well; he was just letting the slope take him down, channeling him into the pond. Now he heard Scovill behind him, splashing through the water. Shit, the guy was close. A few more strides and he'd be in range.

The bottom fell away under his feet. He plunged in and slid beneath the milky calm surface into cool, thick water, holding his breath, frog-kicking along a few feet down. He made a sharp left just in case Scovill was still behind him.

When he stuck his head up, the pond was empty. He craned quickly around for Scovill but didn't see him. Gas drifted across the flat water like early fog. He kept his head low and only got a whiff of it, but it was getting denser. He sucked air in and out, pumping up the oxygen in his bloodstream. Where the hell was—

Something touched his leg, lightly, tentatively.

He gulped a lungful as he twisted away, surface-diving at the same instant he kicked the bangstick away. There was only one round in the thing. If he could get Scovill to jam it into something other than himself, then he could close in and take him. But for right now, all he could think to do was go deep, evade. So he did, kept kicking downward, clearing his ears.

Down . . . and down. He kept anticipating bottom, mud or sand or silt, had one arm extended for it as he frog-kicked with open eyes through the milky murk. But there wasn't any bottom. His arm brushed a surface once, but it wasn't silt. It was rock, and it sloped down.

Suddenly, he understood. This wasn't a settling pond. It was a sinkhole, like all the others that dotted the karst country. There was no ditch going out, because the water didn't go out. It went down. No wonder Tartar was so foul. It wasn't just sulfur. Every gallon of water Holder used had to be disposed of somewhere. And this was where he was dumping his waste: down into the upper layers of the Styx.

It was smart, but he didn't have time to think about it right then. The guy behind him was occupying all his attention. That and the rock he was pulling himself down along. He wished he had weights. Something about that nagged at his mind. Weights . . . Then a hand brushed his back.

He twisted away and kicked out. Even if he could trigger the power head with his foot, it would be better than getting it in his chest or his head. But his kick petered out into milky emptiness. He couldn't see anything. Go up? Couldn't—the sinkhole was too narrow. Scovill was above him. Wait him out? No, shit, Scovill was breathing off his Spare Air. While all Tiller had was the one breath he'd sucked in before he dove.

It occurred to him that he was probably going to die down here. Pressure leaned on his eardrums. . . . Twenty, thirty feet, the milky light was turning dim. Hearing the squeak and burble of exhaled air, he looked back and up and caught a dark blur that might be the other diver. But Scovill couldn't see him, either, mask or not; it was just too murky, with all the shit in the water.

Pressure squeezed his chest. He was out of ideas. A roaring thump built in his head, and he swallowed to drive back the need for air.

Then, as he'd almost given up, his groping hands slid over slippery wood: fallen, submerged trees, from when the land above was forest, before Holder and Company had mowed it clean and thrown up their factory. Here it lay where it had fallen, the smooth trunks slowly rotting away. . . . He pushed himself in past them and felt it: the bottom. Here was the silt at last, deep and oozy. He clawed up sticky handfuls, spreading inky night around him. The more murk, the better. Then he and the man above him would be equal.

Except Scovill could breathe, and he couldn't.

He sculled across the bottom of the sinkhole, arms groping out in desperation as a scarlet mist vibrated inside his skull. If he didn't head up in a few more seconds, he'd black out. But he could still hear the click and bubble above him. Five more seconds and he'd head up, just hope Scovill missed somehow. It wasn't much of a hope at bangstick range.

His groping hands felt the absence of rock. His staring eyes, nearly blinded by the gas, still could sense darkness.

Kicking hard, he propelled himself into it.

The opening wasn't very large, three or four feet across. He knew ten feet in that he was past returning. He didn't have enough air left in his lungs to get back to the surface, whether or not Scovill killed him en route. So he plunged on, pulling himself with numbing arms deeper into the dark, back bumping against a smooth limestone ceiling, feeling his way as the tunnel turned and the light vanished altogether.

Now he was alone. The cave-dark pressed down into his soul and into his brain, and his lungs screamed, burning, empty. His throat pumped in useless spasms, fighting to stay closed against the fluid blackness that would leave him kicking and clawing at the rock as it filled his lungs. A lifetime of control kept it closed, but with each beat of his failing heart, the lock weakened. He had to have air . . . had to have air . . . had to have *air*—

The ceiling lifted above him and he clawed at the rock, losing it then, the beast in the back of his brain snapping its chains at last. His nails tore on dark stone. Nothing to breathe but dark water. Here was Death waiting in a black cloak . . . Monica . . . Tad . . . the dark—

His face emerged into a lightless pocket clamped against the roof: a tiny sump, a bubble, three or four cubic feet. He sucked it in, indescribably grateful; then he strangled.

It wasn't air. It was cold fetid gas the water had rejected, thick with the nitric fumes of fertilizer and decomposing waste. His lungs squeezed like fists, expelling it. His skull filled suddenly with a headache like bronze screws crushing his brain. But he made himself follow it with another breath, even though he was blacking out.

Something hard probed his stomach. He kicked out, violently but blindly. The shaft struck the sole of his foot, and he kicked again.

A crack, so loud and sharp that he went instantly deaf, split the blackness with a red flash. He twisted and reached down. His probing hand struck something round. He jerked at it and found himself with the little bottle of air in his hand.

In an instant, it was in his mouth; he cleared it and sucked in one deep, heavenly breath of pure air. Then a hand gripped his balls and he doubled helplessly, coughing out the mouthpiece in an involuntary convulsion like a stabbed starfish. He grabbed after it in the dark, but it was gone.

He struck out again and his fingers found a hand. He closed his fist on it with terrific force, bending it back in a sudden access of rage. Another hand whipped across his face, searching for his eyes. He ignored it, bending the arm back and back till bone snapped, the sound carrying clearly in the water, intimate as if it were inside his own head. At the same moment, a blade sliced into his buttocks.

He and Scovill grappled in utter lightlessness, spinning and kicking, slamming into rock that sent new universes blasting and fading out into the eternal darkness. He heard the tank clang as it hit stone, then rattle as it rolled away. Gone. He needed air again, but he couldn't break away to find the pocket. Anyway, the stuff in it was worthless; he'd just about passed out even when he was breathing it.

They were both going to die now, but he wasn't quite satisfied with that. So when the knife came back and jabbed again under his armpit, he drove his elbow backward. Bone crunched as it drove into the other man's face. He hammered it back again and again, and at last Scovill went slack. Galloway pushed him away.

Then he pulled him back.

There was only one place down here he was going to get another breath.

He bent the unresisting head back and pressed his lips firmly to Scovill's. The other diver must have understood then, because he suddenly began struggling again. Galloway held his head back with one arm, holding him by his hair, and drove his fist into his stomach. Face pressed to the other diver's, he sucked in the explosively expelled air, still hot from the other's lungs.

The body crushed to his bucked and shuddered. Then it went quiet. A limply floating hand drifted back, brushing his forehead gently.

He pushed it away and kicked downward. His hand scraped the bottom, plowed through silt soft as wet face powder. It came up empty. No tank. No light. No air.

Kicking slowly, hands extended, he turned in a slow circle through the immense and icy dark that surrounded him. He had no idea which was the way back. The dark crept inside his head. He fell into it, starting to spin, and he put his hands out, hugging the remorseless stone that walled him in like the sides of a coffin.

He came back to consciousness still floating in the black, but with all pain and fear gone. His brain was clear now, burning serene and unwavering for a few final moments off some obscure one-time store of power. The rest of his body was dying. He couldn't feel his extremities, could barely stir his hands. He groped through the silt like a dying eel, expiring far from the sea.

The blackness was so immense, it seemed friendly. In a moment, he'd open his mouth and join it at last. But for another second or so, he still thought, still felt.

He floated in darkness, smiling gently.

He understood with the clarity of a disembodied spirit that the man known as Lyle Galloway had lived a life full of futility and error. He'd made too many mistakes, and learned too little from them. There was too much he regretted for him to be ready to die.

But he was. And, dying, the entity within that had looked out calmly and steadily at all the changing scenery marveled at the shortsightedness and blindness with which he'd lived his life. How fixed his attention had always been on things that in the end had no importance whatsoever. How casual he'd been about those that did—his son, the women who'd tried to love him, the men who'd tried to be his friends.

He drifted upward, the clarity ebbing. Perhaps he'd already breathed the black water of the Styx. Maybe the agony was already over; perhaps he'd drowned while he was unconscious. It didn't matter. . . . His back bumped softly against the ceiling, came to rest.

It slanted up.

He kicked feebly, but there was no response from his dead legs. He reached out with his hands instead and felt rock.

He pulled gently, floating forward. A narrow passage opened. He wriggled into it. Now his brain was shutting down, thought ceasing, the last consciousness of existence shimmering and dissolving like clear water bleeding away into murky nothingness, into the ultimate black.

The cave turned, then angled up, and he saw that it split into two passages. At first, he didn't understand, just floated there. Then the meaning slowly penetrated his dying brain. He had *seen*.

Pulling himself forward, he raised his eyes to a faint wash of light from far above.

The man broke the surface and floated there. After a time, his arms jerked. They reached out with a weak scooping motion. They dragged his body, like that of some dying lizard, very slowly up onto the bank.

He lay there facedown for what felt like hours, just looking at the material beneath his eyes, running his hands through it gently over and over. So beautiful. So soft. Covered with light, made of light itself. . . . The word came back to him: *mud*. His lips moved, whispering it.

Gradually, his attention widened, from what he lay on to the brush-covered slope above, then to the corrugated iron culvert that spilled a trickle of dirty water down into the sink-hole. It wasn't the settling pond, where he'd gone in. He'd done some kind of traverse, come up somewhere else—somewhere unfamiliar. Treetops and palmettos moved slowly against a pale sky. He couldn't tell if it was inside the wire or outside. He felt dizzy and disoriented. He had a blinding headache, and although he could think in words now, he wasn't sure who he was.

He was still lying there, alertness a gradually opening blossom, when he heard a scuffing noise echo from inside the culvert. It was followed a few minutes later by a squat man in a once-expensive but now very rumpled suit with the knees torn out. He had a small revolver in his hand, and he pointed it at the exhausted man in the water.

"Mr. Galloway. What a surprise. Was it you who pulled them in on us?"

Galloway . . . yeah, that was his name. A constellation of images, symbols, events lit suddenly, illuminating with danger what had a moment before been simple and peaceful. But he didn't answer. Holder glanced behind him, into the woods. Men were shouting back there. Occasionally, there was a shot. He stared up at him, remembering a little more each moment. Recalling that this pudgy, narrow-eyed man was responsible for it all—the drugs, the money, the death.

"You had Bud killed," he rasped.

"Me? Kusczk killed himself. Going places he wasn't meant to, seeing things he wasn't meant to see." Holder looked around. "You seen Colten?"

He pointed down into the sinkhole. Holder stared at him, then frowned. "He down there?"

He wished he had something witty to say, but he didn't. "Uh-huh," he finally muttered. "Won't be coming up again, either."

"Oh? Well, I don't have time to talk." Holder gestured behind him. "The facility is going to . . . catch fire shortly. Leaving no evidence, and very few witnesses. So I have to be moving along." He raised the gun.

"How did you find out?" Galloway asked him.

"Say what?"

"About Bud. That he knew about your operation? Did Blanche tell you? Or did Scovill, from something he found out?"

"Blanche?"

"Come on, Holder. Surely you knew about him and your wife."

"About who and my wife?" said Holder. "You trying to provoke me or something?"

"Okay, don't tell me," he said, feeling unutterably tired. "How you found out Kuszck knew about the Styx deal. How you were going to take over an entire aquifer. I thought it was Monica and Arkin. But I was wrong. Either Scovill happened to see it on Bud's computer, and decided you ought to know, or Bud told Blanche himself. By the way, where *is* Blanche?"

"She's back with Arkin. They're going to say they were taken hostage. I thought leaving was a better idea." Holder shrugged. "We disagree sometimes, Bibi and me. That doesn't mean we aren't on the same side."

"Which was where Bud probably went wrong. He thought, since she was running the Conservancy, she might be able to stop you. . . . But it doesn't really matter how you knew. Just that once you did, you set Scovill up to kill him. Bud was smart. He was tough. I wonder how Scovill did it."

Holder frowned. "You really think I'm gonna *explain* it all to you? You really think I have time to do that?"

"No," said Galloway.

"You're right." Holder aimed with both hands, clumsily, as if he was unused to a gun. Still, he was only about ten feet away. He wasn't going to miss a man lying in the mud, unable even to crawl.

The ragged volley rattled off the trees like hail off a tin roof. Tiller kept his eyes closed, waiting for the bullet. Only when it didn't come did it occur to him that he'd heard not just one shot, but three or four, all fired together.

He opened his eyes again. Then he pushed himself heavily up, propping himself in a sitting position with his arms.

Holder was sagging like melting tallow down beside the culvert. As Tiller watched, the gun slid from his hand into the weeds. Tiller's gaze followed the curve of the sinkhole around to the far edge, then up. He stared, wondering if he was seeing things. His brain still didn't seem to be working too well. But the figures standing under the trees didn't look at all like guardian angels.

"Hi, Dad," said Tad. He was holding the biggest revolver Galloway had ever seen. The barrel alone was at least a foot long. Ripper, with him, was carrying a single-shot shotgun, and Rafael, a bright red bandanna knotted around his head, had a little chrome-plated automatic. Their clothes were muddy and torn, their faces smeared with mud.

"You shouldn't have shot him."

"What, we should have just let him kill you? Right."

"But . . . what are you doing here?"

"Chain Saw noticed this culvert last time we were here. Remember? He asked if you wanted to get inside? He figured somebody else would figure it for a way out." Tad stuck the revolver into his belt and scrambled down the slope. He jerked Tiller to his feet, then poked a finger into his side. "You're bleeding like a pig. Can you walk?"

"I think so, just not very fast. Where the hell are we?"

"West of the fence, behind the cops. We better get going. There's more of 'em every minute. A chopper landed down the road a little while ago. We can fade back into the woods, cut back to where we left the car—"

"Car? What car?"

"The one we stole," said Tad patiently, as if he was explaining something to a slow three-year-old. "Another thing. I'm getting tired of saving your ass. You got to start taking better care of yourself from now on. Hear me?"

Galloway didn't answer. He tried his legs, and found they worked. Not well, but they held him up and moved him forward. He looked back.

Billy Holder was lying on his back, wingtips rooted deep into the mud as if searching for sustenance, or as if being gradually consumed. . . . The rank bog plants and water grasses, the hyacinths and hydrilla pushed up hungrily under and around his body. The gray suit was stained with dirt and duckweed. The yellow silk tie was pulled loose, sodden with dark blood. The puffy little eyes stared up, the sky reflected on their irises, but not seeing it. They'd never *see* anything again.

It wasn't a very neat ending, but maybe it would do. If only he'd been able to—

If only he still had *her*—

He stood still, frowning up at where the light came down in slanting, sparkling shafts between the swaying leaves. So beautiful ... It was like a cloud drifting across his mind. Sometimes hardly there. Other times, so thick that he could hardly put two words together. But he remembered her, her smile.

"Come *on*, Dad!"

Without looking back again, he stumbled after them into the woods.

THE AFTERIMAGE

See," said Tad, turning back from the conveyor that carried the canvas duffel away from them, growing smaller and smaller as it headed toward the rubber-strip curtains of the loading area. "They don't search them, or X-ray them or anything. Especially if you show up like ten minutes before takeoff. They just throw it on the cart with everybody else's stuff and off it goes. That's how I got the gun down to Florida. Just threw it in my bag and checked it."

Tiller nodded. He felt empty. He was still weak from twelve days in Tallahassee General, recovering from stab wounds, contusions, oxygen deficiency, decompression sickness, and tear-gas exposure.

He was alive. But he wasn't altogether sure he wanted to be.

He'd seen her twice on the way through the airport. Or rather, he'd seen women who tricked his eye into a second look, his heart into a leap that turned instantly to regret. . . . One had her shining hair, another her profile. Another carried a purse just like hers.

"Dad? You gonna just stand there?"

He turned from the check-in counter and limped back to where they were waiting. The divers from Scuba Florida, Daughtrey and Montagnino. Ripper and Rafael slouched a few feet away, exchanging glares with a baggage guard.

He shook hands with the divers first. "Mark, Tony, you guys are gonna have to carry Fabricante for a while."

"Negative perspiration. At least we got a stake now. You'll have to come back down, go diving with us again."

"Yeah, I'll have to do that."

He waited as Tad said his farewells, giving the tall, gangly Cracker and the dark Cuban quick, embarrassed hugs. He said good-bye, too, good-bye and thanks.

Then they headed up the carpeted ramp, Galloway limping, Tad scuffing his shoes, toward their gate.

He still felt vague at times, the cloud drifting back across his mind. Not as thick, but it was still there. The doctors said maybe it would go away, maybe it wouldn't.

He'd used that in the hospital, when the lawyers arrived. He'd known guys in the oil fields who'd taken hits, taken brain damage. So he acted like one of them. He gave disjointed and contradictory answers. He rambled. Then he'd ask who the man or woman interrogating him represented. He'd rear up in bed, shoot out a finger and yell, "Them! *They're* responsible for this!" The attorneys would go tight in their seats, warn him sternly against libel and nuisance suits, then start looking around for their briefcases.

He didn't think he was going to be called as a witness.

The condition of his heart wasn't as clear. If only he'd given her a chance . . . If only they'd had more time . . . Because she was right: He could have loved her. But whether or not he'd loved her, why couldn't he at least have said he did, there at the end?

It hurt too much to think about. So instead, he thought how the rest of it had turned out.

Zeno's second attempt to take the compound had been as futile as the first, with two more federal officers shot down. In the end, it had taken Army Rangers from Fort Benning to breach the walls of the office building, which was built like a bunker, and dislodge the last resisters.

Coverage of the raid had plastered the headlines for days, with full details of what was growing at FFF and who was involved. Jack Reed, an investigative reporter for the *St. Petersburg Times*, had uncovered the connection to the Styx River Preserve, and Blanche Holder and Arkin and Ferebie were being called before a grand jury.

Billy Holder was missing; no one knew where he was. Tiller figured the gators had gotten the body, dragged it off into the swamp, and hidden it under a big cypress root for later consumption.

The bald guy had turned out to be Carlos Díaz-Báez, a major player and financier. But because he was from Cali, not from Medellín, he was a rival and enemy of Don Juan Nuñez's.

So Galloway was in the clear, for a change, at least as far as Nuñez's organization was concerned.

Victor Fabricante had bought in to the dive shop, with ten points each to Mark and Tony as partners, and he seemed interested in Tartar Springs, too. So eventually, Bud's dream might even come true—a challenging course for advanced cave divers, leading down through tight constrictions and dangerous passages to the immense and sunless sea beneath.

The thing about the weights and other junk in the clavo had nagged at Tiller's mind, but it was Tad who'd figured it out—how Bud Kusczk had gotten all that money out of the country.

Kusczk had bought gold from jewelry supply houses. Using his jewelry-making equipment, he'd cast it in the molds open-water divers used for their weights. Dipped in bright thermoplastic, or into melted solder to make them look like lead, they were indistinguishable from the real thing. Scuba Florida diving parties arrived in Mexico or Freeport with a crate of weights checked through. That looked normal to the customs agents, a bunch of divers and a bunch of weights. But cave divers didn't use belted weights, since their tanks were so heavy. They went home with no weights at all, and what *wasn't* being checked back didn't ring any bells for customs.

Twenty pounds was a normal amount of ballast for a diver to carry. So that just four belts, tossed casually into a stout gear bag or nailed into a wooden crate—that was half a million dollars right there.

And of course the stuff back in Bud's cache—the dinged-up weights on ratty belts Tiller had thought were junk—well, he and Tad had gone in one last time and gotten them the day after he got out of the hospital. And guess what? It wasn't junk at all.

When they got to the gate, their flight was boarding. He and Tad joined the line, followed the others down the narrow metal corridor into the aircraft. The air was already hot, stuffy from sitting on the tarmac, in the sun. They settled into their seats and he reached up to adjust the air nozzle.

304

"You okay, Dad?"

He nodded, glancing at his son. Tad looked more confident now. The diving had helped. Sure, there would be struggles ahead. They were too much alike; maybe that was one reason. God knows, he and his dad, they'd had some screamers. But now he respected his son, and he hoped Tad felt the same way about him. That was progress.

The flight attendant, bending over them, said, "Tray table upright, please. Are you Mr. Galloway? Just thought you'd like to know, your pet's safely aboard. It's in a special cargo area, heated and pressurized. It'll be as comfortable as you are. Now, what can I get you to drink?"

Lunker, the cream Himalayan—an unexpected inheritance, and something living to remember her by.

And another inheritance, of sorts, was riding in the baggage compartment, the last thing he'd expected to be heading back to Hatteras with: some cash in hand at last. Two sample cases full of unmarked bills, and the duffel, so heavy they'd had to pay an excess-baggage fee. He'd made inquiries, but the closest family Monica had left was a second cousin. The cousin was getting the insurance, the savings, and the proceeds from selling the business and house; Tiller couldn't see the point of burdening him with a large sum of unexplained cash and a seabag of precious metal, as well. He couldn't give it back to Díaz-Báez's people, for obvious reasons, and he didn't feel like giving it up to the feds, either. Shit, they were the ones who'd shot her.

He'd thought about it, lying in the hospital. In the end, he'd decided it was as much his and Tad's as anyone else's.

He looked out at his last glimpse of Florida. The incandescent sky, so pale and so brilliant that it was almost white, made him squint. He could almost see her waiting for them at the gate. It seemed like a long time ago.

When the plane started rolling, Tad leaned back and sighed. "So, you gonna send me back to Mom?"

He cleared his throat. "I've got to."

"Why? I mean, I'll go see her, apologize if you want, but why do I got to live there? The school sucks. She doesn't know what to do with me except lock me in my room." He turned in his seat, and Tiller saw something he'd never seen before in his son's eyes: pleading. "Can't I stay with you?"

305

"I don't know," he said. "We'd have to think about where you'd go to school, find a place two people could live—"

"We're rich now. Can't we get a house or something, hang out together for a while?"

He almost smiled. Actually, it didn't sound too bad. But all he said was, "We'll see, Tad. After we get home."